I0576193

SING FOR ME

SING FOR ME

LULA GREENE

ANOTRA

To Mom and Dad for always supporting my dream.

Copyright @ 2026 by Lula Greene

All rights reserved.

The characters and events portrayed in this book are fictitious. Any similarities to real persons, living or dead, is coincidental and not intended by the author.

No part of this book may be reproduced in any manner whatsoever without written permission except in the case of brief quotations embodied in critical articles and reviews.

ISBN: 9798994299531

Cover Design by: Nora from Covers by Sophie

Library of Congress Control Number: 2025928147

1

Christine

"What have you gotten yourself into, Christine?"

She gulped as she gazed up at the dark, ivy covered mansion that looked like something straight out of a gothic novel. Pointed sections of the roof gave the illusion of towers melting into a central keep, but it was one solid, three-story high monstrosity. It was almost ugly, but the intricate stonework around the windows and the black iron details throughout gave the building a regal air that transformed it into something elegant. The whole place seemed shrouded in shadow, despite the sunshine burning up the long driveway's pavement.

The house was doing nothing to calm her ragged nerves. Starting a new job was stressful enough. Having to also live on her new employer's isolated upper-state New York estate?

Terrifying.

What did a house like this say about the person who owned it?

Christine gave her head a sharp shake, as if that would dislodge her anxious thoughts.

"Get it together, idiot," she murmured. "This is the chance of a lifetime."

With a deep, calming breath, she reached out and pushed the ornate button for the doorbell. It only took a moment for the door to swing open, and Christine was face-to-face with a stern looking older woman dressed in a black pantsuit and white blouse.

"Can I help you?" The woman's tone was polite, but just south of cold. She regarded Christine with a razor-sharp brown gaze.

"Ummm...yes." Christine was taken aback by the woman's intense scrutiny. She cleared her throat to try and gain her bearings. "I'm Christine Davidson. I'm Mr. Roux's new personal assistant."

The woman stared at her a moment more before nodding. "Yes, we spoke on the phone. I'm Mrs. Giry, Mr. Roux's housekeeper."

Christine caught herself before she raised a brow in surprise. Housekeeper? The woman appeared dressed for a board room, not dusting the fireplace mantel.

"Uhhh, of course. I hope I haven't arrived at a bad time..."

"Your timing is fine, my dear." Mrs. Giry took a step back, clearing the doorway. "Please, come inside. Do you have any luggage?"

"I have a few bags in my car," Christine answered, adjusting her purse strap on her shoulder as she stepped over the threshold and into the house.

The blend of gothic and contemporary continued inside, but there was an added element of luxury, like that of a French chateau. The floor of the low-lit foyer was black marble, webbed with veins of white. A lush crimson rug stretched the length of the room towards a spiraling staircase that led up to a second-story landing. The steps were made of the same marble as the floor, and the railing of black iron matched the exterior of the house. Two identical mirrors with gold frames dominated the walls on either side of the hall just before the stairs, and twin, stone console tables stood beneath them with identical white-rose flower arrangements.

Christine gazed to her left and right, and two open doorways led into two side rooms. They were both dark, and she couldn't make out many details from where she stood, but one room appeared to be a parlor with a fireplace and decorative, cushioned chairs arranged in front of it, and the other room was empty save for a black grand piano, which sat in the center of the space.

As Mrs. Giry began moving towards the stairs, Christine tilted her head up and froze in amazement. A huge, gorgeous chandelier hung from the high ceiling. Black chains attached to a round, black base held it aloft, and the body was a mass of silver spikes, from which rained delicate strands of crystal. It gave off a soft white glow that seemed to illuminate the darkness around it rather than dispel it. The piece was beautiful, modern, and somewhat frightening. Christine couldn't tear her eyes from it.

Mrs. Giry cleared her throat, snapping Christine from her awed haze.

"Please, follow me," the older woman said.

"Yes, of course." Christine fell into step behind the housekeeper.

They made their way up the spiral staircase to the second floor. The space they entered was darker. Mrs. Giry began to lead her down a hallway with canvas portraits in dark colors and framed posters of music albums decorating the walls. Christine recognized a few that she herself owned.

After passing several closed doors, Mrs. Giry came to a stop at the very end of the hall.

"This will be your room." She motioned towards the door in front of them, moving to the side so Christine could reach it.

Taking a hesitant step forward, Christine turned the brass knob and pushed the door open. After so much darkness and shadow, she was surprised by the brightness of the room. The walls were a honeyed beige, and the furniture was painted white. There was a desk, a vanity, a chest of drawers, a TV stand with a large black flat screen sitting on top, and two little nightstands. A queen size upholstered sleigh bed sat against the wall opposite of her, with a light blue coverlet, decorative pillows, and crisp white sheets. Sunlight poured in through a large bay window with a cushioned white bench, the white gossamer curtains tied back so as not to obstruct the view. She could see through a doorway to her right into a large walk-in closet, and an open door on her left revealed a private bathroom.

Christine could only gape in wonder. *This* was to be her new home?

"It's...beautiful."

Mrs. Giry, who had entered the room behind her, crossed her arms over her chest and gave a curt nod of her head.

"Mr. Roux had it redesigned after you accepted the position. You are of course free to make any changes to the space you wish, but he wanted you to be as comfortable as possible."

Christine was floored. This was far more than she'd expected. The kindness behind the gesture touched her.

She turned to face Mrs. Giry. "When will I be able to meet Mr. Roux? I'd like to thank him for his generosity."

The housekeeper tilted a perfectly plucked brow. "Mr. Roux will introduce himself to you later this evening. For now, you are to rest and get settled, and I am to go over the rules of the house with you."

"Of course." Christine supposed such a fine house would have a few small rules for its more temporary occupants.

Mrs. Giry cleared her throat before beginning. "The first and foremost is that you are not to disturb Mr. Roux under any circumstances. He is a very private man, and prefers to keep to himself."

Christine blinked, certain she'd misheard.

"But, Mrs. Giry, I...I'm his personal assistant. How am I to do my job if I can't interact with him freely?"

The sharp-eyed housekeeper pursed her lips in clear disapproval.

"Mr. Roux will contact you as he sees fit, most likely by email or text message, to instruct you in your day-to-day tasks."

"You mean...I'm not to even *see* him? That seems..." *insane, outlandish, impersonal* "...inefficient." Was she really expected to work for a man who couldn't be bothered to face her?

Mrs. Giry lifted one bony shoulder in a shrug. "Efficiency is not always the way of great artists. Eccentricity is most often the trait of the creatively-minded."

"I suppose..." Still, the arrangement made Christine uneasy. Even the most introverted artists she knew interacted with the people closest to them. Employment-wise, it didn't get much closer than personal assistant. When she thought about it, though, the perks of the job continued to outweigh the strangeness of the situation.

Perhaps it wouldn't be as strange as she anticipated?

"You must keep the rooms of the house lowly-lit at all times, with the exception of your personal quarters," Mrs. Giry continued. "All of the rooms are open to your use, except for Mr. Roux's private areas. His study and bedroom are off-limits to everyone but myself, unless through invitation. If Mr. Roux requests you drop something off, you may leave it outside his doors. There are also security cameras in all common areas of the house, but not in bedrooms or bathrooms. You are able to visit whomever you would like, but you cannot bring other people into this house."

"What about members of the production team? Or musicians? Investors?" Surely, they would need to entertain people every now and again. When Christine had learned that the headquarters for *Fantôme Records*, Mr. Roux's label, was located on his personal property, she'd been surprised. Why would a recluse open his home to the large amount of people it took to run a label?

Mrs. Giry shook her head sharply. "No. All business-related visits take place in the studio next door. I'm sure you saw the building on your drive into the property?"

Christine had. It had been much more modern in appearance than the house. One story of sleek black steel and glass. So, Mr. Roux didn't open his home to his employees, but he made it so he never had to go out in public to work.

Mrs. Giry continued, "The personal residence of Mr. Roux is not to be opened to anybody without his direct consent."

"And how often does he give his direct consent?"

"Never."

That's what she'd been afraid of.

"Now, feel free to freshen up and settle in," Mrs. Giry said as if nothing about the situation she existed in was at all odd. "I'll fetch your bags, and you can unpack."

"Oh, please, no. Don't trouble yourself. I can get them…"

Mrs. Giry held up a hand and Christine fell silent. "Nonsense. It is no trouble and you must be exhausted from your long trip. Rest, and I will fetch you for dinner at seven o'clock."

Seeing no point in arguing with the woman, Christine nodded her assent. "Thank you, Mrs. Giry."

The housekeeper turned to leave, but Christine stopped her with a hurried question.

"Will Mr. Roux join us for dinner?"

The older woman glanced back over her shoulder. "Mr. Roux prefers to dine alone. As I said, however, he will introduce himself to you later in the evening." Without another word, she walked out of the room and shut the door behind her.

Christine was left alone to wonder how a man who did not wish to be seen could introduce himself.

And was it an introduction she truly wanted to make?

2

Christine

Forty-minutes later, Christine stepped out of her bathroom wrapped in what she was convinced was the softest towel in the world, a cloud of steam billowing around her. Her long red hair, which was a riotous mass of curls when dry, hung wet and straight around her shoulders. She used a second towel to wring out the excess water still clinging to the strands. Though a full wash might not have been what Mrs. Giry had in mind when she'd suggested Christine freshen up, she'd found she couldn't resist when she'd seen the glass-walled waterfall shower.

Glancing around, her gaze fell on her suitcase, duffle, and computer bag arranged neatly on the floor beside her bed. She began moving towards her luggage, intent on digging out an outfit suitable for dinner and meeting her new boss, when something caught her attention out of the corner of her eye. She stopped and looked over at the small desk, which rested against the wall adjacent to the window. A single long-stemmed red rose sat on its surface.

Christine frowned. Had that been there before?

She found a sealed parchment envelope resting next to the flower, her name written on the front in bold, black ink. Picking it up, she turned it over and tore the flap open. Inside was an embossed notecard with the letters ER monogrammed in red on one side. On the other side, a simple message.

Welcome.
Please make yourself at home.

ER

ER. Erik Roux.

Christine furrowed her brow, perplexed. Though the rose was gorgeous and flawless, it seemed an odd gift one would give their personal assistant. First the room, then the flower. Kind gestures, without a doubt, but romantic ones in a different setting. She remembered what Mrs. Giry had told her about eccentricity being a trait of the creative.

Perhaps in addition to being an eccentric, Mr. Roux was also a romantic.

The thought made her grin. What an interesting man he must be.

Setting the card down, she picked up the rose and skimmed the full bloom under her nose. She couldn't help the blush that colored her cheeks, and wondered, not for the first time, what Mr. Roux looked like. When she'd first heard one of his songs, she'd been entranced, and believed such beautiful music could only have been made by an equally beautiful man. She'd scoured the internet, desperate to find a picture of him, but there'd been nothing. Only articles written by other people wondering the same thing as her. The man never made public appearances. His studio was located on his estate, so no one could even spot him coming or going from his home. He had no personal social media accounts, and anything that did appear online about him—that didn't come from a gossip site—came through his label's accounts, and never included an image of him.

It was amazing he'd managed to become so popular and keep himself such a mystery in the digital age. Christine guessed a lot of money and a solid PR team could do wonders for a person hell-bent on keeping his life private while letting his work shine in the spotlight.

She placed the rose back on the desk and checked her phone. It was almost six o'clock, and she wanted to give herself plenty of time to get dressed and ready before Mrs. Giry returned to fetch her for dinner. Moving towards her luggage, she dragged her suitcase onto the bed and popped it open to dig out clothes. Deciding to err on the side of dressy, she chose a navy, long-sleeved bodycon dress that was business appropriate, but subtly sexy. The pencil skirt went to her knees, and the v-cut at the neck could have been considered scandalous were it not for the white collar that hid her cleavage and matched the cuffs of her sleeves.

By the time she'd finished her hair and make-up, it was only six-thirty. Too filled with anxious energy to stay still, Christine wandered around her room, but after a full lap, she found she had nothing to distract her from her thoughts.

What if Mr. Roux didn't like her?

What if she couldn't do the job?

What if he was a tyrant?

A pervert?

Something worse?

Taking a deep breath, Christine decided she needed to walk off her anxiety. Mrs. Giry had told her she was free to use any room in the house, save Mr. Roux's personal spaces, so what harm could there be in looking around? A little exploration would divert her attention and keep her from dissolving into a bundle of nerves.

Decided, she slipped on a pair of nude high heels and made for the door.

It was like day and night between her room and the hallway. She had to take a moment and let her eyes adjust to the dimness. The click of her heels against the hardwood floor echoed off the walls as she made her way along the corridor. In her worried mind, the sound was thunderous.

It wasn't long before she came upon another door. Feeling somewhat like a child about to get into mischief, Christine paused to listen for any sign of Mrs. Giry approaching before she reached out and turned the doorknob. The room was dark, but she found a switch on the wall to her right as she stepped inside. She flipped on the lights, and the room was encased in a soft glow. It was another bedroom, much simpler than her own in decoration and setup. A four-poster bed and armoire were the only furniture, and the walls were gray. Given the fact there were no sheets on the bed, Christine doubted anyone occupied the room. The space reminded her of a blank canvas, ready for someone to bring color to it, but kept on a shelf in the meantime with all its potential hidden from sight. She wondered if this was what her room had looked like before Mr. Roux had remodeled it.

There didn't appear to be anything else of interest, so Christine turned off the light and backed out into the hall, pulling the door closed behind her. Not having encountered the bogey-man, or, even more frightening, Mr. Roux himself, Christine felt less nervous as she moved further down the hallway. The next room she came upon was another bedroom, identical to the one before. Two more dark bedrooms and a half-bath dominated by black marble later, she found herself crossing the landing that overlooked the foyer. Glancing down, she saw no sign of Mrs. Giry, and so continued on in to the opposite side of the house.

She expected more dark, plain bedrooms, but found herself gasping with delight when she opened the next door. A cozy library greeted her. Mahogany shelves lined the walls of the deep room, every one filled with books. There were no windows, but a massive fireplace with a marble mantel dominated the far wall. Lush leather chairs were arranged in front of it, and a long mahogany table stretched along the room to Christine's right. The floor was covered in a thick, dark crimson carpet. Hanging brass wall sconces lit the space with enough light to read by, but not enough to be overbearing.

Christine wanted to explore more. To see what types of books her new employer collected. Just as she stepped into the room, however, a sound further down the hall caught her attention. She froze, listening.

It was music.

Someone was playing the piano, and it was breathtaking.

Her heart began to race and she gulped as a lump formed in her throat.

It had to be Mr. Roux. Though her common sense was screaming for her not to go snooping, her curiosity was too much to bear. She turned from the library and began walking in the direction of the fantastical melody.

She passed door after door without so much as a glance, turned to the left when the hallway ended in front of her, and continued in the new direction. The music grew louder and bolder with each step she took. The voice in her head telling her this was a terrible idea was drowned out. She felt pulled...possessed.

She had to find the music's source.

At last, she reached the end of the hallway and came upon a set of tall double doors. The piano's tune was coming from the other side. She wanted nothing more than to push the doors open and discover what lay beyond, but her cautious inner voice managed to break through at last. Christine paused, her right hand resting on one of the door handles. What was she thinking? She was seconds away from breaking one of the rules Mrs. Giry had given her barely an hour ago. This had to be the entrance to Mr. Roux's private domain. Still, the urge to see him, to follow the music, was so powerful she struggled to fight it. She knew it could cost her job. She'd be out on the streets before sunrise.

Yet, her hand twitched to twist the knob.

"Just what do you think you are doing?" A sharp voice startled Christine, breaking her trance. She yanked her hand away from the door with a gasp.

The music stopped.

Turning, Christine met Mrs. Giry's glare.

The older woman had her hands on her hips, her expression dark and unforgiving.

Christine gulped. "I...I'm sorry. I don't know what came over me." The excuse sounded lame even to her ears. "The...the music was just so...so..." There was no right word to describe it. "...gorgeous." That didn't do it justice.

Mrs. Giry crossed her arms over her chest.

"You're going to have to learn to control yourself if you have any hope of maintaining your position." She rolled her eyes, but some of her anger seemed to fade. "Come along. Dinner is ready."

Confused, Christine blurted, "I'm not fired?"

"Not today, girl. Mr. Roux is a big believer in second chances. I warn you, though...you won't get a third."

With that, she turned and began marching back down the hallway.

Christine looked back at the doors. Silence greeted her, but the memory of the music continued to make her blood hum as she hurried to follow Mrs. Giry to the dining room.

3

Christine

Dinner was an awkward affair.

The small hope that Mr. Roux would join them was crushed the instant Christine walked into the large dining room and found the long table set for two people. Mrs. Giry took the seat at the head of the table. Christine sat to her right. A tall black man with a buzz cut who appeared to be in his fifties or so entered the room from what Christine assumed was the kitchen, carrying a bottle of wine. Mrs. Giry introduced him.

"This is Darius. He is our part-time chef."

Christine smiled and took the man's hand to shake.

"Very nice to meet you."

He smiled, flashing even white teeth. "The pleasure is all mine, Ms. Davidson. Please let me know if there are any dishes you are particularly fond of, or dietary restrictions I should be aware of."

Christine felt herself relax for the first time since she'd entered the house, warmed by Darius' kind brown eyes and gentle speech.

"No dietary restrictions to speak of. I'm quite fond of chicken marsala, but I'm really not a picky eater. I enjoy most any type of food."

Darius' grin widened. "I love a woman who loves food." Releasing her hand, he stepped back and looked between her and Mrs. Giry. "Your first course will be out momentarily." With that, he disappeared back into the kitchen.

In the silence that followed, Christine felt her back stiffen once more with the tension that Darius' presence had temporarily relieved.

Though the darkly decorated formal room would have been enough to make Christine uncomfortable, it was Mrs. Giry's coolness that stole the show. Christine maintained the sense that the woman was no longer angry at her impertinence, but she did not attempt small talk as they waited for their food, nor crack so much as a smirk. Christine feared this might be Mrs. Giry's regular demeanor. If she was the only other full-time employee of Mr. Roux's, was this how their time together would always be?

The thought made Christine's stomach twist.

When Darius returned with their first course, a delightful smelling tomato basil soup, Christine wanted to breathe a sigh of relief. Her respite was brief, however, as Darius placed the bowls of steaming soup before them, poured them each a glass of crisp Riesling, offered his hope that they would enjoy the food, and then departed the dining room once more. Mrs. Giry bowed her head for a moment, catching Christine off guard.

Was the woman praying?

Before Christine could determine what to do, Mrs. Giry raised her head, picked up her spoon, and began eating. After a moment of hesitation, Christine followed suit.

The painful silence continued to stretch between them.

When she had finished her bowl and wine, Christine mustered up the courage to speak.

"How long have you been working for Mr. Roux?"

Mrs. Giry froze, looked up, and blinked as if she'd forgotten she wasn't alone.

Clearing her throat, she responded, "A very long time." She returned her attention to her bowl.

When it became clear she wouldn't expand on her answer, Christine tried again.

"Do you enjoy working for him?"

Mrs. Giry didn't bother to look back up. "Yes."

Christine wanted to roll her eyes in frustration. She scrambled to find a topic that didn't revolve around Mr. Roux. There must be something else they had in common that they could talk about?

"Do you enjoy music, Mrs. Giry?"

At last, it appeared Christine had snagged the woman's attention. She gazed up, and there was a gleam in her eye. Not quite excitement, but interest at the very least.

"I love music."

Christine couldn't help but smile at the reverent tone the woman used.

"Do you play anything?"

Mrs. Giry shook her head, and then opened her mouth to say something just as the kitchen door flew open. Darius returned, wheeling out a cart with covered plates on top. He pulled up to the table, and with a flourish, removed the lids from three steaming dishes.

"Ladies, this evening you will be dining on stuffed Cornish game hens glazed with honey, roasted asparagus with lemon, and red garlic mashed potatoes."

The food smelled divine, and Christine's mouth watered as Darius began preparing her plate.

He gave her generous portions of the asparagus and potatoes, but Christine didn't mind. She was starving and doubted she'd have any trouble finishing the meal. He also served a Pinot Noir and switched out their dirty glasses for clean ones so as not to mix the flavors. Christine was impressed with his attention to detail and dedicated service. Did he put so much thought into every meal, or was this night an exception?

She supposed she'd find out.

Once Darius had placed their plates before them, he asked, "Will there be anything else, ladies?"

Mrs. Giry gave a shake of her head. "No, thank you, Darius. We'll ring you when we are ready for dessert."

Darius nodded. "Very good."

With a smile to Christine, he took his cart and departed the room.

Christine was eager to start the conversation back up from where they'd left off, and didn't bother to touch her food before asking, "I beg your pardon, Mrs. Giry, but before Darius arrived, you were about to tell me if you played an instrument?"

Mrs. Giry swallowed a bite of her chicken, her cheeks tinged pink. "I do not play anything. I was a dancer."

Christine was surprised and intrigued by this revelation. She reexamined Mrs. Giry with a discerning eye. The woman was older, and though slight, had lost the tone and sharpness of youth. Yet Christine could see in her lithe frame and delicate features the remnants of a ballerina.

"Did you dance professionally?"

Mrs. Giry nodded, though the move was hesitant. "Yes. I lived in France and danced in the Paris Opera Ballet for four years. Before that, I danced for several smaller companies in the United States and Europe."

Christine couldn't help but feel a little bit of awe. She wasn't a dancer herself, but knew it was a difficult, competitive career. For someone to get as far as the Paris Opera Ballet was impressive, to say the least.

"Four years doesn't seem like a long time."

Mrs. Giry's lips thinned. "I retired when I was twenty-eight. I could have stayed a few more years, if not for..." She stopped, pain flashing in her eyes.

Ballet careers were never very long, but Christine could guess what cut Mrs. Giry's short.

"Were you injured?" she asked in a gentle tone.

Mrs. Giry swallowed, avoiding Christine's gaze. She cleared her throat and snapped, "It doesn't matter now. That was a lifetime ago."

Christine didn't push further.

The rest of their meal was eaten in total muscle-clenching silence. Christine worried she'd overstepped her bounds...again...and lost all chance of Mrs. Giry warming up to her.

It was a blissful relief when, at last, they finished their food and Mrs. Giry rang the little bell that was resting next to her plate. In moments, Darius came through the kitchen door, once more pushing his cart. If he noticed the chill that now existed in the air between Christine and Mrs. Giry, he made no mention of it.

"Ladies, I hope you enjoyed your meals!"

Christine managed a smile for the chef as he cleared their plates and replaced them with smaller dishes of fluffy meringue, whipped cream, and fresh strawberries. He switched out their wine for a sweeter dessert one as well. Though the thought of staying in that room one more second was painful, Christine did not want to turn another member of the staff against her, so she tucked into the plate without hesitation. It was delicious, but she struggled to eat it at a pace that didn't give away her desperation to escape.

At last, it was Mrs. Giry who broke the silence.

"Mr. Roux has instructed me to escort you to his study following dinner."

Christine perked up, surprise and excitement stealing her breath.

"I'll actually meet him? In his study?" *His private domain you told me no one was allowed to enter?*

Mrs. Giry eyed her like she was a nuisance. "You'll be able to discuss your day-to-day duties and his expectations of you. If you have any questions, you'll have the chance to ask him directly."

Christine didn't miss the fact that the older woman hadn't answered her question. As much as she wanted to push, however, she didn't. She was on thin enough ice with the housekeeper. Whatever she encountered after dinner, she'd deal with the situation alone.

When dessert was completed, Mrs. Giry didn't wait for Darius to return to clear the table. She patted her mouth with a napkin and stood without a word. Christine hurried to her feet as well, startled by the woman's sudden movements. Mrs. Giry began walking towards the door that led back out into the hallway, and Christine followed after her. They moved through the big house in silence, ascending the staircase and turning right when they reached the second-floor landing. Mrs. Giry led Christine back down the hallway she had been exploring earlier, back towards the doors she'd been so close to opening in order to discover the source of that enchanting music. The hallway was quiet now and appeared somehow darker and more foreboding than it had before.

Christine gulped as they came to a stop in front of the large double doors. Her curiosity had shifted into anxiety, and she grew nervous at the prospect of meeting her new employer. She was almost too afraid to step any further forward.

Mrs. Giry turned to her. "Mr. Roux's study is beyond these doors. You will go inside and sit in the chair provided for you in front of his desk. You will not touch anything. You will not open any drawers or other doors. You will speak only when spoken to, and you will refrain from asking Mr. Roux any personal questions. Is that understood?"

Though her tone might have been a touch colder than before, Mrs. Giry's stern expression was no more severe. Christine took a small amount of comfort in that.

She nodded. "I understand."

The housekeeper gave a quick tilt of her chin and pushed the doors open.

4

Christine

Christine stepped into the room.

The click of the doors shutting behind her reverberated in her ears like a cannon blast.

She paused to take a breath and calm her shaking hands, gazing around the dark but luxurious study. Mahogany built-in bookshelves lined the walls on either side of her, and a large floor-to-ceiling window dominated the wall opposite her. Its draping curtains were pulled back to reveal a clear night sky and gorgeous full moon.

To her left sat a beautiful grand piano, the second she'd seen so far, and no doubt the source of that haunting melody that had drawn her to this room earlier. Its cover was closed, and the bench rested beneath the hidden keyboard. She wondered if he had continued to play while she and Mrs. Giry had had dinner.

Turning to her right, Christine took in the huge executive desk, which matched the bookshelves and other wood features in the room. The large-back executive leather chair sat empty behind it, as did the matching, smaller chair before it. Remembering her instructions, Christine took another deep breath and walked across the room, her heels sinking into a plush oriental rug. When she reached the desk, she lowered herself into the smaller chair, crossed her ankles, laid her hands in her lap, and waited. She didn't dare speak, though she feared her thundering heart would be audible to Mr. Roux when he made his appearance.

The only other sound was the soft tick of an antique clock resting on the bookshelves behind the desk.

Christine watched the clock's hands. It was coming on 8:30 PM, later than she'd thought. She didn't wear a watch, and hadn't thought it appropriate to bring her cellphone to dinner, so she'd had no way of knowing how long that excruciating meal had dragged on. Would her meeting with Mr. Roux be as painful and awkward an affair?

She shivered with dread at the thought.

"Cold, Ms. Davidson?" a deep voice spoke from behind her.

Christine gasped and jumped in her seat, startled. She hadn't heard the door open...hadn't heard him approach. Instinct had her turning her head to look at him.

"Don't." The command was sharp.

Christine froze, at a loss for what to do.

"Sir, I..."

"Face forward, Ms. Davidson." Then, in a gentler tone, "Please."

His change in tenor didn't make the order any less nerve-wracking. Why wouldn't he allow her to look at him? What was he hiding?

How did she know it was even Mr. Roux?

For the first time since she'd arrived at this strange house, Christine felt a tremor of fear course through her. Fear for her safety.

"You'll have to forgive my...peculiarities," he continued. Strange though it was, the sound of his voice soothed Christine, calming her erratic heartbeat. It was a beautiful baritone. Melodic. It reminded her of the music he'd been playing earlier.

She licked her lips and gulped. "Sir...I...I'm not really sure what to do. This is not a situation I expected."

The sound of his chuckle sent a rush of heat through her body.

Holy shit. What was that?

Before she had time to process her strange reaction, he was speaking again.

"I imagine this all is rather unexpected, Ms. Davidson. Still, I promise you have nothing to fear from me. As I'm sure Mrs. Giry informed you of, I am very protective of my privacy. Which means, somewhat unfortunately, that until I can trust you, I'll be taking certain precautions in our interactions."

Though a small voice in her mind tried to stop her, Christine couldn't help the words that slipped from her lips.

"My job will be quite difficult if I don't have your trust, sir."

A heavy silence stretched between them, and Christine wished she could take her words back.

You idiot...

At long last, his voice filled the room. "I'm sorry to say that I'm too much of a cynic to trust others easily. Here, trust is earned, not given."

"I see..." She didn't, not really, but what else could she say? Christine wasn't ready to walk away from this job. Not yet, anyway.

"You are, of course, under no obligation to stay once I have made my provisions for this position clear." His tone shifted to business-like with such smoothness, it caught Christine off guard. "If, once I have explained fully my expectations, you do not feel you can meet them, you only have to say so and we can part ways with no ramifications. I'll even offer compensation for your travels getting here."

It was as if he expected her to walk away. Sure, his behavior was odd and eccentric, but it wasn't something she didn't think she could get over in time. Were his other expectations for her so much worse, or did he truly have so little trust in people?

"That's very generous of you, but I believe this job too good of an opportunity to pass up so easily."

"We'll see, Ms. Davidson," he murmured. "You come highly recommended of course, although I am curious why a graduate of Columbia Business School would give up a rather cushy corporate job and seek out and accept an assistant position she is so clearly overqualified for?"

A question many of her close friends had asked. A question her mother would have demanded an answer to.

Christine hesitated before replying, wary of the truth, but also determined to gain his confidence.

"Business administration isn't exactly my passion."

"And what is?" His tone turned husky with curiosity. It made her heart flutter.

She swallowed. "Music, sir. I love music...have always wanted a career centered around it."

"You love music, yet aren't a musician?"

This was the painful part. "I wanted to be. I could have been. My father was a renowned musician himself and told me I held great promise, but I didn't have the opportunities to pursue my passion when I was young."

A thoughtful quiet followed her admission.

"Your father wasn't by chance Gerard Davidson? The violinist?"

Christine gulped and began fidgeting in her chair, her hands clasping and unclasping in her lap.

"He was."

"Very interesting..." His words were released like a breath, and she imagined she could feel them run down her back even from across the room. "You must have been quite young when he died."

"Yes," she whispered. Young and scared. Alone with a resentful mother, and no way to achieve her dreams. "My future as a musician died with him. My mother wasn't as keen that I should pursue that life as he had been."

"She wanted a business woman, I suppose? A stable future for you and herself?"

"Something like that." They'd also been so poor they couldn't afford the luxury of music lessons of any kind. She kept that to herself, however. At the moment, Mr. Roux was simply curious. She couldn't stand it if he pitied her.

"Well, be that as it may, I did not hire you for your passion for music, though I can appreciate it. I've hired you because you were by far the most qualified of the applicants, though I do wonder if you'll grow bored with such a position?"

Christine couldn't help the burst of laughter that escaped her. "Sir, I can assure you already, I will be anything but bored here."

She snapped her mouth closed as soon as the words were out. How stupid was she? There was no way he wouldn't take that as an insult.

She thought she might have caught him off guard with her reply, which did not help her anxiety. He was silent again, and a strange tension settled between them. Was he shocked? Annoyed? Unused to having his words thrown back at him?

The sound of footsteps made Christine's breath hitch.

He was moving towards her.

She forced herself to remain still, facing forward as he had ordered.

He stopped when he stood behind her, so close she could feel the heat of his body.

She held her breath, trying not to smell him even as the spicy scent of his cologne wrapped around her.

"Are you not afraid of me?" His voice was low, but curious.

She frowned at the question. *Was* she afraid of him?

"I...I'm certainly intimidated," she admitted. "Your behavior is not at all what I expected, and I do wonder how we will be able to work together with your restrictions on our interactions, but...no. I'm not afraid." She paused. "Should I be?"

More silence. More strange tension.

"No, Ms. Davidson. You have nothing to fear from me."

Though she wasn't naïve enough to believe a total stranger who refused to let her see his face, something in his words rang true. Her gut told her she was indeed safe with him.

She would go with his flow, but she would proceed with caution until she had a firmer hold on her situation.

As he said, trust was earned, not given. He would have to earn hers just as she would his.

"Still, you might not be so eager to keep this position once I've explained things."

The first prickling of dread poked at her stomach.

Mr. Roux moved away from her, and she shivered at the chill left in his absence. He began to pace, his shoes shuffling against the thick rug.

"My expectations for you, while peculiar, are not strenuous," he began, businesslike once more. "I expect you to be ready for work promptly at seven in the morning. You will be given daily tasks and instructions via text and email. You will be provided a phone and laptop for these and other business purposes. Should you have questions about your tasks, you may send me messages using the same means, or else ask Mrs. Giry."

Christine frowned. "Am I to take that to mean we won't be seeing...*talking* like this regularly?"

His chuckle had heat spiking her blood again. She was too afraid to ask herself why that was.

"No, Ms. Davidson. Until I can be sure you are trustworthy, we will not interact like this again."

She bit her tongue as the *Why?* fought to escape.

Instead, she murmured, "Yes, sir."

He paused in his pacing, and she tensed, waiting to see what he would do next. When his footsteps resumed, she let herself relax.

"You will handle my schedule and appointments, take messages, sort mail, maintain paperwork and the like."

Basic assistant responsibilities, she thought with disappointment.

"Sir, will I assist with any music production?"

Another lengthy silence. Mr. Roux appeared to enjoy his dramatic pauses.

"Myself and Mrs. Giry handle the bulk of production." Christine felt her heart begin to sink. "However..." she perked up again "...it is not beyond the scope of your position to step in when extra hands are needed."

She couldn't help the grin that split her face. "Are there any albums currently being produced?" Though it had been five years since the label had released new music, perhaps they had plans that she could get in on the ground floor of?

"No." The word stabbed and deflated her like a pin in a balloon.

"Oh." She felt herself sag in her chair.

"Sorry to disappoint, Ms. Davidson."

Christine sat up straighter, embarrassed that she'd let her disappointment show in such a blatant manner.

"No, sir. I apologize. It's just...well...I was hoping..."

"You were hoping to get in on the ground floor of my latest creation. Perhaps have a hand in it yourself?" The ease with which he guessed her intentions stole whatever explanation she was attempting to give him right from her lips. "If a new project presents itself, you may have that chance. Unfortunately for you, it has been quite a while since I've felt...*inspired* enough to produce new music. You may have to settle for overseeing our current distributions." Before she could reply, he finished with, "Any other questions, Ms. Davidson?"

She had so many questions, but she didn't know where to begin. Didn't know what he'd bother to tell her.

He must have taken her pause as affirmation that he had explained everything to her satisfaction, because before she could figure out what to say, he was speaking again.

"Then I bid you good night."

Startled, Christine tried to ask him to wait, but could only manage a whispered, "Sir...?"

The sound of a door opening and shutting had her whirling in her seat, but it was too late.

The room was empty.

Mr. Roux was gone.

5

Christine

By the time Christine returned to her room, she was exhausted. The evening had proven more mentally draining than she'd anticipated. Not for the first time, she had the smallest inkling of doubt about keeping her job in this strange house with its strange owner.

Kicking off her shoes, she let herself fall back into the plushness of her new bed. She stared up at the ceiling, replaying every odd moment of her interaction with Erik Roux.

The situation she found herself in was strange, of that there was no doubt. Protecting his privacy was one thing, but to not allow her to see him...

What had happened to make him so wary of people?

It wasn't his oddities, however, that stood out as the most startling aspect of their encounter. It had been her reaction to him.

His voice had left her heated.

She couldn't understand how only his voice could have had such an impact on her. It was deep and beautiful. Even now, the memory of his dark timbre had her shifting her legs in an unconscious attempt to ease the small ache she felt at their junction.

Was it possible to be attracted to someone she'd never laid eyes on?

Christine again wondered what he looked like. She closed her eyes and tried to picture someone in the realm of tall, dark, and handsome, but failed to produce a solid image. Instead, a large, shadowy figure dominated her imagination.

Frustrated, she popped her eyes back open.

Curiosity, frustration, and arousal swirled within her as she thought of her new, enigmatic boss.

"Erik Roux," she murmured his name, and then bit her lip as her face flushed. *What type of man will you turn out to be?*

* * *

Erik

"*Fuck.*"

The curse came out as a growl.

That meeting had not gone as planned.

He hadn't expected Ms. Davidson to be so alluring.

Nothing in her resume had prepared him for that.

His mind whirled, the darkness that haunted him creeping at the edges instead of overwhelming him as usual. It'd been so strange, how she'd walked into the room and seemed to bring the light in with her.

Shaking his head, he tried to push the thought away.

Erik paced the confines of his bedroom like a caged tiger. This was not good. He couldn't keep her on as his assistant. The attraction he felt for her the moment he'd seen her had shocked him to his core. He'd watched her enter the study from a hidden compartment by the room's two-way mirror. Her curly red hair had flowed around her slim shoulders, and her rather conservative navy dress hugged her delectable curves. Amber eyes had sparkled with curiosity as she'd gazed around, taking in her surroundings. A slim nose, sharp chin, and full pink lips had left him speechless as she'd made her way to the chair in front of his desk. It'd taken him a moment to collect himself before he'd been able to step out and interact with her.

Beautiful. Mesmerizing. An angel had stepped into his shadowed world.

An angel he wanted to bend over his desk and make sing with pleasure.

An angel that put impossible thoughts into his head, and had his heart beating with the deceptive tendrils of hope.

Yet, there was no hope for him.

Blue eyes stared at him in disgust...

"Even that mask cannot hide what you are..."

He shook his head to ward off the memories he tried to keep hidden. His fingers strayed towards his face and traced over the hard, cool surface that hid his deformities. It was an absentminded gesture, born of anxiety and uncertainty.

It reminded him of what he was, and what he could never be. What he could never hope to have.

Ms. Davidson's presence was no blessing, but more torment.

He didn't know what to do. His first thought, *Let her go.*

His second thought, *Fucking idiot.*

Coming to a halt, he snarled in frustration.

He couldn't fire her. It wasn't her fault *he* found her so attractive. It wasn't her fault her presence would be torture for him. He could handle torture. *She* shouldn't be punished because he was a weak fool.

Erik released a huff of breath. He could be professional, damn it. He *would* be professional. Ms. Davidson would have nothing to fear from him. He wouldn't darken her world with his ugly face and twisted soul.

Touching his mask again, he felt the darkness that had been dispelled in her presence begin to retake him at last.

His interest in her didn't matter. There was no chance in hell she would ever reciprocate, so why concern himself with fanciful notions?

"How could I ever want such a wretched creature?"

He just had to keep his distance, and all would be well.

Ms. Davidson's allure would dim with time. Nothing could hold back his darkness for long.

* * *

Christine

"Ms. Davidson..."

Christine groaned and cracked open her eyes in confusion. Had someone said her name? Her room appeared empty. Snuggling deeper into her soft bed, she closed her eyes to go back to sleep.

"Ms. Davidson, I need you. Wake up."

Her eyes shot back open. No, she hadn't imagined it. Sitting up, she gazed around her new room in bewilderment. Was it darker than it should be? She blinked, but couldn't seem to penetrate the thick blackness surrounding her. Her eyes widened when they landed on a shadowed mass in the corner by her window. The curtains were drawn, shutting out the moonlight, but she could still make out the figure who stood there.

"Mr. Roux? Is that you?"

He said nothing in reply, but began moving towards her. Strange...she felt no fear at his approach. Instead, a sense of anticipation hummed in her blood.

"Mr. Roux, what are you doing here?"

Her heart began beating harder and harder. She clutched her sheets and rubbed her legs together as a tell-tale throbbing began deep in her core.

Mr. Roux stopped when he stood next to her bed. Though he was close enough where she should have been able to discern some of his features, even in the dark, she could make nothing out. His face was a black mask.

He reached out a hand that she couldn't see and cupped her chin, pulling at her lip with his thumb.

"You are so beautiful, Ms. Davidson. I find it impossible to resist you."

"What do you...?" she whispered, but he swooped down on her before she could finish. Lips fused with hers in a searing kiss that left her breathless, and he pressed her back into the mattress and pillows. He was on top of her the next second, rendering her all but blind as his large form blocked what little view of her room there was. Still, she felt no distress, only excitement, and a desire so powerful it robbed her of rational thought. Strong hands began to explore her body, stripping her of her oversized t-shirt and panties.

As he touched and caressed her, her skin heated with pleasure, and she grew wet with need. He kissed her throat, stroked the sides of her torso, licked at her collarbone, and squeezed her hips. Her mind couldn't grasp what was happening. Why was she not afraid? Why was she not fighting him? This was wrong. He was her boss. He'd come to her room without permission.

Yet she couldn't seem to care. All her mind and body wanted was his touch and the release it promised her.

She gasped when his hands covered her breasts.

"I want you, Christine," he growled at her ear. "Do you want me?"

"Yes." She tried to wrap her arms around him, but found no solid body above her.

Frowning, she tried again.

There was only air, but his hands on her were heavy. She felt his weight and warmth against her, but none of the friction that existed when flesh met flesh. It was as if he was there...but wasn't. Like a ghost. No, something more tangible than that. A phantom.

His fingers inched from her breasts to her belly. When they reached the juncture of her thighs, she let out a cry as they probed her wet heat.

"I'll make you sing, beautiful Christine. You'll sing for me." His disembodied voice floated around her. The pleasure was overwhelming, but how she longed to see him.

She was bombarded with sensation. His hands were everywhere on her, yet they hadn't left her sex. His mouth and tongue kissed her from head to toe, yet he continued murmuring in her ear.

Christine was confused, hot, and so close to coming, nothing else mattered.

"Scream for me, beautiful," he ordered. "Tell the world who owns you."

Between his voice and his touch, she was helpless to resist. She could only obey. As she reached her peak, she screamed his name.

"Erik!"

* * *

With a cry, Christine woke. She stared, wide-eyed at her ceiling in confusion. Her body was hot, covered with sweat, and her breaths were ragged. Her sex throbbed with the aftershocks of her very real orgasm.

Sitting up, Christine gazed around her room as she had in her dream. It wasn't as dark. The moonlight was able to filter in through the gauzy curtains. She could see that she was alone. Letting out a deep breath to calm her racing heart, she recalled the details of her dream. It now made sense that she hadn't been afraid. It had been a fantasy.

A very visceral fantasy.

About her boss.

Christine felt her cheeks heat as embarrassment washed through her.

She'd just had the most intense sex dream of her life about her brand new, faceless *boss*.

Who she'd only ever spoken to once!

With a groan, she collapsed back into her pillows. Good God, she'd just met him! If she could truly qualify their encounter as meeting each other, that is. How could she dream something so vivid and *intimate* about a man she didn't know?

His voice, though...

Desire bloomed deep within her when she thought of his voice. The dying throbbing between her legs came roaring back to life.

God, that voice. He could enslave her with that voice. Command her, and she would obey without hesitation.

She shook her head. Where had *that* thought come from? Command? Obey?

Tell the world who owns you.

Her blush deepened.

Christine had never considered herself submissive in bed. So why did the mere thought of obeying Mr. Roux's commands leave her short of breath?

She shook her head again. Enough. She needed to pull herself together. It would be beyond unprofessional to begin her new job with inappropriate thoughts of her employer on her mind.

Still, her body refused to calm down. She squeezed her thighs together, but it did nothing to ease the ache.

A quick glance at the alarm clock on her nightstand showed her it was five thirty in the morning. She had half an hour before she needed to be up to be ready for work on time.

Perhaps she could indulge in her fantasy just a little more.

After all, she technically hadn't officially started her job yet...

Christine didn't need more convincing. The throbbing continued to increase, demanding relief. She ran her hands down her torso, let her fingers slip beneath the waistband of her panties, and gave the scenes from her dream free reign to play.

6

Christine

"Good morning, Ms. Davidson."

"Good morning, Mrs. Giry." Christine offered the older woman a warm smile, hoping it would be returned.

It wasn't.

"Mr. Roux has instructed that I give you this." Mrs. Giry produced a sleek black smartphone from her blazer's pocket and slid it across the table.

Hiding her disappointment, Christine picked up the phone. She and Mrs. Giry were back in the large dining room for breakfast. Darius, offering Christine the smile and cheerful morning greeting Mrs. Giry had not, had served up two plates filled with eggs benedict and bacon. Christine was not used to such hearty breakfasts, but found everything so delicious, she finished her plate.

At that moment, Darius returned from the kitchen with a steaming pot of tea.

"Freshen your cup?"

His presence brought immediate ease to the tension stiffening Christine's shoulders.

"Thank you, Darius, yes."

Once the chef had returned to the kitchen, Christine turned her attention back to her new phone, swiping her finger over the screen to unlock it. She was surprised to find a text message waiting for her.

E. Roux:

Good morning, Ms. Davidson. Please come to my study when you have finished breakfast.

Christine blinked in surprise. His study? Again? Her heart began to race. Images from her dream flashed through her mind, and she fought them back as her cheeks heated.

"Ms. Davidson? Are you feeling all right?"

Startled, she met Mrs. Giry's quizzical stare. She had to clear her throat before answering.

"Ummm...yes. Sorry. I just received a text from Mr. Roux asking me to go to his study once breakfast is over."

Mrs. Giry arched a dark eyebrow, but Christine couldn't tell if it was in disapproval or surprise. Perhaps both.

"Indeed? Well then, I would suggest you finish your meal quickly. Mr. Roux is not a man who likes to be kept waiting."

"Yes, ma'am." Leaving Mrs. Giry's presence became a singular priority. Christine continued to struggle to get a read on the woman, and couldn't tell if Mrs. Giry hated her or not. She had no idea why she would, but Christine couldn't imagine someone being so cold to people they liked.

Making quick work of her tea, she excused herself from the table. She could feel Mrs. Giry's eyes on her as she hurried from the dining room. When she was in the hall and out of sight, she paused and released a breath of relief. The respite was short lived, however. She needed to hurry to Mr. Roux.

She was once more assaulted with images of her dream, and felt her whole body tingle despite the release she'd given herself less than an hour before.

Her steps were hesitant as she made her way up to the second floor and down the hall. She had no idea what to expect. What if he was there? What if he wasn't? How could she face him if he was? How could she do her job if he wasn't?

Christine's mind was buzzing when she reached the doors to his private rooms. She paused, wondering if she should knock. Deciding it better to be safe than sorry, she raised her hand and rapped her knuckles against the wood.

She was greeted by silence.

Should I be surprised?

Disappointment lanced through her as she pushed the doors open and stepped inside.

Mr. Roux was nowhere in sight.

Gazing around, she pondered what it was she was supposed to do. She pulled out her phone, but there was no new message.

"I knew this would happen," she grumbled.

"Knew what would happen, Ms. Davidson?"

Christine jumped at the sound of Mr. Roux's voice, and then whirled around, expecting him to be behind her.

He wasn't.

"It's no use looking for me." His voice seemed to surround her. "I'm not there."

Confused, Christine turned towards his desk. A small speaker sat on its surface, facing her.

"Sir?"

"Yes, Ms. Davidson?" he answered, his voice ringing from the speaker.

She sighed. "I see."

"I sense disappointment in your tone, Ms. Davidson. Yet I did tell you we would not meet again as we did last night. Not so soon, anyway."

"Yes, you did say that." Bending down, Christine studied the little speaker. It was wireless, and unlike a regular intercom system, there was no call button that she needed to push to talk with him.

"The room is wired with cameras and microphones. I will be able to see and hear everything you do in there, and we will be able to communicate as if I was there with you."

He sounded so calm and casual about his elaborate nanny-cam system. Christine quirked a brow.

"That is extremely creepy. You do realize that?"

Mr. Roux's chuckle came through the little box, and Christine had to force herself not to react. She didn't trust that he wouldn't see her bite her lip or sigh in wonder at the sound. By his own admission, he had eyes everywhere.

"Mrs. Giry explained that I have cameras all over the house, didn't she? Apart from bedrooms and other private areas, that is."

Christine wandered around the room, searching for the hidden cameras as she replied, "Yes, she did warn me. She didn't say anything about microphones, though. That's a little NSA-ey, don't you think?" She shifted through the books on one of the shelves, but found nothing.

"The microphones are only set up in this room, specifically to create easier communication between us. When you are in other areas of the house, I will text or call you on your new work phone."

"Thank you for that, by the way." She peered inside a large stone floor vase, which appeared to be very old, and she was sure very expensive. No camera there either.

"I can assure you, Ms. Davidson, you will not find any of the cameras." His tone was amused. Christine rolled her eyes, exaggerating the gesture so he was sure to see it.

"It's hardly fair that you can see my every move, yet I'm not allowed to see you at all."

"My house, my rules."

Christine couldn't help but smile at his quip. She hadn't expected a sense of humor from him. Coming to a stop in the middle of the room and facing the speaker, she placed her hands on her hips.

"Fine. I get it. I don't get to see you yet. I promise not to push the matter anymore. Now, what would you like me to work on this morning?"

"Your acquiescence is a great relief," he responded in a dry tone. Then, turning business-like, he explained, "This morning I want you to familiarize yourself with my calendar, my filing system, the business structure of the label, and my typical means of communication. I want us to get to a point where you can do your job without my guidance being a necessary constant. The first step towards that is for you to learn how I operate."

Christine nodded. "That makes sense."

"On the desk, you will find your new laptop. All necessary programs have been installed, and an email account has been set up for you that is linked to my own email and calendar. You'll be able to keep track of my appointments and correspondence that way."

She walked towards the desk, spotting the brand new silver laptop. Picking it up, she sat and opened the computer. It asked for login information.

"Sir, what is my username and password?"

"Your username is cdavidson, all lowercase, and the password is Gounod."

Christine paused in the middle of typing, frowning as the word he'd used pulled at something in the back of her mind.

"Gounod? Is that even a word?"

His bark of laughter startled her. She gaped at the speaker. That sound was more alluring than his chuckle.

"A composer. A favorite of mine, truth be told."

Realization struck. "Faust. Charles Gounod. He composed Faust."

"Very good, Ms. Davidson." The purr of approval in his voice had her flushing. Ducking her head, she pretended to focus on her computer screen, praying he didn't notice her blush.

She typed in the password.

"Now, open your email..."

For the rest of the morning, Mr. Roux walked her through every piece of information she would need to fulfill her duties. He was patient with her, thorough in his explanations, and encouraging of the questions she had. They spoke with an ease that surprised her, especially given the barrier of the speaker. She was able to push aside memories of her dream and focus on her work, a feat that alleviated much of the tension she had started the morning with. They found a flow that carried them past noon.

"We'll stop here for now," Mr. Roux declared. "You should go to the dining room for lunch."

Closing her computer, Christine stretched her arms above her head, easing her stiffness from sitting in one spot for so long.

Lowering her arms, she asked without thinking, "Will you be joining us?"

Silence.

Christine realized her mistake too late.

"You said you wouldn't push the matter anymore." His voice was cold.

Sitting forward in her chair, she gazed around the room, hoping he could see the regret in her expression. "No! I'm sorry...it just slipped out. I didn't mean..."

"It's all right." It didn't sound like it was all right. The easy atmosphere they'd developed over the course of the morning vanished, and Christine felt her shoulders stiffen with dread.

"Mr. Roux..."

"You did well, this morning," he interrupted. "You will be with Mrs. Giry this afternoon."

"Wait! Mr. Roux..."

"Good day, Ms. Davidson."

The speaker went dead.

7

Erik

What had he done?

What a fool he was.

He'd ruined it.

She'd been enjoying his company the whole morning. Or, rather, she'd been enjoying conversing with him. He didn't know if his voice alone qualified as company.

Still, she'd been comfortable speaking with him. Had appeared at ease, despite the odd circumstances of her new position.

Then he'd gone and fucked it up.

He knew she hadn't meant to offend him. She hadn't even realized what she'd asked him. It had been a simple question. One that should have had a simple answer.

"Will you be joining us?"

"Yes, I'd like that."

But no. He couldn't.

Erik pushed away from the desk of monitors in his security room, images from around his home playing out before him. Mrs. Giry was in the library, dusting shelves with one hand as she spoke on her cellphone with the other, her expression stern.

Darius was in the kitchen, putting the finishing touches on the day's lunch, which increased Erik's guilt.

Christine was still sitting in his study. She appeared stunned.

He balled his hands into fists as his anger rose, but it was at himself. She had every right to be confused. Shocked, even. He'd been a complete ass to her.

But that was what his darkness did. It twisted his perceptions of the world. Made him paranoid and cruel.

It's what you deserve, monster.

His hands fell limp at his sides, and he rested his head against the back of his leather chair.

For a short time that morning, when they'd been able to talk with such ease, he'd felt the wicked tendrils of hope wrapping tighter around his heart. He'd begun to think that perhaps he could show himself to her. Maybe she wouldn't mind? Maybe she wouldn't be terrified?

Maybe she wouldn't be disgusted?

His behavior towards her, however, was a stark reminder that his ugliness was more than skin deep.

It was soul deep. He was broken beyond repair, and no amount of easy conversation would change that.

She would never want more from him.

He would never deserve her.

He was such a fucking fool.

* * *

Christine

Christine felt glued to her chair. She couldn't make herself move. All she could do was stare at the speaker and remember the icy tone of his parting words.

She'd messed up, and she didn't know how to fix it.

With a start, she realized, even if he was no longer speaking to her, it didn't mean he was no longer watching her. The thought made her shiver, but if it was from trepidation or something else entirely, she couldn't be sure. Raising her chin, she forced herself to rise to her feet and turn towards the door.

Christine said nothing as she left the room, but a part of her hoped *he* would.

The silence that followed her was deafening.

She stepped out into the hallway and let the door shut behind her. With a dejected sigh, she rested her back against the wood and gazed ahead, lost in thought.

No doubt, she was angry at herself, but she was also angry with *him*. Considering all the oddities of her job, he wasn't giving her much of a grace period to adjust. Did he have to go so cold on her because she made one mistake? Did he have *no* patience?

She ran her palms against the door. Guilt softened her, and she recognized she was trying to turn herself against him to protect her own damaged pride.

No, perhaps she wasn't angry at him after all. She wished she was. It'd make his rejection easier to swallow.

What was it about him that she found so fascinating?

Shaking her head, she resolved not to think about him anymore. Or, at least to try. She hurried down the hall and away from him, determined to continue with her day as if nothing had happened.

As if she didn't still have his deep, hypnotic voice ringing in her head.

Christine let out a soft groan as she crossed the second floor landing and began to descend the stairs.

She was such a fool.

* * *

Lunch proved less awkward than dinner. Darius had prepared a light meal, salad and a selection of sandwiches with meat he'd sliced himself, and then joined Christine and Mrs. Giry in the dining room to eat. While Mrs. Giry remained silent and stern-looking, Darius was a delightful companion, more than willing to indulge Christine in conversation.

"How has your first day been going?" he asked with a smile on his round, ruddy face. He sat across from her, next to Mrs. Giry, who was distracted by something on her phone.

Knowing she couldn't tell either of them the whole truth, Christine plastered on a grin and answered, "So far so good, I'm happy to say. Mr. Roux is a very easy person to work with," *Unless you say the wrong thing,* "and has been very thorough in his explanations of how he likes things to be run. I feel very at ease with my expected responsibilities." *Though far less at ease about my next encounter with our captivating employer.*

"Glad to hear it!" Darius exclaimed. "I'm happy that Mr. Roux has been so welcoming to you. He's an odd one, no doubt, but he's an easy man to work for once you get used to him."

Christine considered the chef for a few seconds, mulling a question over in her mind she wasn't sure she should ask. It was one she knew Mrs. Giry wouldn't approve of.

"Darius, do you *see* Mr. Roux all that often?"

Mrs. Giry's head snapped up, and she glared at Christine. Darius appeared startled, but recovered himself after a beat. Still, he didn't look comfortable when he offered his answer.

"I...I do see him. Not as often as Mrs. Giry, but..."

Overcome by excitement, Christine blurted, "What does he look like?"

Darius froze.

"That is quite enough," Mrs. Giry snarled, slapping her hand down on the table. "Darius need not be subjected to your inappropriate questions..."

"Amelia..." Darius attempted to interject.

Mrs. Giry shot him a cold look.

His expression was contrite. "My apologies, Mrs. Giry."

"No, I'm sorry," Christine said, regretting the question. "I shouldn't have asked you that. Mrs. Giry's right, it was inappropriate."

Darius offered her a small, but kind smile. "No need to apologize, my dear. Curiosity isn't a crime."

"In this house, it can be." Pushing to her feet, Mrs. Giry leaned over the table towards Christine. "You will mind your tongue, Ms. Davidson, if you wish to remain employed here."

Feeling like a child mid-scolding, Christine nodded. "Yes, ma'am." She needed to get a hold of herself. Twice now in one day her big mouth had gotten her into trouble.

"If you are done with your meal, we will get back to work." With that, the older woman turned away and headed towards the dining room door.

Christine shot an apologetic look towards Darius, abandoned the rest of her food, and stood to hurry after Mrs. Giry.

* * *

The first half of the afternoon was spent touring the house. Mrs. Giry showed Christine every room available to her, including an indoor swimming pool and sauna. She gawked at the opulence of the massive home. Mrs. Giry even took her out to the backyard, where a beautiful garden stretched from the house's huge stone terrace. The sunshine hurt her eyes after being in the low-lit interior of the home all day, but Christine let her head fall back to bask in the rays. White lilies and rose bushes were artfully arranged around a large stone fountain. A cherub stood in the middle of the fountain, a vase in its hands spilling over with water.

"This place is wonderful!" Christine turned to Mrs. Giry with a smile. "Thank you for bringing me out here."

The older woman was regarding her with a calculated look in her eye. It made Christine nervous.

"I brought you out here so that we might speak frankly, Ms. Davidson, without the risk of being overheard."

Taken aback, Christine sputtered, "W...what?"

"How old are you, Ms. Davidson?"

Where was this coming from? "Ma'am?"

"I'd peg you at about twenty-six or twenty-seven."

"Ummm...twenty-seven, Mrs. Giry."

The woman nodded. "Still very young indeed."

Frowning, Christine asked, "Why do you ask?"

Mrs. Giry didn't answer for several moments as she continued to stare at Christine. "You're quite lovely. Is the color of your hair naturally so red?"

The conversation was growing more confusing with each word. "Yes, it is. Mrs. Giry, please, why are you asking me these questions?"

"He likes you." She crossed her arms and lifted her chin. "Quite a lot for as short a time as you've been here. It's rather remarkable, though somewhat understandable given your beauty."

Stunned, Christine could only gape at the housekeeper. He liked her? Who? *Mr. Roux?* No way could that be true after her earlier foolishness.

Still, the thought sent a thrilling buzz coursing up her spine.

"How do you know he likes me?"

"It's obvious. The original plan was for you to spend your whole day with *me*, and I would teach you how to do your job. He did not inform me that those plans were changing. The first I heard of it was his text message to you at breakfast. There was no need for him to take up his time with your instruction, and then he ignored my messages all morning demanding an explanation."

Her words were accusatory, but Christine was delighted at the revelation. Still, she felt guilty that Mrs. Giry had been undermined on her account. It explained the woman's foul mood towards her.

"Mrs. Giry, I'm very sorry." *Though I can't say what I'm sorry for, exactly.* "I didn't mean to cause any type of issue between you and Mr. Roux."

Tilting her head, Mrs. Giry seemed to consider her apology. At length, she released a sigh and looked away.

"I suppose there is no real need for you to apologize. You only did what you were instructed to do." She met Christine's eyes again, and her voice grew hard. "Still, his interest in you has been immediate and out of character. I would advise you to tread carefully when it comes to Mr. Roux."

"Would he try to take advantage of me, somehow?" *Why* did that thought not fill her with unease? Why did it instead *excite* her?

Mrs. Giry scoffed. "No, you foolish child. I'm not worried about what *he* might do to *you*. Mr. Roux is a gentleman, and a professional. He would never do something to put his career and the label in jeopardy. I'm concerned about what *you* might do to *him*."

"What I might do to him?" Christine was baffled. What could she possibly do to Mr. Roux?

A flash of something crossed Mrs. Giry's expression. It might have been...sorrow.

"That man has been through enough. He doesn't need you coming in and giving him false hope for a future."

The conversation started pissing Christine off.

"What does that even mean?"

"It means you aren't to be trusted!" Mrs. Giry spat. "If you allow him to like you, he'll start thinking he can open himself up to you, but I know if he does you'll reject him."

"How can you think so little of him?" Christine snarled, affronted.

"I think the world of him! It's you who will disappoint him. Who will hurt him. A woman like you could never appreciate the true beauty of that man."

"A woman like me?" Christine had never hit another person in her life, but the thought of slapping Mrs. Giry across the face was very tempting.

"You only want him for his money and connections," the older woman hissed. "I've seen it before, and it nearly destroyed him the last time..." Mrs. Giry gasped, slapping her hand over her mouth, as if she hadn't meant to say that.

Christine froze. "The last time? What are you talking about?"

Mrs. Giry's face burned red, and she turned her back to Christine. "Nothing. Forget I said anything."

It dawned on Christine where this strange conversation was coming from. Mrs. Giry was *protective* of Mr. Roux, because she'd seen him hurt before, and she thought Christine would hurt him again.

Her heart softened toward the woman, her anger washing away.

"Mrs. Giry, I promise you my intentions are in no way to take advantage of Mr. Roux. I'm here because I love music, and his more than most. I just want to exist in his world. Nothing more."

Silence stretched between them, Christine's words hanging in the air like a lifeline.

At length, Mrs. Giry turned back around. Her expression was guarded, but some of the coldness had left her eyes.

"I hope you're telling me the truth."

"I am."

Raising her chin, Mrs. Giry murmured, "We'll see."

Turning, she walked back towards the open French doors of the house. After a moment of hesitation, Christine followed. Though she felt relief at the tenuous peace she'd seemed to have established with Mrs. Giry, her mind was in a riot over the woman's words.

"...he doesn't need you coming in and giving him false hope for a future."

"I've seen it before...it nearly destroyed him..."

Christine's heart ached, wondering what had happened. Was that previous heartbreak the reason he was so wary of people?

More questions about her new employer joined the ones she'd already been obsessing over, yet despite all that, one thought dominated her mind.

He likes me.

She tried, and failed, to hide her grin.

8

Christine

Mrs. Giry led Christine back through the house towards the foyer and into the parlor she'd seen when she'd first arrived. The space wasn't large, but it was cozy with its marble fireplace and sitting area. Mrs. Giry directed her to a table with a single chair sitting near the large window. There was a stack of manila folders on top of the table.

"Now, enough touring for today," Mrs. Giry said. "There's still time left for you to get some actual work done."

"Um, Mrs. Giry, I was hoping to see the recording studio..."

The housekeeper gave a firm shake of her head. "Not today. Mr. Roux has not indicated when he would like you to see that facility, so for the time being you are to work in the house." She picked up the folder sitting on top of the stack. "These are bids from several music vendors. We are looking to update some of our recording equipment, as well as bring in new instruments, and have reached out to each of them in regards to pricing. You are to go through these papers and summarize each bid."

Christine wanted to groan at the tediousness of the task, but kept her mouth shut.

Mrs. Giry continued. "You likely won't get through all of them today. This room is yours for as long as the task takes you. Any questions?"

Though she hated the idea of reading through all those papers, Christine shook her head and offered the woman an easy smile.

"It should be a piece of cake."

Mrs. Giry arched an eyebrow. "Go ahead and keep telling yourself that." She dropped the file back on the pile and walked out of the room.

Christine allowed her groan to escape. With a dejected sigh, she settled into her chair, grabbed the first file, and flipped it open.

It was going to be a long evening.

* * *

Glancing up from her reading for the first time in what had to be hours, Christine realized it was growing dark outside. The room was dim, the main source of light the standing lamp by the door. How long had she'd been working?

She checked her phone. Three hours had passed, and she wasn't even halfway through the pile of documents.

Sighing, she decided she would take a break and stretch her limbs.

Pushing to her feet, she threw her arms above her head, parts of her spine and neck cracking with the movement. She rubbed her tired eyes and wondered if she should turn on another light to save them from strain. There was something about the shadows playing around the room that she liked, however. They made the space cozy. Glancing towards the covered window, she decided against a lamp. Instead, she pulled open the heavy curtains to let in the rising moonlight.

Grinning, she gazed outside towards the grove of trees that lined the property. Their long shadows stretched across the meticulously manicured lawn. Christine could see the recording studio from where she stood, though the windows of that building were dark. She wondered if anyone else came on to the property during the day to work there. Mrs. Giry hadn't mentioned any other employees, but there had to be more. Perhaps she would meet them once she'd earned Mr. Roux's trust.

She watched the rising moon, a feeling of nostalgia overtaking her as she remembered an old song that had been a favorite of her mother's.

Opening her mouth, she let the familiar lyrics slip out.

"Magic in the moonlight...On this lover's June night...As I see the moonlight...Shining in your eyes..."

As she sang, she walked back to the table and picked up the file she'd been working on. She became lost in the song, moving around the room as she thumbed through the papers without seeing the words typed on them, her voice growing louder as the world around her began to slip away...

"Lovely."

Christine gasped. She dropped the file on the floor and whirled around as papers scattered at her feet. At first, the room appeared empty, but as her eyes adjusted to the dark, she could make out a shadowed figure in the far-left corner, half concealed by the thick curtains she'd pulled open minutes earlier. She felt her heart begin to thunder.

He was there. With her. Not a disembodied voice instructing her from afar, but a flesh and blood man mere steps away. If he would move to the side a few steps, she would be able to see him in the moonlight.

Yet he didn't move. He stayed hidden, and though she knew he was looking right at her, the corner was so dark she couldn't even see his eyes.

The silence stretched between them until she was able to regain her voice.

"Sir, I didn't hear you come in."

"I apologize for taking you by surprise. I have secret passages that I use to avoid running into anyone."

There was a tinge of *something* in his voice that made her heart clench. It wasn't quite sorrow, but not so simple as loneliness. It almost sounded like longing. Perhaps her eccentric hermit boss had ventured out of hiding because he wanted something more than his solitude.

Why come to her, though? Especially after their debacle of a morning...

"I want to apologize for this morning..."

"Don't speak of it. It's not worth revisiting."

Christine blinked, confused. If he didn't want to speak of it, why was he there?

"Is there anything else I can do for you?"

The curtains rustled as he adjusted his position.

"No. I came because I heard someone singing, and I found you. You have a beautiful voice, Christine. It's raw and unrefined, but lovely nonetheless. I couldn't help but seek out its owner."

She felt her cheeks flush at the compliment.

"You're very kind, sir, but I'm not a singer."

He chuckled, and she felt the heat in her face stretch down to the rest of her body as the dark sound washed over her.

"No, you're not a singer." A flash of white. Had he grinned? "But, you could be. With the proper training."

Christine gulped. "Training, sir?"

The curtain shifted again. "You said that you were unable to receive any kind of music lessons as a child, yes?"

He couldn't possibly be offering her what she thought he was. "Yes. After my father died, my mother...well, we couldn't afford it." Gerard Davidson had been as talented at spending as he had been at music, leaving Christine and her mom deeply in debt once he'd passed. That hadn't helped motivate her mother in any way to help Christine pursue her own dreams of music.

"It's not too late, you know. With raw talent such as yours, I don't imagine it would take much instruction to perfect it. I could provide you with that instruction, if you'd like."

Christine didn't respond for several moments as she processed his words. Could this really be happening? Could Erik Roux, a modern music legend, truly be offering to teach her to sing?

There had to be a catch.

"What would you ask for in return for your lessons?" She hated how timid she sounded.

There was a pause, and she could feel his eyes on her.

At length, his deep voice rumbled over her.

"What would you be willing to give?"

Anything. The thought popped into her head before he'd finished speaking, and she was startled to realize it was true. *My mind, my body, my soul. Whatever you asked for, I'd give it to you.*

She did not speak those words out loud.

"Sir, I'm not sure..."

Taking pity on her, he cut her stammering off. "I only tease. I would not think of coercing you into any arrangement you were not comfortable with. You are a marvelous employee, and I offer my tutelage free of charge or expectation. I simply hate to see such potential wasted."

Though his words should have relieved her, she found herself somewhat disappointed. What had she expected him to say? That he demanded her body as payment? What was *wrong* with her?

Yet the mere thought had her fantasies running wild. Him giving orders.

Her obeying.

He was speaking again, his voice breaking her from her thoughts. "Ms. Davidson?"

Shaking her head, she said, "I'm sorry sir, what did you say?"

A note of amusement entered his tone. "I was asking if you would like to take me up on my offer?"

"Oh, absolutely! It would be an honor. I don't know how I could ever thank you."

"I'm sure you'll think of something."

Though innocent enough, his words sent a delicious shiver down her spine. A few ideas came to mind...

"I'll leave you to your work, then. Good evening, Ms. Davidson."

"Good evening, Mr. Roux."

The heavy curtain waved, and the next second, he was gone.

9

Erik

He'd done it. For good or ill, he'd spoken with her, and his infatu-ation had intensified. Lying in his bed, staring at the ceiling, he pon-dered his next move.

Erik had stewed all afternoon about his morning encounter with Ms. Davidson. He'd paced the floor of his security room, watching as she and Mrs. Giry explored the house. His obsession with Ms. David-son was troubling, the suddenness of it startling. Yet, he couldn't fight her pull. She'd appeared fascinated with everything that Mrs. Giry showed her, her beautiful amber eyes wide and awed. He wanted those eyes staring up at *him* in awe as his fingers ran through her wild red hair.

Little chance of that happening, though, especially after the way he'd treated her that morning. If she ever saw him, at worst her gaze would fill with terror or disgust. At best, with pity.

He'd forced himself to walk away from his wall of monitors once Mrs. Giry had taken her outside and out of his sight. It wasn't healthy, his fascination with her. He was turning into a manic stalker. Was growing disgusted with himself. Slipping out of his security room, he'd wandered through the hidden passageways of the house. When he was feeling restless, he would walk the length of the passages to burn off steam. As he'd meandered, he'd pretended he was trapped within the walls so that he was not tempted to seek out Ms. Davidson.

It was during his skulking in the dark that he'd heard her singing.

Her voice had entranced him, though he could not say for sure he would have found it so entrancing had it not been hers. Still, she had a good voice, whatever his bias. Like a doomed sailor following the song of a siren, he'd gravitated towards her, slipping into the parlor without her noticing to hide by the window.

If possible, she appeared more beautiful than the night before. She'd been wearing a black, knee-length pencil skirt and white silk blouse. Her hair had been tamed, pulled back into a loose knot at her neck. Her feet had been bare, her black high-heels abandoned as she'd danced around the room.

She'd been a vision in the moonlight.

He hadn't been able to stop himself from speaking to her.

To his surprise, she hadn't been angry with him. Hadn't rejected him. She'd even attempted to apologize to him for the morning, but he hadn't wanted to hear it. Instead, he'd proposed to be her music teacher.

What had he been thinking?

He needed to distance himself from her, not find new ways to be close to her.

Sitting up, he considered the only options available to him. He could rescind his offer to teach her. That would be the most logical solution. However, her voice was so lovely, and he really did hate to see such raw talent wasted. Plus, the excitement in her eyes had been so intoxicating, he didn't think he had it in him to take that from her.

He wasn't that much of a monster.

But could he teach her, work with her, and not desire her?

No. It was impossible.

Erik dropped his head into his hands with a groan. If only he could have her, just once. Then perhaps the worst of his desire would be sated, and he could move past her.

It wasn't an option, though. He knew that. Still, he yearned.

"No woman will look upon your face and want you between her legs. They'll scream and run as if the devil himself is in pursuit."

He gnashed his teeth, his mind cracking, more memories threatening to surface. With a growl, he left his bed and stalked towards the door. Throwing it open, he entered his study and made his way towards his piano. He would pour himself into his music until he could think of nothing else. Not her. Not his torment. Nothing but the melody he created.

Sitting on the bench, he slid his fingers across the keys, the cool feel of them like a salve for his soul. Closing his eyes, he released a slow breath and began to play.

The music consumed him, as it always did, and for the length of his song, he wasn't a monster. Wasn't a tortured soul yearning for a woman he could never have. A devil lusting for an angel.

For the length of his song, he was free.

* * *

Christine

Christine woke the next morning before her alarm went off again. She lay in her bed, staring at the ceiling, replaying the events of the previous day over and over in her head. Her stomach growled. She hadn't gone to dinner after she'd left the parlor because the thought of dealing with Mrs. Giry after her encounter with Mr. Roux had been too exhausting.

The memory of her conversation with Mr. Roux filled her with equal parts giddiness and trepidation. It had been unexpected, to be sure, but when he'd offered to be her teacher...

It was a dream come true.

He was going to teach her to sing.

She was going to *sing*.

It was too unbelievable for words.

When her alarm sounded at last, she switched it off and slid out of bed. Though she wondered what tasks Mrs. Giry would have for her that day, she couldn't help but wonder if Mr. Roux would try to talk to her again.

She checked her phone, but there were no messages.

It's still early, she told herself, though the reassurance didn't stop the nervous churning in her stomach.

He'd said he'd be her teacher, but he hadn't told her where or when her lessons would be.

What if it had all been a ruse?

Her thoughts swirled as she prepared for the day. As she stepped out of her room, Christine shook her head, forcing her growing doubts aside.

He was trying to earn her trust as much as she was trying to earn his. He wouldn't disappoint her. She just had to be patient.

Resolved, Christine squared her shoulders and raised her chin. She wouldn't let herself be distracted. She would focus, do her job, and wait for word from Mr. Roux.

He would contact her.

She was sure of it.

* * *

By midafternoon, she was less sure.

The work day was nearly over, and she hadn't heard anything from Mr. Roux. No texts. No emails. No hidden interactions.

Her hope in him was beginning to slip away.

She'd powered her way through the long day, but as the hours slipped by, it had become more and more difficult to concentrate. Mrs. Giry had set her up in the parlor once again, and after she'd finished going through and taking notes on the rest of the bids, she'd been tasked with budget work and updating Mr. Roux's calendar.

No surprise, the calendar did not take long to update. Mr. Roux was not overburdened with social engagements.

The rest, however, was another matter.

Though she would claim no skill as an accountant, even she could see that *Fantôme Records'* finances rested on shaky ground. It seemed that a label with a single signed artist could only go so far when it relied exclusively on redistribution and didn't produce new music.

The operating budget, which she was expected to oversee, was tight. She couldn't quite believe they expected to stay running with it. She chewed on her lip as she scanned Excel sheet after excel sheet, trying to make sense of the numbers.

They only gave her a throbbing headache.

Deciding she needed a break, Christine stood up from her little table, slid back into her shoes, and left the parlor to make her way towards the kitchen in search of a cup of tea and a snack.

When she entered the dining room, she froze at the voices coming from the kitchen.

Frowning, she stepped out of her shoes to ease closer to the kitchen door without making a sound. Mrs. Giry and Darius were speaking. Unable to help herself, Christine leaned against the wall so she could listen in on their tense conversation.

"I'm at my wits end, Darius," Mrs. Giry said. "I don't know what else to say to try and convince him."

"Does he understand how bad things are?" Darius asked.

"Yes! He does, but he can't seem to bring himself to care enough."

"Oh, dear."

Christine frowned. Were they talking about Mr. Roux?

"He's going to lose everything if he doesn't do something." Mrs. Giry sounded more agitated than Christine would have thought her typical cold-demeanor capable of.

"You can't force a person to create," Darius pointed out.

Mrs. Giry huffed in frustration. "*He* doesn't have to create. He could sign new artists, hire more engineers to mix tracks. He doesn't have to have a hand in every piece of music that comes out of this place."

Christine was shocked at Mrs. Giry's blatant criticisms of Mr. Roux. The woman had been so protective of the man the day before.

Darius released a deep sigh.

"Amelia, you know he hasn't been the same these last five years. That woman broke him. Not just his heart, but his soul."

Woman? What woman? And why was Christine jealous of her?

"I know, Darius." Mrs. Giry's voice went soft, almost sad. "But it's not just about him, not when it comes to the label. I'd hoped that his hiring a new assistant after all this time meant he had plans to restart things, but he's told me nothing. He has no new plans, no recording sessions scheduled. We can't keep going like this."

"Have you told Christine any of this? Does she have any idea how bad things are?"

There was a brief bout of silence before Mrs. Giry admitted, "No, I haven't told her outright. He forbids it. I'm sure he doesn't want to scare her off, but I gave her the operational budget files and told her she was to oversee them."

"Amelia!"

"She has a right to know!"

Christine had to hold back a squeak of surprise. She'd wondered why Mrs. Giry would deem to put the budget in her care. Had Mrs. Giry truly been looking out for her? Or was she just trying to scare her away?

And why did Mr. Roux not want her to know about any of this?

"Was that really your motivation, or did you want her to get a whiff of the impending disaster and flee? I know you don't like her..."

"Darius, please. Whether I like her or not is of no consequence. That girl should know that there's no future here. Not for her, and not for us if things don't change."

No future...

The dark figure from her dream flashed through her mind, and she felt her heart clench. Would she have to leave Mr. Roux before she ever got the chance to really know him?

Christine didn't think she could hear any more. Pushing from the wall, she hurried on the balls of her feet towards the dining room door, picking up her shoes along the way. Once in the hallway, she stopped, unsure where she should go. Back to the parlor, and those damning files? Or back to her room to...what? Pack? Hide? Cry?

Vibrations from her phone made her jump. Fishing the device from her pocket, she saw she had a text message from Mr. Roux at last.

Come to the study.

She stared at the message for several seconds before tucking the phone back into her pocket. She didn't think, didn't want to, just acted. Running through the house in her bare feet, Christine hurried to the man who haunted her mind.

10

Erik

Erik paced his study, impatient as he waited for her to arrive. He'd resisted the urge to contact her, but his resolve had weakened as the day had gone on. As the afternoon began to wane into evening, he'd broken down and texted her.

He couldn't ignore her, he reasoned. He'd promised to teach her.

Yes. That was it. He was simply keeping his word.

He shook his head in disgust of himself, knowing he was justifying behavior that Ms. Davidson had every right to be wary of.

Still, he'd use the lessons as an excuse to be near her. He wasn't strong enough to deny himself her presence.

A sudden, tentative knock on the door had his heart thudding with anticipation.

She was here.

Backing his way into the shadows of the room, he pressed against a panel on the wall which revealed a hidden door leading into his secret passageways. Stepping inside, he let the panel close behind him. He made his way towards the two-way mirror built into the wall of his study next to his piano. From there, he could see every inch of the room. When he was settled, he waited for her to knock again.

Pushing the button on the intercom next to his mirror, he said, "Come in." His voice reverberated throughout the room, loud enough for her to hear.

After a moment, the door opened and Christine stepped inside.

He lost his breath at the sight of her. She'd let her hair hang loose around her shoulders today, and the color appeared brighter against the green of her sheath dress.

"Mr. Roux?" she called.

He pushed the button. "Hello, Ms. Davidson."

She jumped at the sound of his voice, but didn't appear startled for long, though he noted the look of disappointment that crossed her expression. Had she been hoping he'd be in there with her?

No such luck, Ms. Davidson.

Closing the door behind her, she moved to stand in the middle of the room. She crossed her arms and gazed around.

"I received your text," she said, her voice tinged with frustration. He found it oddly satisfying. "I'm here. What is it that you need, sir?"

He grinned at her impertinence. "I would think that's obvious."

Erik watched as she swiveled her head from side to side, her eyes scanning the corners and ceiling of the room.

"Not using the speaker this time," she observed.

Sharp woman.

He held the button down. "No, not this time. This room also has its own intercom system so I can speak to visitors while I watch them from..." Erik stopped, hesitant to reveal his hiding spot.

Christine tilted her head, however, and narrowed her eyes. "Watch them from where?"

She swept her gaze around the study again before locking in on the mirror. With slow, deliberate steps, she moved closer. Erik observed her in silence, curious as to what she would do.

Coming to a stop, she murmured, "You're back there."

His body tensed, and for a heartbeat, his paranoia made him believe she could see him through the glass. He let out a deep breath, though, remembering that was impossible.

Pretending he hadn't heard her, he asked, "What was that, Ms. Davidson?"

Her eyes flashed with something resembling defiance, and it thrilled him.

She raised her chin. "You're behind this mirror, aren't you? Watching me?"

He didn't see a point in lying to her. "Yes."

She placed her hands on her hips. "Why do you insist on putting me at such a disadvantage?"

He grinned. She'd said as such before, but he wanted to tease her. "What do you mean?"

"You are able to see me, whether I like it or not, but I don't have the choice to see you. It puts me at an automatic disadvantage when we interact, as I can't read you the same way you get to read me. That's not exactly fair, sir."

She was right, of course. It was unreasonable of him to insist on anonymity and not give her the same luxury of choice.

Unfortunately for her, it was not something he was willing to compromise on.

"As I believe I've said before, my house, my rules."

He chuckled when she rolled her eyes and didn't even try to hide it from him.

"Is there a point to my being here, sir?"

The clear fact that she was not intimidated by him was more refreshing than he could have anticipated.

"Didn't I tell you I'd teach you to sing, Ms. Davidson?" Her eyes went wide in surprise. "I intend to keep my word."

Her lips parted. "Oh...I see."

Unable to resist, he decided to tease her more. "Do you still wish me to instruct you? If not, you're free to go..."

"No!" she exclaimed, losing her composure for a moment. He watched, fascinated, as she regained her control before continuing. "I mean, no, I do want you to instruct me. I can't thank you enough for this opportunity..."

"Don't thank me yet," he interrupted. "I don't intend to go easy on you."

"Of course, sir. I'm ready to work hard. I'm yours to command."

Oh, Ms. Davidson, you are treading on dangerous ground with such promises...

"Very good," he said, keeping his hungry thoughts to himself. "Shall we begin?"

* * *

Christine

An hour later, there was a part of Christine regretting her declaration of assurance that she could handle the hard work he'd promised. He hadn't exaggerated, and she'd had no idea how exhausting a singing lesson could be. They hadn't even done that much. After he'd guided her through a warm-up, it'd been mostly breathing techniques, correcting of her posture, and testing her vocal range. Still, he'd had her go through chords again and again until her throat was sore. When she'd voiced her discomfort, he'd informed her in a firm tone that she was relying too much on her vocal cords, and needed to engage her diaphragm.

By the end of their session, she was filled with doubt.

"Rest your voice tonight, and drink plenty of water," his disembodied instructions filled the room. She kept her gaze locked on the mirror, knowing that's where he hid.

"Yes sir," she croaked, pulling her hair off her neck to cool her heated skin. Moving towards a loveseat near the piano, she sat.

"I told you I wouldn't go easy on you."

"You did."

Silence followed, and she waited to see if he would break it first. Though he remained a mystery, she was managing to catch glimpses of his personality through their exchanges.

He was patient, but a perfectionist.

He spoke with confidence, and was commanding with music, but there was a hesitancy when they spoke outside of that context.

The more she picked up, the more fascinated she became.

At length, he murmured her name. "Christine..."

Her breath caught in her throat. It was the first time he'd used her first name. She could only manage a whispered, "Yes, sir?"

"I...I want you to..."

She sat up straighter, her gaze on the mirror unwavering.

"You want me to...what?"

"I...I want you to know..." he stopped, and she was frustrated that she couldn't see him to read his body language to know where his hesitation was stemming from. "I want you to know that you...have a very beautiful voice."

While the compliment was pleasing, Christine was disappointed at his words. She couldn't say why, however, because she didn't know what she wanted him to say instead.

"Thank you, sir."

An awkward tension settled in the room, and Christine had the distinct feeling that he wanted to say more to her. He was holding himself back, however, and it maddened her not to know why.

"We'll meet every day for an hour," he ordered, slipping back into his instructor persona. "When you are done with your work day, report here for your lesson. Is that agreeable?"

Though it was a question, she didn't feel she had much of a choice.

"Yes, Mr. Roux. That sounds very agreeable."

"Then that will be all for the evening. I will see you tomorrow, Ms. Davidson."

"Yes. Until tomorrow, Mr. Roux."

* * *

After that first lesson, Christine fell into a daily routine. Every morning she would wake, eat breakfast with Mrs. Giry, and spend the day working either in the parlor or out in the garden. Some days she would eat lunch with Mrs. Giry, and other days Darius would bring her meal to her so she could continue working. She never brought up the conversation she had overheard between them, but it came to her mind often. There wasn't anything she could do about it herself, and if her time at *Fantôme Records* was limited, she wanted to make the most of the opportunity while she could. It wasn't her work which fascinated her, though, as it was all pretty basic responsibilities that would be assigned in most any type of office setting.

No, it was her nights that excited her, when she would visit Mr. Roux's study for her singing lessons.

Though he kept himself hidden away during their sessions, she could sense him on the periphery of the room, and his mere presence made her heart race.

His deep voice, while firm in his instruction, seemed to wrap around her until she was consumed by him.

"Breathe, Christine..."

"You're still not engaging your diaphragm..."

"You were flat on that note..."

He didn't go easy on her, and there were moments she wondered if she could ever meet his high expectations. He would pepper his criticisms with praise, however, building up her confidence when she doubted her own abilities.

"That's lovely, Christine..."

"You are a natural, truly..."

"I could listen to you sing all night..."

Yet, as her voice grew stronger and her skills improved, Christine found herself growing more and more anxious with each lesson that passed. In all their interactions, she sensed he kept himself distant from her, and not just physically. He did not talk about himself, or ask her questions about herself. It was clear he was trying to keep the exchanges from turning too intimate, but it drove her crazy. The more time they spent together, the more desperate she grew for him.

To see him.

To touch him.

She had no doubt her growing desire for him was reciprocated. There were moments when he would let his guard down, would slip up for just a second, and she would catch hints of how much he wanted her as well. His voice would grow husky when he complimented her. He'd once made particular note of her hair, admitting to being fascinated by its color, and she'd heard hunger in his tone.

He wanted her. She wanted him. Yet, he kept her at arm's length, making it clear that he wouldn't be the one to initiate the first move.

It would have to be her. An intimidating prospect, to be sure, and one she hesitated moving forward with. However, she knew she could only take so much.

It was at the end of her first month in the house that she at last reached her limit.

Christine made her way to the study, per usual, but paused outside the door.

She released a deep breath, building up her courage before she walked into the room. It was now or never. She wouldn't make it through one more session with him and the distance he forced between them.

Resolved, Christine squared her shoulders and raised her fist to knock on the door, giving him ample warning of her arrival before she let herself inside.

"Mr. Roux?" she called as she did every evening. Making her way across the room towards the mirror, she waited for him to reply.

"Good evening, Ms. Davidson."

Disappointment lanced through her. Every day she hoped he wouldn't interact with her through the intercom, but would stand in the study with her. Every day, she was left wanting.

Today would be different.

"Are you ready to begin...?"

"Sir, I need to speak with you about something."

There was silence, and she wondered if he was taken off guard by her boldness. Not that she could tell unless he spoke. The thought had her clenching her jaw.

"What is it you need to speak about, Christine?"

She hesitated with her next words. This was where it would get tricky.

"Would you come in here, before I tell you?" She held her breath as she waited for his reply.

It took several moments, and his words were cautious when he finally spoke. "Why do you need me to come in there to speak to me? We are speaking now, aren't we?"

Deep breath in. Deep breath out.

"Please, sir. I promise I won't look at you. I'll keep my gaze locked on the wall, if that is what you wish." To emphasize her promise, she turned her body away from the mirror and stared at the wall next to the door.

"I still fail to see the necessity of my physical presence."

She had known it would be difficult to convince him, but frustration welled up within her anyway.

"Please, sir...I just need you near me!" As soon as the words were out, she froze. She hadn't meant to cry out like that. Hadn't meant to let slip how desperate she was.

Christine waited, fearful. Tears began to form in her eyes as time stretched on without a response from him. Had he left? Had she just ruined everything?

All the sudden, she heard a noise behind her. It sounded like a small door opening and closing, and then footsteps followed. She dared not move, keeping her gaze locked ahead even as the temptation to look his way grew with every one of his steps.

He stopped when he was so close behind her, she could smell the familiar sharp scent of his cologne.

"Well, you have me here, Christine. Now what?"

His voice, clear and deep, free of the interference and distortion of electronic devices, sent a delicious shiver rushing down her spine.

She felt paralyzed, unable to move or speak. Fear and doubt began to poke at her plan, and she struggled to get any words out in response to his question.

"Christine, what do you want?" His tone was tinged with frustration.

Closing her eyes, she took another deep breath, shaking away any thoughts of failure.

It's now or never, she thought. *There's no turning back.*

"I have a request of you, sir."

11

Christine

"What is it that you want from me, Christine?" There was caution in his tone, as if he knew what she was going to ask him.

Christine gulped, but raised her chin before answering.

"I want to see you, sir."

"Impossible."

That's what she had been afraid he would say. Still, the words stung.

"Why?" she whispered.

He released an audible breath, and she wondered how he showed his frustration. Clenched hands? Taut jaw? Lips drawn into a hard line?

It frustrated her yet again not to know.

"I'm afraid your interest would...dissipate, if you saw me." His tone was firm, but there was a quiver of vulnerability underlying his words.

"I very much doubt that," she admitted on a breath.

Silence. Again, she wondered at his body's way of communicating his feelings. These interactions would be much easier if she could observe him.

"You cannot see me," he snapped at last. "What else could you want?"

She closed her eyes as disappointment washed through her. Still, she recognized the opportunity for what it was, and was not going to leave this interaction empty handed. Saying the words out loud, however, proved difficult.

Opening her eyes, she stared straight ahead.

"If I cannot see you, then I want...I want you to touch me."

Silence once more. This time, however, the tension between them crackled.

"You don't know what you're asking."

"I know exactly what I'm asking."

He snarled. "Do you know how hard it has been to resist you until now? You are treading into dangerous territory, Ms. Davidson."

His words made her shiver, but not from fear.

"I said, I know what I'm asking."

"I'm your boss."

She fought a grin. "I don't care."

"I'm your teacher."

"Still don't care."

"This is highly inappropriate." Amusement crept into his words and, to her delight, anticipation.

"Perhaps, but that just makes it more interesting."

His next words were hesitant. "I...I don't want to hurt you. To take advantage of you."

Tenderness swelled within her. He was so dark and temperamental, yet so gentle and considerate. The contradictions within him only made him that much more intriguing.

"I know," she murmured, wishing she could touch him. Kiss him. Hold his hand. Offer some comfort and assurance. "You won't."

He might. An evil little voice whispered in her head. *He could take your heart and rip it to shreds if you let him.*

The thought startled her, but before she could dig for its source, she sensed him move behind her.

"Christine." His breath warmed the back of her neck as he spoke her name.

Her entire body reacted in an instant. Her breath shortened, her stomach clenched, and her breasts grew taut. Heat rushed through her, and her sex began to throb with arousal.

He hadn't even touched her, simply whispered her name, and she was melting for him. It terrified her how much power he had over her.

She prayed he didn't realize it himself, because she couldn't afford one more disadvantage against him.

He skimmed a bare finger up her arm. The touch was unexpected and jarring after so long without physical contact. Christine flinched with a cry. She could feel the trail of his finger on her skin even after he took his hand away, as if he'd burned her.

"So sensitive," he murmured. "One small touch, and you're shivering. But with what, my dear? Fear? Or something much darker?" Before she could respond, his lips brushed her ear.

Her knees almost gave out.

"Please...Mr. Roux..." she whimpered, though she wasn't sure what she was begging for. For him to stop his torment? For him to continue? It was maddening, knowing he was so close, feeling him just at her back, but not being able to see him and touch him herself.

"When we're like this, I'm not your boss," he murmured, nipping the shell of her ear with his teeth. "Call me by my first name."

Christine bit her lip to try and contain her smile. "Erik."

She felt his own grin spread against her throat. His tongue dipped out to lick at her skin.

She gasped, desperate to feel him with her own hands

He'd never said she *couldn't* touch him. Her only order had been to stay facing away.

Feeling bold and drunk on lust, Christine reached her left hand back. When her fingers touched the cloth of his pants, she trailed them up his leg before gripping his thigh. A thrill ran through her when she found it hard with muscle.

So, her phantom didn't only exercise his mind.

He hissed in a breath, tension radiating off him, but he didn't remove her hand.

"What are you doing?" he demanded in a strangled voice.

"I'm not sure," she answered with all honesty. "I just need..." *To feel you. To touch you. To be wrapped up in you.* "I need you."

He pushed up against her back, dislodging her hand from his thigh. His chin met the top of her head. God, he was so tall! His heat engulfed her, and both his hands gripped her hips to pull her even tighter against him. Christine moaned when she felt his hardening length grind into her.

His hands began to slide up her torso, gliding over the silk of her blouse. They were large, with long, slender fingers, but strong as they gripped her. Up, up, up they traveled until he cupped her breasts and gave a gentle squeeze. She covered his hands with her own and felt that shock again when skin touched skin.

He brought his lips to her shoulder, darting his tongue out as he made his way up her throat. She tilted her head to give him better access.

When he reached her ear, he groaned, "I need you too."

Christine couldn't help herself. She had to feel more of him. Releasing his hands, she slid her arms back and up towards his face. Her left hand met smooth skin and sharp features, but her right hand met...leather?

Confused, Christine froze, and that seemed to snap him out of his own lust-filled haze. His right hand left her breast and snatched her wrist, pulling her fingers from his face.

"No," he growled, wrapping her arm around the front of her torso and trapping it against her. He grabbed her other arm and did the same, forcing her to hug herself as he maintained his grip on her wrists. She struggled against him, but couldn't break his hold.

"Erik..."

His grip tightened at the sound of his name.

"No. I did not give you permission to touch me."

Why? She couldn't begin to guess, but the leather on his face baffled her. Was he wearing a mask?

His lips were at her ear again. "Stay like this. Do not move." He let her go and stepped back. Curiosity had her obeying him without thought.

What was he planning? How long was she expected to wait?

A silky piece of cloth appeared before her eyes. She blinked in surprise, but didn't move.

"Will you allow me to blindfold you?"

Christine hesitated in answering. She'd never been blindfolded before. It would put her at his mercy, make her more vulnerable than she'd yet to be with him. Her mind worried, wondering if she could trust him, but her body screamed at her to submit.

With a slow, careful nod, she gave in to her own desires. "Yes."

He brushed his lips against her ear again. "Excellent."

Erik pulled the cloth over her eyes. It wasn't thick enough to block out all light, but she was blinded to the room. She released a deep breath as he secured it at the back of her head.

He stepped away from her again, and she felt a moment of panic. What was he going to do? She almost loosened her arms, but forced herself to stay still.

"Don't worry, Christine. I'm not going to hurt you."

She almost cried out. He was standing in front of her! If she wasn't blindfolded, she'd be able to see him. The thought almost had her ripping the cloth from her face, but she knew this was a test. It was why he hadn't bound her hands. He wanted to see if she would obey him, even when faced with her greatest temptation.

Gritting her teeth, she raised her chin and kept her arms tight around her.

His large hand cupped her cheek. Heat spread from that point of contact to the rest of her body.

"You are lovely beyond words," he murmured.

"Erik..."

Her breathless moan was cut off when his lips crashed down on hers. She let out a cry of delight, and he took full advantage, sweeping his tongue into her mouth. It became more and more of a struggle to keep her arms locked. She was desperate to reach out and touch him, but she knew she hadn't passed his test yet. His other hand came up, and he tilted her head so he could deepen their kiss. Christine melted into him, pressing her body as close to his as she could.

He moved from her mouth, kissing across her jawline, then down her throat. His hands slid down to her breasts, and he gripped the front of her blouse as if he would tear it open.

Christine waited with bated breath, but then everything stopped. He didn't strip her, instead releasing her and letting his hands fall away.

"Erik...wha...?"

He let out a long sigh as he dropped his head to rest against her shoulder.

"Christine, what are you doing to me?"

He spoke so softly it was difficult for her to hear him.

She bit her lip. "I don't know. Perhaps the same thing you're doing to me?"

His body stiffened against hers, but relaxed again after a heartbeat.

He chuckled, and she felt the vibration of the sound against her throat.

Turning his face, he brushed his lips against the base of her neck before lifting himself up and away from her. With a gentle touch, he reached out and pulled her arms apart, smoothing his hands down to guide them to rest at her sides. He ran a finger down her cheek until he reached her chin. Cupping it, he pulled her face forward, the force of the action making her gasp.

His lips touched hers, and at first he kept the contact light. Then, as if he couldn't help himself, he grew more aggressive, pressing his mouth flush against hers. She clenched her hands into fists to keep from reaching out and grabbing him, but she parted her lips in the hope of coaxing his tongue inside. He didn't oblige her, however, and pulled away again.

"That's enough for now."

He removed his hands from her, and the room grew quiet. It took Christine several minutes to realize he was gone. Reaching up, she tore the piece of cloth from her face and whirled around, searching the room for any sign of him.

She threw the cloth to the floor, frustration and anger boiling up within her. They'd been so close! She'd passed his test, damn it.

So why was he still pushing her away?

1 2

Erik

What had he done?

Erik stared out his bedroom window at the night sky, his thoughts rioting. He couldn't get Christine out of his head. Not that he'd had luck with that the past month, but that had been *before* he'd known what she tasted like. She'd been an obsession. Now, he feared she would be his addiction.

His blood remained heated from their encounter, his body tense, his cock hard. He couldn't remember ever reacting to a woman so strongly. Not even Carla. Erik shook his head before unwanted memories rose to the surface. He had enough demons to deal with at present.

Tainted...broken...monster...

They'd crossed a line tonight. *He'd* crossed a line. She was his employee. His student! He'd taken advantage of her. No matter how insistent she'd been, he should have remained firm. Yet, his willpower had crumbled in the face of her own desire.

Out of everything, that's what baffled him the most.

She'd wanted him. *She'd* pursued *him.*

He couldn't wrap his head around it. His lust for her was torturous, but understandable. She was gorgeous, brilliant, kind, and her voice could melt the coldest of hearts.

For her to lust after him, though?

Life had never been that generous.

"How could I want such a wretched creature?"

Resting his hands on the windowsill, he pressed his forehead against the cool glass and closed his eyes, images of Christine flooding his mind. They way she'd looked with her beautiful face blindfolded, her mouth his to devour. She'd been so obedient. So pliable to his commands.

The memory made his cock twitch. He winced as his arousal began to turn painful. His eyes flashed open and he pushed away from the window. He knew it wasn't about to go away on its own.

Not when Christine's scent lingered in his nostrils.

Turning towards his bed, he unbuckled his belt. As he stripped, he swore to himself that he would never cross that line with her again. Spending in his hand to thoughts of her would be enough. It *had* to be enough.

It was all he deserved.

* * *

Christine

Once again, Christine found herself lying sleepless in her bed, staring at the ceiling, thoughts of Mr. Rou...of *Erik* swirling in her head.

Thoughts of him, and what he'd done to her.

She touched her fingertips to her lips. They still tingled from his kiss.

Letting out a sigh, she let her arm drop back down to her side. She wasn't fool enough to think a single kiss would make things better between them, but it did change things. He'd acknowledged his desire for her and acted upon it.

She shivered when she remembered how he'd commanded her. Christine had never considered herself the submissive type, but with him...

There was something thrilling about letting him take charge. About letting him take control of her body. About putting her pleasure entirely in his hands.

The thought had her flushing, her blood heating.

Still, the fact that he'd blindfolded her bothered her. Not that she hadn't enjoyed it to some degree, but he hadn't done it for her benefit. He'd done it for his protection. She'd done everything he'd asked, and he still didn't trust her. Had left her wanting in more ways than one.

The thought was like a bucket of cold water to her arousal.

Frustrated, she sat up and slapped her hands against the mattress. What did a single kiss matter if he maintained this infuriating distance between them?

She hugged her knees to her chest, despondent.

What was she going to do? What *could* she do? Any attempt she'd made to get to know him better had been met with total resistance. Their brief physical encounter was the only real headway she'd been able to make.

Leaning back against the headboard, she furrowed her brow and bit her lip as a thought struck her. She wanted more than just sex from him, true. She wanted to know him, to experience his creative genius and passion for herself, but he kept himself guarded. His body, though, was a different matter. Though he continued to hide from her, he'd turned bold when he'd touched her.

Maybe that was the key. If she could seduce him, convince him to explore the wild physical attraction between them, perhaps he would come to trust her with more. If she made herself vulnerable to him, he might make himself vulnerable in turn.

Christine let out a groan, dropping her head into her hands. When had she become the type of woman to throw herself at a man? How pathetic was she?

She just couldn't get his touch out of her mind. His voice. His kiss.

Maybe her desire for him was intensified by her curiosity? Maybe she'd simply been too long without a man? Maybe she was a glutton for punishment and drama? Whatever the reason, she couldn't fight how much she wanted him. Couldn't fight the pull towards him.

The intensity of that pull scared her. She knew, if she wasn't careful, she could lose herself to it. To him.

But a part of her thought it was a risk worth taking.

* * *

"Ms. Davidson, I would like an explanation."

Surprised, Christine looked up from her laptop to find Mrs. Giry standing in the doorway to the parlor. As usual, the woman looked pristine in a gray pantsuit with her shining hair pulled back in a high bun.

Christine had kept her distance from Mrs. Giry ever since their conversation in the garden. She could appreciate the woman's protectiveness of Erik, but she didn't appreciate being accused of playing the role of gold digger. Mrs. Giry had been accommodating, limiting their interactions to work-related necessities.

Christine doubted the reason for her current interruption had anything to do with work.

"An explanation for what, Mrs. Giry?"

What could I have possibly done now?

The housekeeper moved into the room and crossed her arms, glaring down at Christine.

"I've noticed you've been spending your evenings in Mr. Roux's study."

Narrowing her eyes, Christine nodded. "Yes. That's correct."

"Why?"

Christine flinched at the harshness of Mrs. Giry's tone. She was baffled. Had Erik not told the woman what they were doing? Why would he keep it from her?

Deciding the best option was honesty, she admitted, "Mr. Roux has been giving me singing lessons. We meet at night in his study for them."

Mrs. Giry's brow furrowed, and she appeared as confused as Christine felt.

"Singing lessons? That's all?"

"What did you think we were doing?"

The older woman's cheeks flushed red. "I wasn't sure."

Liar. Christine could guess what Mrs. Giry had believed was happening. She felt her own cheeks heat as memories of her kiss with Erik flashed through her mind.

"Mrs. Giry, did you think that Mr. Roux and I...that we...?"

The woman shook her head. "Whatever I thought is not the issue here. Why is he giving you singing lessons? What is your goal?"

Christine raised her hands. "I don't have any goal. He offered to teach me. I didn't seek him out if that's what you think."

Mrs. Giry took a full step back as if she'd been struck. Christine raised her brows at the housekeeper's strange reaction. She paled, looking for all the world like she'd seen a ghost.

"Mrs. Giry? Is everything okay?"

"He...he *offered* to teach you?"

Christine shrugged. "Yes. Why? Is that unusual?"

Mrs. Giry's throat worked up and down as she swallowed her shock. "Uhhhhh...yes. It is a bit." She moved to stand in front of the table and bent down to rest her hands on its surface. Dark eyes keen, she studied Christine for several moments.

"What are you doing?" Christine asked, uncomfortable under the older woman's scrutiny.

"What is it about you that has him acting this way?" Mrs. Giry murmured, though she didn't seem to be directing the question towards Christine.

"Mrs. Giry?"

With a start, the woman snapped out of her daze. Shaking her head, she pushed off the table and stood straight once more. Her expression grew stern.

"If it is Mr. Roux's desire to teach you, I am in no position to argue against the matter. I warn you, though, if I find out you have some ulterior motive at play, I will rid this house of you myself." With that final threat, she turned on her heel and marched from the room.

Christine watched her go, too shocked to say anything in response.

* * *

That evening, as Christine made her way to Erik's study, she mulled over Mrs. Giry's puzzling behavior. She couldn't get the woman's murmured question out of her mind.

What is it about you that has him acting this way?

Christine knew Erik teaching her had come as a shock to the housekeeper, but she had backed off her condemnation against Christine once she'd realized it was something *he'd* initiated.

It'd been years since he'd released any music, but was it so unusual for him to share it with those around him?

She was still lost in thought when she reached the study door and knocked. Listening for his bid she come in, she frowned when there was no response. She knocked again, but was once more greeted by silence.

Panic began to take hold. What if he was ignoring her after last night? What if he regretted it?

What if he made her leave?

She hit the door with her open palm and cried, "Erik? Are you in there? Please answer me!"

Several more seconds passed before, to her shock, the door swung open on its own. She hesitated to enter, thrown off by the unexpected development. At length, she took a step forward, and then another, and another, until she was over the threshold and inside the room.

He was nowhere to be seen.

She jumped when the door shut behind her. Though her instinct was to whirl around, practice kept her facing away.

"You startle too easily, Ms. Davidson," Erik teased with his dark voice.

"Well...it's easy to be startled when your routine is thrown off," she stammered. She had expected him to be back behind the mirror and that she would need to coax him back out.

Yet, here he was. Waiting for her.

Unpredictable man.

He didn't come closer, but she heard the rustling of his clothes as he moved behind her.

"Christine, I have a confession to make."

Gulping, she replied, "And what is that?" She kept her eyes locked straight ahead, her arms at her sides.

"Despite my best efforts, I haven't been able to push you from my mind." Unsure whether to be insulted or flattered, she remained silent and let him continue. "Last night, after our indiscretion, I resolved myself to never cross that line with you again."

Disappointment gripped her like a vice. So, he *was* going to ask her to leave...

Tears began to form in her eyes, but she gasped when a breath of air tickled her neck. He was right behind her, so close she could feel his heat, yet she hadn't heard him approach.

"Then I spent the night with my cock in my hand, and you on my mind. I came harder than I ever have in memory. All because of you."

Heat spread from her core, engulfing her body, and she whimpered as his soft words flowed over her.

"Erik..."

"I tried to be a better man than I am, Christine. I tried to let you go, but I can't. I'm not a good man." He grabbed her shoulders and pulled her back against him. She cried out when she slammed into his hard body. Growling at her ear, he said, "You're mine now, Christine, and God have mercy on us both."

He released her and stepped away, leaving her shaky on her feet. She managed to stay upright, but she had to lunge forward and grab the back of one of his desk chairs for support.

Everything he'd said overwhelmed her, and she struggled to get her rioting emotions in check. Elation, lust, terror...all battled for dominance. Taking deep, steadying breaths, she managed to calm herself enough that she could stand without support.

"Christine," his voice floated to her and touched her like a caress. "Turn around."

13

Christine

Whatever calm she'd managed to claim evaporated with his command.

"W...what did you say?"

"I said, turn around."

Turn around. To face him.

To see him.

Christine's mind screamed at her to obey, but her body remained paralyzed. She felt like she was standing on the edge of a cliff, staring down in the empty abyss, the choice to jump or step away before her. To step away would mean returning to safety, to the life she knew, and the strict definitions of their relationship as employer and employee. To jump was to risk it all in the terrifying, yet alluring unknown. She'd thought this decision would be so easy when it wasn't an option, but now that he'd offered it to her, she hesitated.

"This is your one and only chance, Christine. Turn around, or I never touch you again. The choice is yours."

The thought of never feeling his hands and lips on hers again snapped her from her indecision. Taking a deep breath to brace herself, she turned to face him.

She went numb with disbelief at the sight of him.

He was *beautiful*.

Black hair framed an angular face with a strong jaw. He was tall, towering over her, even in her heels, and his body was lean and muscled beneath his black button-up shirt and slacks. Bright blue eyes captured hers, daring her to look away.

One thing marred his appearance, though. A black mask covered the right half of his face from the top of his forehead down to his chin, also hiding his nose.

He watched her as she studied him, and she realized he was wary, waiting for her to react.

Swallowing, she said the first thing that popped into her head.

"The mask is a little dramatic, don't you think?" She arched a brow and couldn't stop a small grin.

He appeared startled by her response, but his lips curled into a slow half smile and he touched the black mask with the tips of his fingers.

"I'm a creative genius," he replied in a dry tone. "I operate most effectively within the dramatic." Though his words were light, there was a tension that remained in his shoulders, communicating his discomfort.

Christine scrambled to ease the mood. "Are you a comedian now as well? I've never heard you make a joke before."

Erik shrugged, sliding both his hands into his pockets. The motion drew Christine's attention to his narrow hips and long legs. Dressed in black from head to toe, including the mask, he had a dangerous, roguish air to him that had her breath hitching.

Perceptive man that he was, he noticed.

His blue eyes narrowed, and his full lips tilted up into a smirk.

"Something the matter, Christine?" His tone was teasing, and filled with something...dark. Something titillating. Something that had her heart racing.

"N...no. Nothing's the matter." God, she sounded like an idiot. And a liar.

Like a predator stalking its prey, he began to move towards her with slow, deliberate strides.

Gulping, Christine tried to focus on anything but the lust that started burning through her. She was too overwhelmed to let things escalate any further at that moment, no matter how desperate she was to have him. She needed a little bit of time to process everything and make sense of her swirling thoughts and feelings.

He was drawing closer. She needed to distract him.

"Why do you wear it?"

He froze midstride. "What?"

"The mask. Why do you even wear the mask?" What was he so desperate to hide?

He grew guarded at her question, and she wondered how honest he would be.

"The mask contains the monster."

Christine frowned in confusion. "What does that mean?"

Erik ran an agitated hand through his ink-black hair. "My face is not...I was born..." He struggled to explain. "It's not something I enjoy talking about."

His obvious turmoil tugged at her heart. She thought he wanted to confide in her, but wasn't sure how he could.

"It's okay," she muttered. "You don't have to tell me. Or show me. It's none of my business. I'm just...I'm just glad you've finally let me see you."

Yet, she couldn't help her curiosity. She had the nagging suspicion that his appearance was only the tip of the iceberg when it came to explaining his mask and self-imposed solitude. After all, how terrible could his face really be?

He slid his hands back into his pockets, and gazed at anything and everything in the room but her.

"You must think I'm crazy."

That was the last thing she wanted him to believe. Pushing her own misgivings aside, Christine moved towards him.

"I don't think you're crazy," she insisted. "I think you're amazing."

She threw her arms around his neck and pushed up onto her toes to kiss him. She could tell she'd shocked him when his body stiffened against her, but then he was wrapping her in his tight embrace, pulling her closer as he devoured her mouth in turn.

Her eyes slid closed, but she wanted to keep them open. To keep looking at him.

She didn't think she would ever get enough of the sight of him.

Tearing his mouth from hers, he ran his lips along her cheek and jaw, chanting her name like a prayer. She cupped the uncovered side of his face, careful not to reach her other hand up towards his mask. Instead, she let it fall against his hard chest and curled her fingers until she clutched his shirt.

He spun them around and began to back her up, and she didn't resist until her back met the wall behind her. Shoving his knee between her legs, he rested his thigh against her sex. She grasped at his hair with one hand, and began working her other hand in between the buttons of his shirt. He returned his mouth to hers, and they lost themselves in each other. For a blissful moment, the whole world melted away, and all Christine cared about was the man in her arms. His hands slid from her waist up to her breasts. Taking a soft mound in each hand, he squeezed. Christine squirmed under his touch, rubbing herself against his hard thigh.

A breathy moan escaped her lips.

He broke his mouth from hers with a self-satisfied smirk.

"Your eyes are glazed," he observed, staring down at her. "You look drunk on lust. Do you want me that badly?"

Christine pressed herself flush against him and groaned, "Yes."

"You are delightful, Ms. Davidson."

He dropped his head to kiss her again. She managed to undo the top few buttons of his shirt and slid her hand along his hard chest. Growling against her lips, he dropped his hands from her breasts to her thighs, and began moving them upward, bunching the material of her skirt around her hips. He exposed more and more of her soft skin until he revealed her panties. Breaking their kiss once more, he glanced down as he stroked the lace of her thong.

"Mmmmm, I like this."

Christine whimpered when he pressed his thumbs harder into her.

"Oh, God," she groaned.

"Does that feel good, angel?"

She could only nod, her words stolen as pleasure swept through her. Smirking, he continued to stroke her through the barrier of her underwear. Christine couldn't understand why he didn't try to touch her flesh directly. Was he *trying* to torture her with the dulled sensations, strong enough to make her squirm and pant, but not strong enough to get her off?

The thought turned her on even more, and with a start, she realized she *liked* the torment.

Closing her eyes, she dug her teeth into her bottom lip as excitement and frustration made her undulate against him, desperate for the release he kept just out of reach.

"What's the matter?" he teased in her ear. "Do you want something? It seems like you do, but I can't quite tell what it might be."

"Bastard," she moaned. She dug her nails into his chest. He chuckled.

"Tell me what it is you want, angel, and maybe I'll give it to you. I'm feeling generous today, after all."

He pressed his thumbs harder, but then lightened his touch again.

Christine dropped her head back against the wall with a groan. "Please...let me come..."

Stroking his lips across her cheek, he murmured, "As you wish."

With one hand, he pulled aside her panties, and with the other, stroked his fingers along her hot folds.

Christine cried out, her body jerking, his touch like lightning after so much teasing.

It wasn't long before she was climbing to her peak. She clawed at his chest and arms.

"Erik..."

With a snarl, he crushed his mouth to hers in a brutal kiss as he cupped her sex and vibrated his whole hand against her. She crashed over into her orgasm with a scream that he caught with his lips.

As she began to come down from the height of her pleasure, she felt her knees shake and buckle. Erik wrapped his arms around her, catching her before she slumped to the floor.

"My God," she breathed, resting her forehead against his shoulder.

They stood like that for several moments. Christine felt herself growing shy, which was strange. It'd been years since she'd felt that way around a man she'd been intimate with.

At length, he stepped back from her, steadying her before dropping his hands away. The sudden absence of his touch left her cold. She had to fight to keep from hugging herself.

Christine raised her eyes to his, and was surprised to find his gaze guarded. It was as if a curtain had fallen, hiding any trace of emotion from her. She felt her heart clench at the sight.

"Erik..." she began with a murmur.

She froze when he reached out and cupped her cheek, caressing her skin with his thumb. His expression turned soft, but the distance remained. Even after what had just happened between them, he was holding himself back.

"You're so beautiful, Christine. I think I could grow addicted to your body."

Just my body?

He leaned in to kiss her on her forehead before dropping his hand and stepping away.

"Should we get on with your lesson?" His tone turned business-like, and it took Christine a moment to catch-up with him.

That was it? They were just going to move on as if nothing had happened? She hadn't even had the chance to touch *him*. A quick glance down was all the evidence necessary to know that he was in as much need as she had been. Yet what could she do if he insisted on pulling away? She'd already pushed him further than she'd thought possible. Perhaps she should allow him some space for the time being.

She nodded. "Yes, sir."

He visibly relaxed, as if she'd given him permission to breathe again.

Yes. Giving him space was for the best. She would not put pressure on him, and would win his trust.

Still, even as she reasoned herself through their situation, her gut was tight with apprehension. The truth was, she might already be falling for him, but she didn't know if that was something he would allow.

* * *

Erik

Her voice was improving, but Erik found it difficult to concentrate on her music when the scent of her hot sex lingered in the air. When the lesson was over, he was almost grateful. He didn't know how much longer he could control himself around her.

"You did very well today, Christine," he told her as she readied to leave.

She looked at him, and he had to fight his instinct to hide away from her. He wasn't used to having someone's eyes on him. It was unnerving, but at the same time, with her, it was a relief.

"Thank you, sir," she responded, her tone brusque. He knew he'd thrown her off with his drastic change in behavior after wringing her orgasm from her, but in that moment, when her face had been overcome with the bliss of her pleasure, he'd recognized the danger she posed to him. He was at risk of growing more than obsessed with her. He was at risk of falling, heart and soul, for this woman. As much as that terrified him, it was nothing compared to the fear of him dragging her down into his darkness, corrupting her soul as much as his own.

He couldn't do that to her. She deserved so much more, but he knew he couldn't walk away from her either. He was already addicted.

Better to keep a distance between them, and eventually she would grow tired of him and be the one to walk away. He wasn't strong enough to do it himself.

"I'll see you tomorrow."

She appeared surprised by the statement. "You will?"

He frowned. Had she thought he was ending things between them? Even if he wanted to, even though it was the best thing for her, that wasn't an option on his end.

Moving towards her, he took her chin in his hand and tipped her face up so he could kiss her lips. She squeaked, startled, but was melting into him in seconds. He didn't try to deepen the kiss, knowing he wouldn't be able to part with her until she was squirming in his arms again, but he was hesitant to break away from her all the same. He wanted to stay there, in that moment, with her warmth and soft body against him. Before he lost himself in her again, he pulled away. For a moment, he let himself gaze down into her beautiful amber eyes, imagining how different things could be if he wasn't so damaged.

She stared back up at him, a question in her gaze that she didn't voice.

"Sleep well, Ms. Davidson," he murmured, releasing her chin.

Christine lingered a few moments more before nodding. "Good night, Mr. Roux." Turning, she walked out of the room without a backwards glance.

When the door shut behind her, Erik reached up to trace his fingers along his mask. He cursed his deformities. He cursed his darkness. He cursed everything that had left him broken and twisted inside.

Tainted...broken...monster...

"*The devil's child...that's what you are...*"

No matter what he might hope, he would always be a monster, a devil, unworthy of the touch of an angel.

14

Christine

Two steps forward, three steps back.

Christine let out a sigh as she left her bedroom and began walking down the hall towards the second-floor landing. It had been two weeks since Erik had allowed her to see him, and though they continued to meet for her lessons every evening, her worries from that night continued to plague her.

Though he would greet her with hungry kisses and a heart-stopping orgasm before each session, his gaze would grow shuttered once she'd finished coming and he would limit his physical contact with her until a chaste good-bye kiss at the end of the hour. At no point would he speak to her about anything other than music. It was beyond frustrating, and she didn't know what to do to make things progress between them.

Apart from his emotional distance, however, it had become apparent after that first night that he was holding himself back physically as well. The second night they'd been together, he'd stripped her panties from her as soon as she'd walked through the door. He'd also freed her breasts to pet and suck, but he hadn't removed any of his own clothing. The next night, she'd tried to push things further by gripping him through his pants, but he'd removed her hand, kissed the inside of her wrist, and moved on to her lesson as if nothing had happened.

That he wouldn't let her touch him the way he touched her hurt her almost as much as his refusal to open himself emotionally did. Yet, as aggravating as the situation was, she knew she'd go back to him that evening just like she had every evening before. She couldn't stay away from him. Was growing addicted to his touch.

But how do I move us forward?

Christine pondered the question, so lost in thought that she didn't hear the front door of the house open.

"Hello?" a sweet, feminine voice called from the foyer. "Mama? Erik? I'm home!"

Christine froze, shocked at the casual use of Erik's first name. A strange sting of jealousy had her stomach twisting. Curious, she continued down the hallway until she stood at the railing of the landing.

A girl, not much younger than Christine herself, stood framed by the sunlight streaming in through the open front door. Long blonde hair swished from side to side as she looked around, her emerald eyes bright and expectant. A short-skirted blue sundress displayed long, toned legs and highlighted her lithe, elegant frame.

The girl's eyes turned up and latched onto Christine. Her beautiful face lit up with an immediate smile.

"You must be Christine!"

Taken aback by the girl's exuberance, Christine stammered her reply.

"Y...yes I am. How did you...?"

"I'm Meg. Meg Giry. My mother has told me so much about you!"

That shocked Christine more than the girl's disarming friendliness.

A startling shriek had her gripping the railing.

"My darling!" Mrs. Giry appeared from beneath the landing, rushing towards her daughter. The two embraced with excited giggles, and Christine felt certain she had stepped into a parallel universe where Mrs. Giry smiled and enjoyed the company of others.

Suddenly, the hairs on the back of her neck stood up, and she recognized Erik's imposing presence before she turned her head and found him standing on the opposite end of the landing, gazing down at the pair of hugging women. His mouth was curled into a small smile, and there was a fondness in his gaze that Christine had never seen there before. He'd never looked at her that way, yet he couldn't seem to turn his eyes from the beautiful blonde Meg.

The sting of jealousy grew into a painful stabbing.

"Megan," Erik called out. "I'm so glad to see you."

Meg and Mrs. Giry broke apart from each other, and the girl looked up with a huge grin on her angelic face.

"Erik!" she cried, moving to the stairs. She had a noticeable limp, favoring her left leg as she walked. Mrs. Giry shut the front door, and then turned to watch the exchange with a warm smile. She didn't so much as glance at Christine.

Once she'd reached the landing, Meg launched herself into Erik's arms, hugging him with as much enthusiasm as she had her mother. Christine felt like a voyeur, watching something she shouldn't.

Her throat tightened as Erik pulled away from Meg to look down at her. His large hands remained on her shoulders, and Christine lost her breath at how perfect the two appeared together. Her, bright and beautiful. Him, dark and striking.

"You look so lovely, Megan," Erik observed, his fondness for her clear in his tone. "I'm glad to see New York hasn't changed you overly much."

Meg rolled her eyes, but her smile remained. "Erik, you know I hate when you call me Megan. And what did you expect? I'd go to New York and turn as dark and brooding as you?"

He rolled his eyes. "How is your ankle? Amelia informed me you'd hurt yourself and wished to stay here while you recovered."

Meg sighed, rubbing her hand against her thigh. "It's just a sprain, though it wouldn't be so bad if it were the first time. The company's given me some time off to heal and strengthen it back up. It's nothing too serious, though. I should be good to go in a few weeks."

"Ah, so you'll demand my hospitality for that long?" His tone was teasing.

Arching a brow, Meg replied, "I know it will be a strain on your hermit-lifestyle, having one more mouth to feed, but I'm sure you'll survive."

Christine was astonished at the boldness of Meg's words, and worried how they would affect Erik. She was shocked when he released a burst of laughter.

She'd never heard him laugh before. Not a true, carefree laugh. It was mesmerizing.

Watching them, Christine came to a stark realization. There was a dynamic here, amongst the three of them, that she'd never fully understood until that moment. They were a family.

She was an outsider.

Unable to handle standing on the outside looking in, Christine turned to make a quiet exit.

"Christine, where are you going?"

His voice wrapped around her like a web, trapping her in place. With no small amount of hesitation, she turned her head to glance back. Erik and Meg were standing side-by-side, no longer touching. Christine met his blue gaze, and heat shot through her at the blatant desire she saw there. What was he doing, looking at her like that when another woman stood next to him?

"I thought I'd give you all time alone together," she lied. Did her voice sound strained? She took a breath before continuing. "I'm sure I'd only get in the way of you catching up."

To Christine's surprise, Meg hurried towards her with a look of genuine concern.

"Oh, no Christine, don't go!" There was no hint of malice or falsity in her tone. "Please, I'm sorry. I didn't mean to barge in and make you feel awkward. Stay and hang out! I'm *desperate* to get to know you." She made her eyes big as she clasped her hands against her chest.

Does she truly want me around? Christine thought, baffled. Perhaps Mrs. Giry had not informed Meg of her and Erik's...arrangement.

There was no way the girl would tolerate Christine's presence otherwise. It was clear she and Erik were close. Perhaps intimate.

The thought stung Christine more than she liked.

The real question might be could *she* stand being around *them*?

"I...I really don't think..."

"We insist!" Meg declared, reaching out and grabbing Christine's hands. Glancing towards Erik, Christine saw that he was watching her with an intensity that startled her.

"Indeed, Ms. Davidson," he rumbled, "we do insist."

Christine gulped. Something in his gaze made her wary, but also excited her.

"Very well."

"Excellent!" Meg exclaimed, oblivious to the growing tension between Christine and Erik. "I'll go see if Darius has something to eat, and maybe open a bottle of wine. We can relax and chat and get to know each other."

Christine broke away from Erik's hot stare to look at the girl. There was eagerness in her expression. Something inside Christine softened at the sight, and she smiled.

"That sounds great."

"Fantastic! I'll meet you both in the living room." Before either Christine or Erik could say a word, Meg bolted down the stairs and disappeared in the direction of the dining room and kitchen. Christine watched her go, and then glanced towards Mrs. Giry. The older woman was studying her with a shrewd gaze, but said nothing as she began to follow after her daughter.

Only when Mrs. Giry was out of sight as well did Christine return her eyes to Erik. His were locked on her, as intense as before.

"What is it?" she whispered.

"Why did you try to run away?"

She hadn't expected that question at all. "What do you mean?"

Erik eased towards her, and she took an instinctive step back. He smirked.

"When you were trying to disappear to your room," he explained, his voice low. "It was obvious you were trying to escape." He stopped when he was less than a foot from her. "Tell me why."

Christine's heart began to race at his nearness, and she was overcome with the urge to reach out and touch his chest. She fought it, however, and kept her hands locked together behind her back. Unable to look away from him, she pondered her answer. It was no use to lie, he'd be able to tell. Yet the truth felt so silly. She'd been jealous of Meg, and hadn't wanted to see him and the girl together.

She couldn't quite bring herself to admit that, however. Instead, she murmured, "She made you laugh."

He didn't say anything at first, just continued to stare at her.

At length, he asked, "Were you jealous?"

Embarrassed, Christine dropped her chin. She couldn't bring herself to look at him when she admitted with a whisper, "Yes."

Christine saw his arm rise out of the corner of her eye. He placed a finger under her chin and raised her face back up towards his.

A smile played at his lips. "I can't remember the last time a woman was jealous over me."

Rolling her eyes, she pursed her lips in agitation. "Don't look so pleased with yourself."

He chuckled, leaning down to place a sweet kiss on her lips. She whimpered at the contact, but it wasn't enough. Sliding her hands up his chest, she clutched his shirt to bring him closer, opening her mouth beneath his. With a groan, he deepened the kiss, his arms wrapping around her in a tight embrace.

The passion that seemed to always simmer between them flared up as their tongues danced. Christine grew desperate for more, wanting his skin against hers, his weight pressing down on her, his heat engulfing her...

Instead of taking things further, however, Erik tore his mouth from hers. She tried to reclaim it, but he dodged her with a smirk.

"Now, now angel, none of that." He put her at arm's length. "We have company, remember? It would be rude to keep them waiting longer than we already have."

Christine felt a flare of annoyance, and then disappointment. Was he not as affected by their kiss as her? Did he not want her as much as she wanted him? How else could he so easily refocus his attention on Meg?

Yet, as she stood before him, she noted his heavy breaths. They made his chest rise and fall, as if he'd just sprinted along the hall. His hands were clutching her shoulders with more force than was necessary, his arms tensed and straining, as if he fought to keep himself from embracing her again.

Perhaps he wasn't so unaffected after all.

Though every inch of her body strained to continue what they'd started, she recognized the rightness of his words. They shouldn't keep Meg and Mrs. Giry waiting.

Stepping out of his reach, she nodded her head. "You're right, of course. We don't want to be rude." She made to move past him towards the stairs, but he stopped her with a hand around her arm.

"Don't think for a moment that we won't finish this later," he growled. "Your reprieve from me will be a brief one."

Christine bit her lip, but even that couldn't hide her smile of delight.

Erik took her hand and led her down the stairs. His grip was firm, and she curled her fingers around his. Strange how such a simple act could feel more intimate than most anything else they'd done together so far. It was affectionate, not lustful, and though that certainly remained, the show of tenderness had her heart thumping.

She expected him to release her once they reached the living room, and was shocked when he didn't, opening the door and walking inside linked together for everyone to see.

Meg sat on the plush sectional, and Mrs. Giry was beside her. Darius was there was well, opening a bottle of red wine. All three turned to stare as Erik and Christine entered the room.

Christine didn't miss Mrs. Giry's eyes dart down to their joined hands. The woman pursed her lips, but said nothing.

Bright smile wide, Meg exclaimed, "I didn't know you two were together."

Breathless, Christine struggled to form words to reply and explain the notion away.

Erik beat her to the punch.

"We're keeping it casual for now." He glanced towards Christine, who stared back wide-eyed. Moving his gaze back to Meg, he continued, "Exploring possibilities, as it were."

Meg nodded. "Hey, nothing wrong with that. As long as Christine's cool with it, and you're not being a creep, Erik."

It amazed Christine how the girl teased him as if it were nothing. She couldn't imagine having that kind of easy relationship with him, not when he intimidated and fascinated her in equal regard. Christine wondered at the two's connection once more. While it was growing clearer that no romantic feelings existed between them, there was an openness there that Erik did not allow to exist between him and Christine.

Jealousy reared its savage head once more. She tried to squash it, but her insecurities weakened her and made her more susceptible to the negative emotion. If only Erik would give her a little more reassurance of where they stood with each other...

"So, Christine, my mom tells me you're a singer?"

Taken aback, Christine glanced at Mrs. Giry. The housekeeper avoided her eye, but there was a flush on her cheeks.

Turning her attention back to the girl, Christine replied, "Your mother is too generous. I'm not a singer, not really..."

"But she will be," Erik interrupted. There was pride shimmering in his blue gaze. "She is quite naturally gifted, and only needs someone to help her refine that gift."

Meg's jaw dropped. "Wait, are you teaching her, Erik?"

Why is this so surprising? Christine wanted to shout.

Erik nodded. "Yes. A rare occurrence, I know, but when true talent is before me, how can I resist?"

Christine wanted to grin like an idiot at the praise. It was one thing when he said those things in the privacy of his study, but for him to speak of her so highly in front of others...

At that moment, Darius offered Christine a glass of wine, his smile kind. She took the drink without hesitation and thanked him.

"So what's Erik like as a teacher?" Meg asked.

Christine took a sip of her wine to give herself time to gather her thoughts. *Don't you know?*

"He's strict," she answered. "Very strict, but not in a mean way. He's very patient and...hands on." She couldn't help the last part. Glancing his way, she saw he was amused by her little inside joke. He squeezed her hand, which he had yet to release.

"Well, that's not surprising," Meg nodded, raising her glass to her lips for a drink. Christine almost spit out hers as a laugh threatened to overtake her. Instead, she managed to force the wine down with a cough.

"Are you okay, Ms. Davidson?" Mrs. Giry asked with polite concern.

Taking a deep breath, Christine forced a smile. "Yes, my apologies. It went down the wrong pipe."

"Best to drink more slowly then, I think," Mrs. Giry said with an arched brow.

Christine had the feeling her innuendo hadn't gotten past the keen housekeeper.

The small party sat together and chatted for about an hour. Meg dazzled them with stories of her exploits in New York, and Christine was happy to remain quiet and listen. She sat in a cushioned chair next to the couch, and to her glee, Erik perched on the chair's arm, staying close to her.

When Darius, who had left them to prepare supper, returned to announce their meal was ready, Christine felt reluctant to leave her seat and Erik's side. He declined to eat with them, as usual, and she was disappointed despite the normalcy of the situation. Meg did not seem at all surprised, and left the room linked arm-in-arm with her mother.

Christine made to follow them, but Erik stopped her with a hand around her wrist.

"What is it?" she asked.

He leaned down so his mouth was next to her ear.

"When you come to your lesson this evening, I want you to wear nothing but that silk robe of yours. I have something special planned."

Christine gasped as heat infused her.

"You couldn't have waited until *after* dinner to tell me this?" How was she supposed to maintain her composure and focus on Meg and Mrs. Giry with this command on her mind?

He smirked. "Your anticipation for the evening will only heighten the fun."

Releasing her wrist, he stepped around her and left the room without another word.

Christine watched him go, breathless, exhilarated, and ravenous, though she no longer had an appetite for food.

15

Christine

Dinner seemed to last for hours as Christine's blood hummed with her anticipation. When she was able to excuse herself at last, she rushed to her room to change. Hurrying towards Erik's study, she clutched her robe around her and kept a sharp eye out for any sign of Mrs. Giry or Meg. No matter how excited she was for what Erik had in store for her, she'd die of embarrassment if either woman caught her running through the halls half-naked.

It felt strange, yet freeing, wearing only her robe. The material caressed her body, and cool air rushed past her most intimate parts as she moved. Those sensations, combined with the expectation of what was to come, had her wet and eager by the time she reached the study door, which was yanked open before her knuckles could scrape the wood.

He'd been waiting for her.

Erik stood framed in the doorway, tall and dark, hunger burning in his eyes as they raked up and down her body. The hand holding the top of her robe tightened on instinct, but she forced herself to relax beneath his gaze.

"I was getting ready to hunt you down."

Christine blinked. "But I'm not late."

"I know, but I'm not a patient man." He grabbed her arm and yanked her forward. She slammed into his body, and he stole her breath with a demanding kiss as his hand tangled into her red curls.

Before she could gather her wits, he ended the kiss and pulled her into the study, shutting the door behind them. His hand engulfed hers as he led her towards another set of doors across the room. She held the top of her robe together, her heart pounding with anticipation, her blood humming with nerves.

When they reached the double doors, Erik stopped and faced her, his grip on her hand firm. His gaze was heated, but his mouth was set in a thin line, the skin around his mask tighter than usual.

"I want to try something with you, Christine," he began in a clear, even tone. "This isn't my usual taste, but the thought of doing it with you..." A small moan broke from his throat, and he squeezed her hand. She didn't think it was voluntary. He took a moment to compose himself before continuing. "In order for you to tap in to your true potential, you must be familiar and comfortable with not only your voice, but your body. This exercise I have planned will help you with that."

She couldn't speak, could only nod as she bit her lip. His free hand shot out to cup her face, his thumb stroking at her bottom lip, tugging it from her teeth. She saw his Adam's apple bob.

"Before we go in, I need you to come up with a word to stop me if the exercise becomes too much for you."

That gave her pause, draining a bit of her growing lust.

"You mean a safe word? You're not going to whip me, are you?" The idea frightened her. She didn't have a high pain tolerance, and any time a partner had tried to simply spank her in bed play, she'd found no pleasure in the experience.

His mouth relaxed into a grin, and he stroked the back of his fingers against her cheek.

"No, angel. I do not wish to whip you. I do not want to harm you in any way, but I *do* want you to be helpless. To be open to new sensations. I also want you to feel secure, and to know you can stop me at any time with a word, should the experience become too much for you. Now, please, choose a word. It cannot be *no*, or *stop*. You may protest in the moment out of trepidation, but not mean it, and I don't want there to be any confusion between us. Choose a word you would not normally say in an everyday situation, much less a sexual one. That way, if you speak it, I'll know you are serious and I will stop what I'm doing to you immediately."

Though she remained nervous, she felt comfort in the fact that he was so concerned about her wellbeing. She trusted that he wouldn't harm her or cause her discomfort. In every one of their encounters so far, he'd only ever wanted her surrender in order to heighten her pleasure.

But what word would she choose?

She thought for a moment before it struck her.

Gazing up at Erik, she murmured, "Gounod."

His eyes crinkled as his smile widened, and he brought her hand to his lips.

"Very good."

Without further comment, he turned and opened the doors. Moving to the side, he made way for Christine to enter ahead of him.

With hesitant steps, she walked into what she realized was his bedroom. Her eyes fell on a huge, stripped bed, apart from a dark fitted sheet and mountain of pillows. Attached to the metal headboard were two padded leather cuffs.

Her gaze remained locked on the bindings, even as the doors shut and she felt Erik move to stand behind her. His heat surrounded her as his lips skimmed the top of her ear.

"What are you thinking?" His voice was a dark whisper that made her shiver.

"You want to tie me up." It wasn't a question.

He grasped her upper arms, pulling her back against his solid form. "And blindfold you."

Air whooshed from her lips. "How will that help my singing?"

With a gentle touch, he turned her to face him. She had to crane her neck to meet his smoldering blue stare.

"As I said, I want you to come to know your body. I want to blind you so your other senses take over, and I want to make you helpless so you have no choice but to feel everything. I will touch you and play with you, and you will pay attention to every noise you make. You will learn the sounds your body is capable of, and determine their sources to better control your voice when you sing. Do you understand?"

She thought she did, but the idea of being tied up and at his mercy intimidated her as much as it captivated her.

He skimmed his hands up her shoulders to cup her face.

"If, at any point, you feel uncomfortable or want me to stop, say your word."

Christine nodded.

"Say it out loud for me."

"Gounod."

"Good." He kissed her forehead. "Do not forget it." He met her eyes once more. "Are you ready?"

Was she? She hoped so. She was nervous...anxious, not knowing what he would do. Still, she trusted him. Trusted his process. Trusted her voice to him.

Trusted her body to him.

Taking a deep breath, Christine nodded.

"Out loud, angel."

"Yes. I'm ready."

He dropped his head to kiss her lips. His movements were slow...lulling...meant to drug her with lust and calm her.

Christine felt herself relax under his ministrations. His hands grazed down her torso until they reached the silk belt of her robe. He didn't break their kiss as he pulled the loose knot free, and then his hands were on her bare skin. They slid back up her body to push the material from her shoulders. It pooled around her feet, leaving her naked next to his still-clothed form.

He continued kissing her as he backed her towards the bed. She didn't resist, letting him guide her until the back of her knees hit the mattress. Only then did he move his mouth from hers so that he could sweep her up into his arms. He stared down at her, his eyes blazing, as he placed one knee on the bed and laid her down. She sank back into the pillows.

Without a word, he proceeded to bind first her left, and then her right wrist. He kissed the fingers of each hand after he'd secured the cuffs. She felt a moment of reservation when she tested the restraints and found she was well and truly trapped. He must have sensed her apprehension. Bracing himself above her with both arms, he offered a soothing smile.

"Remember, angel, you are in full control. You can stop this at any time. You need only speak your word. Do you want to use it?"

Gazing up at him, she took several deep breaths. They hadn't even begun, and she was desperate to know what he had in store for her.

She gave a small shake of her head. "No. I don't want to use it."

His gaze grew hooded, and his tone turned husky. "What do you want?"

Heat rushed through her as his voice washed over her. Her own was a whisper.

"I want you."

With a groan, he kissed her again, but it was not gentle as before. It was demanding. A feasting, rather than a tasting. His goal was not to calm her, but to whip her into a frenzy.

He succeeded.

When he broke from her, she was panting and sweating. She pulled against her bonds, desperate to touch him and pull him back to her.

He grinned as she struggled.

Moving to the end of the bed, he grabbed her ankles and pulled her legs apart, opening her wide and exposing her to his hungry gaze. Bending them at her knees, he pressed her heels to the back of her thighs.

"Hold yourself like this."

Though it proved a difficult task, both because of the awkwardness of the position and her own embarrassment, Christine held herself still as Erik bent down and pulled two leather straps from beneath the bed. With quick, sure hands, he wrapped the straps around both legs so she couldn't straighten them, and then lifted her halfway off the mattress so he could attach them together with a buckle against her lower back. Once she was secured, he dropped her back down. She bounced with a surprised shriek.

"Are you ready for what comes next?"

"Erik..." she gasped.

He crossed the room to the antique dresser. Opening one of the small drawers at the top, he dug around, searching for something. When he returned to stand beside her, he held up a silky black sleep mask.

She'd almost forgotten he meant to blindfold her. Apprehension trickled into her once more, but she was too curious and eager for him to touch her again to use her word.

"Relax, angel," he cooed as he slipped the mask over her head. "Just let yourself feel."

The mask contoured around her eyes, blinding her. She felt panic at the darkness, but took a moment to reorient herself to her surroundings. Every dip and curve of the mattress around her seemed more luxurious, the silkiness of the sheet and pillows more pronounced, and the chill in the air brisker. Her ears began picking up every little sound in the room as she tried to identify Erik's location. She'd never noticed the soft hum of the air conditioner before, and the crinkling of the sheet whenever she moved was stark in the silence.

Yet, as hard as she tried, she couldn't hear him. She could sense him, his presence was strong in the room, but she couldn't pinpoint him. The idea that he could touch her anywhere, at any point, from any direction, had her heart racing. Her breaths deepened, and she felt each inhale and exhale expand and deflate in her chest.

Something caressed her right calf. She let out a startled cry and heard Erik chuckle before he touched her with his toy again. Once her initial shock passed, Christine could tell that the object was a feather, though a rather large one by the amount of skin it was able to cover.

Perhaps a peacock feather, as the strands felt thin and set further apart than those of a thick ostrich feather.

With the lightest touch, Erik ran the feather from her calf up to her inner thigh. It tickled, and she couldn't help the giggle that broke from her as her leg jerked to escape. The giggle was a shallow sound that originated in her throat, leaving her mouth quickly as she reacted to the feather's contact. He ran the feather down the length of her other leg, and the giggle morphed into a shriek that shot from the base of her throat. It was one step away from a full-on laugh.

"Enjoying yourself, angel?"

She couldn't stop her mouth from splitting into a grin.

"This is not what I expected," she admitted.

The mattress dipped with his weight, and she felt his breath against her cheek.

"And just what were you expecting?" he rumbled in her ear.

She whimpered, a shallow sound that came from the middle of her throat.

"Erik..." All laughter was gone, replaced once more by her need to touch him. To feel him.

He skimmed his lips along her jawline and brushed them over her mouth. It wasn't enough, and she strained forward to capture him. He alluded her with a dark chuckle.

"Let's try something else, shall we?"

He left the bed, the mattress shifting again. More silence. Christine stilled, trying to hear him. Trying to pick up any hint of what he had planned for her next.

She heard a drawer open and shut.

Then, a soft buzzing sound.

What is that?

The buzzing grew louder, but she couldn't figure out where it was coming from. All of the sudden, something firm, cool, and rubbery touched her in the middle of her chest. She yelped as gentle vibrations reverberated between her breasts.

He moved the toy down to her belly, causing her to suck in a breath and concave her stomach.

"So responsive," he murmured. She whimpered as he moved the vibrator lower still. It was growing hard to concentrate on the sounds her body made.

He reached the juncture at the top of her legs and paused. She squirmed as he let the toy rest on her pelvis. His hands smoothed down her hips and stroked her thighs. He seemed in no hurry, his movements slow, almost reverent, all while the vibrator pulsed against her. Short, shallow sounds escaped her throat as her breathing grew ragged. The combination of sensation, sightlessness, and anticipation was heightening every instant of contact until it felt like her body was one hot, exposed wire, ready to release a shock with the slightest touch.

She jolted when he brushed his lips across her belly. A gasp, originating from deep within her stomach, burst forth when he swirled his tongue around her navel. While he distracted her with his mouth, his hands continued moving along her legs. The mattress shifted again as he slid down the bed, settling between her spread thighs. He lifted his mouth from her stomach and picked the still buzzing vibrator up as well.

Christine held her breath as she waited for his next move.

She cried out when his fingers brushed between her wet folds, the sensation catching her by surprise.

She shrieked when he placed the vibrator flush against her core, shocking her entire system.

"How is it, my angel?" he asked, his voice teasing but heated. He used his free hand to grope her breast and pinch at her nipple. "Does it feel good?"

It was agony and bliss all at once. The vibrations were so powerful, they were almost painful against her tender flesh, yet she wanted more. She dug her heels into the mattress, thrusting her hips up as her hands opened and closed uselessly above her. Sounds she'd never heard herself make before slipped from between her clenched teeth. Growls, whimpers, and squeaks...animalistic sounds that grew more carnal as her pleasure increased. He continued to attack her from both ends, one hand on her breasts, the other on the vibrator humming between her legs.

Christine thrashed her head from side to side as she tried to tighten her thighs around his body, but the leather strap held firm. His mouth found the hollow at the base of her throat, and he dragged his tongue up her neck to her jaw.

"Erik..." His name was a desperate plea.

He didn't respond, but brought his mouth crashing back down to hers, taking in her cries as she drew closer and closer to her peak.

Breaking away, he murmured, "You are everything I could ever want." Then he sealed his lips to hers again.

Don't say things like that to me, she thought. When he spoke to her that way, he made her feel hope, but every time she felt hope with him, he would do something to take it away from her again. As her body writhed beneath him, her heart throbbed with a deeper longing.

She wanted more from him. More than he was willing to give.

Her thoughts swirled, her focus torn between her confused emotions and the promise of her physical release. He kept kissing her, touching her...the buzz of the vibrator filled her ears.

Yet it wasn't enough. She didn't want the vibrator between her legs. She wanted *him*. She wanted to touch him...hold him...feel him inside her as she came.

Why couldn't he let her have that? Why did he continue to keep her at a distance?

His mouth left hers. "What is it you want, Christine?" His voice was a low rumble, tender yet demanding. "Do you want me to let you come?"

She did. She didn't! She was desperate for release, but feared what she would be left with once it came. He would leave her again. Draw away from her and return to his isolation. He would leave her physically sated, but emotionally hollow. The thought had her gut twisting in pain. It was too much...her impending orgasm...his inevitable abandonment...her loneliness...

Tears burned in her eyes as he pushed her to the very edge of pleasure...

"Gounod!" she cried.

He removed his hands from her instantly, the vibrator disappearing with them. The room went quiet as he switched off the toy. Tears began to fall down Christine's cheeks as the blindfold was ripped from her face.

"Christine? What's wrong?"

She gazed up into Erik's concerned, and confused, face. Holding himself above her on straightened arms, he remained close without touching her. He'd taken off his shirt, and his pale bare chest rose and fell with his heavy breaths. His dark hair was tousled, but his mask remained in place, as secure as ever. He was so beautiful, her heart ached.

Christine wanted to cover her face with her hands, but they remained handcuffed to the bed.

"Please..." she whimpered. "Let me go." She jostled her arms.

He moved without hesitation, unstrapping her legs, and then fetching a small key from the nightstand to unlock both cuffs. When her hands were free, she threw her arms across her face and tried not to sob.

"Christine, please. Tell me what's wrong. Did I...did I hurt you?"

The worry in his tone made it harder for her not to cry.

"No, you didn't hurt me."

"Then what's the matter? Did you not enjoy this exercise? We don't have to do it again if you don't want to, I promise."

She shook her covered head. "It's not that. I did enjoy it..." *Until I remembered what would come after.*

"Christine, why won't you look at me?"

"I just can't."

Silence stretched between them, and the tension in the room grew until Christine felt like she would choke on it.

"I don't know what to do to make you feel better," he admitted in a soft voice. The fear and hurt which layered his words made him sound younger. Vulnerable.

Christine lowered her arms and met his gaze. Slowly, she reached up to cup her hand against his covered cheek. He backed away from her, the move so instinctive, she wasn't sure he'd meant to do it. Still, it reinforced what she'd feared.

She let her hand drop back to the mattress.

His eyes filled with remorse. "Christine..."

She shook her head. "You still don't trust me."

His shoulders tensed as he grabbed the bedsheet on either side of her head. "That's not true."

Closing her eyes, she offered him a sad smile. "Yes it is. You wouldn't flinch from my touch if it wasn't true."

Letting out a deep breath, Erik hung his head. It might have been in shame, or it might have been in frustration, she couldn't tell. Whatever the reason, she knew it didn't bode well for her.

"I'm sorry," he murmured at length, though he didn't raise his face to look at her. "It's not that I don't want to, it's just that..."

"I know you were hurt before," she admitted with a whisper.

His head shot back up, his gaze wild for a second before he got himself back under control.

"How do you know that?"

His hard tone frightened her. She knew she was treading on dangerous ground.

"That doesn't matter...and I don't know the details. I do know it's related to why you haven't produced music in so long..."

He shot away from her, flinging himself from the bed. She scrambled up, following him.

"You don't have any right to know that," he snarled, tangling his fingers in his hair. He started to pace back and forth, like a caged animal.

Feeling vulnerable in her nakedness, Christine found her robe on the floor and covered herself.

"I'm sorry. I didn't mean to hear what I did, but you refused to explain anything to me..."

He whirled on her. "So you thought you'd go poking into my life without my permission?"

Christine gasped and shook her head. "No! No, I wouldn't do that. I know hardly anything, and only that by accident. I just want to know why you're keeping me at arm's length, and..."

"Is this not enough of a reason?" he roared.

Flinching, Christine had to fight not to take a step away from him. She knew it wouldn't help her win his trust.

"You don't frighten me, Erik," she responded in an even tone.

With a shout, he swept his hand across the dresser resting against the wall next to him, sending everything on its surface crashing to the floor. Glass shattered, and Christine wanted to jump away from the chaos. She forced herself to stay still, however, clutching her robe tighter to her body.

"You're a fucking fool if you aren't frightened!"

Christine's heart raced, but she kept her voice steady. "You would never hurt me."

Erik ceased his tirade, coming to a standstill in the middle of the room, his back to her. His heavy breathing made his shoulders rise and fall, and sweat glistened on his pale skin. It wasn't until his breath had calmed that he spoke, his words low and dark.

"Maybe not physically, but there are other ways to bring about pain."

A tear trickled down Christine's cheek. "I know you don't want to bring me pain. I know you're afraid that you will..."

"Get out."

Christine froze, her mouth dropping open. "What did you say?"

He didn't look at her as he clenched his fists at his sides and repeated with a roar, "I said *get out!*"

Though he was angrier than she'd ever seen him, his dismissal of her was like a slap across her face. He wouldn't even talk to her...wouldn't let her explain.

He was pushing her away, yet again. Nothing had changed.

Lip trembling as she fought not to sob out loud, Christine turned and fled out the door. He didn't try to stop her.

With every step she took away from him, she felt her heart crack a little more.

16

Christine

"So, this is where they stash you during the day, huh?"

Christine looked up from her laptop to find Meg, dressed in jean-shorts and a white peasant blouse with sandals, leaning against the parlor doorway. Her long hair was braided over her shoulder. She was the pinnacle of hipster chic, apart from her heavily wrapped ankle.

Chuckling, Christine joked, "They say I can leave, but it's *highly* suggested that I don't."

Meg giggled as she limped into the room. She stopped next to Christine's table, and hopped up on top of it like it was a kitchen counter and not an overpriced antique.

"What brings you to my little corner of paradise?" Christine asked, leaning back in her chair.

Meg shrugged. "I was just wandering, bored out of my mind, and thought I'd come bug you a bit since you're currently the most fascinating person here."

"Me?" Christine shook her head. "You have very low standards for what you consider fascinating."

"Well, you're the newbie who I know next to nothing about, so in my book, that equals *fascinating*!"

Christine grinned in bafflement. "If you say so."

Cocking her head, the girl asked, "So what's your story, anyway?"

"My story?"

"Yeah. Where are you from, what are you like, what are your hopes, dreams, and deepest, darkest secrets?"

Needing time to adjust to Meg's bluntness and open curiosity, Christine stuck with the basics.

"Well, I was born in New York. My dad was a violinist, and my mom was a nurse."

"Wow, really different types of people there, huh?"

Christine couldn't have agreed more. "Yes, you could say that. My dad was creative, passionate, and spontaneous, but that often translated to unreliable. My mom was more practical, serious, and organized, but she didn't have as much fun with life as my dad."

"They still together?"

Sadness stabbed at her. "No. My dad died when I was a kid, and my mom passed away last year."

Meg pressed her hand against her mouth. "Oh, my God. I'm sorry Christine. I didn't mean..."

Christine cut her off with a wave of her hand. "You couldn't have known, don't worry about it." Still, she wasn't keen on sharing too much more. "What about you? What's your story?"

Shifting back to her casual friendliness, Meg shrugged. "Eh, there's nothing too exciting to tell. You already know my mom, so I'm sure you've seen firsthand how much of a charmer she can be." Christine couldn't hold back a snort at the wry description. Meg's lips curled. "My dad was never in the picture. Mom doesn't really talk about him, but it's whatever."

Though it would have been understandable, Christine could detect no trace of sadness or evasion in her tone. It appeared the girl was truly unburdened by her father's absence. "Obviously, I followed in my mom's footsteps and became a dancer. I live in New York with my girlfriend and dance for the New York City Ballet Company, and really, that's about it."

Christine blinked. "Girlfriend?"

Meg raised a brow. "Chelsey. We've been together two years now." Narrowing her eyes, she broke out into a huge, teasing grin. "What?

You relieved? Find out I'm gay, and not your rival for Erik's affections?"

Christine gasped as her cheeks burned with embarrassment. "No! It's not that...I mean, I didn't..."

Meg let out a laugh. "Hey, I'm just kidding. You'd never have to worry about me anyway. Even if I was into guys, Erik's basically my brother."

Christine tipped her head against the back of her chair. "I'm sorry. I shouldn't have made assumptions, it's just that you and Erik have such an easy relationship. I can't help but feel a little..."

"Jealous?"

Her face grew warm again. "Yes."

"I know he's not an easy guy to be around, but if it makes you feel any better, I've never seen him like this with anyone but you."

Bringing her head back down, Christine scooted forward in her chair. "What do you mean?"

"I've just never seen him so..." Meg squinted as she thought of the right words. "...so light, I guess. No, that's not really right. Casual? I don't know how to phrase it. It just seems like less of the world is weighing on his shoulders."

Christine bent her head to hide her smile.

Meg jumped down from the table.

"Hey, you need a break. Come hang out with me in the garden. It's such a beautiful day, it'd be a crime for you to stay cooped up in here."

The invitation was tempting. "I'd love to, but I don't want your mom to get angry with me. I'm already her least favorite person in this house."

Meg grabbed Christine's hand, yanking on her until she was forced to stand.

"Oh, never mind my mom. She's all bark. I love the woman, but she needs to loosen up once and awhile. Don't worry, I'll take the blame."

Smiling, Christine gave in with a nod. "Well, in that case, let's go."

Linking arms, the two strolled out of the parlor, leaving the monotonies of the work day behind them.

* * *

Erik

The music surrounded him, filling him body and soul. It flowed from him like blood from an open wound, just as much a life source for him. The piece was new, something he'd been working on for only a few days, but it was turning out to be one of his most brilliant compositions.

And it was all thanks to her.

Playing a few more chords, he paused to edit a note on the paper in front of him. When the air cleared of music, a different sound tickled his ears.

Laughter.

Curious, Erik stood from his piano and moved towards the window. Pushing aside one of the curtains, he gazed out into the sun-covered garden below. He was surprised to see Christine and Meg sitting together on a stone bench next to the spouting fountain, talking as if they were old friends. The sight warmed him, yet made him nervous all the same. What might Meg be telling Christine? The girl knew more about his past than he cared for, and she was not one to maintain confidences.

His eyes rested on Christine, and his chest ached. She was so beautiful with the sunlight streaming through her red hair and her eyes bright with merriment. He was overcome with longing for her, and regret for his actions the previous night.

He'd frightened her. His temper had overwhelmed him, and she'd run from him.

When she'd told him she knew he'd been hurt, panic and shame had made him stupid. He fisted the curtain as he watched her. He hadn't reached out to her, hadn't tried to apologize, but what right did he have to her forgiveness? Her understanding and compassion? He didn't deserve her, and she didn't deserve such a desolate fate as being chained to him.

She deserved the sun.

Letting the curtain fall back into place, Erik stepped away from the window. Making his way back to the piano, he sat at the bench and resumed playing, letting the music drown out the sound of her laughter.

Yet, he couldn't banish her from his mind.

He was a selfish bastard, because despite knowing he should stay away from her, he wanted more of her adoring stares and sensuous smiles. He didn't want her to hate or fear him. She was a light in the darkness, and he was the ill-fated moth worshiping her warmth, desperate to escape the shadows.

He wanted to apologize, but that alone seemed inadequate.

His fingers danced across the keys, filling the room with song. With *her*. She had become his inspiration, pushing his genius to new heights, and filling him with a drive to create he hadn't felt in years.

His gaze scanned the piles of music littering the floor around his piano. All the songs he'd composed in his solitude, but never intended to share with the world. Some were good. Most weren't.

None compared to the song he was writing for her.

And he wanted the world to hear it.

He wanted her to sing it.

Erik froze. He knew what he could do. To earn her forgiveness. To bring back her smiles. To make her greatest dream a reality.

He knew what he could do for her, despite his darkness, his ugliness, and his brokenness.

He would give her his music.

He would give her the world.

17

Christine

Three days passed before Christine saw Erik again. They hadn't spoken directly since she'd ran from his room, and she hadn't dared return without his permission. All she'd heard from him were a couple short text messages with mundane tasks to complete. They hadn't had another lesson. She wasn't sure if there would be any more.

Not being able to speak with him, see him, and touch him had proven more painful than she'd anticipated. Keeping her distance grew more impossible every day, and she'd convinced herself to reach out to him when her phone had buzzed.

I need to see you in my study. Now.

The tone of the message hadn't been all that inviting, but her heart leapt at the words nonetheless. She'd wasted no time, hurrying from her table in the parlor. As she grew closer to his private domain, though, her steps began to slow, her thoughts anxious. Three days of nothing, and then this? What could he want?

What if he'd decided she was too much of a nuisance to keep around?

Her throat seized at the thought of having to leave, but she shook her head to banish the unwelcome idea. Squaring her shoulders, she picked up her pace, determined to dismantle the tension between them. She wouldn't *let* him let her go.

Reaching the study's door, she opened it without knocking, stepping into the room with more confidence than she felt.

She stumbled at what greeted her.

Erik stood behind his desk, dressed all in black, looking powerful and beautiful. Christine's lingering anger with him vanished as relief at seeing him again washed through her. It wasn't his presence that had her tripping on her own feet, however. Mrs. Giry and Meg were waiting with him, the younger seated in front of his desk, the older woman standing behind her daughter.

All three stared at her as she struggled to regain her footing.

"Christine!" Meg shot up from her chair and hobbled to her. "Are you all right?" She grabbed Christine's arm, steadying her.

Gulping, Christine offered the blonde a shaky smile. "I'm fine. Thank you Meg, but why...?"

"Please have a seat, Christine." Erik's voice cut through the room, the sound jarring to her ears having gone so long without hearing it.

Though she still felt off balance, she tried to appear calm as she made her way towards the desk with Meg. The girl helped Christine into the second chair before reclaiming her own.

Christine had to take a deep, calming breath before she could look up at Erik. His gaze was locked on her, but she couldn't read his guarded expression. The silence that stretched between them was suffocating.

"What is this about, sir?" she asked.

Her question seemed to snap him from whatever trance he'd been under. He blinked, looking from her to the Giry women next to her, and back again.

"I wanted to gather you all here to inform you of a decision I have made."

When he didn't immediately elaborate, Meg piped up. "Enough with the dramatics, Erik. What decision have you made?"

Christine clutched her hands in her lap as she waited for his answer. What if he said he wanted her to leave? What would she do?

"I've decided to produce a new album."

Shock and relief wrestled for dominance as his words washed over her. She glanced towards the other women to see their reactions to his announcement.

Meg gasped in excitement, and Mrs. Giry appeared stunned.

"Sir..." the elder Giry stammered. "What brought about this change of heart?"

Christine looked back at him, and his bright blue gaze was focused on her once more.

"Christine did."

She couldn't move. Couldn't breathe. They stared at each other, she too afraid to turn away, his eyes daring her to.

At length, she whispered, "Why?"

Placing his hands on the desk, he leaned forward. "You've *inspired* me, Ms. Davidson. Your hard work and talent deserves to be shared with the world. I want you to be part of the album."

Christine felt her jaw drop.

"*What?*" she exclaimed. "You can't be serious..."

"I agree with Ms. Davidson, sir," Mrs. Giry declared, disbelief in her tone. "She's nowhere near ready to be featured..."

"I don't mean for her to be the main attraction of this album," Erik corrected.

Christine frowned.

Meg furrowed her brow. "Then who do you have in mind?"

"I intend to have Carla Dicelli as the main name on the project."

"Carla Dicelli?" Christine cried in disbelief. "She's an international superstar! How do you propose getting her attached to the project?"

Erik didn't answer. In fact, he ignored her, his attention focused entirely on Mrs. Giry.

The housekeeper had gone pale, and she was staring at Erik as if he'd sprouted a second head.

"Erik, why would you bring *her* on?"

His voice was steady, his eyes fierce. "Wouldn't you agree, Mrs. Giry, that a star like Carla Dicelli would ensure a hit album that could

save our label from the downward spiral and crashing we've been flirt-
ing with for over a year now?"

Mrs. Giry moved her mouth up and down, as if she was trying to
speak, but couldn't produce words.

At length, seeming at a loss, she admitted, "Yes, I do. But sir, it's
been so long, do you even have enough material for an album?"

"Even though I haven't been sharing it, I have continued composing these last five years," Erik assured her. "I have more than enough
written already that we can fast-track the process."

Mrs. Giry looked like she wanted to say more, but instead let out a
defeated sigh. "As you wish."

Clapping his hands together, he replied, "Then we're in agreement.
Christine will have a single on the album, and you'll reach out to
Carla's people to make the necessary arrangements. You still have her
agent's information, correct?"

Christine watched, fascinated, as Mrs. Giry nodded. "Yes, sir."

Frowning, Christine looked from Mrs. Giry to Erik, noting the tension that now existed between the two. There was something wrong.
Something to do with Carla Dicelli. There was a connection there,
that much was clear, but given Mrs. Giry's reaction, it was not a good
one. Curiosity ate at her, but she was careful not to say anything. The
strain between Mrs. Giry and Erik was palpable, and she was afraid to
intervene.

Yet, she couldn't help but wonder how Erik knew Carla Dicelli?
Had they worked together? How close were they?

Had they been lovers?

The thought stole Christine's breath, but she dismissed it. There
was no way that could be true. If Carla Dicelli and Erik Roux had
ever been romantically involved, it would have blown up all over the
tabloids. Erik wouldn't have been able to hide from that bright of a
spotlight.

Still, despite her reassurances, the idea lingered in Christine's head,
nagging her with its possibility.

She glanced towards Meg, wondering if she might have insight into Erik's connection to Carla Dicelli, but the girl looked as confused as Christine.

Erik grabbed her attention again. "Meg, Mrs. Giry, that will be all thank you. Christine, I'd like to speak with you in private."

As they stood to leave, Meg cast Christine a concerned look. Christine wished she would stay, wanted to beg her not to go. Mrs. Giry's glance was icy, but the two women left the room without hesitation or argument.

The sound of the door latching made Christine jump, and dread settled in her stomach as she kept her gaze cast down. She was overwhelmed, couldn't imagine what he was thinking, and struggled to process her own emotions.

His gaze was on her. She could feel it burning into the top of her head.

"You won't even look at me?"

She knew it made her a coward, but she *was* afraid to look at him. What would she see in his eyes? Anger? Lust? Regret?

Or, worst of all, would she see nothing?

"I'm sorry, Erik. I'm just stunned."

"Look at me."

A spike of anger shot through her at his tone. How dare he command her after days of silence!

She snapped her eyes up to his, and lost her breath as she fell captive to the electric blue. It took her a moment to regain her senses.

"Don't talk to me like that," she snarled.

He folded his arms across his chest. "You work for me. I'll talk to you however I like."

"You're a bastard."

"Maybe, but you didn't seem to mind it all those times I made you come."

Christine gasped, horrified. "How *dare* you."

Something flashed across his face that might have been remorse, but he schooled his features into an expression of smugness before she could make any sense of it.

"You're beautiful when you're furious."

Pushing to her feet, Christine turned to leave the room.

"Wait!" He hurried around his desk and blocked her path to the door. She glared at him.

"Get out of my way."

He shook his head. "No."

Christine didn't know what to do. If she tried to get around him, she might touch him, and she didn't think she could resist him if that happened, despite how angry he was making her.

"What do you want, Erik? Why are you doing this?"

He released a breath as he glanced away from her, his smirk and previous confidence gone.

"I...regret my behavior the other night."

Christine's anger began to cool at his words. "You do?"

He nodded. "Yes. I know you didn't mean to offend me, and I acted irrationally." He turned his gaze back to hers. "I shouldn't have told you to leave."

Her heart began to race, but she forced herself to maintain a calm exterior. "Why is that?" She wanted to flinch at the breathless hitch in her voice.

Of course he heard it, and his expression turned smoldering. Moving closer to her, he cupped her cheek. She fought not to lean into his palm.

"Because I should have begged you to stay, and then lavished you with so much pleasure you'd have been unable to move from my bed."

His words heated her blood, but they weren't quite the soothing balm she needed.

"That doesn't sound like an apology."

The corner of his mouth twitched.

"I'm sorry, Christine. Truly, I am. I'm sorry I lost my temper and lashed out at you that night, and I'm sorry I've not reached out to you since then. I...I'm not used to this sort of thing."

"What sort of thing?" She cursed the hope that fluttered in her heart.

Erik stroked his thumb along her cheek.

"I'm not used to wanting someone the way I want you. I'm not used to, well, being *used* to someone."

"You were going to tell me to leave, weren't you?" She'd been agonizing over that question since she'd ran from him that night, and for her own peace of mind, she had to know if it had ever crossed his.

"No, I wasn't going to ask you to leave." His immediate response had her hope swelling. "But..." Her hope stalled "...I was determined to stay away from you. To return to when things were strictly professional between us."

Christine swallowed against a lump in her throat. "Why did you change your mind?"

Leaning down, he rested his forehead against hers.

"No matter how hard I try, I can't forget the feel of your skin. The softness of your lips. The little cries you make when you're in the throes of your pleasure. These things are seared into my mind, making it impossible to go back to the way things were and pretend I'm not, even now, aching for you."

She squeezed her eyes shut as that hope burst into full bloom in her heart.

Damn it. Christine knew she was an idiot, but she couldn't help herself. Not when he said things like that.

Opening her eyes, she gazed up at him.

"I'm aching for you too."

She caught the flash of his grin before his lips descended on hers in a gentle kiss. Christine didn't want gentle, however, not after days without his touch. She cupped his face and deepened the kiss, opening her mouth to invite his tongue in to twine with hers. Groaning, he complied, wrapping his arms around her and holding her tight. She whimpered when she felt his erection pressing into her belly.

Erik moved his hands down to the backs of her thighs and lifted her up, parting her legs to wrap around his waist. Never breaking their kiss, he walked them to his desk and laid her on its surface. Pulling back, he smiled down at her as his hands went to work undoing the button and zipper of her slacks. Once he pulled them and her underwear off her legs, he knelt on the floor in front of her.

Christine pushed up onto her elbows to stare down at him, excitement coursing through her.

"Erik..."

He pushed her thighs apart, his eyes flashing with hunger.

"Try not to scream too loud. We don't want to startle Mrs. Giry."

Before she could manage a word in reply, he dropped his head and dragged his tongue along her flesh. Christine fell back on the desk with a cry, then remembered his warning and slapped her hands over her mouth. He ravaged her with his lips, teeth, and tongue, and she writhed as pleasure pounded through her. She'd never had someone perform oral sex on her with such enthusiasm. With past lovers, it had always been a burden, one they would force themselves through in order to please her. With Erik, though, she could tell he relished the act. He took his time, extended her enjoyment by bringing her to the edge, only to back off right before she came. Each time he did this, the sensations grew stronger, and she knew when he finally let her fall, the orgasm would eviscerate her.

When Christine could take no more, was on the brink of madness, she pleaded with him.

"Erik...please...no more...let me come!"

He lifted his head, grinning. "What are you talking about, angel? This is my apology. I need you to know how deeply and truly sorry I am. I don't think you understand quite yet."

She moaned. "I do understand! I really, really do. You're very sorry...I can tell. Just please, please, please...stop teasing me!"

His chuckle reverberated against her thighs, making her tender core clench. She gasped as pleasure and pain mingled.

Letting out a dramatic sigh, he said, "Very well. If you're sure you know how sorry I am..."

She nodded, her desperation growing. "I am. Very sure."

"All right, angel." He dove back into his task with a greater frenzy than before. Christine reached down and tangled her fingers into his hair, determined to keep him down there until she'd reached her peak. When her pleasure began to rise once more, she closed her eyes and prayed he'd keep his word.

He did, and the orgasm that crashed through her had her screaming at the top of her lungs. She didn't care if Mrs. Giry, Meg, or the whole world heard her.

When the tidal wave passed, Christine lay limp and panting. Erik sat back on his haunches, caressing her legs as she caught her breath.

"How was that?" he asked, tone smug.

Christine couldn't help the grin that curled her lips. "Apology accepted."

Chuckling, he stood and helped her to sit. She blinked several times as her vision swam, but once everything came back into focus, she noticed the sizeable bulge tenting his trousers.

Biting her lip, she reached out towards it. "Now it's my turn..."

Erik stepped away from her and grabbed her wrist.

She frowned, confused, and looked up into his face. He was shaking his head, his gaze shuttered.

"No, no, angel. No need for that." His tone was teasing, but there was a hard edge to it. "This was about me apologizing to you. It's not a punishment if I receive relief."

"But I don't want to punish you."

The corner of his mouth quirked up, but his expression was guarded. He was drawing away from her again.

"You're too kind, my sweet." He kissed her hand, but remained out of reach. "Now, we should get back to work. I've contacted my financial managers to come in and discuss funding the album. They'll be arriving tomorrow, and we need to prepare."

He released her hand and moved around his desk. Christine was left to slide to the floor and retrieve her clothes as he continued to explain the upcoming meeting. She half-listened, consumed by her jumbled thoughts.

He'd apologized, which was good.

He still wouldn't let her touch him, which was not good.

She realized no matter how much he may want her, or how much he claimed to trust her, if he didn't let her touch him, none of it mattered.

Nothing had changed.

Forcing a small smile, she pretended to be okay. She pretended to be absorbed in her work.

Yet inside, the hope she'd felt from earlier drooped, withering like a dying flower.

18

Christine

"Sir? Mr. Montgomery and Mr. Richards are here to see you," Christine announced as she entered the study the next day, guests in tow.

Erik was sitting behind his desk. He wore a three-piece black suit with a white shirt and black tie. With his mask, he looked powerful, and dangerous. Like the Devil himself, ready to make a deal for someone's soul.

The look was effective. She heard Mr. Montgomery's audible gulp behind her.

Standing, Erik spread his arms to invite them forward.

"Gentlemen, welcome. Please, have a seat."

Both men took hesitant steps further into the room before collapsing into the chairs in front of Erik's desk. When they'd arrived at the house, their expressions had been cautious, though their greetings polite when Christine had invited them in. She didn't blame their wariness as they'd followed her, imagining that Erik's sudden summons had caught them off guard. He couldn't be an easy man to work with in ordinary circumstances, and this situation was far from ordinary.

Once it appeared the men were settled, Christine turned to leave, but Erik stopped her.

"Ms. Davidson, I'd like you to stay." He had resumed his seat, but waved his hand at the empty air next to him. Confused, but not wanting to show it in front of the other two men, she moved to stand at Erik's side.

Turning his attention back to his guests, he began. "Now, gentlemen, I've invited you here because I wish to produce a new album, but have been informed we don't have the necessary funds available for the project. As my financial managers, I wanted to get your insight on this matter."

Both men looked stunned, and Christine wondered if it was because of the news about the album, or the downplaying of the label's financial situation. She almost felt sorry for them, having to balance Erik's vision with the company's reality.

It was the shrewd-eyed Mr. Richards who spoke first. Of the two, he seemed the least intimidated by Erik.

"Sir, as you're well aware, *Fantôme Records* has been sliding on a negative trajectory for the past few years. There haven't been any new projects to bring in new revenue, and while the money made of the redistribution of old albums has kept things afloat, even that revenue is starting to decrease and..."

Erik cut the man off.

"I know this already. If this new album is a success, if should reinvigorate our finances. My question, Mr. Richards, is how do we finance the creation of the album in the meantime?"

"You could find an investor," Mr. Montgomery blurted before Mr. Richards could respond. Mr. Montgomery blinked his large, round eyes, as if surprised he'd spoken. His partner glared at him.

Erik appeared interested in the idea. "An investor? I suppose that could work. Did you have anyone in mind, Mr. Montgomery?"

Looking as if he wanted to be anywhere in the world but sitting in that room, Mr. Montgomery stuttered, "Well...there are several individuals who come to mind, sir. My first pick, however, would...would probably be Phillip Chagny."

Christine frowned as the name sparked something familiar in her mind. She couldn't quite put her finger on why, though...

"Phillip Chagny? Who the hell is that?" Erik questioned.

Mr. Richards stepped in to relieve his partner. "A major real estate developer who our firm has recently taken on as a client. He's looking to diversify his financial portfolio. An investment in your company might prove appealing to him."

Erik leaned back in his chair and steepled his fingers as he considered the suggestion.

"Very well, put something together to present to him, and see if the man will bite." Erik looked between his two managers. "Let me know as soon as you receive his reply."

"Yes sir," they said in unison.

"That'll be all, gentlemen."

Both men appeared startled by the abrupt end to the meeting. Erik ignored them, indicating to Christine to see them out. She stepped forward with a hospitable smile.

"Right this way, gentlemen." They stood, wide-eyed, mouths agape, and she ushered them toward the door and back out into the hallway.

As she guided them back through the house, Mr. Richards glanced at her.

"Do you enjoy working for Mr. Roux, Ms. Davidson?"

Christine met his calculating gaze.

"Very much so, Mr. Richards."

He looked skeptical. "Such an odd man. I imagine he's very particular about things?"

They began descending the stairs to the first floor as she replied, "He is, but that is the way with creative geniuses, I suppose." She didn't like the line of questioning. Didn't want to engage with the man any more than was polite.

"Hmmmm."

"As long as you enjoy the work, that's what matters," Mr. Montgomery piped in, oblivious to the building tension between Christine and his partner. She couldn't help but smile at the man. He reminded her of a stuffed teddy bear.

"Yes, I believe that as well, sir."

They reached the front door, and she opened it for them, bidding them goodbye as they made their way outside towards their vehicle. Shutting the door behind them, she let out a breath of relief, thankful that strange exchange was over.

Christine made her way back to the study and found Erik still sitting behind his desk, looking lost in thought. When she entered the room, he raised his head and offered her a small smile.

"Tweedle Dee and Tweedle Dum make it out okay?"

She grinned, making her way across the space.

"Yes, they made it out fine." She perched on the edge of the desk next to him. "They seem like *interesting* individuals."

Erik grabbed her hand and began to play with her fingers.

"Hmmmm, yes. Interesting."

She tilted her head and watched him as he watched their hands.

"Erik? What are you doing?"

Gripping her hand, he pulled her so that she slid in front of him. She let him arrange her so she sat with her legs closed together between his. Not sure what he would do, she waited as he continued to entwine his fingers among hers.

With a deep sigh, he dropped his head into her lap and wrapped his arms around her waist.

"Erik!" she shrieked, surprised. She quickly realized he wasn't attempting to do anything to her. He was just resting on her. *Cuddling* her.

"You smell good," he mumbled, turning so that the uncovered side of his face was against her thighs. "You're warm, too."

You beautiful, strange man.

She began stroking her fingers through his hair. He let out a contented hum and closed his eyes.

Christine stared down at him as she continued to pet his head. He looked so weary. So vulnerable, lying in her lap. He had left himself unguarded to her. If she wanted to, she could reach down and take his mask from him before he could stop her.

It was tempting. Oh, God, it was so tempting.

But she kept her free hand at her side.

She cared more about him than about seeing his face, and she wasn't willing to risk the tentative trust she'd managed to build with him just to satisfy her curiosity. Playing that logic like a mantra in her head to keep from slipping up, Christine continued to comb through his hair until his breathing evened out and she realized he'd fallen asleep.

She froze. He'd never slept in front of her before, and she didn't think he'd done so now on purpose. How exhausted must he be? Should she wake him?

No, not yet. Leaning back on one arm, she kept stroking his hair, finding a strange sense of satisfaction in the act. It was as if they were a real couple, sharing these types of intimate moments every day. She knew it wouldn't last. The moment would pass, and they'd go back to being whatever it was they were. So, she didn't think about anything else, and just let herself be in the moment with him.

It was over too soon.

Perhaps twenty minutes passed before he began to stir. His visible eye slid open, and he blinked in confusion before raising his head to gaze at her.

"I fell asleep?" he asked, as if he couldn't believe it.

Christine nodded, dropping her hand from his hair, smiling despite her disappointment that he'd burst their peaceful little bubble.

"Yes. You're clearly exhausted. Perhaps you should go rest in your room."

She moved to scoot off the desk, but he gripped her thighs, holding her in place.

"You didn't take it off."

Christine stilled, careful to keep her expression neutral.

"Take what off?"

He squeezed her in warning. "My mask. You didn't take it off."

"Of course I didn't."

He narrowed his eyes. "Why?"

She rolled hers. "Are you really asking me that?"

"Just answer the question."

Licking her lips, she met his gaze straight on. "Why would I do the one thing that is sure to destroy whatever trust in me you have? I'm not an idiot, Erik, and I'm not here just because I'm curious." She pushed his hands from her, annoyed, and slid from the desk.

"Then why are you here?"

The whispered question made her pause, her hands frozen in the act of straightening her skirt. That he felt the need to ask her that made her heart hurt.

With a sigh, she met his baffled blue eyes. "I'm here for you, Erik."

Not waiting for him to respond, feeling too vulnerable about her confession, she turned and hurried from the room without a backwards glance.

* * *

Erik

I'm here for you, Erik.

The woman would be the death of him.

What could she mean by such an impossible statement?

He leaned back in his chair as he pondered the question. Her expression right before she'd ran from the room wouldn't leave his thoughts. She'd been wounded by his words, yet she'd still made that confession.

She was doing things to him he didn't understand. He still couldn't believe he'd fallen asleep on her like that. Yes, he'd been working into the night finalizing pieces for the album, planning the arrangements and selecting musicians, which left him exhausted, but to let his guard down like that? He hadn't allowed it in years.

Memories began to surface; ones he had spent more time than he cared for hiding away in the back of his mind. He forced them back down, but knew they wouldn't stay there for long. *She* was coming, after all this time.

With her arrival, the memories would break free, and with them, the pain and rage.

Mrs. Giry had been right to question him. He knew he wasn't in his right mind, but he also knew he would do anything for Christine. Her voice on his album, with *that woman* featured, would open the world to her.

Singing was Christine's dream. Music lived in her soul.

He'd make her dream come true, whatever the cost.

Then, she would leave him. The world would claim her, and he wouldn't be able to follow.

Still, even that devastation would be a small price to pay to see her shine. Even if her brilliance didn't reach him in the shadows.

19

Christine

"Phillip Chagny will be arriving today. Is everything prepared?"

Christine glanced up from her bowl of oatmeal and met Mrs. Giry's questioning gaze. Next to the housekeeper, Meg sat eating her own breakfast and scrolling through her cellphone, oblivious to the conversation unfolding beside her.

"Yes," Christine answered, wiping her mouth with her napkin. "I mean, I believe so. I wasn't given any special instructions."

Mrs. Giry frowned. "Our potential investor comes to meet with us, and Erik gives you no specific instructions?"

That's not what I said, Christine thought. *He didn't give me* special *instructions...*

Instead of voicing her annoyance, however, she shrugged.

Mrs. Giry's lips tightened into a line. She stood, startling Meg.

"This simply will not do."

Christine watched as the housekeeper turned and marched from the room, her heels clicking against the floor.

Meg stared after her mother with wide eyes.

Turning to Christine once Mrs. Giry was out of sight, she asked, "What was that all about?"

Christine shrugged again. "Your guess is as good as mine." She returned her attention to her food. Meg, however, having been pulled into the live drama around her, placed her phone on the table and focused in on Christine.

"So, are you excited?"

Looking back up, Christine furrowed her brow. "About what?"

Meg rolled her eyes. "The album, stupid."

"Oh! Yes, of course." Excited. Terrified.

Not at all sure she was ready.

Meg chuckled. "I know it's probably intimidating, what with Carla Dicelli on board, but Erik wouldn't include you if he didn't think you could handle it.

Christine nodded. "You're right, I know." A thought rose up that had been haunting her on and off since Erik had announced the new album. "Meg? Can I ask you something?"

"Of course. What is it?"

Glancing around to ensure they were alone, Christine leaned forward and lowered her voice. "Do you know anything about Erik and Carla Dicelli?"

Pursing her lips, Meg scrunched her face as she thought for several moments.

At length, she answered, "There's not much I can tell you. I know they dated before Carla made it big. He produced her first album, and wrote a lot of her first songs."

"How did things end between them?" Mrs. Giry's stark expression at the news Carla would be involved with the album flashed through Christine's mind.

"Well, I don't know the details. I was in school when they were together, so I wasn't really around. Whatever happened, though, it wasn't pretty. Erik was never very keen on interacting with people, but after Carla, he went full-hermit. Shut down any music production that was happening, withdrew into himself. Basically cut himself off from humanity."

Christine's heart hammered. "When...when did they break up?" Though she could guess at the answer, she needed to hear it out loud.

"Five years ago."

Five years. It had been five years since Erik had put out new music.

He'd stopped because of Carla.

Because she'd broken his heart.

He'd been in love with her.

Jealousy lanced through Christine with such ferocity, it startled her.

"I see."

Meg grabbed her hand and gave it a gentle squeeze.

"Hey, that was then. Erik's finally moving on, and he wouldn't be if it weren't for you."

Except he's not moving on. He still keeps me at a distance...still won't let me touch him.

She kept the thought to herself, however, and offered Meg a smile. "You're right. It's not worth thinking about."

Meg's grin was encouraging. Her phone buzzed in that moment, stealing her attention.

"Oh, it's Chelsey. Sorry, I've got to take this."

Grabbing the phone, she headed towards the dining room door before Christine could reply, answering the call.

"Hey babe, what's up?"

The door swung shut behind her.

Alone, Christine stared down into her oatmeal, but she no longer had an appetite.

* * *

"Thank you for meeting us today, Mr. Chagny," Mr. Richards said from where he stood next to Erik's desk.

"Of course," Phillip Chagny replied. He was seated in front of the desk. Christine had been surprised when she'd greeted him at the front door by how young he'd appeared. Handsome as well, with slicked back brown hair, bright amber eyes, a strong jaw darkened with stubble, and a tall, lean figure. He was dressed in a crisp three-piece gray suit that screamed money and class. Mr. Chagny looked between the two financial advisors and Erik. "I'm very interested in this project."

Mr. Montgomery, who stood next to Mr. Richards, clapped his hands together. "We're so happy to hear that, sir."

Christine, standing at Erik's side, glanced down at him. He was silent, leaning back in his chair with his elbows perched on the arm-rests and his fingers steepled in front of his mouth. His sharp blue gaze was locked on Mr. Chagny, but his eyes gave no hint as to his thoughts.

"Well, if we are all in agreement, Mr. Montgomery and I will write up a contract..."

Christine raised her brows at Mr. Richards' words. They'd barely been in the meeting twenty-minutes, and while Mr. Chagny had agreed to the number Mr. Richards and Mr. Montgomery had pre-sented to him, she had anticipated more of a negotiation. Erik had yet to speak. Surely it couldn't be this easy to procure an investor?

"I do have a few stipulations I'd like included in the contract," Mr. Chagny said.

Mr. Montgomery's expression sagged, though Mr. Richards was able to maintain his own composure. Erik let his hands drop from his mouth.

"Of course, sir," Mr. Richards nodded. "Just what would those be, exactly?"

Mr. Chagny brought his hands together in a casual knot before an-swering. "First, I wish to be kept abreast of the album's development. I am a very hands-on individual, and like to see exactly how my money is being spent. I will be on site throughout the process."

Christine felt Erik tense next to her, but he still said nothing.

Mr. Richards glanced towards Erik, and when he didn't receive any sign of outright disagreement, he turned back to Mr. Chagny. "Of course. You will have full access. What else?"

"I have a band I would like included in the project. I can vouch for their talent myself."

Mr. Richards looked at Erik again. This time, he offered a stiff chin jerk, which Mr. Richards seemed able to interpret.

"They must perform for Mr. Roux and receive his approval first."

Mr. Chagny's eyes slid towards Erik. "Of course."

"Anything else?" Mr. Montgomery managed to compose himself enough to speak.

To Christine's surprise, Mr. Chagny's eyes landed on her. Erik gripped the arms of his chair.

"Ms. Davidson, wasn't it?"

She nodded.

Mr. Chagny smirked.

"I want Ms. Davidson to serve as my personal assistant when I am on site, and to *walk* me through the process of the album's development." He looked towards Erik. "You don't mind sharing her, do you Roux?"

There was a lecherous gleam in his eyes. Christine's stomach tightened in disgust.

"Ms. Davidson is not an object for me to pass around," Erik spoke at last, his tone hard. "She is my employee, and will also have a song on the album. She will be far too busy to babysit your pompous ass. We either have a deal without her included, or we have no deal."

Christine stared at Erik with wide-eyes, feeling as shocked as Mr. Richards and Mr. Montgomery looked. Had he just blown this deal? For *her*?

Her treacherous heart fluttered.

Erik and Mr. Chagny stared each other down for several long moments. Christine worried that their potential-investor would explode and storm out, or worse, take a swing at Erik.

She was startled when he opened his mouth and released a bark of laughter.

"Very well, Mr. Roux. We have a deal without the inclusion of Ms. Davidson. I'm nothing if not reasonable, and I appreciate a man who would choose his integrity over my fortune."

"*My* integrity was not in question," Erik growled.

His quiet hostility didn't appear to faze Mr. Chagny. Pushing to his feet, he turned towards Mr. Richards and Mr. Montgomery.

"Send the contract to my office once it is complete, gentlemen."
He reached out to shake their hands. Both men appeared stunned, and
Christine couldn't blame them. She was still trying to figure out what
had just happened herself.

"Ye...yes sir," Mr. Richards managed to stutter.

Turning back to Christine, Mr. Chagny winked. "Until next time,
Ms. Davidson."

Erik appeared ready to leap up and attack the man, so she stepped
forward. "Allow me to walk you out, sir."

"No." Erik's voice boomed, making Christine jump. He stood, glaring at Mr. Chagny. "Mr. Richards and Mr. Montgomery will show you
out."

Both men gaped at Erik.

"But, sir..." Mr. Richards began.

"Get out! All of you!" Erik roared. Montgomery and Richards each
looked horrified at the show of rage. Chagny looked delighted.

"You will be a fascinating man to work with, to be sure."

"I said out!" Erik slammed his hands on his desk.

Christine moved to herd the men out the study door.

"Thank you, gentlemen. That will be all."

Mr. Montgomery and Mr. Richards gawked at her, but allowed her
to guide them out into the hall. Mr. Chagny strolled after them, offering Christine another wink.

She shut the door behind them.

Whirling around, she opened her mouth to berate Erik, but he was
already in front of her.

Grabbing her shoulders, he pushed her up against the door as his
mouth descended on hers in a bruising kiss.

Surprised, her body reacted on instinct, her fingers plunging into
his hair, and her lips parting to let his tongue slide in. His hands
moved down to clutch her hips, pulling her against him so he could
grind his length along the juncture of her thighs. She let out a gasp,
and then a cry when he brought one hand back up to clutch a breast.

It was then that she remembered the men who had just left their presence.

They could still be right outside the door.

She tore her mouth from his. "Erik, stop! They might hear!"

He growled against her throat. "Let them. Let that bastard hear you scream, so he knows who you belong to."

Christine rolled her eyes and shoved at his chest. "I'm not your property, Erik. You said as much yourself, remember?"

He resisted her pushing hands for a few seconds, but eventually acquiesced and stepped away.

"I know," he sighed, running a hand through his mussed hair. "I'm sorry. That son of a bitch just brought the caveman out of me."

Lips swollen and chest still heaving, Christine made no reply. Phillip Chagny had been disgusting, but Erik's defense of her had been thrilling. She held back saying so, however. It would make her too vulnerable to him. She was growing cautious with him, working harder to guard her heart from his grasp.

He released another sigh and let his hand drop. Meeting her eyes, he offered a soft smile.

"I know what would lift my mood."

Christine blinked. "What?"

"Showing you the recording studio."

She gasped as excitement shot through her. "Really?"

Erik nodded. "Yes. I should have shown it to you weeks ago. Now that we'll be reopening it, you'll need to become familiar with the facility."

She smiled. "If you insist, sir."

He grinned at her teasing tone, and then offered her his hand. "I do."

Christine slipped her palm into his. He turned and led her to an empty section of wall and pushed against the molding in the center. A panel shifted and moved to the side, revealing the entrance to a secret tunnel.

"Erik?"

He glanced back at her. "I have an underground passageway between this house and the studio."

Christine arched a brow. "Do you ever go outside?"

Erik chuckled. "Only at night." Turning, he tugged her with him into the passageway. She followed, unsure if his answer had been a joke, and suspecting that it wasn't.

20

Christine

The passageway took them to a small office with little furniture and a door that locked from the inside. Erik led her out into another hallway, which he explained stretched through the whole building. The one-story facility was modern in design, with gray walls and light wood accents. While the right side of the hallway had several doors, the left side only had one. Erik stopped, opened it, and stepped aside to let Christine enter first. She gasped, recognizing the control room, with its large mixing console, monitors, and collection of speakers varying in size. Through a window above the console, she could see into the live room, one big enough to hold an orchestra. A grand piano sat in one corner, a full drum set in another.

"We also have an isolation booth, and a vocal booth," Erik said, pointing to two doors flanking the console on either side.

She spun around, flashing Erik a smile. "This is amazing."

"I'm glad you like it." He leaned down to murmur at her ear. "Now, do you want to try it out?"

Christine frowned. "What do you mean?"

"I want you to sing for me, angel."

"Here? Now?"

He nodded. "Yes. Here. Now."

Christine's stomach twisted. It was one thing to sing when it was just the two of them in his studio, but the thought of singing here, in this space, was intimidating. It was too real. Too professional.

She doubted she was good enough.

"Erik, I don't know..."

He tilted her chin up with a finger. "You misunderstand. It wasn't a request."

Christine gazed up at him. "Don't record me."

The corner of his mouth tilted. "I won't. We'll use this opportunity to get you used to the space."

After a second to think, she took a deep breath. "Okay."

Taking her hand, he walked her towards the door to the live room. Her heels clicked on the wood floor as they moved to stand in front of the window. Erik positioned her and told her to stay still. His hands on her shoulders sent tingles down her arms.

When he spoke, his breath caressed her cheek. "We're going to do an exercise, angel."

"An exercise?"

"Yes, an exercise. To help you with your nerves and keep you from growing distracted once this place is full of people."

She gulped as her breathing grew faster. "What kind of exercise, exactly?"

He brushed his lips against her ear. "I want to play with you while you sing. If you can make it through the song, I'll grant you any favor you want."

"And if I don't?"

Erik chuckled. "I don't need a prize. The game itself is what I want."

Her core clenched. "You want to play with me?"

"I want you to give me control of your body, just like last time."

"And if I feel you're going too far?" She remembered how he'd pushed her to her emotional limits the last time they'd *played*. The experience had been overwhelming, but the pleasure had been stunning.

"What is your safe word?"

"Gounod." Her voice was little more than a whisper.

"Do you accept my challenge, Christine?"

She bit her lip as she considered his offer. If she kept her emotions in check, she would reap the benefits of his masterful hands and mouth. Could she do it, though? Last time, she'd been taken off guard by the intensity of the experience, but this time she had a better idea of what to expect.

At length, she answered, "Yes."

He released a breath that fanned over the back of her neck. Had he been holding it as he waited for her answer?

"Start singing."

Licking her lips, Christine opened her mouth to obey. As the song burst forth, she felt his hands slide to the zipper at the back of her dress. When he began to pull it down, she faltered.

He stopped.

"Defeated already, angel? Pity. We've only just begun."

Taking a deep breath to compose herself, Christine resumed singing, and he continued undoing her zipper. When he reached the bottom of her dress, he slid his hands beneath the parted cloth at her waist. Christine jolted at the skin-to-skin contact, and her voice pitched, but she didn't stop her song.

"Very good, angel."

He traced his fingertips up her back to her shoulders and pushed her dress down her arms. It pooled around her feet and she shivered as the cool air of the room caressed her skin. When he ran his hands down her arms, goosebumps followed in their wake. She forced herself to ignore the sensations, maintaining eye contact with her reflection in the window and watching her mouth move, like a dancer spotting a turn.

Erik caressed the back of her neck with his lips. Her voice hitched, but she managed to continue without missing a lyric. With swift movements, he removed her bra and it joined her dress on the floor. He cupped her breasts with a quick squeeze, but then moved his hands up to her hair.

"I love your hair," he rumbled, plunging his fingers into the thick mass. His touch grew rougher as he played and tugged at the strands. The more turned on he made her, the harder it was to engage her diaphragm.

His hands returned to her breasts and he pinched her nipples as he dragged his mouth along the column of her throat. Her voice grew breathless, but she fought to get the words out, bringing her hands up to cover his. She felt him grin against her shoulder.

"Tsk, tsk, angel, I didn't say you could move." He lifted her arms up and back to wrap around his neck. "Keep those right there, or there will be consequences."

She clutched his hair, but obeyed.

He inched one hand from her breast down her torso, his destination clear. When his fingers played at the waistband of her panties, she clenched her legs together at the rush of heat that burst from her core. Her voice grew pitchy, but she didn't stop singing.

Erik slid his hand into her underwear. The moment his finger made contact with her clit, Christine let out a loud moan, breaking her song.

His other hand left her breast and slapped her backside.

She let out a surprised shriek.

"Erik!"

"I told you there would be consequences." He spanked her again, and he was not gentle.

Her ass stung, and she didn't think she liked it. He hadn't struck her the last time they'd played. She'd never enjoyed this kind of thing before.

When he slapped her a third time, she opened her mouth to use her safe word, but he began massaging her tender flesh.

She froze. The stinging turned into a delicious tingle that had her arching her backside into his hand.

"Oh my God."

"You're not singing, angel." His palm whipped across her ass as he began stroking his finger against her clit. She released a pained groan, pulling at his hair in desperation.

"I...can't!" she exclaimed, undulating her hips to increase the pressure.

"Are you raising the white flag?" He stopped moving his fingers. She dug her nails into his scalp.

He chuckled.

"Damn it, yes! I give up. You win!"

Erik took in a breath. "Victory is *so* sweet."

His fingers began moving again, but at a far more rapid pace. She was close, could feel her release nearing with each second.

Just as she reached her peak, he spanked her one more time, harder than any of the other blows.

Christine screamed as she exploded in his arms. The combination of pleasure and pain was overwhelming. She prayed for it to end, but at the same time hoped it never would. Erik was murmuring in her ear, but she couldn't hear him. She was coming undone, and wasn't sure if she'd be able to put herself back together again.

When her orgasm began to subside at last, her legs shook before giving out. Erik caught her under her arms.

"Are you okay?" he asked, the triumph in his tone tinged by his genuine concern.

Christine could only nod. He swooped her up into his arms and carried her back into the control room. Setting her down on a sofa against the back wall, he returned to the live room to retrieve her clothes. Christine slumped against the couch, exhausted. He grinned at her when he returned.

"Tired, angel?" He handed her the dress and bra.

"You could say that." Her throat felt raw, and her voice croaked.

Erik frowned and knelt in front of her, taking her chin in his hand.

"Damn it. I pushed you too hard. You'll need to rest your voice."

Christine nodded. She studied his face as his blue gaze examined her. He was so beautiful, even with the mask. Maybe more so because of it. She wanted to see him, though, to know him in a way that no one else did.

She wanted his trust.

Reaching up a hand, she gripped his wrist. He met her gaze with a frown.

"Christine, what is it?"

She didn't speak. Leaning forward, she pressed her lips to his in a tender kiss. He didn't respond right away, was perhaps too startled. After several heartbeats, however, he returned her kiss.

Christine was the one to end it at last, pulling back from him and breaking their connection.

He blinked at her, his brow furrowed.

"What was that?"

She shrugged. "Nothing. A thank you, I suppose."

"A thank you for what?"

"For putting your faith in me." *Now just put your trust in me.*

The corner of his mouth curled in bemusement. "You don't need to thank me for that."

"Yes I do." She made to stand, and he moved back. Picking up her dress from the couch, she pulled it on and turned to present the zipper to him. He secured the garment without question. Facing him again, she smiled. "We should probably get back."

He continued to stare at her as if she was a puzzle he couldn't quite solve, but found entertaining nonetheless.

Spreading his arm towards the door, he said, "After you."

With her chin up, she headed out into the hall. Erik followed her, but she didn't look back at him.

She didn't trust her eyes not to give away how hard she was falling for him.

21

Christine

The next week, *Box 5* arrived to audition for Erik.

Christine stood in the lobby of the recording studio as the band members and their crew filed in with their equipment. Mrs. Giry was there as well, barking instructions and directing them to the live room. Though she was only there as backup, Christine couldn't help but thrill at the activity. It wasn't just excitement over the album, but a genuine glee at having so many new people around.

"Christine? Christine Davidson?"

Startled, Christine spun around and her gaze locked with a young, handsome man standing by the doorway. Disheveled blonde hair, twinkling brown eyes, and a strong jawline, the man was a striking figure and somehow familiar.

Frowning, she asked, "I'm sorry. Do I know you?"

The man hurried to stand before her, a wide smile splitting his face.

"It's me, Christine. Rick! Rick Chagny. Remember?"

Recognition slammed into her. "Oh my God, yes!"

Without thinking, she closed the distance between them and threw her arms around him in a tight hug. He squeezed her to him in turn, and when they parted, he was laughing.

"I can't believe it. What are you doing here?" he asked.

"I could ask you the same thing!"

He spread his arms, swinging his head from side to side as members of the band and their crew continued to flood into the studio.

"I'm with the band."

Christine couldn't believe it. What were the odds of them meeting again after so many years like this? Then it clicked.

Chagny. He must be related to Phillip Chagny. *That's* why she'd recognized the name.

"What are you doing here, Christine?" he questioned again.

"Oh, actually, I'm Mr. Roux's personal assistant. I'm helping with the coordination of the recording sessions."

Rick's eyes widened. "*You're* Erik Roux's personal assistant. Wow. How'd you land a sweet gig like that?"

Christine shrugged with a grin. "I was highly overqualified and very convincing in my interview."

Rick let out a bark of laughter, and Christine found herself swept up in the sound. It was so light and easy, a laugh that was only possible when a person was without any kind of care or worry. It was so different from Erik's dark chuckles.

A sense of unease settled over her at the thought of Erik. She glanced around the lobby, half expecting to find him lurking in the shadows watching her. His moods had been unpredictable as of late. She knew the stress of the album was weighing on him, but there was something else she couldn't name that seemed to be adding to his burden.

"Christine? Helloooooo, are you in there?"

Blinking, Christine refocused her gaze on Rick.

"Sorry. I'm just overwhelmed, and so happy to see you."

He chuckled. "I get it. What are the odds, right? We haven't seen each other since, what? Sixth grade?"

Christine couldn't help a grin as memories flooded through her.

"That summer music camp. Seems like that was ages ago."

"Because it was." Rick frowned, his brow crinkling. "You never came back after that summer. What happened?"

She had to swallow as sadness threatened to overshadow her nostalgic happiness.

"My father died that fall, and my mom...we just couldn't afford camp after that."

Rick's gaze turned sympathetic. He was expressive, every emotion visible in his expressions. She found it refreshing.

"I'm so sorry, Christine. I remember how much you loved your father, and how passionate you were about music, even back then. To lose both at the same time...that must have been so hard."

Her heart eased at his words, her sadness dissipating. She was relieved the grown-up Rick before her still had so much of the boy she'd known in him. He was sweet, gentle, and understanding. All the things her childhood heart had loved about him had survived through the years.

"It was, but I was able to find a new path for my life."

Gazing around the room, Rick said, "You seem to have done pretty well for yourself, all things considered."

"Yes. I suppose I have."

At that moment, one of the crew yelled out Rick's name.

He waved a hand and replied, "I'm coming." Facing Christine again, he flashed her an adorable smile. "I've got to go, but can we catch up sometime?"

Christine nodded. "I'd like that."

"Great!" He leaned in and gave her a quick peck on the cheek. It was an innocent enough gesture, but it caught her off guard. Rick was gone without another word, and Christine found herself gazing around the room, hoping there were no cameras hidden in the walls.

* * *

Erik

The amount of people invading his home made his stomach roil in agitation. Erik didn't like people. His experiences with people were rarely good. Mrs. Giry, Meg, and Darius were one thing. Christine was his ultimate exception.

This horde, though? He wasn't sure he'd be able to handle their presence.

He watched from his security room as the band scurried in and out of his studio like ants carrying their burdens back to the colony. Mrs. Giry was handling everything with ease, as she always did, which went a long way to calm some of his anxiety. He'd sent Christine down as well to be his representative if need be, but she'd kept herself out of the way for the most part, watching the chaos from the corner of the room.

God, she was beautiful. Erik wondered if he'd ever be able to look at her without losing his breath. Her hair was loose around her shoulders, and she wore a gray pinstriped dress. It was everything he could do to not just stare at her instead of paying attention to the activity surrounding her.

A man suddenly approached her. Young, handsome...there was something familiar about him. Christine turned to look at him, and after a moment of confusion, recognition lit up her face.

Did they know each other?

Erik's whole body tensed and jealousy surged through him when she smiled at the man. They talked, that was all, but there was an ease between them that had Erik grinding his teeth. He couldn't remember the last time he'd been able to be as comfortable around someone as the two appeared with each other, and never had he felt that way around Christine. She had him on edge, second guessing himself at every turn. He was so consumed by her when she was near, it was maddening.

This man was all confidence when he spoke to her. Collected. Friendly.

Everything Erik wasn't.

Everything Christine deserved.

Erik was a rational man. He knew his jealousy stemmed from his insecurities. The two were just talking, and it wasn't like he had any real claim on Christine...

Just then, the blonde bastard leaned in and kissed her on her cheek. Erik wanted to fucking kill him.

He curled his hands into fists and took several deep breaths as he fought down his spike of rage.

Calm down, you idiot. Murdering the asshole would only drive Christine away.

The ringing of his cellphone was a welcome distraction. Picking it up from the console, he looked to see who was calling.

His stomach dropped to the floor, and his worries about the blonde asshole were pushed to the side in the face of something much worse.

"Shit," he murmured before clicking the button to accept the call. Putting the phone to his ear, he offered a cold greeting. "Hello, Carla."

22

Christine

Christine rushed into the study to find Erik staring out the window into the gardens below. She stopped, panting, having run from the studio up to the house. He turned towards her with a raised brow.

"Are you okay?"

She wanted to stamp her foot in frustration.

"You said there was an emergency and to hurry up here!"

"Well, I appreciate your haste." He moved from the window towards the bar cart in the corner and poured two glasses of amber liquid from a crystal decanter. He offered her one.

She frowned. "You know I don't like bourbon."

"Take it. You'll need it, trust me." He forced the drink into her hand, and then took a long swallow of his own.

Christine stared at him in shock. She'd never seen him like this before. His hand shook as he drank.

"Erik, what's going on? Why did you call me up here?"

She'd been helping Mrs. Giry oversee the last of the band's setup when she'd received a text from him.

We have an emergency. My study. Now!

He moved back to the cart to pour himself another glass. "We're receiving an unexpected visitor this afternoon. As if this day wasn't fucking stressful enough."

Christine placed her glass on his desk.

"Who else is coming?"

There was a sudden flurry of activity out in the hall. The sound of sharp footsteps could be heard approaching the door.

Erik stiffened next to her. "Damn it. She's already here."

Christine frowned up at him. "*Who?*"

His jaw clenched and his eyes burned with rage. "Carla."

The study door flew open and a gorgeous woman strolled inside, long dark hair flowing behind her, the silky skirt of her floor-length gown swirling around toned legs revealed by a thigh-high slit.

"Erik, darling," she purred, coming to a stop and batting emerald green eyes. A cruel smirk played at her blood-red lips. "It's so good to see you again."

Erik gnashed his teeth. "I can't quite say the same, Carla."

The woman's eyes flashed, jumping to Christine. She frowned.

"Who the hell are you?"

Christine blinked. "I'm Christine Davidson, Mr. Roux's personal assistant."

Carla Dicelli's gaze raked her up and down. Lips curling, she glanced back at Erik.

"My, my, Erik. She's rather young, even for you."

"That's enough, Carla," he growled. "Leave Christine alone."

Rolling her eyes, Carla hissed, "I'm not going to talk with you in front of the help, Roux. Get rid of her."

"Christine is not *the help*. She is my assistant, and she sits in on my meetings. Without exception."

Carla cocked her hip and smirked. "What? Too afraid to be alone with me, Erik? Afraid you won't be able to control yourself?"

Christine did not like the suggestive way the woman spoke. She shot a glance at Erik, who appeared to be struggling to keep his anger in check.

"I have no fear of losing control around you, Carla. You're here on business, nothing more."

Flipping her hair over her shoulder, Carla ignored him and turned her attention back to Christine.

"Has he fucked you yet?"

Shocked, Christine couldn't find words to respond.

"Carla!" Erik snarled.

The woman's grin widened. "I take that as a no. I'm not surprised. He's not an easy one to get into bed, but once you do, let me tell you sweetheart, he's a great lay. You're really missing out."

"That's enough!" Erik's voice boomed. "Shut the hell up, Carla. I'm not so desperate to have you on this album that I'll allow you to speak to my employees like this."

Carla shrugged. "That might be true, but we both know the album won't be as big of a success without me, and from what I hear, you are in desperate need of a *huge* success, aren't you?"

Christine couldn't believe the cruelty dripping from the woman's words. How was it possible the two had been together?

"Did you come here just to piss me off, Carla? Production doesn't start for two weeks."

Carla shrugged. "I heard you were auditioning a band today. Though I assume your assistant here simply failed in her duties to inform me, I thought it important that I come down and see them for myself."

"Christine failed at nothing. It was never my intention to invite you."

Christine bit her lip to hide her grin at his easy dismissal of the overbearing woman.

The diva narrowed her eyes. "Well, since I'm here anyway, I'll join you for their performance."

Erik opened his mouth to spit a retort, but a knock on the door interrupted him.

"What is it?" he snapped.

The door opened, and Mrs. Giry stepped inside, followed by Phillip Chagny.

"Sir, Mr. Chagny is here for the audition." The housekeeper kept her gaze directed away from Carla, ignoring the woman so blatantly, Christine was impressed.

Erik glared at Mr. Chagny. "I didn't say you could be here."

Mr. Chagny ignored him and stepped further into the room. He caught Christine's eye and smirked, but turned his attention to Carla without any other acknowledgement of her presence. It was a relief.

"Ms. Dicelli," he said, taking the woman's hand in his and bringing it to his lips. "It is a true honor to meet you. I'm a fan."

Carla's smile was like a cat who'd caught the canary. "Mr. Phillip Chagny, I presume? The sponsor of our little project?"

Christine imagined the woman sinking her blood-red nails into Phillip's shoulders, just like claws, and refusing to let him go. Although, from what she'd gathered of the two in her brief interactions with them so far, she thought they might actually be perfect for each other.

Chagny's smirk was cocky. "Indeed I am." Turning to Erik at last, he said, "I see no reason why Ms. Dicelli and myself shouldn't be here today. I have a lot at stake financially in this album, and Ms. Dicelli should have a sense of who she is working with."

Christine could tell that Erik was fuming, but he managed to keep a cool exterior, apart from his fisted hands.

"This is my production, Chagny. You may be footing the bill, but that doesn't mean you get to come into my home and my studio and tell me how to make this album."

Phillip waved his hand, a dismissive gesture that had Christine's own blood boiling.

"Of course not, Roux. You have total creative control, as we agreed. We also agreed, however, that I would be able to be present for every step of the process." Turning back to Carla, he offered her his arm. "Shall we? I believe the band is preparing as we speak."

Taking his arm with a seductive smile, Carla allowed Phillip to lead her from the study without a backwards glance at Erik or Christine. They swept past Mrs. Giry, whose reddened cheeks were the only indication of her own pique.

Glancing at Erik, Christine held her breath. His expression was guarded, and she couldn't tell what he was thinking.

At length, he took a deep breath and released it with deliberate puffs.

Meeting Christine's questioning stare, he said, "Let's go."

He was moving towards the door before she'd processed the command, and she hurried to catch up with him. As she passed Mrs. Giry, the two locked eyes, and Christine could see her own worries reflected in the housekeeper's bright gaze.

23

Christine

The tension in the control room was thick as they waited for the band to ready themselves. Christine stood off to the side, trying to stay out of the way of Erik, Carla, and Phillip. She hadn't missed how Erik positioned himself between her and the others, almost as if he were shielding her. His continued protectiveness had her traitorous heart racing.

Christine forced her attention away from the three imposing figures in the room with her to the live room. The band was making final adjustments to their positions and instruments. She smiled when she spotted Rick in the back sitting behind a drum set, remembering how much he'd loved playing percussion instruments when they had been at camp. Besides him, there were four others. Standing in front of Rick was a tall, dark haired man with a bass guitar, and a shorter red haired man strumming the strings of his electric guitar. A young black woman with a halo of curly hair stood behind a keyboard, and another girl with platinum blonde hair stood in front of a microphone at the head of the group.

At that moment, Rick gave them a thumbs up, letting them know the band was ready.

Erik reached forward and hit a button on the console. Pressing another button, he said, "We're recording. Go ahead."

Box 5 began playing their first song, and Christine was surprised by how good they were. She hadn't expected them to be terrible, but she hadn't expected to be impressed either. Peeking up at Erik, she couldn't tell what he was thinking. He was scrutinizing their performance with a neutral expression, but his eyes were laser-focused.

Once the band had finished, they flowed into their second song after a brief pause. Erik said nothing, continuing to observe them with a discerning gaze.

Two songs later, he hit the button on the console again and said, "That's enough."

The band stopped playing and waited, staring into the window of the control room. Christine could tell how nervous they were, and tried to offer a reassuring smile.

Erik continued to study them for several more moments.

"So? What do you think?" Mr. Chagny said at last, his impatience clear in his tone.

Erik shot him a glare. "I'll be honest, Phillip, I didn't anticipate your little brother's band to be any good. I agreed to the audition as a courtesy." He gazed back out into the live room. "However, they have genuine talent and skill." Pushing the console button once more, he announced, "You're in."

The tension was shattered by his words, and the quaking musicians broke out in excited whoops and celebratory hugging. Rick caught Christine's eye through the window and winked. She grinned, surprised to find her cheeks heating in a blush.

"Does my opinion not matter?" Carla snapped.

Erik shook his head. "No, it doesn't."

Phillip turned to the incensed diva. "Do you not approve of them, Ms. Dicelli? Please, be honest. I will not be offended."

Carla didn't bother to hide her interest in Phillip as she looked him up and down before answering with a purr. "That's not the case at all, Mr. Chagny. I agree that they have more talent than I expected. I simply wished for the opportunity to say so." She shot Erik an icy glare, which he ignored.

"Of course you have every right to." Phillip took her hand and brought it to his lips. Christine arched an incredulous brow as the woman lapped up his attention. Phillip caught her watching them and winked. Her natural response was much different than when Rick had done the same. Revulsion took the place of giddiness. Phillip was a womanizer, there was no doubt, and she suspected he was the kind of man who took *no* as a challenge.

Pivoting away from him, she rolled her eyes, and almost smacked right into Erik's broad chest.

He gazed down at her with a frown. "Are you okay?"

She nodded, unable to speak as his nearness and heat consumed her. Something in her expression must have given her thoughts away, because his eyes darkened with hunger.

"I've been around too many people today," he murmured. "Let's go back to the house, and you can help me relieve my stress."

She squeezed her thighs together.

"Yes sir."

His hand rested on the middle of her back as he began guiding her towards the exit.

"Christine, hold on!"

She stopped and looked to find Rick hurrying into the control room. She turned back to Erik, who was staring at her with narrowed eyes, his hand pressing into her back as if trying to push her forward.

"Would you excuse me a moment, sir?" Her voice was shaky, and her shoulders stiffened as she waited for his response. There was a part of her that wanted him to tell her no, and sweep her away to ravage and keep her all to himself. That petty part of her wanted him to be jealous, because it would at least be an indication he cared for her beyond their physical arrangement. At least enough not to want another man to steal her from him.

Instead of any of that, however, he dropped his hand, and with an expression that told her nothing, said, "Of course, Ms. Davidson. Take your time. I'll head back now."

Without another word, he turned and left her standing there.

Her heart sank. He'd walked away from her so easily, as if she meant nothing.

Blinking away sudden moisture in her eyes, she raised her chin and turned to find Rick standing behind her with a large smile.

She plastered one on herself.

"Congratulations! You all were incredible."

An adorable blush colored Rick's sculpted cheeks.

"Thanks. That had to be one of the most terrifying things I've ever done." He looked past her. "Was that really Erik Roux?"

Christine was careful to keep her expression from betraying the hurt even the sound of his name produced. "Yes. You'll have to forgive him for leaving already. He's not much of a people person."

"That's what they say. Was he wearing a mask? It was kind of hard to see from the other side of the glass."

She chose her words with extreme care. "Mr. Roux is a very private man, and doesn't typically let people see his face. The fact that he showed up in person for your audition is an indication of how impressed he is with you." No reason to tell Rick the truth. That Erik had had no expectations his band was any good, and had only shown up in person to keep Carla and Phillip from running the show.

Rick appeared appropriately awed. "Well, please thank him for me when you get back to the house. It was a true honor to play for him."

Christine nodded. "I will. Was there anything else you needed, Rick?"

His eyes lit up. "Yes! Actually, I wondered if you'd like to go out sometime? To catch up?"

Surprised, Christine struggled to find words to respond.

He must have taken her silence as hesitation, because he added, "It'll be very casual. No pressure at all. I'm sure now that we're working together, there might be some issue with us going out, but we can just go as friends if you'd like."

Blinking, she was at last able to retrieve her voice. "Oh, no, that's not the problem..." Was there a problem? Erik had made it very clear there wouldn't be more between them, so why shouldn't she go out with Rick? She took a moment to look at him. *Really* look at him. He was handsome, no doubt, and kind as far as she could tell. Perhaps a bit naïve, but it made him endearing. Like a puppy. Rick was the opposite of Erik in so many ways, and while he didn't spark the same kind of passion in her that Erik did, she didn't deny that she was attracted to him.

He wouldn't hide from her, or make her play games to earn his trust.

He wouldn't just walk away from her when he should stay and fight for her.

"I'd love to go out with you." The words flew from her mouth before she realized she was saying them, but once they were out, she refused to regret them.

Impossibly, his smile grew wider. "Great! How about tomorrow night? I could pick you up about seven?"

"Sounds perfect. I'll see you then." With her head high, she turned from Rick towards the door. Once in the hallway, she turned left instead of right, choosing to walk up to the house in the open air and sunshine rather than Erik's dark tunnel.

24

Erik

Erik sat at his piano, staring at the music in front of him, but he couldn't focus on the notes. He was too distracted, waiting for Christine to return from the studio. His ears were perked, listening for the telltale sound of high-heels approaching the study door.

He knew it was irrational, but he was angry. At her, and at himself. She hadn't hesitated to stop when Chagny had called for her, throwing off the cloak of lust that had covered her moments before. The fool Chagny made no secret of his desire for her. It was clear in his big, dopey, puppy-dog eyes. There was no way Christine couldn't see it, and still she was willing to put Erik aside for the boy. It had hurt him. His pride had taken a hit, yes, but it had poked at the darkness in him only she was able to dispel.

The darkness that told him he was a monster, one a beauty like her could never want.

Yet, more so than at her, he was angry at himself. He had no right to feel jealous or possessive of Christine. He hadn't promised her anything, and she wasn't tied to him. She was free to speak to whomever she wanted. So, he'd let her do so without argument, when his heart had screamed to sweep her away.

He didn't know if he'd made the right choice.

The clip of heels in the distance had him perking up like a damn dog. He picked up a pencil and pretended to work.

He didn't turn around when the door opened and shut behind him. She didn't approach him right away either. The scratch of the pencil against the paper was the only sound in the tense silence that stretched between them.

At length, he heard her release a sigh.

"I thought today went well, all things considered."

So, she was going to pretend everything was fine. Very well, he would follow suit.

"I thought so too."

More silence.

Erik was desperate for her to say something to assuage his fears. To tell him that she was sorry she went to Rick and wasn't interested in him at all.

"Is there anything else you need from me, sir?"

He clutched his pencil so hard between his fingers, he was surprised it didn't snap. Her business-like tone was infuriating.

Taking a deep breath, he replied in kind. "No. That will be all today, Ms. Davidson."

She didn't leave, and he hoped she lingered because she wanted to say something more.

That hope was dashed, however, when at last she said, "I'll see you tomorrow, then."

"Yes. See you tomorrow."

She did leave then. He whipped around when he heard the door shut and almost chased after her, but that evil voice in the back of his head whispered, *You don't deserve her. She wouldn't want you if she saw your face. Don't drag her down into your darkness.*

He stayed frozen on his bench.

In all his years of misery, he'd never wanted to be someone else more than in that moment. He wanted to be whole and handsome. He wanted to be able to light up Christine's face with a smile.

Bitterness filled him. He wished he could be Rick Chagny...a man more suited to stand at Christine's side.

He wished he could be anyone, and anything, but who and what he was.

Yet, none of that was possible. He was doomed to his cursed existence, and Christine, no matter how much she might deny it now, would someday leave him. It was inevitable.

The thought should have grounded him. Made him more aware of his reality.

Instead, it made him see red.

The pencil snapped.

* * *

Christine

Christine tossed and turned most of the night, unable to get her cold exchange with Erik out of her head. When she was finally able to sleep, she dreamed of him again. She was surrounded by darkness, except for a light outlining his frame. His back was turned to her, and no matter how much she ran or called out to him, he remained far away and out of reach. As unattainable as he seemed in real life.

She woke before dawn, and gave up trying to fall back to sleep. Instead, she stared up at the ceiling, replaying her and Erik's stiff conversation, hoping for any insight into what he'd been thinking. Nothing became clear, and she only made herself more anxious. At last, when the rising sun began to peak through her curtains, she pushed her covers away and got out of bed. Grabbing her robe, she left her bedroom and went out into the dark hallway.

The quiet of the house was soothing as she headed down to the kitchen. There had been too much activity as of late, too many people invading the space. Though it had been exciting at first, she hadn't realized how much she enjoyed the peace and solitude of the house. Nothing felt right anymore. Knowing it was selfish, Christine wished that everyone would go away again so it was just her and Erik.

With a sigh, she pushed open the door to the kitchen and was surprised to find it occupied.

"Oh, hi Meg. I didn't think anyone else was up."

The girl, dressed in yoga pants and a tight top, smiled from her countertop perch. A mug of something steamy was clutched in her hands.

"Hey, Christine. Yeah, I like to do sunrise yoga now and then. I was just enjoying the quiet before the madness began."

Christine smiled. If she had to have a companion in these early morning hours apart from Erik, Meg was by far her first choice over everyone else.

"What are you drinking?"

"It's a sweet tangerine herbal tea. It's good for positive energy. You want some?" She nodded towards the kettle on the stove. "There's still water."

Though herbal teas were not Christine's go-to, she grabbed a mug from the cupboard, accepted the tea bag Meg offered, and poured herself the rest of the water. Leaning against the kitchen island opposite Meg, she took a cautious sip.

"How is it?"

Christine swallowed and nodded her head. "Hot, but good. Thanks."

A comfortable silence fell between them as they sipped their drinks.

At length, Christine ventured a question. "So, you do yoga?"

Meg grinned. "It helps keep me flexible for dancing, and works out some of my sore muscles and joints. I'm not too hardcore about it, but I take classes at my neighborhood's YMCA. You practice at all?"

Christine shook her head. "No, but I do Pilates."

"Nice."

The conversation died off again, and Christine was content to let Meg pick it back up if she wanted too. After a few moments, though, she noticed the girl fidgeting with her cup as she glanced between it and Christine. It was clear she wanted to say something, but for whatever reason was struggling with her words.

"Meg? What is it?"

The girl gulped. "I...I want to ask you something, but it's kind of...sensitive."

Christine frowned, suspicion rising. "Okay..."

It took several moments of more fidgeting before she said, "I know you and Erik are...intimate. I'm curious, though, just how...how much of him have you seen?"

Christine let out a little breath of air, knowing what the girl was asking, and embarrassed by her answer.

"I've seen less of him than he has of me."

Meg sighed. "I was afraid you'd say something like that."

"Why?"

Shrugging, she admitted, "He's so afraid of rejection and being hurt, and understandably so, don't get me wrong, but he keeps everyone at arm's length and hides himself away. It's toxic for his soul. With you, though, he's been different. He's been opening up in ways I haven't seen in years, if at all. I was just hoping that, with you, he would..."

She trailed off, but Christine picked the thought back up. "That he would trust me with everything." She didn't add that that's what she'd been hoping for as well...what she was desperate for. As much as she knew she could trust Meg, she couldn't bring herself to talk about how much pain his distance caused her.

How lost for him she already was.

"Yeah," Meg nodded.

Silence fell again, but it was not as comfortable as before.

Christine struggled with what to say and how much to tell Meg. She wanted a confidante so badly, but didn't want to tell Meg more than she would be comfortable with about Erik. Still, one thing kept popping into her head, begging to be voiced...

"Rick asked me on a date."

Meg blinked at her, surprised. "Rick? You mean that hot blonde from the band?"

Christine turned her gaze to stare out the small window over the sink. "Yes. He and I knew each other when we were kids, and he recognized me when he got here."

"Were you two together back then?"

Shaking her head, Christine answered, "No. We were too young, but we had little crushes on each other. I suppose it was a sort of childhood romance."

"That he clearly hasn't gotten over."

That made Christine chuckle. "Clearly."

"So, what did you tell him?"

"I...said yes."

Silence.

"Does Erik know?"

Christine closed her eyes. She set her mug on the counter behind her.

"No," she whispered. "I haven't told him."

"Why?"

Opening her eyes, she set her face into a neutral expression. "Why should I? He hasn't offered me anything permanent. He hasn't made moves to form a real relationship. As far as I'm concerned, I'm free to explore different options."

I sound so terrible...so ugly. I don't want to be this person.

Glancing back at Meg, expecting to find anger or affront, instead she found the girl nodding, sympathy in her eyes.

"You're falling in love with him, aren't you?"

Though she'd long suspected, the words spoken out loud were a shock to Christine's system. Her chest ached, and she wrapped her arms around herself.

"What does it matter if he won't *let* me love him?"

Meg dropped her gaze to her cup, looking deep in thought as she considered Christine's words.

"I think you should go on the date."

Christine gaped at the girl. "What? You do?"

Meg lifted her gaze back up. "Yes. I do. Look, Christine, I love Erik. He's like a brother to me, but you can't force him to open up to you. His ability to cope and live with his shit isn't your responsibility. You need to do what's right for you, not him. Maybe you going on this date will be the kick-in-the-ass he needs, or you could find yourself with a different guy who's more emotionally available to you. Either way, you can't put your life on pause waiting for Erik to figure things out. It's not fair to you."

The girl was proving to be more surprising and insightful than Christine would have given her credit for.

"Meg...that's amazing advice."

Shrugging, the blonde hopped down from the counter, putting her empty cup in the sink.

"I'm not saying I'm a genius, but I'm not, not saying that either."

With a smile and a gentle pat on Christine's shoulder, Meg walked out of the kitchen, returning Christine to her solitude. Now, though, it wasn't so soothing.

25

⚜

Christine

Later that day, Christine sat in front of Erik's desk, taking notes as he rattled off the schedule for the album. It was hard to stay focused as her riotous thoughts and feelings from that morning continued to plague her, heightened by his nearness.

"We'll only have the orchestra for those few days, so there can absolutely be no schedule changes that would interfere with them. I had to call in several favors to get them on board the project with such short notice, so we accommodate them, they do not accommodate us." His tone was clear, professional, and commanding. There was no hint that he was feeling anything like the chaos she was.

It was annoying.

"Also, we'll be sure to keep you and Carla's recording times separate from each other. You shouldn't have to interact with that harpy any more than necessary."

Christine clutched her pen as her irritation grew. Why was he acting like everything was fine? Like it was all business-as-usual? He'd dismissed her so easily yesterday, and now wouldn't even acknowledge it?

"Christine? Are you listening?"

She snapped her head up, too late realizing she had gotten lost in her thoughts and stopped paying attention.

"I'm sorry. I spaced out for a moment. What was that last bit?"

He frowned and repeated himself with pique in his tone. "I said that tonight I thought we could go to the studio and begin work on your song once everyone else was gone."

She lost her breath, remembering the last time they had been alone in the studio.

"I can't tonight. I have plans already."

He straightened in his chair, his visible brow arched.

"Plans? What kind of plans could you possibly have?"

Offended by his baffled tone and the very question itself, she snapped without thinking, "Not that it's any of your business, but I'm going out with Rick Chagny tonight."

He went still, and she felt all the blood rush from her face. She hadn't meant to tell him. Not like that, at least.

She waited with baited breath for his response. Would he be angry? Ask her not to go? Demand that she didn't?

Would he do nothing, just as he'd done when Rick had approached her?

When his eyes shadowed and his expression went neutral, she wanted to cry. He was going to freeze her out again.

"Very well, I suppose I can't demand that you give up your date for work. We'll figure out another time."

He bent his head back to his computer. Christine stared at him, stunned.

That was it? That was all he was going to say?

She swallowed, fighting back hot, angry tears.

"You have no objections to my going out with Rick?" she dared to ask.

He didn't look up when he answered. "Why would I?"

His words were like a slap.

"It doesn't cause a conflict of interest?" Why was she pushing this? Did she want him to hurt her?

He shook his head, but still wouldn't turn his gaze to her. "Who am I to start labeling relationships in the work place as inappropriate? Be a bit hypocritical of me, wouldn't you think?"

He chuckled. He *chuckled*! As if he'd just made a clever joke. As if everything that had happened between them was laughable.

Rage exploded inside her. In that moment, all she wanted was to hurt him as badly as he was hurting her.

"What if I fuck him? Would that cause a conflict of interest?"

His whole body went rigid, and he slowly raised his head up to look at her at last. His eyes were blue fire.

"Is that what you want? To fuck that boy?"

She met his gaze without flinching. "He's hardly a boy, and why shouldn't I? You've given me no reason not to. If *he's* willing to let me touch him, why shouldn't I take what satisfaction he can offer?"

Erik shot to his feet, his anger breaking through his stoic expression. She jumped to hers, refusing to be put at a disadvantage.

"Well, I'm so sorry that you've felt so unsatisfied as of late. Perhaps you should let that imbecile have a go at you. If his wiggling between your legs is what you think you've been missing all this time, who am I to hold you back?" His voice was loud, just short of shouting, but his words were like a whip.

Christine threw her pad of paper and pen onto his desk.

"I don't have to stand here and listen to you insult me. That's a benefit of having no real relationship between us. I can just walk away!" True to her word, she turned and stormed towards the door. She heard him follow her, but she didn't look back.

"You think you can just walk away from me, Christine?" he snarled. "You think you can walk away from me right into that asshole's arms? You think you can forget me? You think he'll make you scream when you come like I do?"

With a shriek, she spun around and found him towering over her. She moved to slap his uncovered cheek, but he caught her wrist in his tight grip.

"Don't ever speak to me like that!" she cried.

He pressed her up against the door, pinning her wrist above her head, and taking ahold of her jaw with his other hand.

"Don't you ever take me for a fool again," he growled. "Go on your date with that idiot. Fuck him, for all I care, but don't pretend for a second that he'll be able to make you feel half the things I can. That he'll be able to stir in you the same passion. It's not possible, Christine. That only exists between *us*."

His words both infuriated and thrilled her. At last, he was acknowledging that something existed between them that was strong, and unique! However, he was still willing to let her run off to another man. It was three steps forward, two steps back, and she was exhausted by the endless struggle.

"Let me go, Erik." She needed to get away from him. To regroup and think. He was overwhelming her already anger-clouded brain.

For a second, she wasn't sure he'd release her. She could tell he didn't want to, but slowly, he dropped his hands from her and stepped back.

They stared at each other, their breaths heaving. Unable to take the tension anymore, Christine turned from him, opened the door, and fled.

* * *

Erik

Erik watched her go, his heart shattering. What had he just done? He'd chased her off and straight into another man's arms. The things he'd said to her had been vile, but she was able to goad his anger in a way no one else ever had before.

Her words had been razor sharp, had hit their mark perfectly, just as she'd no doubt intended. He'd tried so hard to maintain his composure, to pretend that the idea of her and Chagny on a date together didn't tear his insides apart. She just wouldn't let up, and then when she'd said *that*...

What if I fuck him?

Erik had lost his mind.

He began pacing the length of his study, his fury, jealousy, and pain all vying for his attention.

If she slept with Chagny, it would destroy him. There was no denying that.

Yet you refuse to sleep with her yourself. What do you expect her to do?

He gnashed his teeth. That pesky voice of reason was right, of course, but he wasn't feeling very reasonable at present.

Not when images of her and Chagny tangled together tormented his thoughts. It made him sick, the idea of another man touching her, kissing her, wringing her beautiful moans from between her lips. Those moans were *his*. Those kisses were *his*. That soft, sweet body was *his* to caress and treasure.

His determination rising, he turned from the window, intent on marching to her room and demanding she cancel her date. He didn't care if it wasn't his right. He'd *make* it his right. He'd demand more from her. *Give* more to her. She wanted more from him, he knew she did, as much as she might try to pretend otherwise. If it meant keeping her, he'd risk the eventual heartache that would come when she left...

Erik froze, catching his reflection as he passed the two-way mirror above his piano. He was startled, so used to the mask, he tended to forget he wore it. Yet, seeing it was a stark reminder of what he was. Of the monster that lay underneath, which would inevitably drive Christine away.

His determination evaporated like morning mist in the hot sun as he stared at his image, and his darkness began to unfurl and envelope him. With a snarl, he turned his back on the mirror, facing his desk, but the self-doubt and loathing had already taken hold and were pulling him down into a spiral of despair. Memories flooded him...his mother's screams...Carla's disgust...so many looks of pity, he couldn't distinguish the faces. He clutched his head as it began to throb with the pressure of all the pain being poured on him at once. The fear that crippled him and kept him locked away in his hated solitude made him nauseous.

Christine's image became mixed with the chaos. Her smile. Her lust-filled gaze. Her body entwined with Chagny's.

It was too much for him to bear. Grabbing a rose-bloom paper-weight from his desk, he whipped around and roared as he threw it at the mirror. The glass shattered and fell away, revealing the hidden space beyond.

Panting, Erik stared at the mess, and a strange sense of calm fell over him. Without his own image shadowing his judgement, he was able to think more rationally again.

He didn't deserve Christine, of this he was sure, and he still believed she would leave him at some point, but not now. Now, she was his. Now, she still wanted him, and he'd be damned if he'd give her up so easily to the likes of Rick Chagny.

He had to talk to her.

Decided, he left his study and stalked through the house towards Christine's room. Reaching the door, he knocked, but there was no answer. He rapped his knuckles against the wood with more force, but still, nothing. His unstable emotions began to boil again. Was she just going to ignore him? He pounded on the door with his fist.

"Christine! I know you're in there. We need to talk."

"Erik, what the hell are you doing?"

He turned to find Meg standing behind him, hands on her slim hips, expression thunderous.

"This doesn't concern you, Megan. Go away." Facing the door again, he resumed his pounding.

"She's not in there, idiot," Meg snapped. "And why would she answer you when you're throwing a hissy fit?"

He rounded on the girl. "I am not throwing a hissy fit! I need to talk to her. Where is she?"

Meg arched a delicate blonde brow. "She left."

Erik's blood ran cold. "What?"

"She. Left. About ten minutes ago. I don't know what you did to her this time, but she looked pissed."

Just like when they were children and Meg annoyed him, Erik took a deep breath and counted to ten before replying in a much calmer tone. "Where did she go?"

Meg shrugged. "Probably on her date."

"But that's not for hours, yet!" It was his nightmare come true.

"I don't know what to tell you, man. She asked if the band was still here, and I told her I thought they were packing up to leave for the day. She left for the studio to catch them."

He closed his eyes, realizing he was too late.

"Erik," Meg's tone was gentle, her concern clear, "what keeps happening with you two? Why do you insist on driving her away?"

He considered lying, telling her he didn't know what she was talking about. It was *Meg*, however, and he'd never been good at lying to her. She was one of the only two people in the world he trusted with his secrets. With everything. That trust was too precious to him to break, even if it meant swallowing his pride.

Pressing his palms against his eyes, he admitted, "I'm scared, Megan."

"Of what?"

He dropped his hands. "Of how much I want her. Of how much she has come to mean to me. Of how much it will hurt when she leaves."

Grief shadowed Meg's gaze. "Why do you assume she'll leave."

He didn't put his ultimate fear to words, but raised his hand towards his mask.

She pressed her lips together. Meg and Mrs. Giry had both seen him without his mask. They knew the horror that lay beneath.

"Christine's not Carla, Erik."

He rolled his eyes. "I'm not a fool. Christine is not shallow, and she strives to see the best in everyone. None of that matters. Can you guarantee, Megan, knowing what lies beneath this thing, that she won't run? That she'll still want me the way she does now if she sees all of me?"

Meg hesitated, and he knew what her answer would be. "I can't."

He offered a bitter smile. "Even the best of people can be pushed to their limits by the hideousness of my face."

"But she might stay! Erik, Christine loves you, I know she does. She'd have to see past your appearance..."

"She might," he nodded. "For a week. A month. A year. She might try to see past it because she cares for me, but eventually, it'll be too much. Kissing me will become a chore that she despises, and then one day, I'll see the thing I dread most in her gaze."

"What is that?"

"Disgust."

Meg released a heavy breath. "Oh, Erik..."

He waved a hand to ward off her compassion. "None of that matters now. I just need to talk to her."

More sympathetic to his plight, Meg said, "I don't know when she'll be back."

With a sigh, he walked past her towards the stairs.

"Then I'll wait."

He heard Meg follow him as far as the second-story banister.

"How long are you willing to wait?"

Stopping on the bottom step, he looked back up at her.

"As long as it takes."

Not bothering to wait for a response, he made his way into the parlor where Christine spent most of her days. Settling into a chair in front of the cold fireplace, he waited for her to return.

26

Christine

As Rick drove up the driveway to the house, Christine couldn't help the twist of guilt in her gut. She'd had a good time with him. There had been a part of her that had hoped the date would end up a failure, making things easier for her, but it hadn't. They'd had fun together, doing things that normal couples would do. A simple dinner, a few hours at an antique arcade, a stroll through the park, and a drink in a small hole-in-the-wall bar. Their conversation had flowed all night, with fewer awkward silences than most first dates would have.

It had been a lovely evening.

Christine felt sick about it.

On the one hand, she felt terrible using Rick as a means to get back at Erik. His genuine kindness and interest in her deserved better. On the other hand, now that the worst of her anger had worn off, she felt as if she had betrayed Erik. Whatever it was between them was complicated, but she cared for him, and wanted *him*. Running to Rick after their fight no doubt broke whatever trust she'd managed to build between them.

"Christine? You okay?"

She blinked, realizing the car had stopped. Rick was peering at her, brows pinched in concern.

Plastering on a smile, she said, "Yes! Sorry. I was just a little lost in thought."

He grinned, appearing relieved. "Let me walk you up."

Before she could decline, he was out of the car and jogging to her door. Offering her a hand, he helped her out into the cool night air. She tried to pull her hand away, but he tightened his grip in protest. They walked together up the steps to the front porch. Christine felt like a high-schooler coming home from a date, trying not to wake her parents.

The last thing she wanted was for Erik to see the two of them. Taking a deep breath, she faced Rick, ready to tell him good night, and that she couldn't see him again.

Before she could say a word, however, he leaned in and kissed her. She gasped in surprise, and he took the opportunity to deepen the kiss. His hands fell to her waist and pulled her closer. Though there wasn't the same kind of fire as when Erik kissed her, it was still rather pleasant. She let her arms wrap around his neck and indulged in the moment. It was nice having a man so willing to touch her and let her touch him in return. The passion she experienced with Erik was all-consuming, but it was exhausting having to fight for every crumb of affection he gave her. Rick was willing. Rick was selfless. Rick was open and unmasked.

Still, that thrum of guilt nagged at her. Christine broke the kiss and pushed away with an apologetic smile.

"I should be getting in. It's late."

Rick's mouth turned up into a grin filled with boyish-charm.

"All right. I had a great time. Can I see you again?"

Christine couldn't help the answering quirk of her lips, or the words that followed.

"I'd like that."

With another quick peck on her cheek, Rick turned and made his way down the porch steps. She watched him go, waving as he got into his car and drove away. When he was out of sight, she turned towards the door, but couldn't find the strength to open it. Instead, she pressed her forehead against the cool wood and closed her eyes.

What the hell am I doing? Why had she agreed to see him again? It wasn't fair to string him along when she was so hopelessly lost for another man, but...she didn't want to be the kind of girl who let her life go by pining for someone who would never give her what she needed.

She wanted Erik, but she didn't want his darkness.

Rick lived in the light, and she wasn't yet willing to give up on the possibility of living in it with him.

Confused and heartsick, she let out a sigh as she turned the knob and pushed the door open. Stepping into the shadowed foyer, she let the door close behind her.

"Did your *date* go well?"

Christine jumped at the sound of Erik's deep, censorious voice. She gazed around, but couldn't spot him anywhere.

Gritting her teeth, she replied, "Were you spying on me?"

"I've told you before, I see everything that happens in this house."

She rolled her eyes. "Of course you do you enigmatic control freak."

"Freak?" he hissed. "So I'm a freak now, am I?"

Christine stomped her foot. "You know what I mean!"

"Is that *boy* able to give you what you really want?" he snarled, ignoring her. "What you really need?"

Pissed and frustrated by his apparent jealousy, she stormed through the foyer towards the stairs.

"What does it matter?" she shouted. "If you refuse to give me what I want and need, why shouldn't I seek both from someone else?"

Just as she reached the staircase, a hand shot out of the shadows to her right and snatched her arm. She cried out as Erik yanked her towards him, slamming her into his broad chest. He gazed down at her with fire in his beautiful blue eyes. His mouth was twisted in a scowl, and the uncovered parts of his face were taught with tension.

He was furious.

Good, Christine thought. *At least this way he's showing some emotion.*

"You think to play games with me?" His voice was a growl, but it still sent a delicious shiver running down her spine.

She held his stare, refusing to flinch away. "I'm not playing games. I'm being honest." She shoved at his chest to try and dislodge herself, but his hold on her remained firm. Giving up her attempt at escape, she continued, "You can't expect me to stick around when you insist on keeping me at arms-length. I need more!"

"You need more?" His voice rose with his indignation, but his temper didn't frighten her. She knew she was safe in his arms, though he might wish otherwise at present. "I'll give you more."

He brought his head down and slammed his lips into hers. The next moment, they had their arms wrapped around each other and were tumbling backwards. He whirled them around and pressed her against the wall. She moaned into his mouth as his tongue swept in to tangle with hers, gripping his hair with one hand.

"Erik," she gasped.

He brought his hand up and wrapped it around her throat. His hold wasn't tight, he didn't attempt to choke her, but the message was clear.

He was in control.

"You're *mine*, Christine," he growled at her ear. "*Mine*! And nobody, not even that *boy*, will take you from me."

Gritting her teeth, she tightened her grip on his hair.

"You don't own me, Erik," she hissed. "You don't get to ignore me, scream at me, and then throw a fit when I don't wait around pining for you."

He snatched both her wrists. Shoving them above her head, he trapped them against the wall as he pressed his body to hers.

"You don't think I own you?" His voice dropped to a purr, but there was a hard edge to it that told her his anger hadn't lessened. He skimmed his lips down her cheek and neck, and then brought them back up to hover in front of her mouth. She fought to keep her eyes open and her head from falling back in surrender.

"You don't," she insisted, but it was little more than a whimper.

Adjusting his hold so he gripped both her wrists in one hand, Erik brought his other hand down to graze the tops of her breasts. The contact was feather-light, but it felt like he was branding her.

She moaned. His hand began to descend lower.

"I own every part of you," he murmured. "Your mind." He kissed her temple. His hand skimmed her waist. "Your body." He kissed her cheek. His hand reached her hip. "Your soul." He kissed her lips as his hand pulled up her skirt.

Her breath hissed from her mouth when he worked her panties aside and slid his hand against her sex. His thumb brushed her clit, and her thighs clenched. Christine couldn't fight him anymore. Her eyes slid shut and she let her head drop back with a groan.

"So wet. So wet for me? Or for *him*?"

His voice had as much an effect on her as his touch. She wanted to lie, but found it impossible with both his hands and voice stimulating her.

"*You*," she whimpered. "Only you."

She felt his grin against her jaw.

"Good girl." He increased the pressure and pace of his fingers, and if he hadn't had her body trapped between his and the wall, she might have collapsed as pleasure exploded through her. He played her body with the same skill and dexterity he used on the piano, and she was helpless to do anything but accept his sweet torment. It wasn't long before she was climbing to her peak, and just as she was about to topple over into utter bliss, he whispered, "Sing for me, angel."

Christine cried out as her body seized with a powerful release that had her toes curling in her shoes.

Her orgasm continued for several moments before tapering off. Only when he was assured he'd rung the last of it from her did Erik remove his hand from between her legs. As Christine began her descent from heaven, he peppered her face and neck with gentle kisses and let her arms fall free from his grasp. She felt boneless as her body hummed with satisfaction.

"My sweet, sweet angel," Erik murmured.

Christine felt the urgent need to reciprocate the pleasure he'd given her. She wanted to make him as mindless as he'd made her. Reaching down, she laid her hand on the front of his pants and felt just how in need of relief he really was.

Before she could say or do anything, however, he grabbed her wrist and moved it away from him.

"No." He gave a firm shake of his head, blue eyes blazing.

Christine frowned. He was rejecting her again?

"Why not?"

His Adam's apple bobbed. Taking his hands away from her, he stepped back, putting distance between them. Cold rushed over her in the absence of his body's heat. It was nothing, though, compared to the ice that lanced her heart.

"This was about you," he said at length. "I don't want to taint what you've just experienced."

Closing her eyes, Christine tilted her head back against the wall.

"Why do you think your pleasure would taint my own?"

She opened her eyes again to find him watching her with a guarded gaze.

"For a monster like me, there can be nothing but darkness."

"Erik..."

Without another word, he turned and walked away, disappearing into the shadows, and leaving her all alone.

She watched him go, not bothering to call him back to her, and vowing to herself he wouldn't dismiss her again.

27

Christine

Christine had always prided herself on her professionalism and focus. If she was given a task, she would always see it through. She didn't allow herself to be distracted from her work or from her goals. She was organized, precise, and kept her deadlines.

Until she met Erik Roux.

Never before had a man so consumed her thoughts that it affected her ability to do her job. It also didn't help that he was her boss, so she couldn't compartmentalize her personal and professional lives as neatly as she would like.

She sat in the parlor, hands massaging her temples as she stared at the open Excel sheet on her computer, praying for the numbers on the screen to start making sense. They blurred together as she spaced out for about the hundredth time that morning. Her mind kept wandering to the night before and her confrontation with Erik. As a good, twenty-first century feminist, she told herself she should feel at least a little annoyed at his high-handedness with her, yet when she remembered how he had taken control of her body like he *owned* it, her thighs clenched and her core tingled.

He'd left again, however, without allowing her to reciprocate. He'd acted as if he didn't deserve to feel pleasure himself.

It frustrated her to no end. With every moment of bliss he gave her, her urge to return the favor grew stronger.

Why wouldn't he let her touch him?

With a groan, she pushed away from her table, closing her laptop as she stood. Perhaps a break and a cup of tea would help calm her mind.

Walking out of the parlor, she began to make her way across the house towards the kitchen. When she was halfway down the hallway, she heard music and stopped.

Is that Panic! at the Disco?

Curious, she followed the sound. It took her to the end of the hall and a door to a room she'd never been in. She paused, the song *This is Gospel* blasting so loud, she could make out every lyric. Putting her hand on the door knob, she glanced over her shoulder, remembering what had happened the last time she'd followed a song to a strange room. Mrs. Giry was nowhere in sight this time, though, so she twisted her hand and pushed the door open.

To her surprise, she stepped into a ballet studio. Floor to ceiling mirrors lined the walls to her left and right, with two wooden bars cutting across them horizontally at hip level. The wall opposite the door was dominated by two large arched paned windows. Both were uncovered and allowed natural light to brighten up the whole room.

Her eyes fell on the only occupant of the space, with one leg balanced along the bars in a deep stretch. Meg was dressed in a sleeveless black leotard and leggings, a pink sweater and ballet slippers, and had her long blonde hair pulled into a messy bun at the back of her head. In that moment, she raised her torso and met Christine's eyes in the mirror.

"Oh, Christine! I didn't hear you come in."

Christine was not surprised, given the volume of the music.

Meg lowered her leg to the floor and walked towards a small bench sitting between the windows. Picking up a remote, she hit a button and the music faded to a low hum. She grabbed a towel and water bottle, patting the sweat from her forehead and taking a drink as she turned back around with a smile.

"What's up?"

Christine returned her smile and shrugged.

"Nothing, really. I was just on my way to the kitchen and heard your music. I was curious where it was coming from."

Meg's expression turned sheepish. "Sorry if it was too loud. Mom always complains, but it's easier for me to concentrate when I drown out everything else."

Christine shook her head. "No need to apologize, I only heard it when I was close." She stepped further into the room and gazed up at the high, white ceiling before returning her focus to her friend. "How's your ankle feeling?"

"Better. I've been easing back into practice, but still focusing a lot on stretching and strengthening. Your timing is perfect, actually, I was just finishing up."

Christine didn't respond right away, too captivated by the studio. The polished wood floors shone, and the white walls gleamed.

"This room is beautiful."

Meg nodded as she took another sip of water. "Yeah, it is. Erik had it installed when he first bought the place so I could practice whenever I wanted."

Christine couldn't help the small pang she felt in her chest. "It must have been nice, having people not only believe in your passions, but do everything they could to support them."

A heartbeat of silence followed before Meg placed her hand on Christine's shoulder.

"I'm sorry you didn't have that."

Christine met Meg's open gaze, and once again found herself floored by the girl's genuineness. She didn't apologize for her own advantages in life, but acknowledged and shared Christine's sorrow at her lack. There were no excuses, no attempt to make Christine feel better in order to assuage her own guilt. Meg had grown up with the support and resources she needed to succeed in her passion, and Christine had not. It wasn't either of their faults; it was just the way it was.

She grasped Meg's hand and gave it a light squeeze.

"Thanks. Anyway, you said you were finished?"

"Yeah. You said you were heading to the kitchen? Mind if I tag along? I'm starving."

* * *

A short time later, Meg and Christine were sitting around the kitchen island, steaming mugs of tea in hand and a plate of chocolate chip cookies between them. Darius prepared lunch as they sipped their drinks.

"So..." Meg began as Christine reached for a cookie. "How did your date with Rick go?"

Christine froze, hand in midair. Darius stopped chopping onions and whirled to face them, a big grin on his face.

"You went on a date with Rick Chagny?"

Christine shot Meg a death glare. "Yes, last night. He and I are old friends, and we wanted to catch up."

"So? How was it?" Meg prompted, bringing her mug to her lips.

Snatching her cookie, Christine sat back on her stool and thought about her response. Should she also bring up Erik's temper tantrum and the mind-blowing orgasm he gave her when she got home from her date? If it had just been her and Meg, she likely would have. With Darius there, though, it seemed just south of unprofessional.

"It was nice."

Both Meg and Darius stared at her.

"That's it?" Meg scoffed when Christine was not forthcoming with details. "Nice?"

Christine shrugged, taking a bite from her cookie. "Yeah. What? What did you want me to say?"

"I don't know. So it was nice. What did you do? Did he try anything?"

Christine gaped as Meg waggled her eyebrows. Darius tried to muffle a chuckle behind his fist.

"Not that it's any of your business, but he did kiss me." Christine felt her cheeks heat.

Meg and Darius shared an excited glance.

"So, will there be a second date?" Darius asked.

Opening her mouth to respond, Christine found no words would come forth. Frowning, she tried again, but couldn't make herself say the word, *"Yes."*

It was a relief when Meg picked up on her struggle. Her smile softened, and her gaze turned determined.

"Darius, bud, could you give us a minute?"

Surprised, Darius hesitated before Meg raised her eyebrows at him. It was a look he must have been familiar with.

"You got it, but I need to finish lunch."

Meg held up her hand. "Five minutes."

"Deal." Shooting a confused look towards Christine, he turned and hurried from the room.

Once they were alone, Meg said, "Okay. Spill."

Christine released a breath. "I don't know what my problem is. Rick and I had a nice time last night, and I enjoyed his kiss. He asked if I'd like to go out again, and I told him yes, but then I went into the house..." Her fingers tightened around her mug. "Erik was waiting for me. He saw our kiss."

Meg's eyes widened. "Shit. What did he do?"

Licking her lips, Christine wondered how much to tell the girl. Erik was basically her brother, after all. "Well, he was angry, and we fought...but, then...we sort of..."

"Nope, stop." Meg waved both hands in front of her as she shook her head. "I get the gist, just spare me the details. What happened after that?"

Christine's embarrassment was washed away by the discontent that overtook her. She stared down into her tea.

"He left."

Meg didn't ask for clarification, and Christine was glad she didn't have to say more. Silence stretched between them.

At length, Meg said, "Christine, remember when I said you shouldn't have to wait around for him to get his shit together?"

Without looking up, Christine nodded.

"I meant it. Every single word. But do you know what else?"

Peeking up from under her lashes, Christine shook her head.

Meg let out a sigh. "Love is complicated. Hell, life is complicated. You can't change him. You can't fix him. Sure, you can help him heal, but only if he wants to. If you want to walk away, you have every right to and no one would blame you. But, if you want him as he is, and you're not willing to give up on him yet, you have to force him to see that. Fight for him. Push him. Challenge him to take that step forward. You can't wait for him forever, but that doesn't mean you can't nudge him along either."

Christine couldn't help but chuckle.

"How do you always know what to say?"

Meg grinned, rolling her eyes. "Probably just read it in a self-help book somewhere."

There was a knock on the kitchen door, and Darius poked his head inside.

"Can I return to my kitchen, now?"

Meg gave Christine a quizzical look.

Smiling to Darius, Christine said, "You're all clear."

The man ambled in to reclaim his domain. He and Meg began swapping gossip, but Christine remained silent, half-listening to their conversation. She pondered Meg's words as she sipped her lukewarm tea. Instead of waiting for him, she needed to nudge him along...

The question was, how did one go about nudging something immovable?

28

Christine

Christine paced the length of her bedroom, mulling over the plan that had formed in her head throughout the day. Erik hadn't contacted her at all, which meant she'd had nowhere to go and nothing to do but sit in the parlor and stare at those cursed Excel sheets. She'd begun to worry at his silence. By the afternoon, she'd decided if she was going to nudge him, she needed to do it sooner rather than later.

By early evening, an idea had sprung.

Meg had been right. She couldn't keep waiting for Erik to get his emotional baggage sorted out, but she wasn't ready to give up on him. Something had to give between them, or their tenuous connection would snap. She knew she couldn't help him heal from all the darkness and pain that haunted him in one night, but there was one thing she could do to bring them closer.

She would sleep with him. Or, more accurately, seduce him.

Taking a deep breath to secure her courage, she began stripping out of her clothes.

Any time they'd been intimate, it had always been one-sided. He would pleasure her, but would not allow her to pleasure him, though his desire for her was obvious. More and more, she had grown to crave that further connection with him. She wanted to know what his face looked like when he hit the height of his pleasure, and she wanted to bring him to that point. He'd alluded as to why he didn't let her reciprocate when they were together, and also why he hadn't attempted to take their physical relationship further. He thought he would somehow taint her. As if his body was toxic, and she would become infected by touching him.

The idea that he thought so little of himself made her want to cry.

Once she was fully unclothed, she donned her silk robe.

Tonight, she would take things in hand. She would make him see how much she wanted him. How much she craved him. She would push him until his ironclad control broke.

Sex would not solve all their problems, but their willingness to be vulnerable with each other physically might help open some doors for them emotionally. It was worth a shot, anyway. If her date with Rick had revealed nothing else, it was that Erik was the man she wanted, and she would fight for him, even if she had to fight with him.

Opening her bedroom door, she scanned the hallway, but it was so late she would have been surprised to find anyone up and about. With soft footsteps, she hurried down the corridor to the other side of the house. When she came to the study door, she stopped. Nerves assailed her, and for a moment, she second-guessed herself.

What if he rejected her again?

Shaking her head, Christine let out a deep breath. She couldn't let things continue like this. She had to do something to shake him up, and he'd left her few options. Cinching the knot of her robe, she reached out her hand to knock on the large doors.

She waited, heart thundering, listening for any sign that he was inside. After several moments of silence, disappointment made her shoulders sag. Was he just going to ignore her?

The door opened. Christine froze.

Erik stood before her, looking surprised to find her at his threshold. His dark hair was tousled, the top buttons of his white shirt undone, and his sleeves were rolled up to his elbows. Black slacks highlighted his narrow hips, and with his black mask, he cut a roguish figure.

Heat flooded through Christine at the sight of him.

He was frowning down at her, confusion in his bright blue gaze.

"Christine, what are you doing here? I thought you'd be in bed by now."

His tone was formal, almost business-like, but she could hear the nervous crackle underlying it.

Christine squared her shoulders. "I want to talk with you. May I come in?"

He didn't respond right away, and a flicker of doubt crept into Christine's mind. After a beat, however, he stepped aside to allow her entry. She fought not to sigh out loud with her relief.

Once she had made her way to the middle of the room, Erik shut the door and turned to face her, leaning back against the wood as he crossed his arms. He was the picture of nonchalance, save for his clenched jaw.

"What do you want to talk about?"

Embarrassment rushed through her as the moment she had planned for arrived. Could she really do this?

He tilted his head. "Christine?"

She gave herself a mental shake. *Stop being silly. He's seen you naked before.*

But always at his request.

Lifting her chin, she summoned all the courage she possessed.

"I want you to make love to me, Erik."

It was his turn to freeze. He stared at her, blue eyes wide with astonishment, jaw moving as if to speak, but no words came out. At length, he managed to clear his throat and gather his bearings.

"Christine, don't be ridiculous."

"No more excuses," she snapped, resting her hands on the knot of her robe. "You can't keep pushing me away. I want you, more than I've ever wanted anybody, and I know you want me."

"Christine..."

"Stop hiding from me. I don't want to hide from you."

With that, she released the knot. Her robe gaped open, revealing her naked body beneath. With a shrug, she dislodged the garment, letting it pool at her feet. She stood before him, bare, aching, desperate for him to open himself to her.

Terrified that he wouldn't.

Erik stared at her, his eyes raking over her as if he couldn't help himself. At length, he forced his gaze to meet hers.

"Put your robe back on." His words were harsh.

She held his gaze. "No."

"Christine..." Her name was a warning.

"Erik." His was a demand.

"You don't know what you're doing." His stare turned beseeching, but she couldn't decide if he was begging her to leave...or to stay.

"I know what I'm doing," she insisted. "I know what I want. What do *you* want?" *Please, want me!*

He gnashed his teeth, eyes burning with frustration.

In a flash, he was in front of her. Gripping her upper arms, he yanked her into him. She gasped, her hands flying up to press against his chest and steady herself.

"You're playing a dangerous game," he growled. "I don't think you'll like it if you win."

Tilting her head back, she snapped, "This isn't a game. I'm not playing you, and I will love anything you do to me."

His grip on her tightened until it was almost painful, but she didn't flinch. She kept her eyes locked on his, daring him to look away.

They stared at each other for several tense seconds.

"Damn you."

His mouth came crashing down on hers.

Christine cried out in triumph, flinging her arms around his neck and pulling him tighter against her. He cupped her face with one hand and dug the fingers of his other into the flesh of her waist. Desire exploded between them, and all Christine cared about was getting him as naked as she was. She began to work the buttons of his shirt loose, but her fingers fumbled in her haste. Picking up on her struggle, he gripped his shirt in both hands and yanked it open, sending buttons scattering along the floor. She gasped in delight.

Shirtless, his powerful chest and sculpted arms on full display for her, he began backing her towards his bedroom door. As they moved, her foot caught on one of the thick rugs on the floor and she stumbled. Erik caught her before she fell backwards, and then gripping the backs of her thighs, hoisted her up so that her legs could wrap around his waist. He moved his hands to cup her backside and keep her pinned against him.

Breaking his lips from her, he grinned. "I love filling my hands with this delectable ass." He squeezed his fingers, and Christine squealed as excitement and an irresistible tickling sensation had her wiggling in his grasp.

"No! Stop!" She laughed as he continued to torment her, pausing only long enough to open the door and reclaim her mouth with his own. He reached the bed in a few long strides and laid her down without releasing her. She relished his weight on her as he crushed her into the mattress. Her legs hung over the bedframe. His feet remained on the floor.

Erik kissed his way to her breasts as his hands reached between her legs. He took a nipple into his mouth just as his finger stroked along her folds. Christine arched her back as she was hit by double shots of pleasure. He continued a steady assault on her breasts, licking, sucking, and biting at her flesh as his finger worked its way inside her hot sheath.

"Oh, God..." she breathed, throwing her hands over her head to clutch at the comforter.

"You're so soft," he murmured. "So warm. I'll rest my head between these luscious tits later when we sleep. But for now..." He added a second finger as he pulled himself upright. Standing above her, he pumped his fingers in and out of her body, his eyes locked on his hand.

Christine bit her lip as she watched him, the muscles of his arm straining as he worked her. It wasn't long, though, before her eyes slid closed as the pleasure overwhelmed her. She thrashed her head from side to side, stroking her calves along his thighs, the cloth of his slacks smooth and cool against her heated skin. She twisted the comforter in her hands as needy moans slipped from her lips.

"Are you going to come, angel?"

Cracking her eyes open, she found his gaze locked on her face. She couldn't speak. Could only nod. He grinned.

"Then do it. Come for me. Now."

The command, the way he mastered her with his voice and his touch, sent her flying over the edge. Her orgasm consumed her, and she cried out as her toes curled and she dragged the bedcovers to cover her face.

It was several moments before she came down from the euphoric high. Panting, her skin damp with sweat, she pushed the covers away. She gasped when she found Erik standing over her, gloriously naked. He'd removed his pants, and his erection stood large and proud, his hand stroking it to readiness.

His size was intimidating. It wasn't that he was so large she feared he wouldn't fit, but it had been awhile since she'd been with anyone, and he was big enough that she knew the stretch would be uncomfortable. Her hesitation must have shown in her expression, because Erik ceased stroking himself and furrowed his brow.

"Christine, what's wrong?"

She licked her lips as she considered how to respond.

"It's just...it's been some time for me..." God, she'd never felt so embarrassed. She wanted to cover her face with her hands like a teenage girl, but forced her arms to remain firm against the mattress.

He smiled, his relief clear. "Don't worry, angel. I'll make sure it doesn't hurt you." He moved towards the bedside table and opened its top drawer. Curious, Christine pushed up onto her elbows to watch him. He dug around before producing a small bottle and several foil-wrapped condoms. Dropping everything onto the comforter next to her, he moved back to stand between her legs. She picked up the bottle to read the label.

Glancing up at him with a grin, she said, "You are prepared, aren't you?"

He didn't answer, but smirked as he picked up a condom, tore the wrapper open, and began sliding the contraceptive onto his cock.

"A little lube can go a long way," he chuckled at last, taking the bottle from her hands. Popping the top open, he dribbled some of the liquid into both of his palms. He resumed stroking his length with one hand, while the other went between her legs to run along her folds. She groaned when he slipped his fingers back into her, spreading them apart to stretch and prepare her. Christine let her head fall back as the pleasure simmered through her.

It wasn't long before her hesitation was forgotten.

"Erik," she breathed, "that's enough. Please. I don't want your fingers."

His expression was hungry, his chuckle dark. "You don't? Then what do you want, Christine?" He rubbed his thumb along her stiff clit.

Christine moaned, the sound coming from deep in her belly. "Asshole...you know what..."

The bastard shook his head. "Nope. I think you need to tell me. I can only guess, and I'd hate to be wrong. You started this. Now you have to finish it."

Grinding her teeth, she snarled, "Your cock. I need your cock inside me now!"

"As you wish, angel." He removed his fingers from her and pushed his hips forward to tease her entrance with his tip. Taking a moment to rub himself up and down her slick folds, he lined up with her and began to push in.

Even with the lube, the stretch burned, but Christine took several deep breaths, relaxing her body to accommodate him.

"That's it, baby," he murmured. "You can take me. You *will* take me."

He continued to ease into her, rubbing her clit as he moved. Pleasure and pain mingled until the line between them disappeared. At last, he slid in to the hilt, his pelvis pressing against her.

"So much..." She hadn't felt so full in...she couldn't remember that last time she'd felt so full.

"You're so tight," he growled. His hands came down to grip her hips, and he slid out of her before slipping forward again. He went slow, giving her time to get used to him. She knew he wouldn't be gentle for long, however. The hunger in his eyes blazed, and she could see how badly he wanted to take her hard. What surprised her was how much she wanted that as well.

"How is it?" he asked. "Does it hurt?"

Christine shook her head. "No, not anymore."

"Good." He moved her legs so they rested against his torso, opening her up wider to him. Holding on to her thighs for leverage, he pulled out until just his tip remained inside her, and then slammed back in. Christine threw her head back and cried out. He did it again and again, picking up speed between each of his thrusts. Christine's breasts bounced, and she couldn't keep her voice down as ecstasy burst through her.

"That sounds so beautiful, angel," he panted. "Don't stop singing for me."

He reached down and circled her clit in rhythm with his thrusts.

"Oh, God!"

She undulated her hips, seeking more pressure as she felt the tingling of an impending orgasm begin to build.

"Are you close?" he asked through gritted teeth.

Unable to speak, she nodded.

He stopped.

"What...?" She felt frantic, pushing up to her elbows as her fingers curled, readying to claw at him to get him moving again.

He gazed down at her, a dangerous glint in his eyes.

"I'm not letting you off so easily, angel. You need a little punishment before your reward."

She stared up at him with wide-eyes. What was he planning? What would he do to her?

Why did his threat have her grinning up at him in excitement?

"As you wish...sir."

29

Erik

The anticipation in her eyes would have brought him to his knees if he wasn't determined to make this last as long as possible. He'd threatened her with punishment, and she looked greedy for it.

This woman was made for him.

"Say your word."

"Gounod," she purred.

His blood heated at the sound of her voice, and his muscles tensed. He felt like a predator about to pounce on his all-too-willing prey. Pulling out of her, he let her legs drop and grabbed her hips. With a growl, he flipped her onto her stomach.

"On your hands and knees."

She obeyed without hesitation. He took a moment to admire her. The smooth curve of her ass...the graceful dip of her back...that gorgeous hair, wild and curly against her pale skin. She was a vision. A dream.

One he never wanted to wake from.

Grabbing her hips again, he ran his length up and down her backside to tease her. She moaned, and it was music to his ears.

He let his hand crack against her soft flesh, craving more of her sounds.

She jolted with a whimper, but arched her back and swayed her hips as if to ask for more.

Erik obliged. Again, and again. His red handprint stood stark on her ass. When he began to massage it, she groaned and stretched like a cat.

"Please, no more teasing." Her husky voice pushed him to the limits of his control. Lining himself up with her entrance, he pushed into her inch by painful inch. Her breaths turned to pants and she clutched the bed's comforter in tight fists.

He wanted to make it agonizing for her, even if it meant he suffered as well. Then, she might have some idea of how torturous these past weeks had been for him. He'd tried to do the right thing...to keep his distance from her. To give her a chance to escape him. All his efforts had been for not, however. She'd seen to that, pushing and tempting him at every turn. What man could turn down the gift she'd offered? Not just her body, but her trust. Her vulnerability.

He would punish her for breaking him, but he would ultimately reward her because all he wanted was to please her.

When he was at last seated to the hilt, his body pressed tight against hers, he paused his movements and savored the sensation. She was so tight...so hot. The squeeze was almost painful, but he relished it. He delighted in her soft noises as she grew used to the new angle of his invasion.

Reaching forward, he grabbed her arms and pulled them back, bending them at the elbows to bring them together.

"Keep your arms locked together like this," he demanded. With her arms trapped behind her back, she was at his mercy. He was in full control of her body and stability.

She did not protest. She did not use her word. Without hesitation, she surrendered, gripping her forearms to keep herself positioned.

Her trust in him was staggering. For perhaps the millionth time since she'd arrived in his study and offered herself up to him, he marveled at his dramatic change in fortune. He did not deserve her, and yet she fought to stay with him. Her submission was his salvation.

Holding her up, he began to move his hips, short thrusts at first, but he increased his speed at a steady rate. Christine's cries grew louder as his thrusts grew harder. A part of him feared hurting her, but he trusted her to tell him when she'd had enough.

She dug her nails into her arms to keep herself bound.

"Erik! Don't stop! I'm...so close..."

Begging for more. She *was* made for him.

He would let her come, but he wouldn't be done with her. Not for hours.

"Then sing for me, angel. Until your lungs burn."

Her body seized. Ducking her head, she screamed and shook as her orgasm slammed through her. He watched, fascinated, as her back arched and her thighs clutched him.

As her pleasure subsided, and her shaking slowed, he eased her down to rest on the mattress. She lay limp and panting as he slipped out of her. Sitting on the bed next to her, he ran a gentle hand down her glistening back as she caught her breath.

"Are you okay?" he asked.

With what appeared to be monumental effort, she turned her head to look up at him. Offering a tired, but satisfied smile, she nodded.

"I feel so heavy, but it's a good heavy."

He grinned, running his fingers through the ends of her hair.

Her hand slid up his thigh and she heaved herself forward so she could lean over his lap, her intentions clear.

Erik gripped her hand to stop her. "Christine, what are you doing?"

Frowning, she said, "That's not obvious?"

He swallowed the lump that formed in his throat. "It is...I mean...you don't have to."

She sat up and narrowed her eyes. "Are you really going to do this again? Now?"

Confused, he asked, "What do you mean?"

Rolling her eyes, she snapped, "You've pleasured me into oblivion, and now I want to do the same to you. Why won't you let me?"

Erik blinked. "It's not that..."

"Then what is it?" She looked hurt.

Cupping her face, he stroked his thumb along her bottom lip. "Don't misunderstand, angel. I'd very much like this beautiful mouth around my cock. I just don't want things to end so soon tonight."

Her expression filled with relief, and then she let out a small chuckle. "I'm not ready for the night to end either, but I'm the tiniest bit sore from your *punishment*, and need a little break before round two. In the meantime, I'd love to have my mouth around your beautiful cock, if you'd let me."

Erik smirked, charmed by her bluntness. "Well, I find I can deny you nothing this evening, Christine." He slid back to rest against the headboard, spreading his legs in invitation.

Heat filled her gaze. Biting her lip, she crawled to him, and he felt the prey instead of the predator. It was a change in roles he thought he would very much enjoy exploring.

She kneeled between his thighs. Leaning in, she brushed her lips against his, but pulled away before deepening the kiss. Unwilling to let her escape, he reached out to pull her back. She grabbed his forearms to stop him and shook her head.

"No, no," she said with a teasing grin. "I've had my punishment, now it's time for yours."

He tensed, fear prickling along his spine. There was a part of him that wanted to give this to her. To give her control. To show her that trust. Another part, however, a much more damaged part, was afraid of being at her mercy. Of being vulnerable to her whims. Though he wanted to believe Christine was different, for him, vulnerability always led to pain.

She appeared to sense his inner-turmoil. Releasing his arms, she brought her hands up to cup his face. He noted how she took care not to jostle his mask.

Her smile was soft. Her gaze tender. She dipped her head to kiss him again, a gentle caress that soothed away some of his anxieties.

Pulling back, she stroked her thumbs along his cheeks.

"Think of a word."

He lost his breath and his hands came up to grip her waist. Her smile widened.

"I do not want to harm you, but I do want you to be helpless."

His own words of reassurance reused in an attempt to calm him.

"I want you to feel secure, and to know you can stop me at any time with a word. It cannot be *no*, or *stop*."

The care with which she spoke brought tears to his eyes.

"I don't want there to be any confusion between us."

Somehow, she was easing his mind, making him pliable and willing in her hands.

"Choose a word you would not normally say, and if you speak it, I'll know you are serious and I will stop what I'm doing to you without hesitation."

He let out a deep, stuttering breath.

Leaning in, she pressed her forehead to his.

"I promise I won't hurt you."

He crushed her to him and kissed her, pouring every ounce of relief he felt into the connection. When he at last let her pull away from him, her face was flushed, and her eyes sparkled with anticipation.

"What's your word, Erik?"

Thinking hard, he struggled for a moment to come up with one. Then, it struck him.

"Rouge."

She scrunched her brows in confusion. "Where'd that come from?"

He took a lock of her hair and twirled it around his finger. "Red has become my favorite color as of late."

Flushing pink, she bit her lip in an attempt to hide her grin. "But you have to use French just to sound superior?"

"Of course." He grinned.

Giggling, she kissed him again. This time, she lingered, coaxing his mouth open so she could slide her tongue inside.

As she kissed him, she eased her hands back down to his arms and lifted them up to rest against the headboard. He allowed it, his fear from earlier no match for her sweet words and hot kisses.

She pulled back so that her lips hovered over his. "Now, do not move your hands, or your punishment will be worse."

"Yes ma'am." He clutched the headboard, determined to obey.

Christine moved her lips along his jaw, then down his throat. She stopped to lap at his Adam's apple before sliding down past his collarbone to his chest. He gritted his teeth and concentrated on his hands, fighting not to plunge them into her soft hair and force her down his body faster.

This was his punishment. Quick relief was not in the cards.

She kissed across his pectorals, stopping and laving attention on each of his nipples. He couldn't remember a woman ever focusing on them, and was surprised by how good it felt. A soft groan slipped from his mouth. He felt her grin against him.

Moving even lower, she licked the ridges of his abdomen as her breasts brushed against his aching shaft. He fought to stay still and not roll his hips to push his erection between her soft mounds. This was her game, and he wanted to let her play it.

Her mouth hovered over his length. The head was glistening with his arousal. She licked her lips at the sight, removing the condom so she could taste him bare.

Glancing up at him, she purred, "Don't forget, if you move, you won't be rewarded."

Before he could fathom a reply, she dragged her tongue along the top of his cock.

He cried out in shock at the sensation. How long had it been since he'd let a woman touch him like this? Since a woman had *wanted* to touch him like this? She licked from base to tip, and then wrapped her lips around the head. The pleasure was familiar, yet somehow new and intoxicating. She sucked on him, and he moaned, unable to help himself. Christine repeated this process several times...lick, wrap, suck, lick, wrap, suck...until he thought he'd lose his mind.

When his control cracked and his hips jerked, she pulled back.

He growled like a rabid animal. "Don't fucking stop!"

Smirking, she wrapped her hand around him and stroked, but her hold was loose. He wasn't going to get anywhere fast.

"It's not punishment unless it's a little painful," she teased.

With her other hand, she hefted his heavy sack. He dug his fingers into the headboard.

"Put your mouth back on me." His voice was harsh, but she didn't appear frightened. Quite the contrary, she looked delighted.

She leaned down until he could feel her hot breath on his flesh, but she didn't touch her lips to him.

"Christine!"

Meeting his eye, she murmured, "Say please."

His nostrils flared with frustration, but his blood heated with excitement.

"Christine...please..."

"Very good." She engulfed him, and he threw his head back with a shout. Her mouth was so hot and wet, it reminded him of another part of her, which only made him harder.

Bobbing up and down, she licked and sucked him with such vigor, he felt his control straining. His fingers were cramping in their effort to stay attached to the headboard, and his thighs shivered as he fought to keep his hips still. He didn't know how much more he could take. Then, she dipped lower and he felt her throat.

"Fuck! Christine!"

He was close. He could feel his release building, pushing up along his length. If he didn't warn her, he'd spill into her mouth.

"Angel...about to come..."

Instead of moving away, she doubled her efforts. A twirl of her tongue and a gentle tug on his scrotum was all it took to tip him over the edge. He squeezed his eyes shut and roared, shooting into her willing mouth. The pleasure was greater than anything he could remember, and stars burst behind his eyelids as his hips pumped and jerked.

When the waves began to subside, he pried his eyes open and gazed down at the angelic vixen between his legs. She was sucking the last remnants from his tip, her throat working to swallow his release. When she finished, she gave his cock a sweet kiss before sitting up onto her haunches.

Her face was flushed, her hair was wild, and her breasts heaved with her panting breaths. The smile on her face was triumphant.

"How was that?"

He stared at her, for a moment unable to believe she was real. Then, he pounced.

She shrieked in delight as he pushed her back onto the bed and stretched out over her. He cut off her laugh with a hard, grateful kiss. She wrapped her arms around his neck and held him close.

When they broke apart, her eyes were glazed over with lust, and her smile was gone. In its place was an expression of pure need.

He would require more time to recover, but in the meantime he could shower her with his thankfulness.

Pressing his lips against hers in a quick peck, he pushed up onto all fours and began to ease his way down her body.

"Erik..." her breathy voice had his blood sizzling.

He planted a kiss between her breasts and looked back up into her excited gaze.

"Allow me to return the favor, angel."

She let her head fall back and her legs fall open. It wasn't long before her cries were bouncing off the walls, and he grew ready to take her again...and again.

30

Christine

Now that is a woman who has been well-fucked, Christine thought as she stared at her disheveled reflection in the bathroom mirror. It was late into the night, and she and Erik had at last worn each other out. Weeks of pent up sexual energy had exploded in that bedroom, and they hadn't been able to get enough of each other.

It wasn't until they were physically incapable of continuing that they at last stopped.

Christine had left Erik spread out and panting in the bed, staggered to the bathroom to relieve herself, and stopped to assess the aftereffects of their marathon lovemaking on her body. There would be bruises, and she would be sore everywhere, but she wouldn't have changed a moment of their night together.

She flushed thinking of everything they had done to each other. This felt like a turning point. Things had to be different between them now. He hadn't just let her pleasure him, he'd let her *control* him. Let her dictate parts of their coupling. It had terrified him, she could tell, but he'd let her do it anyway.

He'd trusted her.

Her heart skipped with joy.

Running her fingers through her hair, she tried to straighten her appearance before going back out to rejoin him in bed. After several minutes of fussing, she gave up. She was a mess, but he had made her that way.

When she returned to the bedroom, she found him lounging against the pillows, the bedsheet tossed over his lap. His hair was mussed, his eyes hooded, and his smile lazy when he spotted her.

Despite his tousled appearance, his mask remained securely in place. She had taken extra care not to dislodge it, knowing to remove it, even by accident, would have ended things between them in an instant. He needed to be the one to take it off, and she was determined to respect that, even if his continued wearing of it was the one thing that marred an otherwise blissful evening.

"Had I known I could have you walking around my room naked, I'd have let you fuck me ages ago."

She rolled her eyes, but grinned as she sauntered towards him. He threw the sheet back and reached a hand out to help her slide in next to him. Curling into his side, she was amazed at how well they fit together. He draped his arm around her shoulder, and they lay in a comfortable silence, more relaxed than they'd ever been around each other. Christine wanted to cling to the moment and make it last as long as she could. She feared once their bubble broke, the distance between them would return.

"Are you happy here?" he asked, breaking the silence and chipping the bubble.

The question confused her, and she hesitated before answering. "What would make you think I wasn't?"

"I know it can be lonely here. Isolating, even. You're a person who enjoys people, and I wonder sometimes if the solitude is too much for you."

It didn't escape her that he did not include himself when asking if she was happy. She tried not to let that bother her, reminding herself that just because they'd slept together, it didn't mean everything was fixed between them. Still, it made her nervous.

Careful to keep her anxiety from her voice, she replied, "I was lonely in the beginning. It took some getting used to, not having people around, but I don't mind it now. I actually kind of like the peace and quiet, and sometimes get annoyed that there are so many people around lately. I miss when it was just you and me…and Meg, Mrs. Giry, and Darius of course."

He didn't respond for several moments, and with each second that passed, her nerves strained.

At last he murmured, "You are too perfect to be real."

Releasing a shaky breath, she relaxed. "I'm not perfect. Not at all."

His fingers grazed her bare shoulder.

"I suppose nobody is." His voice was soft and somewhat distracted, as if he were pondering something. Perhaps he was at last recognizing she didn't need perfection from him? Or was he retreating back into his self-deprecating darkness?

She didn't want to lose him to his thoughts so soon, especially if they were the latter.

Giving his torso a gentle squeeze, she said, "Erik? Won't you tell me something about yourself?"

The question had its intended effect, shaking him from his growing stupor.

"Hmmm? What do you mean?"

She proceeded with caution, careful to keep things light.

"I just want to know something about you that isn't related to work. It doesn't have to be anything major. Just a small piece of insight." She peeked up at him to gauge his reaction, hoping she hadn't pushed too far.

His expression was thoughtful, but not fearful or angry. She held her breath as she waited to see what he would do.

His Adam's apple bobbed.

"What do you want to know?"

Christine's stomach fluttered. Moving to sit over him, she studied his face. He looked nervous now, his gaze guarded, but he didn't flinch away from her. She would take this slow.

With a gentle smile, she asked, "What's your favorite color?"

His lips quirked, and the apprehension in his eyes eased.

"You know that one already." He ran a hand through the ends of her hair. "It's red."

She bit her lip, giddiness filling her.

"Okay, how about your favorite food?"

"Chicken pot pie," he answered without thinking.

She raised her brows. "Really?"

He smirked. "Why is that so shocking?"

"I'd have thought it would be something gourmet, with truffle or caviar or something decadent and expensive. Chicken pot pie is so...homey."

He nodded, but his smile dipped, and his eyes grew distant. "It was the first meal Mrs. Giry made for me when I was a kid."

Christine froze. She'd unintentionally stumbled into something deeper, and debated whether to ask him more about his childhood, about Mrs. Giry, and their relationship. He might shut down again, and all her efforts throughout the evening would have been for nothing.

Still, it hung heavy in the air between them, and to not acknowledge it might be just as damaging.

"Erik, how did you and Mrs. Giry meet?"

She could see his shoulders tense, and he moved to sit up next to her. Bringing his knee up so he could rest his arm on it, he ran his other hand through his dark hair in an agitated gesture.

Without looking at her, he answered, "She found me when I was nine and then she adopted me when I was eleven."

Christine curled her fingers into the sheets to keep from reaching out to him in relief. He was letting her in! Telling her about his past. She schooled her features, taking care not to let her elation show.

"I see," she said in an even tone. "That would explain her protectiveness of you."

That earned her a half-grin. "She's always been that way. Whenever I was bullied or harassed growing up, she'd step in and defend me without question, and with a ferocity that would startle mother bears."

The thought of Erik as a child, vulnerable, teased and tormented, broke Christine's heart. She couldn't stop herself from reaching a hand out to rest against his uncovered cheek. He leaned into her touch, nuzzling her palm, and rested his own hand on top of hers.

"Were you teased because of what lies under your mask?" It was a blunt question, but there was an air of openness between them, reinforced by their physical connection. She didn't know when they would have a moment like this again.

He closed his eyes and didn't speak, but nodded under her hand.

"Was it an accident?"

His jaw clenched, and he shook his head.

"You were born with it."

Another nod.

Christine didn't say anything else. Didn't ask any more questions. There was pain in his expression that twisted her gut, and all she wanted was to relieve it.

Leaning towards him, she pressed her lips against his. His response was immediate. He wrapped his arms around her and pulled her close, deepening their kiss with a desperation that made tears spring to her eyes. Just as she needed to alleviate his pain, he needed her to comfort him. They fell back against the pillows, losing themselves in each other. Whatever pain still lingered from the past was temporarily forgotten as they both found relief in their pleasure.

* * *

Music filled the air. Such beautiful music, it made her want to cry. Where was it coming from?

Christine cracked her eyes open, and it took her a moment to remember where she was.

She was in Erik's room.

In Erik's bed.

But where was Erik?

Sitting up, she gazed around. It was dark. What time was it? The last thing she remembered was being wrapped in his arms as the aftershocks of yet another orgasm pulsed through her.

The music continued to filter in from the study. Easing out of the bed, Christine padded towards the door, not bothering to cover herself. She peeked into the room and found Erik at his piano, naked save for a pair of black briefs, pouring his soul out in song. The sight took her breath away. She'd seen him play before during her lessons, but she'd never seen him play like *this*. This was him in his true element, doing what he was born to do. Alone, just him and his music.

Christine felt like a voyeur, intruding on a private and intimate moment. Yet she couldn't look away.

All of the sudden, he stopped.

"Come in here, angel," he said without turning to look at her. "It's all right."

She gasped. How had he known she was watching?

Opening the door so she could slip through, she made her way over to him. He turned as she approached, and his eyes flashed with heat.

"How unethical would it be for me to order you never to wear clothes in my presence again?"

She flushed, loving how much he loved her body. When she was within arm's reach, he wrapped his hands around her waist and pulled her close, resting his face between her breasts. He held her like that without saying a word. Though his behavior baffled her, she didn't try to escape, and instead combed her fingers through his hair with gentle strokes.

"That song was gorgeous," she murmured, "but it sounded so sad."

He raised his head to gaze up at her, the moonlight from the uncovered window turning his blue eyes gray.

"It is sad...but it isn't. I wrote it for you."

Christine could have sworn her heart stopped. "I don't understand. You wrote it for *me*?"

He nodded. "Yes. I want you to sing it. You're the only one I want to sing it. I want you to sing it for the album."

Overwhelmed, she struggled to process his words. "But we start recording tomorrow. How can I learn it so quickly?"

"We'll practice." Before she realized his intent, he'd pulled her onto his lap so they faced the keyboard together. Reaching up, he turned on the small, slender lamp sitting atop the piano to illuminate the sheets of music resting against the rack. Had he been playing from memory? Either that or he could see in the dark.

He spread the sheets out so they stood next to each other.

"Here, read the lyrics."

Stunned by what was happening, Christine could do nothing but obey. As she read, she was overcome by the story he'd created. It was just as Erik said. The song was sad, but it wasn't.

"It's a love story," he murmured at her ear. "A love story between Life and Death."

He'd written Life and Death as two figures desperately in love, but tragically separated by the barrier of time. Though they could see each other in those instances when a person's fate hung in the balance between them, they could never touch. Yet they continued to long for each other, never losing hope that one day they could be together.

"Erik...it's stunning," she whispered. She wiped tears from her eyes.

He kissed her shoulder. "You inspired it."

She turned her head to gape at him. "I did? How?"

His brushed the backs of his fingers against her cheek. "You are *my* embodiment of life. Everything that is warm, and sweet, and gentle, I see in you."

She sighed at his words. Yet, if she was life, then was he...?

"Does that mean you're death?" Cold, sad, and lonely?

He buried his face in her hair. "If you are life, then I must be death. We are opposites, desperate for each other, but with seemingly insurmountable odds between us."

Fear trickled in at his words. Was this his way of telling her things wouldn't change between them? That this night was all they would have before the distance returned?

Refusing to believe that, she turned in his lap to straddle him and took his face between her hands. His eyes widened.

"It's a heart wrenching story, but it's not our story. We are not Life and Death. We are Erik and Christine. Our odds are not impossible if we are willing to overcome them together."

Desperation glinted in his gaze. "How can you be so sure?"

Her heart seized. He *had* been warning her things wouldn't change. She wouldn't let them go back. They'd come too far...

"I'm not." She would be honest with him. He wouldn't trust her if she wasn't. "But I'm not willing to give up on you, on *us*, just yet. Please, Erik, tell me you're not willing to either. We'll take things slow. You can take your time opening up to me, but promise me you won't push me away anymore."

They stared at each other, the silence between them painful. At last, he nodded.

"I promise."

She kissed him, relief pouring through her, and he responded in turn.

When they pulled apart, he said, "Will you sing for me, angel?"

Smiling, she nodded.

She turned back around to face the piano. He began to play, and she let the music wash over her as she sang his sad, sweet love song. The hope that she'd fought against for so long burst forth in her heart, and she let it bloom.

31

Christine

The noise and activity of the studio was harsh compared to the quiet solitude of Erik's rooms the night before. Though the bustle was exciting, a part of Christine wished she could return to that private bubble they had formed together.

Unfortunately, duty called, and reality couldn't be avoided.

Christine and Mrs. Giry had been instructed to be Erik's envoys outside the recording sessions. He would remain locked away in the control booth with his handpicked sound engineers, obscured in shadows, but in full control of how his music was brought to life. The two women sat together at the reception desk in the studio's lobby, going over schedules and giving directions to the staff and crew that milled about.

Today, they were working with Rick's band, *Box 5*. It was just a rehearsal, but Erik wanted to fast-track them into the schedule. In a couple days, the orchestra would arrive, and then after that Carla and Christine would record. With all the different elements included in the album, the different sounds, the different musicians and singers, the production was scheduled to take about three weeks.

Christine's duties were straightforward. The schedule was clear. She should be focused and ready.

Yet there was one distraction that nagged at her conscience.

Rick.

She needed to tell him things couldn't progress between them, not after everything that had happened between her and Erik. It wasn't fair to either of them.

Still, she dreaded having to tell him. The last thing she wanted was to hurt him.

She'd decided to wait until the band had finished its session for the day, and take him someplace private so they could talk. Anxiety ate at her as the hours dragged by.

"Is something the matter, Ms. Davidson?" Mrs. Giry's cool, but polite voice penetrated Christine's jumbled thoughts.

Realizing she had spaced out, she turned to face the older woman.

"Yes, I'm sorry. Everything is fine." She flinched, not believing her own words.

Mrs. Giry clearly didn't either. "You've been very distracted today. Perhaps you should take a break if you cannot focus."

Christine's cheeks heated as embarrassment washed through her.

"Really, Mrs. Giry, there's no need. I'm fine."

The woman arched a sharp brow. "If you won't go on a break, telling me what is distracting you might help *me* be more at ease about you continuing your work today."

Christine sighed, knowing it was impossible to fool the sharp-eyed housekeeper. Of the two Giry women, it wasn't the elder she'd anticipated unburdening herself to, but since she was insistent...

"Very well, you win. I need to have a less-than-pleasant conversation with Rick Chagny when the band is finished, and I'm nervous."

Mrs. Giry gave a nod. "There. That wasn't so hard, was it?"

Turning away from Christine, she focused back on the laptop open in front of her.

Christine gaped. That was it?

"You don't want to know more about the conversation? Why it's so serious?"

Without looking up from her task, Mrs. Giry shook her head. "Your personal matters are no concern of mine. As long as you are able to refocus on your work once you've had the conversation, I find no reason to fret over the matter."

Christine didn't know whether to feel offended or relieved. Most people upon hearing such a confession would attempt to gain more information in order to satisfy their greedy curiosity. Mrs. Giry was simply not that type of person. It was strangely refreshing.

"Okay then." Christine turned her attention back to her own work.

"Whatever your conversation, it is always best to be honest." Christine glanced towards Mrs. Giry, but the older woman did not look up as she spoke. "Honesty may sometimes hurt, but it opens up a clearer path to healing than deception ever could."

Though the words were spoken with no amount of warmth, they still eased some of Christine's nerves. She hid her smile.

"Thank you, Mrs. Giry. You are very wise, and very kind."

The woman's shoulders stiffened, but she didn't turn her attention from her computer. Christine returned to her own work with a chuckle.

All of the sudden, the intercom speaker on the desk buzzed. Mrs. Giry pushed the talk button.

"Yes?"

"*Box 5* is done for the day," Erik's deep voice filtered through. "They're heading your way. Remind them of their scheduled time tomorrow before they go."

"Yes, sir."

"Also, send Ms. Davidson to my study once all of the band members have left."

Mrs. Giry shot a glance in Christine's direction. "Of course, sir."

Christine wondered what such an abrupt summons meant. His tone had been clear, crisp, and professional, with no indication whatsoever of his intent. They hadn't spoken since the night before. When she'd woken in his bed again, he'd been gone, already in the studio preparing for the band to arrive. Her only communication from him had been an email that Mrs. Giry had also received with their instructions for the day.

She was nervous to see him, and couldn't help but worry that he would tell her their night together had been a mistake...

"Distracted again, Ms. Davidson?"

Christine let out a shaky breath. "I'm sorry, Mrs. Giry."

"Well, it looks like you'll have one less distraction soon enough."

Frowning, she glanced at the older women, whose own eyes were locked on something over Christine's shoulder.

"Hey, Christine!"

Her heart sank. Turning, she plastered on whatever kind of smile she could conjure.

"Hi, Rick. How did your session go?"

Hands resting in the pockets of his ripped jeans, with his tousled blonde hair and adorable grin, he was a classic heartthrob.

"It went really well. Roux is a stickler for the details, though, huh?"

Christine tensed. She had to get this over with before he said anything awkward.

"He is. Hey, um, could we talk? Somewhere private?"

Rick furrowed his brows. "Sure. Is everything okay?"

Pushing to her feet, she nodded. "Yes, I just have something important I need to talk with you about."

"Okay." Though he looked concerned, he didn't hesitate to follow her when she moved from behind the desk.

Just as they reached the front doors of the building, Mrs. Giry called out, "Don't forget that Mr. Roux wants to see you in his study, Ms. Davidson. Once *everyone* has left."

Christine shot the woman a mortified glare.

Mrs. Giry met her gaze, but Christine could find no animosity or meanness in her dark eyes. Just her usual cool, distant politeness.

Had her words been a jab...or a warning?

"Christine?" Rick reclaimed her attention.

"Right, sorry." She pushed the doors open and they walked out into the late afternoon sun.

* * *

"This place is pretty neat," Rick said, gazing around at the hedges and flowers of the garden. Christine had brought him there knowing it was one of the only places on the property where they could talk without being heard or seen by others.

Glancing up at the window of Erik's study, she was relieved to see the curtains drawn.

"It's peaceful back here," she replied. Leading him to a stone bench, she sat and invited him to do the same.

He met her gaze. "So, what's up?"

She clasped her hands in her lap, struggling to start.

"This is not easy for me to say, Rick. I had a really nice time last night..."

He let out a sigh and his shoulders slumped. "This is the break-up talk, isn't it?"

Christine's eyes widened. "Rick, I..."

His lips quirked in a self-deprecating smile. "Although, it was only one date, so I don't suppose we really qualify as a couple. So not the break-up talk then, but the *I-had-a-nice-time-but-it's-not-going-anywhere* talk."

He was clearly upset, but he didn't seem angry. Not even sad, really, just disappointed.

"I'm so sorry."

He nodded. "It's okay. It was only one date, but if you don't mind, could I ask why? I thought we had a really nice time together."

"We did" Christine insisted. "It was lovely. You were lovely, and if circumstances were different, I really would have loved to go out with you again."

"If circumstances were different? You mean if there wasn't someone you already had feelings for?"

Surprised at his bulls-eye assessment, she ducked her head to hide her blush.

"I thought so. Is it Roux?"

She bit her lip, unable to speak, but nodded.

He let out another deep breath and sat back. "Well, I can't say that I'm shocked. I had a feeling there was something more between you two. He did *not* look happy when you stopped to talk to me after our audition."

"It's complicated."

Leaning forward again, his expression turned stone-cold serious. "You didn't go out with me just to make him jealous, did you?"

"No! Absolutely not." She reached out and clutched his hand in hers. "Things with Erik haven't been easy, but I went out with you because you're sweet. I'll admit, I was angry at him yesterday and was ready to walk away, but I didn't say yes to you to hurt him. I did it because I *wanted* to."

His expression softened. "I get it. I appreciate your honesty, and I understand that things are complicated. I just didn't want to find out I was some kind of pawn because I really do like you, Christine."

She smiled, her heart warming, and some of the tension in her shoulders dissolving. "I like you too, Rick. It's just..."

"You're already in love with him."

She was. *Idiot.* She'd known she was falling for him, and despite how hard she'd tried to guard her heart, the masked bastard had stolen it right out from under her.

"Christine? Are you okay?"

She shook her head, snapping back to reality.

"I'm fine. Really. Just trying to sort this all out."

Rick cupped her cheek. "It's okay. You don't have to figure it out now. I just want you to know that I appreciate you telling me, and not stringing me along. I don't know Roux all that well, and to be honest, he seems super intense and weird, but if you're happy with him, then I'm happy for you."

Are you happy here?

Smiling, she said, "Yes. I'm happy."

"Then that's it." He leaned in and kissed her on the forehead. Sitting back, he dropped his hand from her face and grinned. "I hope this doesn't come off as awkward, but we can still be friends, right?"

Christine laughed. "Of course. I would actually really like that."

Standing, Rick offered a hand to help her up as well. "Good. I'm glad. Now, I've got to get going. The rest of the band is probably wondering where I am, and you..."

"I've got some explaining to do." Her voice went soft as her blood ran cold. She'd gazed up at the study window again, right into Erik's hard blue glare.

32

Christine

Christine hurried through the house and up to the study, terrified of what Erik must be thinking. She hadn't had a chance to tell him she was going to talk to Rick and end things. She could only imagine what it'd looked like to him, finding the two of them together, alone, in his garden.

He must be furious.

When she reached the study door, she stopped. Should she just go in? That felt strange, even now.

Taking a deep, fortifying breath, she raised her hand and knocked.

"Come in." His voice sounded even and calm, which rattled her nerves. If he was disguising his feelings, that would be worse than him yelling.

Opening the door, she stepped into the room. Erik was behind his desk, shuffling through papers. He looked up when she entered.

Though he didn't say anything, he also didn't appear angry. That didn't mean he wasn't, though.

"Look, Erik, about what you saw..."

"You and Rick in the garden together."

She gulped. There'd been a sharp edge in his tone. "Yes."

He leaned back in his chair. "Care to explain?"

Her lips parted in surprise. "You're going to let me?"

He frowned. "Of course. Why wouldn't I?"

Stunned, she moved to sit in one of the chairs facing him. "It's just, most men, at least most men I've been with, would jump to conclusions if they caught their..." *What? Girlfriend? Secretary? One night stand?* "...lover alone with another man."

His nostrils flared. "I'll admit, I didn't enjoy seeing you two together, and I was angry...am still angry, truth be told. However, I'm a rational enough man to know that looks can be deceiving, and I want to trust you Christine. I *do* trust you, even if I continue to question why you would want to be with me." He leaned forward to rest his elbows on his desk. "So, please, tell me what was happening in the garden."

He was being so reasonable. She'd half-expected him to fly into a jealous rage before she could explain anything. Yet, he was trusting her to tell him the truth.

He didn't think he deserved her, but she wasn't sure she deserved *him*.

"I was telling Rick I couldn't see him anymore."

She could see the tension evaporate from his body. He closed his eyes for a moment before opening them back up with a smile.

"Thank God."

Her heart clenched at his relief. Had he been that worried she would leave him for Rick? When the two of them had only just begun?

He was still so insecure. She wanted to do something to assure him of her feelings, to remind him how crazy she was for him.

She wanted to return to the night before and the connection they had found in each other's arms.

An idea came to mind, and she bit her lip to keep herself from grinning. She stood and walked around his desk. Without a word, she took hold of his chair and turned it so he faced her. Erik gazed up at her with a crooked grin and a question in his eyes, but he didn't stop her as she laid her hands on his thighs and pushed his legs apart. Only when she had dropped to her knees did he speak.

"What are you doing?" His teasing tone cracked at the end of his question, revealing his growing excitement.

She glanced up at him, moving her hands to his belt buckle.

"Just living out a fantasy."

His Adam's apple bobbed. She undid his buckle and moved to the button of his slacks.

"And what fantasy is that?" Now, his voice was smoky, almost a growl, his anticipation clear. She shivered with her own growing need.

Christine grinned as she undid the button. "The one where I give my sexy-as-sin boss head under his desk during work hours."

A moan escaped him as she pulled his zipper down.

"How long has this been a fantasy of yours?"

Her smile turned teasing as she looked back up at him. "Oh, it's a *very* new one."

Gripping the top of his pants, she began to pull them down his hips. He lifted himself to assist her, and she yanked them to his thighs. His growing erection strained against the confinement of his black boxer briefs.

"I think you like this fantasy," she purred, running her hand over his bulge, making him groan.

"I think I like this fantasy very much," he gasped.

With a chuckle, and his assistance once more, she slid his boxer briefs down towards his pants, freeing him.

She'd have never used the word beautiful to describe a man's sex before, but in Erik's case, she couldn't think of a more fitting description. Perhaps it was because she thought the man himself so gorgeous.

Taking him in her hand, she began to stroke. He groaned, dropping his head back against his chair, closing his eyes as the pleasure took over. Christine bit her lip as she gazed up at his bliss-filled face. It thrilled her that she could give him this. That he was *letting* her give him this. She wanted to keep watching him, to take note of every change in his expression so she would know when she was pleasing him most.

However, she had promised him her fantasy, and she couldn't wait any longer to live it out.

Dipping her head, she took him deep into her mouth.

Erik let out a startled cry, which dissolved into a delighted moan. He opened his eyes and tilted his chin down so he could watch her.

"God, Christine..."

His hands tangled into her curls, but he didn't attempt to wrest control from her. It was as if he simply needed something to hang on to.

She worked him with lips and tongue, finding more enjoyment in the act with him than she ever had with anyone else. He was not quiet in his pleasure, which she found unexpectedly gratifying. Listening to the noises he made, she paid close attention to the pitch of his tone, how it would shift from a deep rumble that was almost a growl, to a higher groan that sounded like a wordless plea. His voice mesmerized her, even without words or song. It sent a shiver down her spine, and she felt her own arousal grow.

Feeling drugged with lust, and wanting to drive him even crazier, Christine reached a hand to her blouse and unbuttoned the top three buttons, leaving her deep cleavage on display for him. His fingers tightened in her hair, and he snarled as his hips bucked, sending him deeper into her mouth.

"Fuck, you're so beautiful..."

She grinned, feeling bold, and grabbed the hem of her skirt, inching it up her thighs, eager to relieve the growing pressure between her legs...

A sudden knock on the door made them both freeze. Christine met Erik's startled, and somewhat furious, blue gaze as he called out in a harsh tone, "Yes?"

"Erik? I need to go over the details of the album's launch with you."

It was Mrs. Giry, thinking ahead as usual, wanting to talk about the album's eventual launch before the thing had even been recorded. Christine would have giggled, had her mouth not still been full of Erik. Instead, the sound came out a muffled snort. He squeezed his fingers against her scalp in warning.

"I'm busy at the moment, Amelia. Come back in thirty minutes."

Christine cocked a brow up at him, and he shrugged with a grin.

"I'm sorry, but this cannot wait. I'm heading into town shortly to discuss a proposal with a vendor for the party, and I need your approval for the plans before I go. They've arranged a special meeting with me this evening, as their schedule in the next few weeks is packed full."

Erik clenched his jaw and murmured, "She'll refuse to leave until I see her."

Disappointment lanced Christine. So much for her fantasy. She moved to release him and scoot away, but his hands remained firm on her head. Frowning as much as she could, she stared up at him. He met her confused gaze.

There was a tense moment of silence between them, before he growled an order that made her heart thunder.

"Get under the desk."

Releasing her, he allowed her to move away from him. Removing her mouth from him, she stared up at him in thrilled shock before maneuvering her way under his desk on hands and knees. He slid his chair in after her, trapping her between his legs, his still hard cock grazing the bottom of his desk.

"Come in."

As the door opened, Christine grasped him in her hand and brought him into her mouth once more. He tensed around her, but made no sound to give them away.

She heard Mrs. Giry approach the desk, and in a brief moment of paranoia, Christine tucked her feet closer to her body. It wasn't necessary since the front of the desk touched the floor, hiding her from view, but the gesture helped ease her nervous mind. Confident that she couldn't be seen and that Erik's steely-resolve would keep him from hinting at their activities, Christine resumed her ministrations with new, albeit silent, vigor. She grinned when his knees squeezed against her in warning.

"Here is the proposal with our initial bid." Mrs. Giry's firm voice floated down to Christine. Instead of feeling ashamed or scared, the woman's nearness and the possibility of being caught only heightened Christine's excitement. She'd never thought of herself as an exhibitionist, but there were many things she would never have imagined herself enjoying before meeting Erik.

"Very well, let me see it." Erik's voice sounded gruffer than usual, though perhaps only she was able to pick up on that. Christine doubted anyone had dedicated as much time to the study of Erik Roux's voice as she had. She could hear the shuffle of papers as Mrs. Giry handed whatever documents she had to Erik, and he at least pretended to study them for several moments. Christine squeezed his thighs as she lapped at him with her tongue, feeling daring, and wanting to see if she could make him crack. He cleared his throat, an innocent enough gesture if one didn't pick up on the brief, harsh growl at the end.

Mrs. Giry didn't seem to notice.

"The orchestra also needs your finalized selections for the pieces you want them to record." More paper shuffling. More pretending to pay attention.

Christine took him all the way to her throat.

The sound of ripping paper had never been so hot.

"Erik, are you all right?" Mrs. Giry's tone was concerned.

He cleared his throat again. "Yes. My apologies. My anxiety from the day must be getting the better of me. Too many people around." Christine heard the paper move again, and then his hands settled on the desk above her. He must be itching to touch her, to grasp her hair and release his frustrations on her, controlling her and forcing her mouth to take him as he liked. The thought dialed up her arousal. Unable to hold back, she reached one hand under her skirt and plunged it into her panties. She sighed with delight when her fingers met warm, wet flesh.

Mrs. Giry, still oblivious to what was taking place right in front of her, appeared to believe Erik's excuse for his odd behavior.

"I know you aren't comfortable with these kinds of events," she said in a sympathetic voice Christine had never heard before, "but they are good for the label. However, if you would rather cancel..."

"No!" Erik insisted, slapping a hand on the desk. Christine wasn't sure if it was because he was so motivated to see the event through, or because of the little move she'd just done with her tongue. "We will have the event. I will work through it. As you said, it is good for the label."

There was a brief silence before Mrs. Giry replied, "I know that the label is important to you, but could your true motivation for reviving it be more personal than professional?"

Christine would have frowned if she could. What did that mean?

"I'm not sure there is a difference," Erik said. "The label is my life. There's nothing more personal."

"It's just that, ever since Ms. Davidson arrived here..."

Christine let out a squeak of surprise. Erik covered the sound with a cough.

"What would Ms. Davidson have to do with this?" His tone turned dark, making Christine shiver, but not with fear. The hand between her legs moved faster.

Mrs. Giry, however, seemed to have latched onto fear. "Nothing. Never mind. Please forgive me for my rudeness."

"It's fine. Don't worry about it," Erik grumbled. There was a note of impatience to his voice, and Christine wondered if he was going to try to wrap things up. Then she wondered what he would do when they were alone again.

"All this is satisfactory," Erik ground out at length. There was the sound of papers exchanging hands again. She doubted he'd actually read them.

"Very good," Mrs. Giry said. "I will head into town and let you know their counter bid."

"Thank you, Amelia." He didn't sound grateful. He sounded strained.

Mrs. Giry's heels clicked as she crossed the room without another word. The door had barely latched shut behind her when Erik shot away from his desk, pulling himself from Christine's clutches. He reached towards her, wrapping his hands around her upper arms, and yanked her out into the open.

"Little minx," he snarled as he picked her up and dropped her on top of the desk.

"Erik," she breathed, but before she could get another word out, his lips came crashing down on hers. He kissed her like a starved man, devouring her mouth as he ripped open her blouse. Buttons scattered across the floor, but she couldn't make herself care. His hands were everywhere on her at once, petting and groping, before he slid them down to her panties. He didn't bother to remove them, simply pulled them to the side with one hand, and used his other to guide his throbbing cock towards her.

He stopped right before entering her.

"There're condoms in the bedroom."

He hesitated, and she didn't want him to leave her, even for the time it took to fetch a contraceptive. She'd never had sex without a condom before, always too afraid of the potential consequences. Yet, when she thought of it with Erik, she didn't experience her usual fear. She *wanted* to be that close to him...that connected...

"I'm on birth control. And I'm clean."

His eyes widened, as if he couldn't believe what she'd just said. "So am I."

"Then I'm okay with it if you are."

He dipped down and kissed her again as he pushed his hips forward.

She was soaked, having played with herself for so long already, so he slammed into her without resistance. There was a brief spike of pain at the sudden intrusion, which made her gasp, but it dissipated as fast as it had appeared.

He kept kissing her as he laid her back and began moving his hips. He was not gentle, but she didn't want him to be. She moaned against his mouth as her pleasure intensified. He snarled her name. The sound of their bodies slapping together reverberated off the walls, and for a moment, Christine feared Mrs. Giry would hear them and return to investigate. Then, Erik twisted his hips in such a way that she no longer cared. All that mattered was the man above her, and the ecstasy between them.

All of the sudden, he stopped, pulling out and away from her. Before Christine could cry out in protest, he slid her off the desk. Once her feet were planted on the floor, he turned her around and bent her over at the waist, pressing her down flat against the cool, smooth wood surface. Gripping her hip with one hand, he used the other to move her panties out of the way again, and then pushed back into her. Christine released a sound of breathless pleasure as he eased in and out of her. He tangled his fingers into her hair and pulled her head back so she was arched before him. Once he had her positioned to his liking, he slammed his hips against her. She cried out, and he did it again and again, until he was pumping into her at a brutal pace.

Christine couldn't stop the sounds that burst from her throat, the screams and shrieks of pleasure she was sure could be heard throughout the house.

"That's it, angel," Erik panted behind her. "Let me hear that beautiful voice."

She clawed at the desk, dislodging papers and sending files flying. When he loosened his hold on her hair so he could grip her hips in both hands to gain more leverage, she pressed her face against the wood in an attempt to muffle her cries. A firm slap against her buttcheek had her jerking forward with a moan

"Now, now, none of that," Erik growled. "Don't try to hide it from me. Sing for me, baby. Let everyone in this house know who you belong to."

"God, Erik!"

"That's it. Again. Louder!"

She felt her climax closing in, and bit her lip as the pleasure overwhelmed her.

Another slap to her ass had her tumbling over the edge.

"*Erik!*"

With a roar, he followed her with his own orgasm, filling her with his release. When he was reduced to nothing but weak, shallow thrusts, he collapsed on top of her, pinning her to the desk.

She was too exhausted to care. Her body was satiated, her arms and legs limp. Erik's heat enveloped her, and she would have been glad to stay basking in that warmth, had he not begun to crush her with his large frame.

"Erik...too heavy," she murmured.

With a groan, he moved off her. The cool air of the room replaced his heat, and she shivered. He collapsed back into his chair, grabbed her hips, and pulled her into his lap before she could move away. Curling up against him, she closed her eyes and reveled in the feel of his arms and body surrounding her.

He kissed the top of her head and laid his cheek against it.

"What am I going to do with you?" he chuckled.

Keep me, she thought. *Keep me with you, and never let me go.*

She didn't speak those words out loud, however. Instead, she snuggled closer to him and placed a gentle kiss just above his heart.

33

Christine

As work began in earnest on the album, Christine and Erik had less and less time to spend together. He would most often be locked away in the control room of the studio during the day, and worked late into the nights adjusting and perfecting the mixes or the songs yet-to-be recorded. Some days she would only see him during those brief moments when she had to bring him something, or they might etch out an hour to practice her new song together. Still, they were never alone. Whether it was Mrs. Giry, a sound engineer, or a band member, someone was always with them.

Their inability to find private moments together made her nervous, but she tried to ignore her growing concerns, focusing on her own work as the days went by.

The time with the orchestra was particularly intense, as they only had a brief window to perfect the recordings. Once they made it through those few days, *Box 5* recorded their sections.

One thing that alleviated her increasingly depressed mood was her growing friendship with Rick. She had expected interactions between them to be awkward, so was delighted when they were able to move past their attempt at romance with relative ease. He would seek her out between sessions to talk, and they would grab coffee in the mornings together, or go for drinks in the evenings.

Yet, even as she filled her time with work and people, she couldn't stop missing Erik. She wished it could just be the two of them, secluded together in his rooms. When production had first begun, she'd tried to wait for him to finish working in the evenings, but when he bothered coming up from the studio, he was so exhausted he collapsed into bed with little more than a smile and chaste kiss. She'd stopped waiting for him and returned to sleeping in her own room, not out of spite, but because he needed his undisturbed rest.

She was trying to be patient, but she couldn't stop the dark thoughts that swirled in the back of her head. Doing her best to ignore them, she counted down the days until the album was finished and everything could go back to normal.

After two and a half weeks, the end was at last in sight. All that was left to record were vocals, but those were the sessions she had come to dread most.

As Erik had promised, she and Carla would be separated by a day. Carla, who would perform most of the songs on the album, would have several sessions over three days to complete her recordings. Christine, with her single song, would record the evening following Carla.

The thought of Erik and Carla together for that long didn't sit well with Christine. She still didn't know their full history, and if Carla had been responsible for his self-imposed isolation, she wondered at the power the woman had had over him...and if any still lingered.

The morning of Carla's first session, Christine was having breakfast in the dining room with Meg. Mrs. Giry had already excused herself to go to the studio, but Christine was lingering, hoping to avoid running into the diva if she could help it, but hating the thought of Erik dealing with the woman on his own.

"You okay, Christine? You've seemed a little down lately."

Glancing up, she found Meg's concerned gaze locked on her. Christine realized she'd been staring down at her oatmeal for a full minute without eating any of it.

With a shrug, she said, "I don't know."

"Is it Erik?"

She shook her head. "No...I mean, not really."

Meg's brow furrowed. "What is it, then?"

Resting her elbow on the table, she let her chin drop in her hand, debating whether she should unload her troubled thoughts onto her friend. But, if not Meg, who else could she talk to?

"I don't like the idea of Erik and Carla working together."

Meg's expression was sympathetic. "It's nothing to worry about. Erik hates her. Nothing's going to happen."

"I know that. It's not that I'm worried they'll rekindle whatever toxic romance they once had, I'm just nervous that..."

"That she'll do something to hurt him?"

"How is it you can always read my mind?"

Meg grinned. "I'm just that brilliant."

Christine managed a small smile, but then breathed out a heavy sigh.

"Meg, I hate to admit it, but I'm scared something will happen and he'll pull away from me again."

Reaching across the table, Meg grasped her hand and gave it a gentle squeeze.

"He won't."

"But he could!" That was her constant fear, and she very much believed it could happen. All her insecurities came rushing to the forefront of her mind. Even though she'd told herself sex alone wouldn't fix everything, she might have fooled herself into believing they were moving forward. But were they? They hadn't been physical since that time in his study, and hadn't spent another night together. What if he was using work as an excuse to stay away from her?

Meg's hold on her tightened. "Hey! Christine, stop panicking. What has gotten into you?"

"Erik and I slept together," she blurted.

She didn't think it was possible for Meg's eyes to grow any larger. "What? When?"

Christine nodded. "About two weeks ago."

Silence. After a beat, Meg prompted, "And?"

Frowning, Christine said, "And what?"

Meg waved her free hand through the air. "What do you mean *what*? That's huge! Erik's finally letting you in!"

Christine dropped her head. "No, he isn't. Nothing has happened since. We haven't even really talked about it..."

"I'm sure it's just the album keeping him busy." There was a tinge of doubt in Meg's tone however. It almost slipped by Christine, but she caught it and latched onto it.

"But that might not be it, right?" She shot her head up to meet Meg's startled gaze.

"That's not what I said..."

"But you're thinking it."

Meg leaned over and gave her a light smack on the cheek. Christine gasped.

"Stop spiraling," the girl snapped. "You don't know what he's thinking. You need to *talk* to him before you start making wild assumptions. He very well could be pulling away, but that doesn't mean you should let him. You know you have to take the lead with this, Christine. He doesn't know how to open himself up to others. You have to *show* him how if you want to keep moving forward."

Rubbing her stinging cheek, Christine processed Meg's words. She had a point. This was all relatively uncharted territory for Erik, as far as Christine knew. Perhaps she was being unfair. Truth be told, this was all pretty uncharted territory for her too. She'd never been with someone like Erik before. Had never had to put so much work into moving a relationship forward.

She sighed. "You're right. Of course you're right."

"Because...?"

Christine chuckled. "Because you're brilliant."

The blonde smirked. "You bet your ass I am. Now, should we go down to the studio together and make sure that diva bitch doesn't emotionally cripple your man again?"

Pushing to her feet, Christine nodded. "Hell yes."

* * *

Cracking open the control room door, Christine peeked around. There weren't many people in the room. Two men she didn't know sat at the console, pushing buttons and turning knobs as they prepared the equipment. Phillip Chagny sat on the sofa at the back of the room, scrolling through his phone. Erik was nowhere in sight.

Frowning, Christine opened the door wide enough to step inside. Phillip's head shot up at her entrance. He smirked.

"Ms. Davidson, so good to see you. To what do we owe the pleasure?"

She kept herself from rolling her eyes. "I'm looking for Mr. Roux."

Phillip pointed towards one of the windowed doors leading into a vocal booth.

"He's in there."

Turning, Christine's heart stuttered.

Erik stood in the small booth with Carla. They were leaning over a music stand, their heads close as they talked. She was struck by how good they looked together. How natural. Anyone looking at them would never know there was animosity between them.

They were two people who belonged in the same world. Carla could understand Erik in ways that Christine could never hope to, because even if the two hated each other, they were still connected through their music.

Christine had never felt like such an imposter.

Erik's eyes lifted and latched onto hers. All the courage and confidence Meg had given her vanished, and she turned to run from the room.

"Leaving so soon, Ms. Davidson?"

She ignored Phillip as she hurried out into the hall, letting the door slam shut behind her.

Tears threatened to fall. What was *wrong* with her? Why was she such an insecure mess? Why was she acting so weak?

"Christine!" Erik's voice startled her, but she walked faster, heading towards the office in the back. Meg was waiting for her at the front of the building, but she couldn't face her right now. She'd escape to the house through the tunnel...

"Christine, stop!"

She reached the office door, but his hand wrapped around her arm just as she grasped the knob.

"Christine, what are you doing?" His tone was irritated.

That pissed her off. She yanked her arm from his grasp and glared up at him.

"Clearly, I'm trying to get away from you. For some reason, you insist on following me anyway."

He flinched, stepping back with his hands up, as if she would lash out at him.

"What the hell is going on with you?"

She couldn't answer, unable to think of a logical reason for her behavior. The image of him and Carla, with their heads bent so close together, wouldn't leave her mind.

"Nothing. I'm fine. Just leave me alone." She turned the doorknob and stepped into the office. He followed, crowding her into the small space before slamming the door behind him. "You're really not great at listening to people, you do know that, right?" she snarled.

His blue eyes flashed. "I'm not leaving until you tell me what the hell is wrong with you."

She wanted to hit him, and then smother him with kisses. Her frustrations from the last few weeks boiled up and threatened to spill over.

Fuck it, she thought. *We promised to be honest with each other, didn't we?*

"You want to know what my problem is?" She spread her arms wide. "This is the first time we've been alone in weeks, and I'm angry about it."

"Why?" His brow furrowed.

She shrugged. "I honestly don't know. I'm frustrated, and tired, and..." She trailed off, too afraid to say what was on her mind.

"Tell me the truth, Christine," he growled.

Eyes narrowed, jaw clenched, she replied, "Fine. I'm scared that you're pushing me away, and using work to do it."

His mouth dropped open. "Why would you think that?"

Feeling too vulnerable, she hugged herself and didn't meet his gaze. "Why wouldn't I? We've hardly spoken since...since that day. You've given me no indication that anything has changed, and for all I know, you could regret everything we did together."

"How can you say that?" He stepped towards her. She took an instinctual step back, and it did not sit well with him if his thunderous expression was any indication. He pushed forward, backing her up against the desk, trapping her.

She gasped, startled, and he swooped down on her. His lips crashed into hers in a soul-searing kiss. Christine clutched at his sleeves, hanging on for dear life as he overwhelmed her and demanded her submission with his mouth. She was helpless against the onslaught, melting into him without protest. Hoisting her up on the desk, he tied her legs around his waist without breaking their kiss. She wrapped her arms around his neck to maintain her balance.

Their lust for each other blinded them to anything else. Grinding into her, he groaned, and her core tightened. She'd thought she'd wanted him before, but now that she knew what to expect, she was desperate for him. As their kiss grew wilder, Christine slid her hands towards his pants. She began to undo his belt, her fingers frantic.

"Fuck, Christine, there's no time."

"Then make it quick." She managed to loosen his buckle as she kissed along his jaw.

He growled at her ear, his body tensed. His hands came to rest on hers, stopping her, but he didn't move away. She froze, her cheek pressed against his, unwilling to let him go. Two weeks without him...without release...had her primed.

"Please," she whimpered. "I need you inside me. Just for a bit. I promise it won't take long."

His moan was long and defeated. Pushing her hands away, he undid his pants himself. She scrambled to pull up her skirt and discard her panties. When enough of their clothes were out of the way, they came together in a fury. Their mouths crashed, tongues tangled. He palmed her breasts, his fingers squeezing to the point of pain, but she relished it. His hips slammed between her thighs, over and over again. Pushing her so she lay on the desk, he gripped her waist for greater leverage. She clawed as his arms, throwing her head back and forgetting to stifle her cries. One of his hands came up to cover her mouth, and she bit into his palm. He snarled, pounding into her harder.

This wasn't like the other times they had been together. This was violent, animalistic, desperate, and angry. They were fighting each other to see who would reach the peak first, taking their weeks of frustration and anxiety out on each other. As Christine felt her orgasm begin to stir, she knew the pleasure would be brutal. Digging her ankles into his ass, she spurred him on. The desk rocked, inching across the cement floor, the loud scraping barely discernible over the sounds of their joining.

When she came, it was as painful as it was blissful. She screamed against his hand, sinking her nails into his forearms. He continued his punishing pace, drawing out her climax until she was too sensitive to take more and shoved at him. Stepping back, he slid out of her and wrapped his hand around his length. Grabbing her bunched skirt, he pushed it further up her stomach. When she realized his intent, her blood burned, and she spread her legs wider.

Seconds later, Erik tensed, his shoulders hunching. Christine sat up and sealed her lips over is, muffling his roar as he found his own release. It lashed against her, coating her sex and the inside of her thighs.

He slumped forward, his head falling onto her shoulder. After a moment's rest, he cupped her between her legs, smearing his essence and making her shiver.

"I want you to feel me for the rest of the day," he murmured. "Whenever you start to question how much I want you, you'll feel my cum between your legs and know I'm mad for you."

She whimpered. Standing upright, he yanked her skirt back down. She watched, stunned, as he bent to the floor and retrieved her lace panties. With a smirk, he pocketed them and walked out the office door without a backwards glance.

34

Erik

When Erik returned to the control room, Carla was leaning against the console, waiting for him with a smirk.

"She must be a hell of a fuck for you to delay your work."

Henry, the poor sound engineer working with them that day, blushed crimson and ducked his head, becoming suddenly consumed by something on his phone.

Erik glared at Carla. "I will not tolerate your bullshit. Christine is none of your business."

She chuckled, pushing away from the console to saunter towards him. His whole body tensed as she neared.

"You never stopped in the middle of production for a quick fuck with me." Her lips pouted, her voice a deceptive purr, as she traced a finger along his chest.

Close. She was too close.

Her scent was cloying. Her body heat stifling.

Memories he worked so hard to keep buried threatened to break free.

Her dark hair spread out across his pillow...

Her breathy moans when he slid into her...

Her look of revulsion at his face...

He batted her hand away and took a step back.

"Don't touch me."

Her smile was predatory. "What's the matter, Erik? You seem jumpy."

Grinding his teeth, he fought to control his thoughts.

"Let's just get this over with." He pushed past her towards the console.

"Has she seen it, yet?" Her words lashed at him like a whip. "Has she seen the monster you really are?"

He froze. "Henry, could Ms. Dicelli and I have a moment?"

With a relieved expression, the man leapt to his feet and dashed out of the room. The moment the door latched, Erik whirled on Carla.

"What's your fucking game, Carla?" he snarled. "Why do you insist on tormenting me?"

She shrugged. "Perhaps I just enjoy watching you squirm?"

"Fucking tell me!"

Prowling towards him, her hips rolling, she slid both hands up his chest. "Do you really think any other woman would be able to stand it? To stare up at that grisly face as your pounding into her? I couldn't, and I worshipped the ground you walked on."

He clenched his jaw, grabbing her wrists to push her away.

"Christine's not like you."

Her red smile was wide. "Darling, every woman is like me. Some just don't know it, and some are better at hiding it. What she sees now is a mysterious genius with the body of a god and the cock to back it up." With a bold hand, she gripped the front of his pants. "You show her what's under that mask, and she'll forget about your other assets in a heartbeat."

Slapping her hand away, he growled, "What the hell are you doing?"

She bit her lip, but the move didn't stir him like it did with Christine. When she did it, it was mindless, an indication of her lust and excitement. When Carla did it, it was a calculated move, meant to manipulate and seduce. He could see right through her, and it made him sick.

"I miss you, Erik." She snaked her hands around his neck and pushed herself flush against him. He was so stunned by her words he didn't untangle himself from her right away. "She could never appreciate you the way I do. *I've* seen your face, and here I am, still wanting you. Can you say the same for her?"

Narrowing his eyes, he reached up and unwrapped her arms from around him.

"You saw my face and bolted, only crawling back time and again for an easy fuck, and I was fool enough to let you. You were clear in your disgust of me all that time, but I'm no fool anymore. You're not back because you want me. I know you've been dropped by your label. Your voice is starting to fail you, and you're a nightmare to work with. Face it, your career is circling the drain and you being here is a hail Mary attempt to save it."

Her expression soured at his words, and she shoved her hands against him.

"How dare you? I'm here doing you a favor. Believe it or not, *Roux*, I know I owe my career to you. I also know that *Fantôme Records* is teetering on the verge of bankruptcy. You need this album to be a success to save your precious label, not just impress your latest whore."

"Watch your mouth, Carla."

She rolled her eyes. "Face it, you *need* me, but I don't need you. I can turn around and walk right out that door and not come back. Is that what you want?"

To drive her point home, she spun on her heel and began marching to the control room door. Erik balled his hands into fists, so tempted to let her go, to not have to *deal* with her anymore, but she was right.

He did need her.

Goddamnit.

"Wait," he ground out. "Don't go."

Stopping, she glanced at him over her shoulder with a haughty glint in her eye that made him hate her even more.

"Why shouldn't I?"

He growled in frustration. She was going to milk this. Make him beg...

"Because you're right. I need you, Carla."

Looking like the cat who'd not only eaten the canary, but made it grovel beforehand, she walked back towards him with a smile. When she cupped his cheek, he forced himself not to flinch.

"That's a good boy. Now, why don't you go fetch your little man...Harvey, was it? Your fuck break put us behind schedule as it is, and I know how much you loathe falling behind schedule."

It took every ounce of his will power not to throttle her then and there, but like an obedient dog, he went to fetch Henry. With every step he took, he cursed the once innocent dark-haired girl who had walked into his life, and the cold-hearted bitch she'd become.

* * *

It ended up being one of the longest days of his life. He knew working with Carla would be a brutal experience. It hadn't been easy when they'd been together, and she'd only grown more insufferable over the years.

And pitchy.

Her voice wasn't what it used to be, and they'd had to work much later than he'd anticipated because of it. It was well past midnight, and he was just getting to his study. He began unbuttoning his shirt, ready to collapse into bed. When he opened the door, he froze, his heart speeding up.

Christine was tucked under his covers, fast asleep. His lips curled as he made his way across the room, shedding his clothes until he was down to his boxer briefs.

Pausing at the side of the bed, he stared down at her sleeping face. She looked so peaceful, with a small dribble of drool leaking out of the corner of her mouth. Sitting next to her, he wiped the spittle away with his thumb, then ran a gentle hand over her hair.

"Angel. Angel, wake up."

She moaned, her eyelashes fluttering. Cracking open her eyes, she peered up at him. There was delight in her sleepy gaze.

"Mmmm, what time is it?"

He continued to pet her hair as he answered. "Almost one in the morning."

Stretching her arms above her head, she offered a contended smile. "Are you just getting in? Why so late?"

He quirked a brow. "Carla is proving more difficult to work with than I anticipated, which is saying something. I planned for her to be quite difficult."

A small frown creased her forehead. She sat up, dislodging his hand. As if by instinct, his eyes dipped down to watch the sway of her breasts under her large, thin t-shirt. Catching himself, he brought his gaze back up to hers.

The flush along her cheeks made him smirk.

"Are you okay? Did she say anything...?"

He cut her off with a kiss. Her small yelp of surprise was almost as gratifying as the moan that followed. She melted for him, seeming to forget her line of questioning. Pushing her back against the pillows, he slid a hand along her thigh and bunched up her t-shirt to reveal her panties. She gasped into his mouth when he rubbed his thumb along her clothed center.

"Erik, you must be tired..." She didn't sound all that concerned, though, and he chuckled.

"I'm feeling wide-awake all the sudden." He took her hand and placed it against his growing erection. "Besides, how could I possibly sleep with this disturbance? I think you'll have to help me out, angel."

She grinned. "How can I be of assistance, sir?"

When she bit her lip, his blood raced, but the image of Carla doing the same flashed in his mind. Dropping down, he nipped at her lip to pull it from her teeth and erase the thought from his head.

Moaning, she pushed against his shoulder and he backed up, confused.

"What is it?"

Though her cheeks were pink, and she was panting, she held him at arm's length. "You didn't answer my question."

He released a frustrated groan and dropped his head to her chest.

"Why do you want to talk about that woman right now?"

She ran her hands through his hair. "I just want to know that you're okay."

Erik knew she wouldn't be satisfied until he answered, but he debated telling her about Carla's blatant advances on him. Propping his chin between her breasts, he gazed up at her. Her expression was concerned. The fact that she cared so much made his chest ache.

It wasn't worth disturbing her with Carla's deranged behavior. He didn't want her to worry for no reason.

"Carla is a pain in the ass, but that's to be expected. She didn't do anything. I promise, I'm fine."

He felt a small twist of guilt in his gut at her relieved smile, but ignored it. Carla was nothing. She didn't matter anymore.

Christine did. Slowly, but steadily, she was becoming more and more central to his world. Her smile lifted his soul, and her happiness fed into his own.

"I like KitKats, by the way."

Her baffled frown was adorable.

"What?"

Lifting a shoulder in a half-shrug, he explained. "I like KitKats. I also like *Doctor Who* and visiting Coney Island. I hate kale, reality TV, and I really don't like cats either."

She stared at him as if he was speaking a language she couldn't understand.

He grinned. "You wanted to know more about me. It's surface level, but I want you to know that I'm trying. I want to let you in, Christine. I want more with you."

The radiance of her grin was a bright light in his otherwise dark world. She tugged on his hair to drag him up and brushed her lips across his.

"You really don't like cats?" she teased, peering up at him from beneath her lashes.

"Well, I suppose there is one pussy I've grown rather fond of." He ground his length against her, turning her burst of laughter into a moan.

"That's the corniest thing you've ever said to me."

Chuckling, he kissed her again, deeper and with more hunger than the last. As they lost themselves to each other, he let her touch banish his worries, his doubts, and Carla from his mind.

35

Christine

Christine stared down at the sheets of music in front of her, unexpected panic making her heart race.

Could she really do this?

"Ready?" Erik's voice reached her through the large headphones covering her ears.

She raised her head and met his eyes through the vocal booth's glass. The way he looked at her did not help to calm her riotous nerves. He didn't look at her like a lover, or even a friend. Right now, in this moment, he was a composer waiting for his singer to perform.

The thought of disappointing him was nauseating.

Something in her face must have given away her trepidation. His expression softened.

"You're going to be fine, Christine." It was odd listening to him like this, and reminded her of when she'd first started her job with him and he would only speak to her through intercoms and speakers.

Dropping her gaze from his, she shook her head. "I don't think I can do this."

"Christine, listen to me." There was an edge to his voice. A hint of desperation. At the prospect of the album being ruined? That made her feel worse. "You know this song. You've sung it more times than I can count. There is nothing for you to worry about."

Except for you realizing I'm a talentless waste of your time.

"Angel," his voice lost that hint of hardness and turned soothing. "Just pretend it's me and you alone in my study. You're singing for me, and only me."

She raised her eyes to him again, helpless not to. There was a small smile curling his lips, and his gaze was bright with encouragement. The only other person in the room was Henry, the sound engineer. He was focused on the console and monitors in front of him, all but ignoring her and making it easier to pretend he wasn't there.

Returning her focus to Erik, she took a deep breath and nodded.

"Okay. I think I'm ready."

His smile widened. "Okay. Henry, give her the intro..."

The control room door flew open and Carla sauntered in with a sneer. She was wearing a figure-hugging dress that reached her knees, and her long dark hair was pulled up into an elaborate chignon.

"Carla, what the hell are you doing here?" Erik barked.

The look she gave him made Christine want to claw the woman's eyes out.

"Darling, I wanted to come hear your new protégé. See what all the fuss is about." Her fingertips ran down his arm. To Christine's relief, he shuddered.

"You're not supposed to be here. We finished with you yesterday."

It had been a relief, and Erik had said they wouldn't have to see the diva until the release party in two weeks. Clearly, Carla had other plans.

"We did, we did." Carla nodded, sliding onto the sofa at the back of the room. "But I just couldn't leave yet, not without a sampling of Ms. Davidson's mysterious talent. You've been keeping her so sheltered, Erik. No one I talked to was able to tell me anything about her ability. Oh, that reminds me, I hope you don't mind, but I invited a few guests."

At that moment, the door opened again and Phillip and Rick Chagny strolled inside, followed closely by Mr. Montgomery and Mr. Richards. The latter two peered around the room with nervous expressions, as if they knew they shouldn't be there. Rick waved at Christine with a grin, oblivious to his role as Carla's pawn in whatever game of manipulation she was playing. Phillip was smirking, and Christine had a feeling he was fully aware of Carla's intentions and was playing along of his own free will.

"This is a private session!" Erik snarled. "No one is allowed to be here."

"Now, now Roux," Phillip said. "Must I remind you of our agreement? I can be anywhere I want during this production, which is why I accepted Ms. Dicelli's gracious invitation to come listen to Ms. Davidson. She is, after all, the reason you are creating this album, isn't she? I believe I have a right to hear the reason for my generous investment."

Christine glanced at Carla, who appeared enraptured by the exchange happening between the two imposing men. This was clearly what she had hoped would happen by bringing Phillip in. Rick, Mr. Montgomery, and Mr. Richards all huddled close to the door, looking uncomfortable.

Rick's eyes met Christine's, and it was clear he'd realized his mistake. He mouthed, *"I'm sorry"*, and she offered a small smile. Turning her attention back to Erik, she could see he was on the verge of losing control of his temper. His expression promised violence to everyone in that room. She had to defuse the situation before he did something he'd regret, which would no doubt delight Carla.

"Erik, it's okay," she said in as even a tone as she could manage.

He turned to face her, scowling. "It's not. I promised you it would just be you and me..."

"People are going to hear me sing anyway when the album comes out, right? If I want to do this, I can't be afraid to perform in front of an audience." She sounded braver than she felt. In truth, this was a nightmare situation, and her panic returned in full force.

"Christine..."

"Let's just get this over with, and then everyone can leave with their curiosity satisfied." She chanced another look at Carla. The diva did not seem to appreciate Christine interrupting her fun, if her glare was any indication.

Once again, Christine wondered how Erik could ever have been with such a vile woman.

"If you're sure, angel," Erik murmured, recapturing her attention.

She met his blue gaze and nodded. "Yes, I'm sure. It'll be fine."

He didn't look convinced, but he didn't argue with her. With a nod towards Henry, he leaned against the console, folded his arms, and closed his eyes to listen as the music began to play.

Christine focused as the sweet notes of a piano filtered into her ears, and with it came a sense of calm. She knew it was Erik playing. He'd recorded this one song himself so that it would be theirs, and no one else's. A string quartet started up in the background, but his piano was the dominant sound. Her eyes slid shut as the music wrapped around her, and when she opened her mouth to sing, it was without fear or hesitation.

In that moment, it was just the two of them. The unwanted onlookers disappeared from her mind, and all that mattered to her was Erik, his melody, and her song. She poured everything she had into the performance. Her heart, her soul, her body...all that she was, she offered up to the music. To him.

When she sang her final note, it was with her whole being.

As the music faded, she felt like she was waking up from a dream. Opening her eyes, she locked her gaze with Erik's.

He was staring at her in awe.

Peering around, she found everyone else was looking at her with similar expressions. Everyone except for Carla.

She looked murderous.

Disconcerted by their rapt gazes and the heavy silence, Christine removed her headphones and stepped out of the booth.

"What? Why are you all looking at me like that?"

Rick was the first to speak.

"Christine, that was amazing! I had no idea you could sing like that."

Mr. Montgomery and Mr. Richards nodded in agreement, their eyes wide.

Her cheeks heated as she fought an embarrassed grin.

"Really?" Of course Erik had praised her voice and told her she was talented, but a small part of her had never quite believed him. He was, she reasoned, fairly biased towards her. To have others complimenting her was more affirming than she cared to admit out loud.

Phillip stepped towards her, and for once, he wasn't looking at her as if he were mentally undressing her.

"Truly spectacular, Ms. Davidson." He took her hand and brought it to his lips. "I'll admit, I had my doubts. I was sure Roux was only including you because of ulterior motives, but I am man enough to admit when I'm wrong. You are a rare talent, indeed."

To say that his praise shocked her would be an understatement. She had no response. He released her hand and turned towards Erik.

"Commendable work, Roux." There was no hint of sarcasm in his words. "You've created a masterpiece." With that, he headed towards the door, collecting Rick and the other two men on his way out. As he followed his older brother, Rick held his hand up to his ear to indicate he would call Christine later.

She nodded and waved good-bye as the door shut behind him.

Erik was still staring at her in silence.

Feeling exposed and vulnerable under his penetrating eyes, she gulped.

"Please say something, Erik. You're making me uncomfortable."

He didn't respond, but pushed away from the console and stalked towards her. She couldn't read his intent until he'd cupped her face with both hands and pressed his lips to hers with an intensity that made her knees quake. Clutching his shoulders, she was on the verge of mindlessness when the sound of a throat clearing reminded her that they were not alone.

Henry remained at the console, wearing headphones, absorbed in his work.

Carla remained on the couch, watching them with blatant hate in her gaze.

Christine pushed away from Erik. He rolled his eyes, turning to face the diva.

"Why are you still here?"

Chin raised, Carla rose to her feet, casting Christine a look of disdain before answering him.

"I haven't been allowed to offer my feedback, yet." Her voice was an even hiss.

Erik stepped in front of Christine, and she realized he was shielding her. Again. Did he fear Carla would do something? The diva was a pain-in-the-ass, but Christine couldn't imagine her being physical in any way. That'd be too much work for her.

"Your feedback wasn't requested," Erik snapped.

Hands on her hips, she moved until she stood toe-to-toe with him. Christine wanted to step between them and push her away, but she didn't. She remained still. It wasn't her fight. Not really. Carla was Erik's living nightmare, and he had to face her.

Still, Christine placed a hand on his back, reminding him that she was there.

"Chagny was right, the girl is good," Carla began, ignoring Erik's objection. "But we both know she wouldn't even be here if you weren't fucking her. She's nothing but a whore who spread her legs to get you to make her famous."

Erik's shoulder moved, and Christine feared he would slap the woman out of blinding rage. She grabbed his arm, sinking her nails in to hold him back. His shoulder dropped, but his hand remained fisted. Carla didn't miss a single movement, and she smirked.

"Get out of my sight, Carla," he snarled.

She tipped her head back and let out a chuckle. "Face it, Erik. If women couldn't use you for your talent, we wouldn't tolerate you. All you are is a stepping stone to something better." She met Christine's horrified stare over his shoulder. "Trust me, sweetheart. If you've seen what I've seen of this man, you'd run away as fast as you could. Hiding behind that mask and talent is nothing but a pathetic, ugly beast whose own mother despised him. Use him how you need, then dump him before he drags you down into his shit." Looking back up at Erik, she murmured, "He's not worth it."

Christine could only watch in dismay and shock as the woman sashayed her way out of the room as if she hadn't left total devastation in her wake. Carla didn't need to use violence to decimate those she hated. With just her words, Christine knew she had landed a blow that would reopen old, invisible wounds that had just begun to heal over.

Erik stood frozen, and Christine wasn't sure what she should do. She was afraid to move, afraid of how he would react to Carla's cruel words.

He uncurled his fingers so that his hands hung flat at his sides.

"Erik?" she whispered.

He turned his head as if to look back at her, but didn't meet her gaze.

"You did beautifully, angel. We are done for the day. You should get back up to the house." His voice was calm, but hollow.

"Won't you come with me?" She knew what his answer would be, but couldn't stand the thought of him being alone right now.

With a shake of his head, some of the distance they'd worked to overcome together came inching back between them.

"No, I need to finish up here."

Though she loathed doing so, she peeled her hands from his arm and nodded.

"Okay. I'll see you later, then."

She moved around him towards the door. When her fingers touched the handle, his parting words made her freeze.

"I imagine I'll be quite late. It's probably best if you sleep in your own room tonight."

He was shutting her out, and there was nothing she could do about it.

Tears threatened to fall, but she held them back long enough to respond, "If that's what you want." Opening the door, she fled the room before he could see her break.

Not wanting to risk running into anyone, especially Carla, Christine opted to take the tunnel back to the house. She wrapped her arms around herself as she walked, but it wasn't the cold of the corridor that had her shivering. It was the realization that her relationship with Erik was built on shaky ground. He didn't trust her with his pain, and she hadn't felt confident enough to fight for it. She'd walked away, and he'd let her.

Christine didn't know for sure what Carla's true intentions had been, but her words had shattered the illusion of security she and Erik had built around themselves. The small tidbits he'd shared with her two nights ago were nothing. Surface-level fun facts. He'd told her he was trying, and she'd believed him because she'd wanted to. However, at the first sign of true conflict, they'd fallen apart.

He still hid himself from her in so many ways, and though their sex was mind-blowing and their music was magic, Christine knew it wasn't enough. She'd thought she'd loved him, but could she truly love someone she didn't even know?

By the time she reached his study, she was heartsick and more confused than ever. Stepping into his space, surrounded by his possessions, she wondered how much longer they could continue. She wasn't ready to give him up, was in fact desperate to keep him, but she had to acknowledge how tired she was.

Stopping in front of his piano, she ran her fingers over the smooth, black surface of the keyboard cover before pulling the bench out and sitting. Opening the cover, she stared at the keys as if they could give her insight into the man who had consumed her heart and soul. This was the place where he was the most himself, yet she could draw none of his secrets from the silent instrument. Closing the cover once more, she rested her elbows on it and dropped her head into her hands.

She felt like a coward and a fool. A lovesick girl who'd fallen for a broken soul because she'd foolishly believed love would conquer all.

Love couldn't conquer all, but trust and honesty could.

Yet those were the things they lacked most.

With a sob, she let her tears fall. She cried for him and his pain he kept hidden from her. She cried for herself and her foolish heart she'd given away so readily. She cried for the future she'd imagined for them as it began to slip away. She cried because she didn't know what else to do. She was in love with a man who would never fully trust her, and she couldn't even blame him for it. With a few words, a woman they both hated had shattered their world. Christine couldn't imagine what devastation she could bring to someone who loved her.

36

Christine

The next two weeks passed in a haze, and though Christine and Erik pretended with each other that everything was fine, the chasm that had opened up between them was like a gaping wound neither was willing to stitch together. The day following Carla's visceral verbal attack, Erik had found Christine back in the parlor. He'd apologized to her and assured her he was okay, but she'd known he was lying. She'd accepted his apology anyway, but his refusal to confide in her stung.

As Erik worked on completing the album, Christine assisted Mrs. Giry with the planning of the release party. It was an effective distraction, keeping her mind from wandering back to Erik and everything unspoken between them. They didn't see each other often during the day, their interactions limited to the necessary ones that took place between a personal assistant and her boss. Minding schedules. Requesting signatures. Screening phone calls. The occasional coffee run. Emotionless, sometimes mindless tasks that didn't require either of them to confess their feelings or fears.

It was different at night. Once the work day was done, Christine would go to him, or Erik would seek her out, and they would lose themselves in each other. Their passion and physical connection became their one outlet for their frustrations and emotions. The sex was wild, hot, and sometimes dirty. When it was over, however, they'd make small talk like they were acquaintances rather than lovers. Erik didn't tell her anything more about himself, and she didn't ask. They slept in each other's arms every night, but Christine would wake up in the mornings feeling more and more hollow inside.

She was exhausted and afraid if she said anything or pushed any harder, he'd reject her again, and it would be for the last time. A person could only take so much, but she wasn't ready to let him go. She knew something would eventually have to give, however, or there would be nothing worth salvaging between them.

The day of the release party, the house was a flurry of activity. Mrs. Giry had hired extra help to prepare for the evening. A dance floor and stage had been delivered and was being installed in the garden, where the party would be taking place. The house itself would be off-limits to guests, but still Mrs. Giry brought in a cleaning service to scrub the place from top to bottom. Caterers swarmed the kitchen, overtaking Darius' domain.

Christine was overwhelmed by the amount of people around. Though she had helped to plan the event, she tried to stay out of everyone's way and out of sight of Mrs. Giry. In an attempt to escape the chaos, she made her way towards the ballet studio, hoping to find Meg.

As she came upon the dining room door, she found Darius pacing in front of it, his face scrunched up in worry. She stopped, but he didn't seem to notice her.

"Darius? Are you okay?"

His head snapped up and his eyes widened in surprise. "Oh! Christine, I'm sorry. I didn't see you there."

Her smile was bemused. "It's fine. You seem distracted."

Nodding, his eyes glanced towards the door. "I suppose you could say that." He turned his gaze back to her. "I just don't understand why Amelia would let them kick me out of *my* kitchen. Those people don't know my storage system. What if they can't find something? What if they mess everything up? What if..."

He was getting worked up. She'd never seen him like this before. Startled, Christine placed her hands on his shoulders.

"Hey! Calm down, it's okay," she said in a soothing tone. "Just take a deep breath." She demonstrated, and he followed her example. "That's it. Now, I'm sure Mrs. Giry didn't mean to upset you. She likely wanted you to be able to enjoy the party with everyone else and not have to work it."

"I...I suppose that could be true."

She nodded. "Why don't you just go to your room and relax, hmm? Get some rest before tonight, and don't worry about your kitchen. The people in there are professionals, and I'm sure Mrs. Giry gave them a very long lecture about respecting your space." As she spoke, she turned him away from the dining room door and nudged him down the hallway. He let her guide him without resistance as her words sunk in.

"You're probably right," he murmured. "Amelia wouldn't let them ruin my kitchen. I should just go relax..."

He began walking, mumbling under his breath as he continued talking himself from the edge of his panic. Christine watched him until he turned the corner and disappeared from sight. When she was certain he wouldn't come back, she chuckled and continued towards her original destination.

Reaching the ballet studio, Christine didn't pause and opened the door without a thought.

"I'm sorry, babe, but I can't leave yet."

She froze, finding Meg on her phone with her back to the door. It was clear the girl hadn't heard Christine enter the room when she continued talking.

"I know, please don't be mad..." she sounded agitated, and Christine got the sense this was a call she wouldn't be welcome to. Backing out of the room, she tried to pull the door closed as she went. Before she could get away, however, Meg turned and spotted her.

Meg's eyes went wide as Christine's cheeks heated.

Mouthing *"sorry"*, Christine moved to shut the door all the way, but Meg shook her head and held up a finger. Confused, Christine stopped.

"I'm not having this conversation right now," Meg snapped into her phone. "If that's what you want to think, then I can't stop you. Look, I have to go. I'll call you later once we've both cooled off." She hung up without saying good-bye.

Standing in the doorway, feeling awkward, Christine waited until Meg put her phone down on the bench before speaking.

"I'm sorry. I should have knocked instead of just barging in."

Meg offered a smile, but it was sad, and her gaze was distant. "It's okay. Don't worry about it."

It was clear things weren't okay.

"Was that Chelsey?"

Letting out a sigh, Meg nodded. "Yeah. We're kind of having a fight right now."

The girl looked so dejected. Christine had never seen her so sad before. It made her heart ache. Stepping into the room, she hurried to Meg's side and took her hand.

"Do you want to talk about it?"

Meg didn't look up, but her fingers wrapped around Christine's.

"She's mad I haven't come back yet."

Christine frowned. She hadn't given it much thought before, but it had been several months since Meg had arrived at the house. Seeing as she had a relationship and career, the extended stay was strange.

"Why haven't you? Your ankle is better, right? Why *are* you still here?"

Dropping her head back with a groan, Meg released Christine's hand. She moved towards the windows and slid down to the floor with her back against the wall. Christine followed her, though her knee-length pencil skirt made getting to the floor a difficult, graceless task.

"Promise not to tell mom or Erik?" Meg asked, hugging her knees.

Christine put her hand over her chest. "I promise."

Meg dropped her chin to her knees. "Chelsey wants to get married, and I don't."

Bending her legs so they were tucked off to the side, Christine placed a hand on the floor for support as she leaned closer to Meg. "Do you not love her?"

Meg's blonde ponytail whipped back and forth as she shook her head. "No, I love her. I'm so in love with her it hurts sometimes. I just don't feel like I'm ready to get married. I don't even know if I ever *want* to get married."

"Have you told Chelsey this?"

"No," the girl groaned. "I don't want to hurt her, and I don't want her to leave me."

Christine tilted her chin up. "I see. So you've been hiding out here to avoid talking to her."

Meg sniffed. "Like a fucking coward. I even lied and said my ankle wasn't better so that I could extend my leave from work."

Christine arched a brow. "Really?"

"Yeah." Meg's voice broke, and she collapsed into tears. "But of course it's only made things worse, and now Chelsey thinks I'm trying to ghost our relationship. I'm so scared of losing her that I'm driving her away, and I know it! But I don't know what to do." Dropping her head into the circle of her arms, she sobbed until her shoulders shook.

Christine wrapped an arm around her and pulled her into a tight hug, cooing soothing words in her ear as she let the poor girl cry. Meg clung to her like a lifeline. The role flip did not escape Christine's awareness. It was usually Meg consoling Christine's broken heart, yet all that time, she'd been suffering through her own, and Christine had had no idea.

"I'm so sorry, Meg," she murmured into the girl's soft blonde hair. "I'm so sorry you've been dealing with this alone. I've been piling my own baggage onto you, and I never took the time to pay attention to how you were doing."

"It's not your fault," Meg sniffled against her neck. "How could you have known when I never talked about it? I pretended everything was okay with Chelsey because I didn't want to deal with the mess I'd created. Now it's too late..."

"No!" Christine pushed Meg back so they were face-to-face. The girl looked startled. "It's not too late. You just need to talk to Chelsey. Have an honest conversation with her about your fears. If she loves you like I think she does, she will listen. It won't be easy, and I can't promise it won't hurt, but you two can figure this out."

Meg gulped. "I'm so scared, Christine."

She could sympathize. It was so much easier giving the advice than acting on it.

"Call her back. Tell her you're sorry and you want to talk. Invite her here, tonight. For the party."

"What if she doesn't come up?"

"Then you go to her. Inviting her up is a way to let her know you want her to be a part of every aspect of your life, but if she doesn't accept, then that's fine. Wherever you end up having the conversation, the important thing is that you *have* it."

Meg wiped her eyes with the palms of her hands.

"Okay. I can do that. If she says yes and comes up, will you meet her? You don't have to explain anything for me, I just want her to meet my family."

A lump formed in Christine's throat that almost choked her. "Of course I'll meet her. I'd love to meet her."

Meg's lips curled into a shaky smile. "Okay. I'll call her back."

"Good." Using the wall to climb to her feet, Christine helped Meg to stand as well. The girl grabbed her phone, and Christine headed for the door. "Let me know what she says."

Meg nodded. "I will. Thank you so much, Christine."

Smiling, she said, "Of course."

She left the room, closing the door behind her as Meg dialed Chelsey's number and pressed the phone to her ear. For a moment, she considered waiting for Meg to finish the call, but decided against it. Better to give them their privacy.

As she made her way back down the hall with slow, soft steps, she chided herself for being so blind to Meg's troubles. Even if the girl hadn't said anything, Christine should have picked up on *something*. She should have at least questioned the length of her stay before now.

Hugging herself, she wondered what else she'd grown blind too. When had she let herself become so consumed with...herself? She'd never been the kind of person to become so engrossed in her own life that she lost sight of the world around her.

But then, her life had never been worth the attention. Not before Erik. Not before this job. Not before the opportunity to finally make her dream of a life engulfed in music come true.

Her existence used to be bland and empty. She'd checked off every box she'd been told was necessary to be successful. She'd gotten a good, expensive education. She'd gotten a good, well-paying job. She'd lived a lifestyle of simple luxury, not too flashy, but comfortable.

Yet none of that had made her happy. She'd been good at school, but hadn't enjoyed her majors. She'd been good at her job, but had hated it more days than not. She'd had nice things and stylish clothes, but it had all been conservative, clean, and organized. Cold. Empty.

Meaningless.

Now, her life was exciting. She was able to pursue her passions, and she felt more in touch with herself than she ever had before.

Yet, she was still unhappy.

She was frustrated and scared of the state of her relationship with Erik, but there was something else. Something she couldn't put her finger on. She was closer than she'd ever been to feeling fulfilled, yet contentment continued to allude her.

Why?

What else did she need?

When she reached the parlor, she stopped at the threshold and took in the room. It was the first place Erik had heard her sing. It was where he had offered to teach her. It was where, with just a few words, he had acknowledged and affirmed her talent like no one else had before. Yet now, it had become a hiding place. The small corner she was banished to when he didn't want to see her, and the safe space she retreated too when she didn't want to speak with him.

Standing there, staring at the ornate fireplace and cushioned chairs, something clicked in her mind, and she realized what she still lacked.

She was lonely.

It was a shock, because she hadn't realized it until that moment. Erik had asked her once if she was happy, because this house could be so isolating. She'd answered that she was, and at the time she'd believed it was the truth. The reality was she'd been lonely ever since her father had died, and had just grown so accustomed to it, she couldn't separate it from what was normal for other people. When she was by herself, it was easier to ignore.

Here though, in this house, it had grown more and more apparent. Mrs. Giry's aloofness never bothered her, because it reminded her of her mother. She'd clung to Meg's friendship and the girl's genuine interest in her life to the point where she'd forgotten Meg was a person with her own problems.

She'd basked in Erik's attention, relishing his praise as her teacher and his interest as a man because no one had ever looked at her the way he did, or believed in her as strongly. The distance between them hurt all the more because she'd had a taste of an intimacy she'd never known. She'd never had to try to connect with someone before, because she'd never cared enough to make the effort. Yet now she did. She cared with all her being.

She loved Erik Roux, and she wanted to be with him.

However, no matter how much she might try, if Erik wasn't willing to fight for them, she would be doomed to a life of solitude even if she was by his side.

Taking a step back, Christine turned from the parlor and headed towards the stairs. Hurrying up to her room, she made a decision. Tonight, she would take her own advice, and be absolutely honest with Erik. She would put it all on the line, telling him exactly what she needed if their relationship was going to continue. If he couldn't, or wouldn't, work with her in finding a solution to move forward, she would walk away. She didn't want to have to choose between the love of her life and her own happiness. She wanted them to feed into each other, build off each other, but if she had to choose, she would choose herself.

Whatever it took, she would be happy. She would be fulfilled. She would live a life with meaning and purpose. She would never be lonely again.

Even if that meant a life without Erik Roux.

37

Christine

The garden was aglow with hundreds of lights draped above the party, like stars among long strips of gauzy white satin. Six faux-marble pillars stood like sentinels along the hedges, holding everything up. A live band, complete with violinists, a cellist, guitarist, pianist, trumpeters, drummer, and bassist created a backdrop of music for the party-goers milling about the rosebushes and flower beds.

Christine stared in awe at the scene, impressed by the transformation as well as the crowd. She stood at the top of the terrace steps, searching the mass for any familiar face. A much more difficult task given the party's theme.

French masquerade.

There was no doubt in Christine's mind that Mrs. Giry had chosen the theme in hopes that Erik would feel comfortable joining the festivities. Christine had her doubts, however. She glanced up towards his study window. The curtains were drawn, but the light from the room was hard to hide at night. Erik was no doubt locked away in his private domain, set on avoiding the throng of people even if they were all here for him.

Christine turned her attention back to the party. It was his choice whether to join or not, and she wouldn't let his absence ruin the night for her.

"Christine!"

She smiled when she spotted Rick break from the melee to hurry towards her. He looked handsome and sophisticated in his black suit and skinny tie over a crisp, white dress shirt. His face was partially hidden by a black domino. Stopping when he was a couple steps below her, he ran his eyes over her and whistled.

"Wow, you look...just wow."

Christine blushed under his gaze, but found she enjoyed the attention. She'd chosen an emerald green off-the-shoulder, floor-length mermaid cut gown that highlighted her figure and complemented her hair, which she wore in an elegant French twist. Her mask was an intricate golden lace design that covered the bridge of her nose nearly to her hairline. At first, she'd thought she'd feel silly wearing it, but once she'd seen herself in her mirror, she'd felt elegant and mysterious.

"Thank you, Rick. You look quite handsome yourself."

His cheeks turned an adorable pink, which only added to his overall appeal.

Reaching out a hand, he asked, "Would you like to dance?"

Christine hesitated, glancing around, a part of her hoping Erik would emerge from the crowd to sweep her away. He didn't, which shouldn't have disappointed her as much as it did. Plastering on a smile, she took Rick's offered hand.

"I'd love to."

He escorted her to the raised dance floor that stood adjacent to the stage on which the band played. The floor was about half-occupied with other couples, so there was plenty of room for Christine and Rick. He pulled her into his arms, his right hand resting in the middle of her back, his left hand taking hold of hers. They didn't press their bodies together, maintaining a comfortable distance as they began to sway and step to the music.

"This is quite the party," Rick said, gazing at their surroundings.

"Mrs. Giry outdid herself," Christine agreed. She didn't look around, though. She didn't want to appear to be searching for someone.

"Didn't you help?" Rick returned his full attention to her with a puzzled frown.

She smiled and shrugged. "I only assisted Mrs. Giry. It's not like I did any of the actual heavy lifting organizing things."

Rick mirrored her grin, and it was swoon-worthy.

"Still, you had a hand in making the night happen. Plus, none of this would be happening at all if Roux hadn't wanted to put you in the album."

Just the mention of his name got her heart racing. She ducked her head so Rick couldn't see her blush.

"That's not true." Humble words she knew were a lie. Erik hadn't made his true intentions behind the album a secret. It had been for her. He'd broken his five-year music drought so she could have a chance at pursuing her dreams.

Guilt slammed into her. He'd done so much for her, and how was she going to repay him?

With an ultimatum.

Rick tsked. "Of course it is, and so what? You're amazing, Christine. The moment I heard you sing, I understood Roux's obsession."

Something in his tone had her glancing up at him. She gasped when she saw the heat in his eyes he didn't bother to hide. He still wanted her. Her heart jumped as a small part of her responded to his blatant desire. It was nowhere near as strong a pull as with Erik, but it was there nonetheless. She knew if she just pushed up onto her toes and let her lips brush his, he would be hers. No questions asked. No secrets. No darkness.

No distance.

They stared at each other for several tense moments. Christine felt paralyzed, unable to break away, but unwilling to move into him. To fall into Rick's security and warmth would close and lock the door to any hope of a future with Erik, yet she couldn't deny the temptation. It would be so easy...so safe...

"Mind if I cut in?"

A burst of heat exploded in her stomach and she lost her breath at the sound of Erik's baritone. The trance between her and Rick was shattered, and she was horrified with herself for what she had almost done. Their hands dropped from each other, and she took a step back.

Turning her head, she locked with Erik's penetrating blue gaze. He stood within reaching distance, his hands clasped behind his back as he observed them with a lazy aloofness that was in stark contrast with the burning in his eyes. It was clear he was furious, but she couldn't make herself care. He was so beautiful, she was mesmerized. He wore all black, from suit, to shirt, to tie, and a black mask that covered his whole face save his mouth and chin. His hair was slicked back, and he towered over everyone around him, including Rick.

"Is that you, Roux?" Rick asked, though his typical grin was not as bright.

Erik tilted his chin in answer, but kept his gaze locked on Christine.

"You look stunning, Ms. Davidson."

She gulped, her emotions running wild. Excitement, awe, lust, love, fear...there was never a clear winner with this man.

"Thank you, Mr. Roux."

He offered her his hand. "Dance with me."

It wasn't a request.

She turned to Rick. "I'm sorry, please excuse us."

He looked like he wanted to protest, but wisely remained silent. With a nod, he turned and left the dance floor.

Christine focused back on Erik. Fighting to catch the breath he'd stolen, she slipped her hand into his. He pulled her into his arms, pressing her tight against him. There was no comfortable distance for them. The spicy scent of his cologne tickled her nose, and she fought not to rest her head against his chest.

"I didn't think you'd come," she whispered, keeping her eyes on his Adam's apple.

"It's my party." His tone was gruff, as if he were annoyed. "I have a right to be at my own party."

She dared to peek up at him, but he was staring over her head. "I didn't mean it that way and you know it."

"Maybe." His nostrils flared with his agitated breath. "What were you and Chagny about to do before I came along?"

Dropping her gaze, she debated whether to tell him the truth, ultimately deciding against it. If he was allowed secrets, so was she.

"I don't know what you're talking about. We were just dancing."

"Like hell," he snarled at her ear. "He had you naked in his mind, and you were gazing at him like he was some kind of goddamn fairy tale prince. Is that what you want, angel? A fairy tale? Because if so, you won't get that from me."

Anger sparked and she glared up at him. "Oh, I'm very aware of that, *Mr. Roux*. You're about as far from Prince Charming as can be, and I'm the foolish girl who wants you anyway."

His grip on her tightened and he lowered his face until they were a breath apart. "Why? Why do you want me?" There was a desperate edge to his question, as if he genuinely couldn't understand. His insecurity and confusion were like knifes to her heart, but she was afraid to answer him. She was afraid to utter out loud the words she had only just begun to believe herself.

"What do you want from me, Erik?" she murmured instead.

Dropping his forehead to hers, he closed his eyes.

"I don't know how to answer that."

She opened her mouth to ask him why, but then let it close without a word. What was the point if he wouldn't answer? Instead, she let the silence between them stretch as she relaxed into his warmth. There would be another time to speak. To face the hurt and grief that was sure to come. But it wasn't now. Now, she would just let him dance with her.

"Well isn't this the sweetest sight?"

Erik and Christine both froze as Carla's condescending tone ripped through their quiet truce. Peeking over Erik's shoulder, Christine found Carla arm-in-arm with Phillip Chagny. She wore a figure hugging scarlet gown with a plunging neckline. Her black beaded mask had a plum of feathers rising above her right eye like a bird, and her long dark hair was piled on top of her head in an elaborate design that must have taken hours to put together. Phillip was dressed similarly to his brother, in a black suit and tie, with a white dress shirt and black domino. He was smirking as Carla fluttered a scarlet and black fan in front of her chin.

"What do you want, Carla?" Erik demanded to know without turning around. He shifted his hands to Christine's waist, keeping her in place in front of him. Shielding her again?

Carla pursed her lips together in a dramatic pout. "Why darling, we only wanted to congratulate you on the album. From what we understand, it's already receiving rave reviews, and it only dropped this morning. You must be so relieved. It looks like you and the label will be safe from bankruptcy after all."

Erik's jaw tensed as he curled his hands into fists. Christine grabbed his arm to keep him grounded before he lost his temper and did something he wouldn't be able to take back. His eyes dropped to hers, and he gave the barest nod of his head.

She released a breath she hadn't realized she'd been holding.

With slow, deliberate movements, Erik turned to face Carla and Phillip.

"I want to thank you both for your parts in making the album such a success," he said through gritted teeth. Though his voice was anything but pleasant, the two appeared taken aback by his words. He snagged Christine's hand in his own, squeezing it. "If you'll excuse us, Ms. Davidson and I have something important to discuss."

He didn't wait for either Carla or Phillip to respond, and before Christine could protest, he was leading her away from them and off the dance floor.

She waited until she was sure they were out of earshot before asking, "Erik, where are we going?"

Without looking at her, he replied, "Away. I don't know. Somewhere alone."

The thought of being alone with him in that moment scared her. She didn't know what she might say or do with her thoughts and feelings as jumbled as they were. What if she fell under his spell again, losing all reason at his touch? She couldn't let that happen, not until she'd sorted out everything she needed to say to him.

Digging in her heels, she stopped, and he yanked on her arm before realizing it. He whirled on her with a frown, and she pulled her hand from his grasp.

"What are you doing?"

"I don't want to leave the party yet." The excuse sounded lame, but it was the best she could come up with.

She couldn't read his face as well behind his new mask, but his eyes showed his confusion.

"Why?"

Whatever she had expected his response to be, it wasn't that. She looked around at the spectacular scene surrounding them before turning her furrowed brow back at him.

"Look at this, Erik. Look at everything around you. Why would I want to leave this? I want to be here, among people. I want to laugh, drink, dance, and enjoy myself. That's what tonight is supposed to be about, isn't it?" It wasn't a complete lie, but it was far from the whole truth.

The truth is you're a coward, avoiding a confrontation that terrifies you.

Erik gazed at her through narrowed eyes.

"I see," he said in a low voice. It was a dangerous voice. "You'd rather prance around the garden with these vapid strangers than come with me."

Horrified, Christine checked to see if anyone had overheard him. There was no one close enough, but curious faces began to turn in their direction as their tense conversation was noticed.

"This is not the time or place," she hissed. "If you're so uncomfortable, why don't you go back inside? I'm fine here."

There was no mistaking his growing anger, but he kept the volume of his voice down when he snapped, "If that's what you want, then who am I to argue otherwise?"

Giving her his back, he shouldered his way through the crowd back to the house. Christine watched him go, her heart sinking. Their tenuous connection was beginning to unravel, and she feared it was already too late to save it.

38

Erik

When he reached the glass French doors leading from the terrace into the house, Erik fought not to slam them shut behind him. There was no point in shattering them. Still, he was feeling destructive. He grabbed an empty vase standing on a small table near the doors and slammed it onto the floor. It was cathartic, but did little to calm his temper.

"Wow, what crawled up your butt and died?"

He rolled his eyes as Meg came into his line of sight, picking her way carefully through the mess he'd created. She was a vision in a pink floor-length chiffon and tulle dress with drop sleeves and a V-neck, her golden hair cascading around her shoulders, and her bright eyes framed by a solid silver mask with raised designs along its edges. Behind her stood a beautiful woman in a purple evening gown with sheer lace sleeves and cutouts. Her thick black hair was done up in an artful knot on the side of her head, and she wore a mask that matched Meg's. She appeared much more shocked by his violence than his sister.

"I'm sorry you had to see that," he said to the woman, ignoring Meg.

His little sister released an annoyed huff. "Luckily, I informed Chelsey of your tendency to throw mantrums before she arrived."

Erik gaped, embarrassment slamming into him. "You're Chelsey? Megan's Chelsey?"

The dark haired woman stepped forward. To her credit, it seemed the worst of her shock had worn off. She extended her hand towards Erik.

"That'd be me."

He clasped her palm in his. "This is an unfortunate first meeting. I'm afraid I've offered a terrible first impression of myself."

Chelsey's lips curled into a grin. "Honestly? I've seen worse. I work in television, after all. My days are full of drama kings and queens."

Meg giggled as Erik blushed.

"Well, I am sorry. You've caught me at a bad time."

Meg's expression sobered. "What happened?"

He avoided her gaze, and debated whether he should tell her. Deciding she'd likely find out anyway, he said, "Things between Christine and I are tense."

To say the least. Ever since Carla ruined what should have been a moment of triumph for Christine, their relationship had grown strained. He'd avoided talking about the incident, partly to maintain what male pride he had left, and partly to keep Christine from feeling any amount of pity for him, but he feared his silence on the matter had backfired. She'd started pulling away from him, and despite that being the very thing he'd planned for all along, it tore at him from the inside out.

He'd forced himself down to the party to see her and show her that he was willing to make the effort. Towards what, he wasn't sure, but towards *something*. However, when he'd spotted her on the dance floor with Chagny, looking gorgeous and gazing up at the imbecile like he was her goddamn knight in shining armor, he'd lost it. All thoughts of wooing her throughout the night were forgotten, and the only thing that mattered was getting her away from that asshole and back into his arms.

Meg groaned. "What did you do now?"

"What makes you think it's *my* fault?" It was, of course, but the fact that she assumed without knowing the details pissed him off.

"Is this the same Christine you were telling me about?" Chelsey asked.

Meg nodded, and Chelsey made an O with her mouth as her widened gaze bounced to Erik. What had Meg been telling her?

"Just tell me what happened," Meg ordered.

Though he hated to respond to her highhandedness, he also had no one else to turn to. As he recounted the events leading up to his fight with Christine, the image of her face turned up towards Chagny kept flashing through his mind. She'd been about to kiss him.

His blood simmered with rage, and he was tempted to march back outside, haul her over his shoulder like a caveman, and drag her back to his study for a bruising fuck.

When he had finished, both Meg and Chelsey appeared to be mulling his words over with serious thought.

To his surprise, Chelsey was the first to speak.

"I know it's not really my place, but maybe there's some worth in an outsider's perspective?" She paused, and he nodded at her to continue. "I think Christine's scared. I don't know of what, but from what Meg has told me, your relationship hasn't had that smooth of a ride. You better watch out, man. It sounds like she's planning to bolt."

It felt like someone had sucker punched him in the gut. The mere possibility of Christine leaving him, *really* leaving him, sent him into a panic.

"Erik?" Meg's voice was laced with concern. "Are you okay?"

He realized he was gripping his head in both hands as if sheer brute strength was keeping his skull in place. Feeling how twisted his expression was, he was grateful for his mask, which concealed his hideous reaction.

"Sorry," he said, his voice cracking. "I'm fine."

Chelsey's face was ashen, and her eyes were wide. "I'm sorry I said anything. I shouldn't have. I have a problem keeping my mouth shut sometimes."

Meg placed a gentle hand on her partner's arm. "It's okay, babe. Things are just a little intense right now."

Overwhelmed by his rampaging thoughts, and desperate to escape their looks of pity, Erik hurried past them towards the stairway.

"Where are you going?" Meg asked his retreating back. There was a tinge of fear in her voice that he didn't appreciate.

"I need to think," he growled, not looking back. When he reached the stairs, he took them two at a time to the second floor and stormed towards his rooms.

Reaching his study, he slammed the door shut and pounded a fist against the hard wood.

"Fuck!" he bellowed.

Was Christine going to leave him? Not that he could blame her. It was a miracle she hadn't left already.

His heart twisted, and he felt tears gather in his eyes.

Blinking them away, he shook his head. No. He wouldn't break down. Not yet. Not until he confronted her and asked her straight out.

Not until he heard it from her.

Turning, he walked to the window overlooking the garden, pulling the heavy curtain back to gaze down on the party. It really was a remarkable sight. More than he could have hoped for.

Amelia had outdone herself, but instead of showing his gratitude, he'd fled from the celebration like a coward.

He *was* a coward.

An ugly, selfish coward.

No wonder Christine wanted to leave.

The sound of the door opening barely registered as he spiraled downward into his familiar pit of depression and self-loathing.

"Go away, Meg," he grumbled.

"Mmmm, yes, she would be a bore right now, wouldn't she?"

Erik's whole body tensed with growing rage, and he turned with predatory intent to face Carla.

Her red lips were curled up in a smirk. She'd removed her mask, and her eyes glinted as she moved into the room.

"What the fuck are you doing here?" he growled.

Carla raised her hands as if in surrender. "Easy, darling. I come in peace."

Erik scoffed at the notion.

Gliding towards his bar cart, she picked up his tumbler of bourbon and poured it into two glasses.

"I'm serious," she insisted. "I know we hate each other, but tonight, we should put our petty squabbles aside and celebrate. This album will save us both. Christine might prove the star, but it'll be our combined clout that sells this thing."

He glared at her, but couldn't dispute her words. She was right. His label was saved, and so too was her career, if the initial reviews were any indication of the album's success. He hated admitting it, but none of it would have been possible without her.

She gave him her back as she picked up the drinks, and then turned to bring him one. Gnashing his teeth, he took the bourbon with reluctance.

"However this turns out, we're done," he snapped. "I never want to see you again after tonight, am I clear?"

Rolling her eyes, she raised her glass in an invitation to cheers.

"Whatever you say, darling."

He tapped his drink against hers, and they both drank deeply. The liquid burned in his chest, but it felt good. When he finished, she took his glass from him and returned to the bar cart.

"You know, it's funny," she said as she poured another round.

"What is?" Erik asked. He blinked, feeling off-balance.

"The fact that *now* we're officially over," she continued. "Not five years ago when I walked out on you. Not after any of the times I came back for a pity fuck, and you would shout me out of your house when we were finished. At no point did you ever tell me that you never wanted to see me again."

"What's your point?" He was growing light-headed. *After one drink? Fucking lightweight.*

Carla faced him, but she was only holding one glass.

"My point is that we were never really over until *she* came into the picture. You've been mine all these years, whether you liked it or not." She sauntered towards him just as his vision began to blur.

One drink wouldn't be hitting him this hard.

He started to lose his balance, stumbling backwards into the desk.

"What the hell did you give me?" he snarled, but his words slurred.

Her smile was poison. "I'm not ready to give you up, Erik. You're mine, to do with as I please. To play with when I'm bored, and put back on the shelf when I'm done with you. Do you really think you can pass me over for that stupid slut? Think again. I own you, Erik. Your mind, body, and soul. You can hate me all you want, but you'll never be over me. I'll make sure of it."

"You....bitch..." His knees gave out and he slumped to the floor.

"You're not wrong." She downed her second drink and placed the glass on the desk above him. Reaching down, she cupped his cheek with her hand. "I'm a heartless bitch, and you're an ugly, broken bastard. In some respects, we're perfect for each other."

Her image swam in his eyes, but he could see the cruel red curve of her lips. He thought he heard the door open again, but couldn't turn his head to see who had entered. Carla dropped her hand and stepped back. His vision was going dark, but he heard her speaking to someone. He couldn't make out what they were saying.

He wanted to fight. He wanted to curse her and escape, but he couldn't move. As he lost consciousness, his last thought wasn't of Carla. It was of Christine.

And how much he loved her.

* * *

Christine

Despite her insistence to Erik, all Christine wanted to do was go into the house and hide. The crowd was overwhelming, and she was too heartsick to enjoy the dazzling beauty of the party anymore. She wanted to find Erik and apologize for her behavior. Soothe away the pain that had flashed in his eyes when she'd told him to leave.

She was still too scared to be alone with him, though.

She didn't know what she was going to do. Didn't know what she *should* do. So, she stood in limbo, on the peripheral of the party, not a full participant, but too much of a coward to go and face Erik.

"Christine!"

Glancing up, she spotted Meg hurrying towards her with a dark haired woman following close behind.

Christine smiled. "Oh! Meg, is this Chelsey?"

Meg came to a halt in front of her, and her expression had dread pooling in Christine's stomach. There was panic in her eyes.

"What's going on?"

"Did something happen between Erik and Carla recently?"

Christine furrowed her brows in confusion. "You mean on the dance floor?"

"No, not that." Meg shook her head. "Anything else? Before tonight?"

The memory of Carla's cruel words in the studio sliced through Christine's mind like a razor blade.

"Why do you ask? What's going on?"

Meg shot a look towards her girlfriend before returning her gaze to Christine. "We were just in the house talking to Erik. He was upset, and went up to his rooms, so we came out to the party. On our way out, we saw Carla and Phillip Chagny talking behind a hedge, away from everyone else. I didn't like the looks of them, so I snuck up to eavesdrop, and I heard Chagny say something about Erik wanting you, and then Carla snapped that she'd remind Erik of his place. Then she went into the house, and Chagny followed her. Do you know what they were talking about?"

Christine couldn't respond. Her heart began to race, and she picked up her skirts to run towards the house. Meg called after her, but she ignored her. She had to find Erik. Had to make sure Carla hadn't gotten to him. She couldn't explain the sense of terror she felt, but that woman could twist him and break him in ways no one else could. A voice in the back of her head was screaming at her that something was wrong.

Erik needed her.

She didn't stop running when she reached the French doors leading into the house, hardly taking notice of the broken pieces of porcelain scattered across the marble floor. Making her way towards the staircase, she hurried to the second floor and then kicked off her shoes to sprint down the hallway towards Erik's rooms. When she reached the door to his study, she didn't stop to knock. Flying into the room, she paused long enough to realize it was empty. Her feet swallowed up the distance to his bedroom door, which she found cracked. There were sounds coming from beyond it.

Breathless sounds.

Feminine sounds.

Her terror shifted. She went from fearing for Erik's wellbeing, to fearing something impossible.

Pushing the door open, Christine stepped inside and froze at the scene awaiting her.

Erik lay on his bed, but she couldn't see him from the waist up. She couldn't see him, because Carla's body blocked him from sight. The diva's dark hair was loose around her shoulders, and she sat straddling Erik, naked but for a lacy red thong. She was bent over him, moaning.

Christine's heart stopped and she let out a small cry.

Carla sat up and looked over her shoulder, her eyes widening even as her mouth smirked.

"Oh, no. Christine." Her voice was tainted by a cruel chuckle. "We can explain."

Erik shifted under her, and Christine heard him mumble, "Hm-mmm....what? What's going on?" He sounded groggy, and was slurring. Was he drunk? That possibility did nothing to stop the world from tipping on its axis.

He moved, as if he were trying to sit up, but Carla put her weight on him to hold him down.

"Darling, not so fast. Don't forget your mask."

Christine hadn't thought the situation could get any worse. She'd been wrong. Carla's words felt like the hammer on the final nail of the coffin containing her heart.

Erik was in bed with Carla.

Carla was naked on top of Erik.

Erik wasn't wearing his mask.

Carla could see his face.

Christine never had.

Erik pushed himself up, mask in place, and stared at Christine over Carla's shoulder.

"Christine?" He spoke as if he didn't recognize her.

Tears were running down her cheeks, and it occurred to her that her feet should be running as well. Running away from whatever nightmare this was. She turned without a word, a choked sob ripping from her throat.

"Christine!" Erik's bellow followed her into the hall, but she didn't stop. She didn't look back. She did what she should have done the first time she'd stepped into his office and realized he posed a danger to her fragile heart.

She fled.

39

Erik

It felt like a fog was lifting from his mind, Christine's look of horror cutting through the haze that had settled over him and sobering him.

As the room came back into focus, he realized Carla was on his lap, her naked breasts pressed against his bare chest.

She was kissing his neck, moaning like a porn star.

Disgust made his stomach churn.

"What the hell is this?" he roared, grabbing her by the waist and throwing her off him.

Landing on the bed next to him, instead of feigning indignation as he expected, she stretched her arms above her head and spread her legs in invitation. Not long ago, he would have accepted it. As much as he hated her, he'd always fallen back into her arms when she allowed it, giving in to a desire that made him want to scorch his body clean from the inside out. Perhaps he had been grateful all these years because she had seen his face, yet would still give him access to her body. He'd been pathetic, believing she was all he deserved.

Yet now, he felt nothing as he stared down at her.

No desire.

No gratitude.

He felt nothing for her. Her hold on him was broken, because someone else had come into his life, bringing light and love in her wake.

Christine.

His heart stopped when the last of his confusion cleared and he realized why she had looked so horrified. She'd walked in and found him on his bed, Carla on top of him.

Of course she'd believed he'd done the unthinkable.

Shoving from the bed, he stumbled as dizziness hit him.

Rounding on Carla, he demanded, "What did you do? Roofie me?"

Propping herself up on her elbows, she rolled her eyes. "What am I, a frat boy? A roofie wouldn't wear off this fast. I gave you a little something special that some friends of mine concocted for me. It's just something to make you relax."

"Relax and pass out so you can assault me? Set me up in front of Christine?" His shirt was gaping open, and his pants were undone. He began buttoning himself up, his mind still struggling to catch up to the situation.

Carla shrugged. "It was just a bit of fun, no need for such dramatics. And besides, how was I supposed to know the nosey bitch would come up here?"

A spike of anger hit him at her disrespect towards Christine. To his surprise, however, he realized that was the only true anger he felt towards her. He should be enraged and tempted to violence by her actions, but he wasn't. All he felt towards her was pity. He didn't know what had driven her to this, and wasn't sure how she'd managed to pull it off, but there was a desperation to her actions that hinted at a darkness in her she wasn't able to overcome. Maybe that was why he had let himself linger with her for so long. Her darkness had called to his.

Now, his darkness didn't have quite the same hold on him as it used to. It was still there, lurking at the back of his mind, but at some point, he'd stopped fearing it. He'd stopped believing it could control him, and at the same time, stopped believing Carla was what he deserved.

Turning from her, he made his way to the door.

"Where are you going?" she demanded to know.

"After Christine."

He heard her frantic movements, but didn't look back.

"Do you really think she'll still want you after this?"

Pausing at the threshold to the study, he at last glanced back at her. She was kneeling on the mattress, gripping the footboard, her eyes swirling with maniacal anxiety. It was clear she understood that he was walking away from her for good, just as it was clear she wasn't willing to let him go.

"Even if she doesn't, she deserves an explanation."

"You'd really leave *me* for her? I'm the only woman who has seen your face and am still willing to fuck you. I'm the only woman capable of swallowing my disgust to keep you from rotting away, a lonely ghost in this dark, empty house. You'd throw me away after everything I've done for you?"

Before, her words would have jerked at him like a leash, bringing him obediently back to her with his tail between his legs. Now, he heard them for what they were. Emotional manipulation to keep her victim in check.

He was no one's victim. Not anymore.

"Whether Christine accepts me or not is her choice, but I've made mine. And it's not you, Carla. Never again."

Her shriek of rage followed him as he made his way to the hall. Shutting the study door behind him, he blocked her noise, and her, from his mind. A part of him felt freer, as if a weight he hadn't realized rested on his shoulders had been lifted.

Still, fear had a chokehold on him. His words to Carla had been brave, but he didn't truly believe them. If he lost Christine, he didn't know how he would recover.

Carla had entrapped his soul, chaining him to her through pain and loneliness.

Christine had enchanted his heart, entwining them together with passion and love.

He'd freed himself from Carla, and felt lighter for it.

If Christine left him, she'd take his heart with her, which was right-fully hers. He'd be a shell of himself, and he didn't know if he'd be able to recover.

Yet, as much as that prospect terrified him, returning to his former life wasn't an option either. He knew what it was to exist in the light, and he would never be able to find comfort in the darkness again.

He needed Christine. Wanted her fixed into every part of his life.

As he hurried down the hallway in search of her, he prayed she still wanted that as well.

* * *

Christine

No matter how hard she tried, Christine couldn't get the image of Carla and Erik from her mind. She sat on her bed, her dress discarded in a pile on the floor, staring at the wall. Her body felt numb. She couldn't even work up tears to cry. The scene just continued to repeat over and over in her head.

Carla on top of Erik.

Carla naked on top of Erik.

Carla naked on top of Erik, who hadn't been wearing his mask.

The strange part was, that's what hurt the most.

Erik had once trusted Carla enough to show her his face. Though the gesture had been a disaster, with Carla leaving him in disgust, the fact remained that she knew what he looked like. Of all people, that manipulative, cruel witch had been allowed past Erik's most fortified defenses and seen him at his most vulnerable. She hadn't deserved it, and had thrown his trust aside like a piece of trash instead of cherish-ing it like the gift it was. Yet that didn't change the fact that Carla had *seen* him, and Christine hadn't.

Someone pounding on her door snapped her from her daze. Her heart sped up, and she didn't speak, too afraid of what she might say.

"Christine, I know you're in there. Please, we need to talk." Despite the turmoil he had thrown her in, the sound of Erik's voice still made her shiver. Balling her hands into fists, she took a deep breath before responding.

"I don't want to talk right now, Erik."

"I just need to explain what you saw." The doorknob jiggled, but she'd locked herself in the room. She heard his growl of frustration, but he didn't attempt to force his way in.

Pushing from the bed, she moved to the door, pressing her hands against the cool wood as she considered what to do.

"What I saw was you in bed with Carla, practically naked." She kept her tone even. The last thing she wanted was to fly into hysterics and scream at him. She wanted to process everything. To think.

"It's not what it looked like." He didn't sound frantic or desperate, but he did sound nervous. Hesitant. Fearful. Though it was clear he was trying to hide it. "Carla drugged me. She set it up so that you'd walk in on us like that. I'm not sure how she did it, but you have to know I would never..."

"I believe you," she cut him off. It was the truth. She believed him, despite how outlandish the explanation was. It was not difficult to believe that Carla would stoop to such tactics, though she didn't understand why. Christine was also confident Erik would never hurt her like that. None of that was what really mattered, though.

"You do?" He sounded confused.

She nodded before remembering he couldn't see her. "Yes, I do."

"Oh, well, then..."

"If I wasn't in the picture, would you have slept with her?"

Silence fraught with tension stretched between them before he admitted, "Yes."

"And have you slept with her since she left you five years ago?"

More silence. "Yes," he gritted.

Christine squeezed her eyes shut as tears threatened to fall. It shouldn't matter. He'd had a life before her, and had every right to be with whoever he wanted. Even someone as vile as Carla.

But it hurt anyway. It hurt because he'd kept it from her. He'd let that woman back into his home, into his *music*, even with Christine there, and she'd been ignorant of what exactly that'd meant. She'd thought he was letting her into his heart, never knowing that Carla still had her bloody claws embedded in it.

"She's seen your face." It came out as a broken whisper, and with it the tears she hadn't been able to cry earlier.

"Christine, I'm sorry." His deep voice was choked, and she wondered if he was crying too. "Carla's not an issue anymore. I've cut her out of my life for good."

That didn't mean he trusted Christine. He'd cut Carla out, but that didn't mean he'd let Christine in. Pressing her forehead against her door, she closed her eyes in resignation.

She couldn't do this anymore.

"Please go away, Erik."

"Christine..."

"I need time. I need to think."

"About what?"

Releasing a sigh, she murmured, "Everything."

He was quiet again. She waited, wondering if he would stay or go, not sure which option she wanted herself.

At last, his voice floated through the door, sad but resolute. "I'll go, for now. Take the time and space you need, but understand that I'm not giving you up so easily. Whatever it takes, Christine, I will make this right."

There's only one thing you can really do, but I doubt it's even crossed your mind.

She didn't respond, and after several seconds, she heard him leave. Staying by her door, listening to his fading footsteps, she felt as if her heart went with him. The problem was, she didn't know if he really deserved it.

40

Christine

There was a chill in the air. The signal that summer was drawing to a close.

Christine pulled the shawl she'd wrapped around herself tighter as she stared at the garden's fountain. The sun beamed down on her. She'd been awake to see it first rise, its light cutting through the lingering gray remnants of night.

She hadn't slept. Had instead sat on her bed thinking for hours before growing claustrophobic and sick of staring at the same four walls of her room. She'd crept from the house to escape to the open quiet of the garden and watch the sun come up.

As she gazed at the water running from the stone vase to the gurgling pool below, surrounded by the remains of what was supposed to have been a celebration, Christine found herself at a loss. She was hopelessly in love with Erik, but she couldn't pretend it wasn't painful. It shouldn't be so hard to love someone. There shouldn't be so much hurt.

Her life was at a standstill, and she didn't know how to move it forward.

Stay and face the reality that Erik may never trust her enough to truly be with her?

Or leave, and risk never feeling what she felt for him with anyone else?

How could she possibly make a choice with two such impossible options?

"What are you doing out here?"

Letting out a yelp of surprise, Christine turned to find Mrs. Giry standing on the gravel path watching her. As ever, her black pantsuit was immaculate, her hair pulled back from her face. Her gaze, however, was weary, and the lines around her eyes and mouth more stark.

For the first time, Christine realized how much stress the woman must be under. How much pain she must experience, seeing the man she raised from childhood in such perpetual torment. Here was a woman who had dedicated her life to Erik.

Did she regret it?

"I just needed some fresh air."

Mrs. Giry nodded, as if in understanding.

"May I sit?"

Surprised, Christine scooted across the cold stone bench to make room for the older woman. Mrs. Giry sat, her back ramrod straight, her long fingers smoothing nonexistent wrinkles from her pants.

Clutching her hands in her lap, Christine waited, at a loss as to what the housekeeper wanted.

After what stretched into a painful silence, the woman spoke. "You and I have never really gotten along, have we?"

Mouth dropping open in shock, Christine struggled to find words to respond. Mrs. Giry spared her.

"It's my fault, I know. I've been rather cold to you since you started working here. It was unfair of me, but I didn't trust you."

I picked up on that easily enough. Shaking away the snarky thought, Christine managed to speak at last. "Why?"

One word, but that was all she needed.

Mrs. Giry's chest rose and fell with her deep breath, and it was as if the ice wall she'd put up between them crumbled with that rush of air.

"You were young, beautiful, brilliant, and vastly overqualified for your position. I worried that you had ulterior motives for working here. Erik may be a recluse, but he is still an icon in the music world. He's also rich and lonely, and I feared you planned to take advantage of him. I saw the wreckage Carla left behind when she abandoned him, and I wasn't willing to let another woman come into his life and hurt him."

Though the assumptions Mrs. Giry had made were insulting to say the least, Christine couldn't blame her for them. She hadn't been there, but she had a good idea of the mess Carla had created. The consequences of the heartbreak she'd inflicted on Erik continued to bleed into the present, creating more pain every day it lingered. She didn't want to think about the state Erik must have been in at the time. The thought of him so broken was too much for her to bear. She didn't blame Mrs. Giry. A small part of her even admired the woman for her protectiveness.

"Why are you telling me this?" she asked, staring down at her lap.

Mrs. Giry's hands were clenched into fists on her thighs. "I want to help you understand some things better so that you can make a sound decision."

Christine whipped her head up and stared at the woman.

The housekeeper gave a small nod. "I know you're considering walking away from here, from *him*. I don't blame you, and I won't hold it against you if you do. Unlike Carla, you wouldn't be doing it out of malice or to hurt him. You'd be doing it because he's given you no better choice."

Dropping her gaze, Christine admitted, "I don't want to leave him, but I can't waste my life waiting for him to trust me."

"It's difficult for Erik to let people in." Mrs. Giry's tone wasn't accusatory, and she didn't seem like she was making excuses. She was just stating a fact. "With good reason, of course. Almost any time he's tried to, he's ended up hurt. You're right, though. You can't waste your life waiting for him. If he's not willing to open himself to you, that's not your fault."

Christine was taken aback, not only by Mrs. Giry's sudden frankness, but by her understanding. She'd expected the woman to come to

Erik's defense, to try and convince Christine to stay. Instead, she was affirming Christine's choice, whatever it ended up being.

"What if I never feel this way about anyone else?" She voiced her selfish fear, desperate for some kind of reassurance.

Mrs. Giry cast her a look that was layered with sadness.

"That's a very real possibility. Great loves don't happen too often, which is what makes them great. That doesn't mean you only get one, but you're never guaranteed even that." Staring ahead, the housekeeper paused, seeming to consider her next words with great care. "I've had two great loves in my life. Meg, and my husband."

Christine stilled. She'd never heard Mrs. Giry speak of her husband. Of course, she'd assumed the woman had been married, but the fact hadn't been confirmed until now. Not wanting to deter her from speaking, Christine barely allowed herself to breathe, afraid she might spook Mrs. Giry back into silence.

"My husband, Victor, was not Meg's father. He died when I was twenty-eight, in a car accident outside of Paris. I broke both my legs in that accident, and lost the love of my life and my career in one blow."

A gasp slipped past Christine's lips. She'd suspected an injury had ended Mrs. Giry's dancing career, but she'd never imagined the woman had experienced something so tragic.

"What did you do after that?"

With a small, sad smile, Mrs. Giry said, "I returned to New York and was able to secure a position as an instructor at the American School of Ballet, where I'd studied. About five years later, I found Erik in an alley near Lincoln Center. He was a runaway, just a boy. Scared, alone, and desperate to hide himself from the world. I took him in and tried to raise him as my own, but he maintained a strict distance between us. Even then, he had scars that ran deeper than his skin. He was brilliant, though. A prodigy. I did whatever I could to make sure he received the best training possible. His music became his escape, and I would lose him to it for hours at a time. He never made any friends...never tried to. The only person I ever saw him grow attached to was Meg. Three years after I found him, I gave birth to her, the result of a drunken one-night stand with a Naval Officer whose name I can't remember. Erik built this life for us...for her, so she could have every advantage. He built this home so he could create in peace, and I stayed here with him."

"As his *housekeeper*?"

Mrs. Giry chuckled. "He'd have let me stay here for nothing, but I insisted on working for him. He needed help running his label and his home, and I wanted to be as much a part of his life as I could. As his housekeeper, I can stay close to him without smothering him. It's an arrangement that works well for us."

Frozen in place, Christine tried to process everything the woman was telling her. There was so much more pain in Mrs. Giry's past than she could have imagined. Yet, amidst that pain, she had still found room in her heart for a lost little boy overwhelmed by darkness who could never really love her the way she deserved to be loved. Christine gazed at the woman, and it was as if she were seeing her for the first time. No longer did she seem cold and aloof. Instead, she was world-weary and cautious, which made her fiercely protective and loyal to her children.

She was a woman to be admired, and Christine found herself in awe of her.

"Did you ever fall in love again?" she asked. *Did the world ever seem right again?*

Mrs. Giry shook her head. "No, nothing ever came close to Victor."

"If you could go back and change things, would you?"

Meeting Christine's gaze, Mrs. Giry answered without hesitation. "No. I wouldn't."

Bewildered, Christine shook her head, as if she hadn't heard correctly and needed to clear her ears. "What? You're saying if you had the chance to have Victor back, you wouldn't take it?"

Now Mrs. Giry's smile was indulgent, as if Christine were a child asking something simple.

"I loved Victor with everything I thought I had, and I miss him every day. If he hadn't died, though, I'd never have returned to New York. I'd never have found Erik, or had Meg, and I wouldn't give either of them up for anything. Not even him."

Christine felt tears gather in her eyes.

"What does this have to do with me?" she murmured.

Placing a gentle hand on Christine's shoulder, Mrs. Giry said, "Even if Erik is the great love of your life, your life won't end without him. You'll miss him, but you'll move on."

Swallowing, Christine asked, "So, you think I should leave?"

Mrs. Giry shook her head. "Not at all."

Christine frowned, confused. "Then what should I do?"

"I'm telling you all this because if you choose to stay with him, I don't want you to do so out of fear. If you leave, it will hurt, but it won't kill either of you. Choose to stay because you *want* to, because you want to be with him, no matter what."

Meeting the older woman's gaze, Christine asked the question that had been brewing in her mind since their conversation had begun.

"What made you change your mind about me?"

Offering her a full genuine smile for the first time since Christine had moved into the house, Mrs. Giry cupped her cheek and answered, "He's different with you. More alive and engaged with people than I've ever seen him, but that's not what convinced me you were good for him. It was when you brought his music back to life. When Carla left, he stopped sharing it with the world. He still created it, still spent hours composing and playing, but he did so in isolation. Until you. When I heard you sing his song, I knew you weren't after his wealth or prestige. You poured your soul into his lyrics, and I could see your heart as clear as day."

With a soft pat of her hand against Christine's face, Mrs. Giry stood and began to walk back to the house. Christine stared after her, overwhelmed by everything the woman had shared.

"Thank you!" she called out before Mrs. Giry was out of earshot.

The housekeeper turned and nodded her chin without a word, and then disappeared back into the home she had help to create and nurture for the children who were her world.

41

Christine

That evening, Christine made her way to Erik's rooms.

She stared at the closed doors for long minutes as she worked up the courage to knock. Since her talk with Mrs. Giry that morning, she'd spent the day thinking. Working through her hurt, frustration, and exhaustion, she'd still managed to come up with no definitive answer.

But she was ready to talk with him, and to give the tiny spark of hope that still existed in her heart one last chance to take flame. That was it, though. If they couldn't decide to move forward together, she would leave.

She would move on with her life.

Taking a deep breath, she raised her hand and rapped her knuckles against the door.

There was no sound from the room beyond, which was why Christine was so startled when the door swung open. She hadn't heard him approach, yet there he stood, towering over her in his favorite ensemble of all-black, with mussed hair and wild eyes. His gaze was guarded, but she was able to catch the glint of relief in their blue depths.

He swallowed as if he were nervous, his Adam's apple bobbing.

"I was hoping I'd see you today."

She tried to smile, to reassure him that she came in peace, but she was so nervous, it felt more like a grimace.

"We need to talk," she said, giving up on the smile.

He nodded, his expression revealing nothing of his thoughts. Stepping aside, he let her in and closed the door behind her. Coming to a stop in the middle of the room, she faced him. He stood a safe distance away, out of arm's reach, with his hands in his pockets. The air between them crackled with tension, questions, and as always, lust, though it was admittedly diluted in this instance. Face-to-face with him, Christine struggled to begin the speech she had prepared in her head most of the afternoon.

"I'm sorry I didn't tell you about Carla."

Air whooshed from her nostrils, her speech forgotten. She hadn't expected him to rip the band-aid off right away.

"I'm not mad that you were with her," she replied.

"I know."

"I was...*am* mad that you never told me how ingrained into your life she was."

"I know."

Silence stretched between them. Awkward. Formal. Pregnant with the explanations and hopes they couldn't quite put into words.

"I'm not here about Carla," she admitted at last.

He appeared surprised, but he kept his expression in check, careful not to give too much away. Which, ironically, was part of the problem between them.

"What are you here for, then?" There was no confusion in his tone. He had to know, or at least suspect, her real reason for coming to him.

This was her last stand.

They would either move forward together from this point onward, or they would end.

And she would leave.

"I'm trying to figure out if this is worth fighting for."

In an instant, his whole demeanor changed. He went from guarded and wary, to cynical and smirking. Moving towards his bar cart, he poured himself a drink.

"You're here with an ultimatum." He ambled behind her towards his desk, leaning against its front like he didn't have a care in the world. She'd expected he'd throw up all his defenses as soon as he realized her intentions.

It didn't mean his behavior wasn't aggravating.

Folding her arms, she said, "I'm here hoping there's a future for us in which my needs can be met as much as yours."

He scoffed. "Didn't anyone ever teach you not to be with a man you wanted to fix? People don't change, Christine, and you can't force them to."

"I don't want you to change."

"Don't you?" Placing his glass on top of his desk, he folded his arms, mirroring her.

She shook her head, frustration prickling along her spine. "No, I don't. I just want to know you."

Christine had anticipated a fight. He wasn't going to suddenly drop his walls because she asked nicely.

What she hadn't expected was his callousness.

He rolled his goddamn eyes at her.

"You know me well enough."

That was it. Everyone had a breaking point, and with just a few thoughtless words, he'd pushed her to hers. She dropped her arms, bawling her hands at her sides as her anger inflamed and engulfed her.

"I can't do this anymore!" she cried.

"Do what?" he snarled, and it sounded like a taunt.

Christine waved her hand in the empty air between them. "This. Whatever *this* is. I can't do it. All we have is sex and music, and it's not enough for me."

He glared at her. "It's all I can give. All I ever promised you." His tone was so cold, Christine shivered.

She blinked back sudden tears as the last of her hope vanished.

"It's not enough," she insisted with a whisper.

Pushing away from his desk, he stood over her. She had to crane her neck back to meet his hard gaze. "Why?"

Because I love you. She couldn't say the words out loud, though. Couldn't admit to him how weak he made her. How desperate and stupid. She'd known falling in love with him would only end in heartbreak, and she knew he was about to do it. He wouldn't abandon his darkness for her.

She wasn't enough.

The realization left her gutted.

"It doesn't matter anymore," she murmured, dropping her eyes from his.

"Christine..." His voice went soft, confused. Vulnerable. Leaving him would shatter her, but as Mrs. Giry had said, she'd survive. She was too afraid to think of what it would do to him.

It's not my responsibility, she told herself. *There's nothing I can do if he won't let me in.*

Taking a deep, fortifying breath, she raised her face back up to his. He was staring down at her, a question in his beautiful blue gaze.

"I'm leaving," she announced in a strong voice.

He appeared startled. "What? Why?"

"I told you why." She turned from him and began walking to the door, refusing to glance back.

"Christine, wait!"

She didn't stop. Didn't reply. She was scared her resolve would crumble if she said another word to him. Her tears began to slide down her face, but she didn't wipe them away.

Let them fall, she thought. *Maybe they'll wash away this searing pain.*

This was for the best. It was what she had to do. She refused to waste away waiting for him, praying and hoping he would trust her enough to let her into his heart.

Just as she reached the door, she felt his hand wrap around her upper arm. She kept her gaze focused on the door handle.

"Let me go, Erik."

"Never." He yanked her towards him. Christine yelped in surprise as she was pulled back around, and slammed into his hard torso.

Warmth coursed through her at the contact, but anger and frustration flared up to banish it away. Curling her hands into fists, she beat them against his chest.

"Why are you doing this to me?" she sobbed. "Why can't you just let me leave? Let me escape this agony?"

He gripped her wrists, holding her arms against him so she couldn't hit him anymore. That only made her angrier.

"I can't let you go," he growled.

"You can't keep me here!"

"What do I have to do to make you stay?" His voice rose with his desperation.

She tried to pull herself from his grasp, but his hold on her was firm.

"You asshole!"

"Tell me what to do, Christine!"

With a cry of frustration, she stopped struggling and slumped against him, letting her forehead fall on his shoulder.

"Trust me," she answered in a soft voice. "Let me in. Show me there's hope for something more between us. I just...I can't..." She buried her face into his shirt and wept.

Erik wrapped his arms around her and held her while she cried. She didn't want his comfort, and yet couldn't bring herself to pull away from him. The last thing she needed from him was false hope, and holding her while she mourned their doomed relationship was not a grand enough gesture to prove to her that he was willing to put his faith in her.

"I do trust you," he said once her tears had subsided.

Christine sighed against him. "No you don't, and you don't have to. I don't want to force you to feel something you don't. I just can't pretend I'm okay with how things are. It's too hard."

"I don't want you to go."

"I can't stay."

"How do I prove to you that I want you?"

She closed her eyes as hurt swept through her. At length, she made herself lean back so she could look up at him.

"I don't doubt that you *want* me. You make that much obvious, at least."

He shook his head. "Then I don't understand."

Christine couldn't help the sad smile that tilted her lips up. Slowly, she reached up and cupped his uncovered cheek.

"I know you don't. That's part of the problem, but I can't spend my life trying to make you understand, hoping you'll want more of me." She pushed away from him, and he let her go. Hugging herself as she backed away, she fought not to return to his arms. Every step she took away from him felt like walking knee-deep through sand.

"Christine, no..."

"I have too."

Anxiety and fear filled his eyes, and she felt like she'd been punched in the gut. He lunged at her, dropping to his knees in front of her. Startled, she stopped moving. Erik wrapped his arms around her and pressed his face against her belly.

"Don't leave me," he begged.

She wanted to scream. He was making this harder than it needed to be.

"Erik, don't do this." Yet she found herself stroking her fingers through his dark hair, unwilling to back away from him again.

He gazed up at her.

"I can prove that I trust you. That there's hope."

"Erik..."

He silenced her by grabbing her hand from the top of his head and moving it down to his mask.

"Take it off."

Christine's mouth dropped open in shock. "What? What are you doing? I can't..."

He pressed his face into her palm. "Do it."

This was it. The grand gesture she'd been wanting, but guilt slammed into her as her fingers slid across the cool covering. This was his protection. His barrier from the world. The fact that he was willing to shed it for her floored her, but she didn't want to cause him pain.

She knew removing the mask would be agony for him.

"I can't," she murmured.

He laid his hand over hers, pressing her fingers down so that they curled around the mask's edges.

"You wanted proof," he growled. "This is it. Take it."

She let out a startled shout when he didn't wait for her to move her hand, but forced her to grip the mask and tore it away himself.

42

Christine

Christine's eyes widened at the sight of his ravaged face. His skin was puckered in places, but sunken in others, molding too tightly to the bones beneath. The eye socket was set deeper than his other one. He looked like someone had taken a clay mask, and having molded one side to near perfection, crumbled the other with their fingertips.

The sight was a shock to her system, and she let out a gasp that made him flinch.

"Oh, my God, Erik I'm so sorry..."

He shook his head, but wouldn't meet her eyes. "No. It's okay. I know it's...difficult to look at."

Christine knew she'd reacted badly. He was drawing in on himself again, regretting his decision to show her this. Panicked, she dropped to her knees so they were eye-level and took his face in both her hands.

"No, stop. I'm sorry," she insisted, holding him so that he had no choice but to meet her gaze. "It took me by surprise. I don't know what I was expecting, but..." She trailed off, unsure what to say next. Turning her eyes to the disfigured half of his face, she studied it. At first, it was hard to look at and not show in her expression how troubling she found it, but she kept her eyes locked there. She knew part of the issue was that the sight of him was still fresh. Still startling.

It's like immersion therapy, she thought. *Get used to the sight, and it won't be so bad.*

Erik appeared to pick up on the thoughts in her head.

Grabbing the wrist of her hand holding the smooth side of his face, he pulled it away.

"You don't have to do this."

Blinking, she met his hooded stare. Despite his guarded look, his blue eyes were the same as they'd always been. Enchanting, intelligent, captivating. There was a defeated gleam in them, however, that worried her. Did he still think she'd abandon him just like everyone else he'd made himself this raw to?

Tenderness filled her, and her heart ached for him. He looked so lonely. So desolate. There was no hope left in him that anyone would accept him. Even though he'd opened himself to her, revealed the most vulnerable part of him to her, he'd done so expecting she would leave him anyway.

Yet he'd done it, knowing it was the only chance he had of getting her to stay.

Tears welled in Christine's eyes as love for the man before her overwhelmed her body and soul.

He saw her tears, and squeezed his own eyes shut. "Please don't cry. I know it's terrible, but..."

She sighed, though she understood where his misunderstanding came from. Knowing words wouldn't be enough for him, just as they hadn't been for her, she didn't bother to say anything to dissuade his thinking.

Instead, she leaned in towards him and kissed his wasted cheek.

Erik froze, his eyes popping open as she laid another kiss at the corner of his sunken eye socket. He gasped when she moved her lips to his nose, and then down to dab her tongue along his jawline.

"What...what are you doing?" His voice sounded hollow with disbelief.

She sat back so they could meet eyes once more.

"I'm showing you how much I want you." Before he could reply, she pressed her lips against his. He was too overcome by shock to reciprocate, but she didn't let that stop her. She licked the seam of his lips, planted kisses at the corners of his mouth, and stroked her thumb along the puckered skin of his cheek. He grabbed her upper arms, squeezing too hard, but she didn't try to pull away from him.

"Erik," she whispered against his lips, "you're hurting me."

His hands released her in an instant.

Shame mixed with bafflement colored his expression.

"I'm...I'm sorry, Christine..."

"Shhhhh." She lifted both hands and stroked his hair in what she hoped was a soothing gesture. "No need to be sorry. I know you didn't mean it."

He gulped, his Adam's apple bobbing as he struggled to find words.

"Why are you doing this? Don't I terrify you?"

Christine wanted to weep, but fought back her tears. Now was not the time for them. This moment wasn't about her and her feelings. It was about him and his. It was about convincing him that she wanted to embrace all of him. Not just his music and beauty. Not just his face.

But his darkness as well.

"No, you don't terrify me," she explained in a soft tone. "I was startled at first, I'll admit, and I reacted poorly. That doesn't matter, though. I still think you are the most beautiful man I've ever laid eyes on." She moved her hands back to his face, and found his cheeks wet with his tears.

"Don't lie to me," he growled. He clenched his hands into fists against his thighs.

"I'm not lying." She tried to kiss him again, but he turned his face away from her.

"Of course you are." His voice was layered with sorrow and anger. "How can you not be lying? I don't want your pity, Christine!"

Christine shook her head. "I don't pity you. I hurt for you, but I would never pity you."

He didn't appear convinced, and moved to stand. Frightened that she would lose him, Christine hurtled herself at him and threw her arms around his neck, trapping him. She pressed her face to his, clasped her hands into his hair, and pulled his body flush against hers.

"No!" he snarled as he fought her hold. She refused to release him.

"Erik, please," she sobbed into his ear. He went still, but did not touch her. "You begged me not to go, now I'm begging you. Stay with me. Believe me when I say you're beautiful."

"Why? Why should I believe that? Why are you not afraid of me?"

"Because..." She knew what she should say, but she was still afraid to voice her feelings out loud. Yet, it was the only way to make him understand. She had to make herself as vulnerable as him. "Because I love you."

He stilled, becoming as stiff and cold as a statue. She didn't loosen her grip on him, but held her breath as she waited for him to say something. Anything.

When he spoke at last, it was a whisper at her ear.

"I love you too."

His arms wrapped around her as she buried her face in the crook of his neck to hide the tears of joy that began running down her cheeks. Not letting her stay hidden for long, he grasped her chin and nudged her head free before claiming her lips with his own.

Erik kissed her with a desperation that made her tears fall faster. She couldn't hold back her sobs as he murmured, "I love you, I love you, I love you..." over and over again.

This was everything she had hoped for, but hadn't dared to believe possible. She'd come to him half expecting to walk away, but not only had he proven his trust of her, he'd opened his heart to her. Christine would have sagged under the wave of relief that crashed through her, had he not swung her up into his arms. As he carried her towards his bedroom, she continued to run her lips along his face, smooth and crumpled. He laid her on his bed without a word, but that was fine. There were no words left to say. As they stripped, touched, and caressed each other, they explored their new love with their familiar passion.

And as they came together, Christine allowed the hope in her heart to blend into happiness and banish away the last of her doubts about the man who had given her everything.

* * *

Erik

"You're sighing like a teenage girl dreaming of her crush."

Christine grinned at Erik's teasing tone, stretching her arms above her head and sighing for about the hundredth time in the past few minutes as she relaxed into a state of sheer contentment. Her curly hair was wild around her head, her cheeks flushed a decadent pink, and her amber eyes sparkled. His heart clenched as he gazed down at her, still in disbelief that this woman was his.

"Well that makes sense, seeing as I'm as happy a girl with her crush."

It was sometime after their soulful confessions to each other. The night sky was thick with stars outside his bedroom window. It had to be the middle of the night. Erik didn't bother to check the time, though. He didn't care.

He hoped the night would never end.

Resting against the headboard, he closed his eyes with a smile. Her arm snaked around his waist, and she pressed her body against his side. Burying his nose into her hair, he inhaled her sweet scent and hugged her tight.

"How could a devil like me ever deserve an angel like you?"

Christine tipped her head back so that she could meet his eyes. He tensed for a second, unused to open gazes on his uncovered face. After a breath, he forced himself to relax, and felt a thrill when there was no flash of distress or disgust in her gaze.

"You're no devil," she murmured, pressing her lips to his jaw. "You're as much an angel as I am."

He snorted. "With a broken wing, maybe."

Rolling her eyes, she said, "You're exhausting, do you know that?"

"And you're breathtaking."

When her teeth sank into her lower lip and a shy grin curled her lips, he couldn't resist her. Rolling so that she lay under him, he dropped his head and kissed her until she was moaning into his mouth. Her hands cupped both his cheeks. The feel of her palm against his marred flesh was foreign, warm, amazing, and terrifying. He wanted to lean into her touch as much as he wanted to pull away. She arched into him, her legs spreading in invitation, but he pulled back, holding himself above her on bent arms.

"This is real, right?" he asked, still half in disbelief that she could look up at him with such blatant want and need despite his appearance. "This isn't a dream? A trick?"

Though most anyone else would have been offended by his question, she wasn't. She stroked her thumbs along his cheeks, her brow furrowed with her resolve.

"This is not a dream. This is not a trick." She pulled him down to press her lips to his. "I love you, so much it frightens me sometimes, but I don't want to stop. I want to spend every day with you, *seeing* you, touching you, and adoring you. You take my breath away. My heart is yours. My soul is yours. I am yours, and you are mine. For real."

He gulped. "You were ready to leave me, weren't you?"

It wasn't an accusation, but a part of him needed to hear her admit it. Knowing there was a chance he could ever lose her would make him work harder to keep her.

She didn't deny it. Instead, she sighed and shrugged.

"I was, but then you gave me every reason to stay."

Burying his face against her neck, he whispered, "I promise I will always give you a reason to stay."

Her arms wrapped around his shoulders and she hugged him.

"And I promise to never look for a reason to go again."

Their lips found each other once more, and the world melted away as they basked in their love and their hope for the future.

43

Christine

True happiness could change the perspective of a person's world. A once intimidating, shadowed mansion could suddenly become a home. A cold, austere colleague could suddenly become a loyal, caring friend and confidante.

And a tormented, lonely phantom could suddenly turn into the love of one's life.

A week had passed since Christine and Erik had first admitted their love for one another. In that time, the house had returned to normal. No more mass of people streaming on and off the property every day. No more sound engineers. No more band. No more Carla.

Meg had returned to the city with Chelsey after opening up about their own issues. Though Christine missed Meg, and also Rick, she found she wasn't lonely. For the first time in her life, she felt content.

Christine was so blissfully happy, there were moments that she was terrified it would all go away. Experience had taught her that nothing so good could last forever, but Erik's newfound openness and blatant adoration of her alleviated her doubts when they arose.

As he would put it, "Better to know the happiness, and take the risk, than be half-alive."

That wasn't to say that things were easy between them, or that each day was a fairy-tale. Erik had proven his trust of her at last, but that one night didn't erase the years of pain he'd suffered. He still wore his mask when he was around other people, and only took it off at night when it was just the two of them. In addition to his face, he'd begun telling her more about his past. He told her about his birth parents.

His father, a New York real estate developer named Francis had died shortly after his birth. Erik had grown up hearing rumors that the man had taken his own life after he'd seen his infant son's mangled face. Though likely untrue, Erik had lived with that guilt his whole life. His birth mother had been an old money heiress named Marionette.

"She despised me so much, she kept me locked in the house," Erik had explained to Christine one night as they lay entwined together under his sheets. "She used to say I was the Devil's son, and that nothing but pain and destruction would follow me. When I was five, she met a man who wanted to marry her, so she abandoned me to child services."

He had passed through the system, bouncing from foster home to foster home, never able to escape the scorn, ridicule, and terror that came when people saw his face. Eventually, he'd run away.

That night, Christine had clung to him and sobbed for the boy he'd been. He'd held her close, but didn't bother to shed a tear himself.

With each piece of himself that he revealed to her, Christine fell more in love with him.

The sun was shining into the parlor as Christine sat at her table, staring at Excel sheets as if nothing had really changed. Yet, even those didn't frustrate her as much as they used to. Things were looking up for *Fantôme Records*. The album, *Love in the Night*, was a best seller, with her own song *A Matter of Life and Death* climbing the charts and consistently appearing in the top ten most played songs on streaming sites like Spotify, Pandora, and Amazon Music. They weren't quite in the black yet, but they were steadily making their way there.

Mrs. Giry had been back and forth between the estate and New York to oversee promotion of the album, so Erik and Christine had had most of the house to themselves, apart from Darius of course.

It had made it difficult to keep their hands off each other.

Just the night before, Erik had found Christine curled up in his library. Taking her book from her hands, he'd ordered her to hold onto

one of the shelves while he took her from behind. She'd come, screaming his name so loud, her throat had been sore afterwards.

The memory had her biting her lip as a blush spread across her
cheeks.

Still, work beckoned, and while Erik was busy with a phone call to
Mrs. Giry, Christine had slipped away to try and be productive while
she had the chance.

"How is it that you can make staring at a computer screen sexy?"

Biting her lip, Christine looked up and met Erik's eyes from across
the room. He was leaning against the doorframe, arms crossed, mask
in place. She didn't mind the mask, but she had come to prefer his face
without it.

Either way, it looked like her time was up.

"You're going to go right back into debt if you don't let me do some
work," she teased.

He grinned, pushing from the doorway to amble towards her.
When he reached her, he dropped a kiss on the top of her head.

"You know my preference is to always have you naked and screaming my name, but unfortunately I can't have my wish today. I have to
go to the city."

Surprised, Christine stared up at him. "What? You're leaving the
estate?"

He nodded, not looking pleased with the idea.

"Mrs. Giry's run into some difficulties with one of our distributors,
and they are refusing to talk with her without me. It's annoying, and
insulting to her, but they want me there face-to-face."

She could see how anxious the idea made him, and how hard he
was trying to hide it. Cupping his cheek, she offered a reassuring smile.

"It'll be okay. Mrs. Giry will be there, and she'll make sure it's a private meeting behind closed doors."

He gulped, but nodded. "I know. You're right. I need to leave right
away, though, so I can get it over with and come back. Will you be all
right here alone? Darius has the day off."

Rolling her eyes, she chuckled. "I'm a big girl, Erik. I can handle being by myself for an afternoon."

"I'll try to be back tonight."

She curled her fingers around his collar and yanked him down into a kiss.

"I'll be waiting with a reward for being so brave," she purred against his lips.

He grinned. "I've never been so motivated to go to a business meeting."

With a laugh, she kissed him again, and then released him so he could go. His steps were reluctant as he walked away from her.

Pausing at the threshold of the room, he glanced back and said, "I love you, angel."

The words still sent a thrill of emotion rushing through her.

"I love you too. Now go so you can come back."

He winked at her before turning and leaving the room. She watched as he opened the front door of the house and stepped outside. Once he was gone, and the house was silent, Christine released a huff of disappointment. With him gone, there were no excuses for her to not do her work.

Turning her attention back to her Excel sheets, she tried to focus in on the numbers in front of her, but her mind was already busy anticipating Erik's return.

"My God, Erik. I straightened these files last week. How have you gotten them so messed up already?" Christine murmured to herself as she sorted through manila folders of paperwork she had spread out on Erik's desk. As pristine as his study appeared, the insides of his drawers were a mess, and no matter how many times she tried to bring order to them, they always fell back into chaos.

It was late afternoon. Erik had been gone for most of the day, and apart from a text letting her know he'd arrived in the city safely, she hadn't heard anything from him. Though she wasn't worried about him, she did miss him, and it was strange being in the house with no one else around. She'd managed to distract herself with work, but she was running out of tasks to do. In a last ditch effort to keep herself occupied, she'd elected to dive back into his filing cabinets to try once more to organize them. It was boring work, but effective at keeping her mind busy. She was so distracted, in fact, that she didn't hear the study door open behind her.

"My, my, my, what have we here? All alone Christine?"

Christine whirled around, startled, and gasped to find Carla standing in front of the closed study door.

"Carla? What are you doing here?"

The diva stared at Christine. There was a crazed light in the woman's eyes that unnerved her, and she swayed on her feet. Was she drunk?

"I came to take back what's mine," Carla responded, and there was a definite slur to her words.

Fear trickled along Christine's spine, warning bells going off in her head. She couldn't understand why, but she sensed she was in danger. Carla had always been cruel and intimidating, but she'd never felt like an actual threat.

Something about her felt that way now.

"I don't know what you're talking about, Carla." As she spoke, Christine tried to determine an escape route. She needed to get away from the woman. To not be alone in a confined space with her. The diva blocked the main door, so the secret passageway was Christine's best bet. If she could only get to that side of the room...

Carla scoffed. "Please, don't take me for a fool. You know exactly what I'm talking about. You *stole* him from me."

Shaking her head, Christine kept her tone as calm as possible when she said, "Stole who? Erik? I didn't steal him, Carla, you gave him up."

She eased a step to her right.

"I wouldn't move if I were you." Carla raised her arm, and Christine froze at the sight of the gun clutched in her hand. She'd kept it hidden in the folds of her crimson skirts.

Christine's heart began to race and her throat felt like it was closing as panic set in. She fought it, knowing she had to stay rational. She had to *think*.

"Carla..."

"Let's take a walk, you and I." She kept the gun trained on Christine as she moved towards the panel that opened into the passageway. Christine's mind scrambled to come up with a plan. She couldn't leave with her. Clearly, Carla had snapped. She wasn't thinking straight, her mind clouded with alcohol and rage.

"Okay, okay. Take it easy, Carla. Don't do something you might regret." She raised her hands in the air, taking care to go slow and not startle the armed woman.

Stopping next to the panel, Carla narrowed her eyes at Christine, but didn't open the passage entrance. Through gritted teeth, she snarled, "Too late. I've already done plenty of things I regret. What's one more?"

"Why are you doing this?"

Carla blinked, and Christine noticed that her eyes shimmered. With unshed tears?

"It's all falling apart. I can't let it all fall apart! What do *you* have compared to me? Nothing! You don't deserve any of this. It should all be mine!"

Her clear instability ratcheted up Christine's fear. She needed to calm the woman down, help her think rationally again.

"Carla, listen to me," Christine spoke in as even and soothing a voice as she could manage. "Everything will be all right. Just put the gun down, and let's talk."

"Shut up!" Carla shrieked, waving the gun in a menacing arch. "Shut the fuck up! No matter what you say, you're not leaving here. Not after everything you've done!"

Taking deep breaths, Christine had to force words past her dry lips. "What did I do, Carla?"

Tears broke free and began to slide down Carla's cheeks. "You stole him from me, and now you're stealing my career from me. I won't let you."

Christine gulped and tried not to look at the gun. Instead, she fought to maintain eye-contact with her captor.

"What do you mean, I'm stealing your career?" *Keep her talking. Keep her distracted.*

"It doesn't matter now. You won't be around long enough to succeed," Carla snapped. She pressed the panel in the wall to open the passageway. Jerking her gun towards the opening, she said, "You first."

Paralyzed with fear, Christine didn't know if she would be able to move. To disobey, however, would spell out disaster. Forcing one foot in front of the other, she made her way towards Carla and ducked into the passageway. The florescent lights in the ceiling seemed dimmer than the last time she'd gone through this corridor. Or perhaps, her terror was shadowing her eyesight. She heard the panel close behind her, and a sharp shove to the shoulder with a barked, "Move," had her stumbling forward.

She walked without seeing where she was going. When Carla told her to turn, she turned. When Carla told her to slow down or speed up, she obeyed without question. After what felt like hours, but was in reality a mere handful of minutes, she realized where they were headed.

"Why are you taking me to the studio?"

"There's something poetic about killing you in the location of your greatest triumph."

Christine tripped over her own feet, but hurried to right herself.

"Please, Carla. You don't have to do this..."

"You brought this on yourself. If you hadn't seduced Erik away from me, he never would have put you on his album. You're just a whore who doesn't know her place."

Christine's head was growing fuzzy with her fear, but she fought to keep herself sane.

"I don't understand. The album is a success. *You* sang most of the songs on it."

"But it's *your* song that's the hit," Carla snarled as they reached the door to the studio. She ordered Christine to open it, and they walked into the tiny office at the back of the building together.

"Now what?" Christine asked, her voice barely louder than a whisper.

Carla pushed her shoulder with the gun again. "I'm not going to kill you here. We're going to the live room, and you're going to have an unfortunate accident."

Her heart racing so fast her blood pounded in her ears, Christine had no choice but to obey. Opening the office's door, she stepped out into the hallway, Carla close behind.

44

Christine

"How did you know I'd be alone today?" Christine asked as Carla tied her hands behind her back with a silky rope that wouldn't leave marks. It had become clear the moment they stepped into the live room that Carla had prepared for this. A chair stood in the middle of the room. Above it, hanging from an exposed beam in the ceiling, was a noose made of the same type of rope that Carla was binding her with. Christine now understood what Carla had meant by *accident*.

She was going to kill Christine and make it look like a suicide.

"I made sure you were," Carla answered, directing Christine towards the chair.

Panic and fear were making Christine lose her senses, but she fought them.

Buy time, buy time, buy time!

"How could that be possible? Erik was called away because Mrs. Giry needed him."

"Mrs. Giry needed him because I called in a few favors and had their distributor demand his presence," Carla explained as casually as if she were talking about the weather. When they reached the chair, she shoved Christine forward. "Up you go."

Christine froze. This was happening too fast. She needed more time...

The cool metal of the gun barrel pressed into the base of her neck.

"If you'd rather a suicide by gunshot, I can make that happen too."

Christine couldn't stop the whimper that burst from her throat.

Think idiot! You are going to die!

"If you shoot me, they'll know it was murder."

Carla snorted. "Wanna bet?"

Before Christine could stop her, Carla spun her around and pushed her down into the chair. Christine flinched when her bound hands were crushed between her body and the metal backrest. She forgot her discomfort, however, when Carla pressed the gun against her forehead.

"I could shoot you, then burn this place to the ground, destroying the evidence."

Christine's mouth went dry, and she struggled to speak.

"They could still figure it out."

Shrugging, Carla smirked, "Maybe that's a risk I'm willing to take?"

The crazed gleam in her eyes suggested that she was, in fact, willing to risk it.

"Please, Carla, can't we talk about this?"

Rolling her eyes, Carla shrieked. "Would you stop trying to distract me? It's not going to work. You're going to die, and a devastated Erik is going to turn to me for comfort."

Realization struck, and Christine's brain began clicking.

"Why do you want Erik so badly, Carla? I thought you left him years ago?"

The gun shook in Carla's hand, and her gaze was stark.

"Why do you give a fuck?"

Christine widened her eyes, attempting to look innocent. "I didn't know you two were still together. Had I known, I wouldn't have seduced him."

The words tasted like ash in her mouth, but Carla's shoulders relaxed.

"You didn't know? Of course you didn't know. He wouldn't have told you, but he's mine, do you understand? Even if I'm not around, even if he hates me, and even if I despise him. We're bound together forever."

Anger unfurled in Christine's chest at the woman's audacity, pushing back at her mind-boggling terror. It helped her think straight, see clearer, and hone in on the cracks in Carla's armor.

"Why him, Carla? Why are you so fixated on Erik?"

As she posed the question, Christine began to twist her wrists with small movements so that the woman wouldn't notice. They slid against the rope, which was so smooth she thought she could work her hands out if she had enough time.

"He ruined me."

Christine's heart stopped. She almost lashed out in Erik's defense, but the lost look that crossed Carla's face gave her pause. For a moment, she glimpsed a pain she'd never seen in the woman before, and it scared her nearly as much as the gun in her face. There was heartbreak in Carla's eyes. In her own, twisted, terrible way, she might really love Erik.

"I was innocent before him," the diva began, oblivious to Christine's movements. "Bright-eyed, with the whole world ripe for the taking. Then he came along and charmed his way into my life. He told me I was special, and molded me into an artist in his own image. All the while hiding what he really was from me!"

Managing to loosen the rope enough to slip it towards her palm, Christine bit her cheek to keep from yelping in relief. Still, she didn't miss Carla's words, or the insinuation behind them.

"What is he, Carla?" No matter how hard she tried, she couldn't keep her anger from darkening her words.

Carla was so lost in her own mind she didn't seem to notice. "He's a monster. Half-a-man. The first time I saw his face, I felt violated. He'd touched me without showing me what he really was. I ran from him, as fast as I could, but no matter how hard I tried, I couldn't escape him."

Christine gnashed her teeth as her rage bubbled.

Priorities. Escape first, rip her to shreds later.

"Escape him? He came after you?" Erik hadn't told her that, and she wasn't sure how she'd handle the revelation if Carla confirmed it.

It was a relief when the woman shook her head.

"No, he didn't come after me, but he was there, in my mind. He'd latched onto my soul, and refused to let go. I found I couldn't perform the same without him. I was still good. I still found fame and fortune, but I was never as brilliant as when I was with him. As brilliant as *you* are now. I found myself returning to him again and again, but it was on my terms. *He* was the toy, and I was the master." Her gaze sharpened suddenly, and she glared at Christine as her hold on the gun grew firm again. "Then *you* came along, and ruined everything!"

Shit, time's up.

Carla moved so she stood at Christine's side, shoving the gun into her temple.

"Enough talk. Time to die. I promise, I'll make it quick."

Mustering all her strength, Christine yanked her left arm from her bonds with a cry the same moment she threw herself sideways into Carla. Pain shot from her hand to her shoulder, and she was sure she'd just broken her wrist. However, the arm came free, and that meant her right side was free as well. Carla screamed as they went crashing to the floor together.

The gun was dislodged from her hand and went skittering across the room. Christine found her bearings, climbed on top of Carla, and pinned her to the floor. Having only one useable hand made her unstable, however, and Carla was able to throw her off without much effort. Christine fell to her side, her head hitting the floor so hard, stars burst in her vision.

Scrambling to her feet, Carla charged after the gun. Christine staggered to her knees, trying to follow, but her head swam and she was disoriented.

"Why couldn't you have just died quietly?" Carla snarled, reaching her weapon. Swinging around, she aimed for Christine and readied to pull the trigger...

"Carla, stop!"

Both women froze at Erik's booming voice. Christine wanted to sob in relief when she saw him standing in the doorway, his expression thunderous, his stance wary.

"Erik," Carla gasped, her face draining of color. "You weren't supposed to be back yet."

He entered the room as if a wild animal was loose inside, which, Christine supposed, wasn't far from the truth.

"We kept getting the ring around, and I grew suspicious," he said in a low, even tone. "I left Mrs. Giry in the city and came home. When I arrived and didn't find Christine anywhere in the house, I checked the security footage. Why are you doing this, Carla? This isn't like you."

He was making his way step by cautious step towards Christine.

"Stop!" Carla shouted, training the gun on him. "Don't move! Don't get close to her. This is all her fault. She needs to die so things can go back to how they were."

Raising both hands, Erik diverted his course and began moving towards Carla. She didn't turn her weapon from him, but her hands began to shake.

"Carla, please stop this." His voice was gentle, soothing. Christine watched in complete terror as he slowly closed in on Carla. "Just tell me what you want so we can leave here and put all this behind us."

Carla's throat bobbed as she swallowed. Her expression was fearful, her gaze anxious and confused. It became apparent the woman didn't want to shoot Erik.

That didn't mean she wouldn't if provoked, however.

"You're mine," the crazed woman hissed. "Don't you see that? You always have been. She can't have you!"

Erik nodded, his hands still up, his steps still slow. "Okay, I get it. I'm yours. That doesn't mean you have to kill Christine. I didn't realize I meant so much to you, and I'm sorry."

Bile rose in Christine's throat, but she forced it back down. She knew he didn't mean what he was saying, but the words still stung.

Taking a deep breath, she kept her body still, not wanting to distract Carla. Their best chance of walking out of that place alive was if Erik could calm the woman down, however he had to.

"You're sorry?" Carla whispered. The hope in her gaze made Christine's gut twist. "Really? You'll get rid of her and come back to me?"

He was drawing closer to her. A few more feet, and he'd be able to reach the gun.

"Let's just get out of here, and you and I can talk."

Carla's forehead furrowed. "Do you promise to get rid of Christine?"

"You don't need to worry about her."

Carla's gaze flashed. "Say that you'll get rid of her."

"Carla..."

Her grip tightened, her voiced hardened. "Say it!"

Erik froze.

"All right, calm down. I'll get rid of Christine."

The air in the room was thick as silence greeted his words. Christine counted the seconds that passed with her heartbeats.

At last, Carla said, "I don't believe you." She turned the gun on Christine.

"No!" Erik roared, diving at her. Colliding with Carla, they both went tumbling backwards towards the floor.

The gun went off.

Blood sprayed.

Erik's mask slid across the floor.

Christine screamed.

She lunged to her feet as Erik rolled off Carla, who was shrieking and clawing at the blood spattered on her clothes. Blood that wasn't hers. The gun lay next to her, forgotten.

A crimson stain spread out beneath Erik as Christine dropped to her knees at his side.

"Erik, no!" Tears streamed down her face. She wanted to take him in her arms, cradle his head in her lap, but she was afraid to touch him, unsure how seriously he was injured. "Are you okay?"

He groaned. "It's just my shoulder. I'll be fine."

A sob of relief ripped its way out of her chest. "Oh my God." She bent over him, raining kisses across his whole face. "I love you, I love you, I love you."

"Carla," he growled.

Christine gasped, having forgotten all about the woman in her dread for Erik. Spinning to face her, Christine froze at the sight of Carla curled on her side, crying hysterically. Hurrying to grab the gun, she returned to Erik's side, fished his phone from his pocket, and dialed 911.

Carla was no longer a threat, so Christine ignored her, all of her focus and care zeroed in on Erik. As gently as she could, she lifted his head to rest on her lap. She slid her blazer off, balled it up, and pressed it against his wound to try and stop some of the bleeding. He grimaced, but grasped her hand with his uninjured side. She let her throbbing hand rest on his torso.

Gazing up at her, he murmured, "I've never been more terrified in my life than when I saw Carla pull a gun on you on the security footage. I thought I would be too late."

Her tears continued to fall, but Christine managed to smile for him. "It's okay. *I'm* okay. You need to rest."

Something moved in her peripheral vision, and she whipped the gun up from where it lay beside her on the floor.

Carla, positioned on her hands and knees, stopped crawling towards them and blinked wide, blank eyes.

"Did I kill him?" she whispered, seeming unaffected by the weapon Christine was pointing at her.

"No," Christine gritted out. "But you will stay the fuck away from him."

Ignoring her, Carla began to creep towards them again, her eyes locked on Erik. Pointing the gun away from her, Christine fired a warning shot. That got the disturbed woman's attention. She stopped again. Fear flashed in her gaze.

"I said stay away from him," Christine hissed. Pointing the gun towards the far corner, she ordered, "You go over there. If you try to get away, I will shoot you in the leg."

Carla gulped and scuttled to obey, huddling against the wall.

Christine kept one eye on her, but turned her attention back to Erik.

His grin was exhausted.

"She's not herself," he muttered.

"I know."

"I want to get her the help she needs."

Her heart beat faster, and she fell a little more in love with him. "I know you do."

His grip tightened on her hand.

"I love you, angel. I'll never leave you alone again."

Bending down to kiss his forehead, she whispered, "Stop talking and rest. If you die, I'll never forgive you."

His chuckle was music to her ears.

* * *

"The doctors say Carla suffered a psychotic break brought on by extreme stress, and exacerbated by the alcohol and drugs in her system. She's been admitted to a facility in the city for treatment, and once she's deemed healthy enough, she'll carry out the rest of her prison sentence. Since she took the deal and pled guilty, she's only been charged with a misdemeanor and will likely be out of jail within the year. As part of the agreement, however, she will then attend rehab for her substance abuse."

Christine watched Erik's expression out of the corner of her eye as Mrs. Giry brought them up to speed on Carla Dicelli. She didn't miss the flash of guilt that crossed his features. Resting her hand on his uninjured shoulder, she gave it a reassuring squeeze.

"I want her to be taken care of. I want to make sure she gets well again," he said. "I also want her to have a career still waiting for her when she is."

Mrs. Giry let out a sigh, but nodded. "Of course, sir."

Christine could understand her frustrations. She continued to struggle with his leniency towards Carla after everything she'd done to them, but she knew that Erik felt responsible for her suffering. Whether his guilt was justified or not, he intended to take care of the woman who'd broken his heart, for the sake of the innocent girl she'd once been, and he'd once loved.

After jotting down a note on the pad of paper resting in her lap, Mrs. Giry raised her head and asked, "Is there anything else, sir?"

"No, thank you."

Standing, Mrs. Giry hesitated to leave. Her expression appeared pained.

Erik frowned. "Is something wrong?"

Licking her lips, she raised her chin. "I just want to say that I'm glad you are all right. When I'd heard what had happened, I was...terrified. The thought of losing you was more than I could bear."

She had in fact been a wreck when she'd shown up to the hospital, desperate to know that Erik was okay. After Christine had reassured her he would live, the woman had collapsed into her arms and wept.

There was a moment when no one spoke or moved. Then, with ginger movements so as not to jostle his shoulder or disturb his sling, Erik stood from his chair. Making his way around his desk, he pulled a surprised Mrs. Giry into a one armed hug.

"I love you, Amelia," he murmured.

Mrs. Giry's eyes swam with sudden tears, and she wrapped her arms around his waist.

Christine turned her face away, feeling as if she were intruding upon the moment.

When the two pulled apart, Mrs. Giry's cheeks were wet and her smile was shaky. She wiped a finger under her eye.

"Well, I should be going."

Christine smiled at the woman as she made her way from the room. Moving around the desk, she took Erik's hand in hers.

"Are you okay?"

His grin was light, despite the tinge of sadness in his gaze.

"Yes. I am."

Pulling her in, he kissed her. What was meant to be a light peck quickly turned into something deeper. It had been days since they'd been able to be together because of his stay in the hospital and injured shoulder. Christine hadn't realized how hungry for him she was. She'd been too consumed by her worry for him. He seemed just as desperate for her, burying his hand in her hair and angling her head to deepen their kiss. When they broke apart, they were both panting.

"Christine..."

She shook her head. "The doctor said you need to rest."

"Fuck the doctor. Better yet, fuck *me*."

She giggled. "You'll hurt yourself."

Taking her hand again, he led her back around the desk to his chair. Sitting, he patted his lap in invitation.

"If I'm not the one doing the work, we should be fine, right?"

Biting her lip, she couldn't deny that she was tempted. He grabbed her waist and yanked her down so she straddled him.

"Please, angel?" he whispered in her ear. "It's been too long since I heard you sing."

Draping her arms around his neck, mindful of her cast, she pressed herself against him, defeated. Not that she ever stood a chance of resisting him.

"As you wish, sir."

His chuckle vibrated her lips as he took her mouth. She wrapped herself around him, giving into her desire. Into their passion. Into their love.

He'd put music into her soul, and she would always sing for him.

45

EPILOGUE

Christine

"Five minutes, Ms. Davidson!" a stagehand announced from the other side of her dressing room door.

"Thank you, I'll be right out!"

Turning back to her mirror, she finished touching up her lipstick. Thank God her hair wasn't a mess.

"Damn, we still had five minutes?" Erik said with a teasing lilt. "I let you finish too soon."

She glanced over her shoulder at him, catching him tucking his black dress shirt back into his pants. Grinning, she rolled her eyes.

"You cut it too close as it was. I always appreciate your stalwart attention and determination, but it all kind of goes against the definition of a quickie. Which, we shouldn't have done in the first place."

Chuckling, he strolled up behind her and planted a kiss on her bare shoulder.

"How can I resist you when you're so beautiful? I think you overestimate my willpower."

She met his gaze in the mirror and smiled, her heart swelling. God, how she loved this man. A year together, and the depth of her feelings continued to surprise her.

He placed his hands on her hips. "Are you ready for this?"

She took a moment to study her reflection before answering. The woman that stared back looked like a princess out of a fairy tale. Her off-the-shoulder white ball gown was covered in lace and strategically placed crystal beading that would shine when the stage lights hit them. Her hair was pulled back into an elaborate chiffon, and a crystal headband matching her dress rested on her head like a tiara. She'd never felt more beautiful, and despite the nerves that always came with performing live, she didn't doubt that she was prepared.

Her teacher was a genius, after all.

Placing her lipstick on the counter, she nodded.

"Yes. I'm ready."

"Remember to breathe."

"I will."

"Don't be intimidated by the crowd."

Her breath caught in her throat. "I'll try."

He nipped the shell of her ear with his teeth. "I'll be watching offstage, waiting for you when you finish. Then, we'll celebrate your great triumph with a trip. Anywhere you want."

She flashed an eager smile, excitement shooting through her. "Paris?"

His blue eyes twinkled. "Perfect."

Turning in his arms, she brushed her lips against his.

"You're perfect."

"You're ridiculous."

Maybe she was, but in her eyes, he was perfectly imperfect. Her broken, dark angel who hid himself from everyone but her. She reached up and tapped a finger against his mask.

"The next time we have sex, I want this off."

He turned his head and caught her finger in his teeth, giving it a gentle bite before replying.

"As you command, my lady."

There was another knock on the door.

"Two minutes, Ms. Davidson."

Shit. "I'm on my way!"

Wiggling out of Erik's hold, she made her way out of the dressing room. He followed her as they hurried towards the back of the stage. The nerves she thought she'd had under control began to riot, and for good reason.

It was no small thing to sing in Carnegie Hall.

As she neared her entry point, Erik reached out and snagged her hand, spinning her back to face him.

"What is it?" she whispered, hyper aware that they were almost out of time.

He cupped her face in his hands. "When you're out there, forget about everybody else. You're singing for me, okay? Just for me."

She smiled as her nerves began to die back down. "Always for you."

He pressed a kiss to her forehead. "Now, go blow them away angel."

Nodding, she said, "Wait for me."

He grinned. "Always."

Letting her go, he stepped back. She turned to hurry towards the stage, to bask in the lights, to follow her passion, and to bear her soul through his music.

All the while knowing that as she stood out in the spotlight, her phantom would be waiting in the shadows, sharing in her glory.

Lula Greene is a romance author living in the Midwest with a soft spot for morally gray heroes and bad boys with hearts of gold.

www.ingramcontent.com/pod-product-compliance
Lightning Source LLC
Chambersburg PA
CBHW011448100726
47899CB00010BB/3206